THE HOUSE OF KILLERS

SAMANTHA LEE HOWE

One More Chapter
a division of HarperCollins*Publishers*
1 London Bridge Street
London SE1 9GF
www.harpercollins.co.uk

HarperCollins*Publishers*
1st Floor, Watermarque Building, Ringsend Road
Dublin 4, Ireland

This paperback edition 2021
First published in Great Britain in ebook format
by HarperCollins*Publishers* 2021

1

A catalogue record of this book is available from the British Library

ISBN: 978-0-00-844457-0

This novel is entirely a work of fiction. The names, characters and
incidents portrayed in it are the work of the author's imagination. Any
resemblance to actual persons, living or dead, events or localities is
entirely coincidental.

Printed and bound in Great Britain by
CPI Group (UK) Ltd, Croydon CR0 4YY

USA Today-bestselling author Samantha Lee Howe began her professional writing career in 2007 and has worked as a freelance writer for small, medium and large publishers, predominately writing horror and fantasy under the pen name Sam Stone.

Samantha's breakaway debut psychological thriller *The Stranger in Our Bed* was released in 2020 by HarperCollins division One More Chapter. The book rapidly became a *USA Today* bestseller.

To date, Samantha has written 19 novels, 3 novellas, 3 collections, over 40 short stories, an audio drama and a *Doctor Who* spin-off drama that went to DVD.

A former high school English and Drama teacher, Samantha has a BA (Hons) in English and Writing for Performance, an MA in Creative Writing and a PGCE in English.

Samantha lives in Lincolnshire with her husband, David, and their two cats, Leeloo and Skye. She is the proud mother of a lovely daughter called Linzi.

samanthaleehowe.co.uk

facebook.com/SamanthaLeeHoweThrillers
twitter.com/SamanthaLHowe
instagram.com/samanthaleehowe

Also by Samantha Lee Howe

The Stranger in Our Bed

For David, Linzi, Tracey and Andrew

'Never hope to see heaven: I come to carry you to the other shore, into eternal darkness, into fire and ice.'

— Dante Alighieri, *Inferno* (tr. by A. S. Kline)

Prologue

NEVA

Five years ago

When Neva wakes, she focuses on her own reflection in the skylight above her bed. She doesn't think about her next kill.

At this time of day, the glass is a mirror; she studies her face. Youthful. Innocent, big blue eyes are framed with perfectly shaped brows. Her hair is long and golden blonde – some would call it strawberry. She's the very picture of mental and physical health. Her bone structure is faultless, cheekbones defined to model excellence, jawline pronounced. She's a natural beauty but she's simple too; with the right make-up and clothing she can be instantly forgettable.

The light changes, breaking her meditation. Part of her face becomes obscured. For a moment her immaculate structure appears skull-like, then the sun breaks the spell as it rises up above her head.

She never thinks about why she is here, or how this started. The beginning was a lifetime ago. It doesn't matter. She is a killer for hire and her reputation precedes her work. Death is simply a process by which she gets paid. It brings no delight. It gives her no emotion at all.

The burner phone by her bed pings. Neva moves from her self-imposed trance. The image of herself, transiently glimpsed, has disappeared for the day. Turning on her side, she picks up the phone. There is only one number stored. Neva reads the instructions, then she swings her long legs over the edge of the bed and stands.

There are no mirrors in the bathroom.

Neva showers and brushes her teeth. She pulls up her hair, wraps it around her head and pulls on a tight netting that flattens it to her skull. She tucks in any remaining strands with practised ease.

In the bedroom, she opens the wardrobe on the left-hand side. The outfit of the day hangs alone and will be discarded once used. Today she will be a redhead. On another day she may be a brunette. When the wig is in place, she goes to her dressing table. In the top drawer are several pairs of contact lenses, all different colours. Neva puts in a pair of brown lenses. She blinks, lets them settle in her eyes, and then applies make-up. When she's finished, the person looking back in the mirror does not resemble the girl she saw in the skylight. This is a mature and sophisticated woman, tanned, lean, confident in red lipstick.

Neva returns to the now empty wardrobe. In the back, she opens a panel and looks at her weapons, lined up on the rear wall. She smiles at the hidden store, which she knows is a cliché. She takes her favourite blade and straps this to her wrist in an automatic holster that will release the weapon into her hand when needed. She pulls on a jacket over the skirt and blouse she's wearing. Then she studies her guns. She takes a small pistol from its casing in the wall. After checking that the chamber is full and the safety is on, she tucks it into the back of her skirt. With some spare bullets stowed in her pocket, Neva is ready.

The gun is for any contingencies; her weapon of choice today is the blade. A blade requires close contact, but is silent. Where she plans to make the kill, any noise will be an issue. She pauses, grounding herself in the moment. Her mind goes blank and then she hears the mantra. It runs through her head like an earworm song. When the chant finishes, her head is as ready as her physical body.

Just before she leaves the room, she pulls on a pair of black court shoes and drops a scrunchie into her pocket, as well as some anonymous cash. She does not take any cards or any form of ID.

Neva's home is in Lincolnshire, on land that sits back from a main A-road. She's in the heart of 'spook central', surrounded by RAF bases – a source of personal amusement as she hides in plain sight.

Leaving via the back of the house she crosses a field, avoiding the droppings of the family of foxes she knows live nearby. The smell of cut grass wafts across from the farm on the other side of the road as the farmer, out early, cuts and leaves it to dry in the sun. It is the height of summer, a hot one for a change, and Neva enjoys the tranquillity of living in this flat countryside.

She leaves the field and makes her way towards a large breeze-block building. She owns this storage space, but it lies empty except for the nests of spiders that inhabit the rafters of the corrugated roof. Parked there, ready for her use, is a blue Mini. She's never been in this car; it was left here for her use for this particular job. She pulls on surgical gloves, then opens the driver's door and climbs in. The keys are already in the ignition. She starts the engine, then drives the car away from her land.

Two hours later she is on the outskirts of London. She parks the car and leaves the keys where they are. Slamming the door shut, she glances around, then removes the gloves, stuffing them into her pocket for possible use later on. She crosses the road and heads down into the nearest tube station.

Exiting the tube at Waterloo, she glances at her watch. Not far now. Her mark will be on the Strand in an hour's time. Neva will be there first. She walks from the station and passes over Waterloo Bridge. A group of Japanese tourists pose on the bridge with the London Eye behind them. She observes but does not engage with them, passing by unseen among the throng of people walking to and from the station. Neva is aware of the odour of pollution; exhaust fumes, the waft of urine coming up from below the bridge, and the smell of summer-hot bodies assault her in contrast to the clean and pure air of the countryside where she lives.

She reaches the Strand. Pausing as she waits to cross the

road at the lights, she looks at her destination: the Savoy Hotel.

In the lobby, Neva sees her target. She has committed her face to memory. She's mousy-looking, forgettable, but Neva observes the guile behind this nondescript disguise. The other woman, her mark, is a rival. Another of her kind. This does not concern Neva – fulfilling her contract does – but she's aware that this will not be a simple kill.

She watches the woman cross the lobby and enter a lift. She doesn't follow. Instead, she observes which floor her kill exits. Her codename is Ansell.

Taking the stairs, Neva goes to the third floor. As she walks along the corridor, she sees a room that is marked 'Staff Only'. Neva quickly picks the lock and goes inside. Then she shuts the door behind her. Inside, she finds what she expected. This is a small cleaning-service room. There is a sink next to shelving that is filled with cleaning products and stacks of fresh towels. An empty laundry basket stands in the corner. Hung up on the walls are several maid uniforms, and a cleaning trolley sits in the centre of the room. Neva doesn't use the uniform or the trolley. She doesn't touch anything. Instead, she waits behind the door, her favoured blade now firmly in her hand.

She breathes. Focuses. She quells the rush of adrenaline that threatens her equilibrium. Her heartrate slows; she's fully in control of all her reflexes.

A short time later, she hears the sound of someone else tampering with the lock. She presses herself back against the wall. Her mark has been given a target of her own in the hotel; Neva knew she would resort to this simple trope to gain access to his room.

Ansell pushes open the door, glances round, and then slips inside, closing it behind her. Neva's knife cuts through the air in an arc as her target bends forward, just out of reach as she feels the shift in the atmosphere. Ansell turns to face her killer, then throws herself forward.

Neva grapevines backwards with the skill of a dancer. She feels the skim of a blade as it brushes against her jacket collar. As if in slow motion, a wisp of red hair flicks into the air. Neva swings her knife upwards. Her opponent hops backwards out of reach, but Neva only misses by a breath.

The woman is smaller in height, but she's strong and toned. Her wig comes away in the struggle. Beneath it is a hairless, shaved scalp. She's not young; she's past her prime. The thought crosses Neva's mind that perhaps this is why *they* want Ansell retired.

'*You!*' Ansell says. 'I trained your generation. I know your every move.'

Neva blinks. How does Ansell know anything of Neva's generation?

'I've retired younger and stronger than you...' Ansell spits.

Ansell's face contorts as she throws herself onto Neva.

'It's not my time,' Ansell says, swinging her knife at Neva. There is desperation in her every move.

The younger assassin loses footing and stumbles, slamming back into the door, but as Ansell falls forward, knife stabbing, weaving, and thrusting, Neva brings her blade back up between them. She is not frantic like her opponent. She is calm, controlled. She doesn't think; she *reacts*. The blade hits home. Up, sharp, under the ribs and straight into Ansell's heart.

Ansell's face twists, her mouth falls open, and her eyes widen. The knife in her hand drops to the floor.

'I am death…' Neva says.

Neva turns the blade, ensuring maximum pain and certain rupture. All the time she is looking into Ansell's eyes, she sees … fear. And something else… Is Ansell, despite her struggle to stay alive, resigned to her fate? The thought of this acquiescence sends the blood pumping through Neva's veins and it's uncontrolled adrenaline, emotion, she is unused to.

Ansell slumps against her. Neva pushes the body back, but holds onto her knife. There is a judder as the steel catches on a rib before it is free. Ansell's corpse collapses to the ground, head cracking against the concrete floor. Blood pools from her chest wound and around the body.

Neva looks down at her. Her chest heaves as she catches her breath. She forces back the adrenaline once more. Ansell did not go easy.

She looks down at her skirt suit and blouse. Blood stains the fabric; her hands are smeared too.

'What a mess,' she says.

At the small sink she scrubs her hands. She watches the red turn to pink and then run clear. There is a slight tremor in her hand. She presses it against her chest. Steadies the shake. Frowns

Then Neva takes the burner phone from her pocket and snaps Ansell's picture, before sending it to its destination.

A few seconds later a text arrives.

PAYMENT MADE. CLEAN-UP ALSO REQUIRED.

This is an unusual request. She glances at the body. Ansell will never say her mantra again; Neva murmurs it, like a eulogy over the body.

She empties her jacket pocket, placing the bullets, her gun, money and the scrunchie down on the sink drainer. She strips away the skirt suit and blouse and throws them into the large washing basket.

In her underwear, Neva kneels. She lifts Ansell's carcass into a sitting position and then hefts the body to its feet. With a twist of her body she turns and lets Ansell fall forward over the basket. Then she pushes the corpse down onto her discarded clothing.

Looking around the room, Neva assesses the damage. Using the towels from the shelf, she mops up Ansell's blood from the floor. She throws the stained towels into the washing basket over the body. Then she pours neat bleach into the mop bucket and begins to cleanse the concrete, removing all signs of the murder.

When she's finished, Neva returns to the sink. She washes the bucket, rinses the mop, and then thoroughly cleans herself, removing the tan make-up and the red lipstick. Any towels she uses go into the washing trolley. She wipes any surface she touches. The room is cleaner than when she arrived.

She pulls on one of the maids' uniforms and slips her own court shoes back on. Then she removes the red wig and the netting. Neva runs her fingers through her long hair and scrapes it back and ties it with the scrunchie. Then she picks up her gun, bullets, and cash, and drops them into the uniform pocket.

Making sure the body and all soiled towels are covered, Neva wheels the washing basket out of the cleaner utility room and into the corridor.

In the service lift, she takes a breath; she almost imagines Ansell swimming through the sea of towels upwards to reveal the crime of her death.

Neva shakes herself. She feels ... *nothing*, her mind insists. Her mantra runs over and over inside her head, capping the tumble of stray, irrational thoughts and emotions that she's unused to.

By the time the service lift reaches the ground floor, Neva is back in control of her mind and body.

Chapter One

MICHAEL

Three years ago

I'm in my office when the folder lands on my desk. On the cover in bold is printed 'TOP SECRET' in important-looking capitals. *What secrets lie inside?* The search for criminals and the study of their minds excite me. I feel a buzz course through me as I pick up the folder.

I don't look up at the person standing by the door, the same man that placed the folder in front of me; I've been expecting this.

The file relates to the cold-case job I've been invited to apply for. An upgrade in security access, pay grade, and fieldwork. All the things I've been working towards my whole life. I feel the cusp of opportunity finally knocking.

I was recruited to MI5 in my first year at university. It was one of the strangest moments in my life. I was called into the dean's office, told to sit down, and then I had to sign the Official Secrets Act before anyone spoke to me. Once I signed the document, an agent came in and my life changed dramatically. I wasn't given much chance to think; it was a take-it-or-leave-it-now deal. I didn't hesitate. Who would refuse a break like that?

After that, the government paid for all of my education, and now I'm an efficient profiler as well as a registered operative. I'm even licenced to carry a firearm. I've never looked back.

Encouraged by my father, a detective at the time, and my godfather, Uncle Andrew, I worked hard. I took Andrew's advice because he has his own corporation and connections with the Ministry of Defence. As a result, I excelled in all areas, rising to the top of my class. The man who recruited me said it was essential to be the best. I believed him, and took his faith in me as an important sign. I remember the excitement of being singled out as someone different, strong, unique. I'll admit, it was flattering.

That same feeling now accompanies the receiving of this folder. I'd been chosen to see this. They needed my input. All those years of studying had given me confidence and expertise as a psychological profiler. My contributions have solved cases, saved lives, but I was acutely aware that I was only as good as each case they gave me. I had a feeling this one would be difficult.

'You can open the file, Michael,' says the man by the door.

I look up at the use of my name and find myself face to face with a man I've seen many times around the building: Security Agent Ray Martin. This man has clearance I can only dream of. I hadn't known he was behind this. I might have been nervous if I had.

'What's in it?'

'Something that may interest you, as a profiler.'

I nod. My adrenaline quells a little. This might be nothing much. I calm myself as I open the folder because I don't want Ray to see my excitement. You should never appear too keen at a job interview, and I had no doubt that this was one.

On the first page I see a photograph showing the burnt-out remains of a hotel laundry van.

I speed-read the information provided in the document, noting how elements of the content have been crossed through with impenetrable black marker. Will Ray Martin explain why so much of this has been redacted?

'We're expecting you to take the job,' Ray says.

'What does it involve?'

'I want you to be part of a special taskforce. It's newly formed and has a specific role within MI5,' Ray says.

I learn for the first time that my role in MI5 isn't going to be the traditional one after all, nor is the agency as transparent as they appear.

'As you know, the official line is that the agency's aim is to "gather intelligence" and we actively say agents have no power to arrest anyone. This is true to an extent but there are branches and divisions that do have that kind of power, and more,' Ray continues.

'I know this, of course,' I say. 'It was part of the recruitment briefing.'

'This taskforce is officially called Archive,' Ray says.

His wording fascinates me; it tells me more about the type of taskforce Ray is running than a full explanation does. I know then that I am being invited into something unique. Archive is not as innocuous as it sounds.

'The brief I was given said we'd be looking at cold cases. That you wanted a second opinion on one such case,' I say, keeping my voice level.

'That's certainly true,' says Ray. 'But there's more to Archive than that. We look at other things too. Current issues. Some cases we'll crack; some will be ongoing as we try to put together the pieces of a complicated puzzle.'

'Solving puzzles is what I do,' I say.

'Few people in MI5 are senior enough to know that Archive even exists,' Ray continues. 'With acceptance of this job come some extra requirements.

'Such as?' I ask.

'You'll be using your expertise to its full capacity. But secrecy surrounding the cases and what you do at Archive will be paramount. You can't share it with anyone. Family, friend, or lover.'

'It's that serious then?' I say, knowing that Ray means every word. 'I can do that. But why me?'

'During your study years you spent time asking questions and not always accepting the obvious explanations. We've been watching you.'

I'm beginning to understand why so much time and money has been spent on me. It's a question I'd raised time and again when, at the end of the training, they gave me a simple office job.

I'd talked about it with Uncle Andrew. He'd encouraged

me to stick with MI5 and it appears that his advice was correct.

Andrew had always been in my life and, though he wasn't really an uncle, my twin sister, Mia, and I called him that until we reached our twenty-first birthday. On that day he asked us both to refer to him as Andrew. Mia and I were happy to, but Andrew was more than that to us. He was a constant, unlike our parents, who were always more interested in each other than in their two children. Though I don't say they aren't proud of our achievements. My father encouraged my choice of profession, and Mia and I had been given the best of everything. But even now, it's Andrew I go to for advice. And Mia who comes to me for help and comfort, just as she did when we were children.

While I'd been plodding along in the new MI5 desk job, I'd expressed my disappointment to Andrew without telling him anything specific. Within twenty-four hours I'd received the call and was invited to apply for this new role. I couldn't help thinking that Andrew had somehow pulled strings, but it didn't matter to me. I wanted to do more – regardless of how the role came about – and I'd prove myself worthy if I hadn't already.

'What do you see in this file?' Ray asks, bringing my thoughts back to this crucial task.

'The van was used to cover up another crime.'

'How do you know that?' Ray asks.

'The extent of the fire. It's not a standard robbery, joyride, and burn-out. It's thorough. Meticulous. There was no DNA found at all anywhere,' I explain.

'This was one of our cold cases until recently. Now it's

become current. We have remains that we believe are connected.' Ray sits down opposite me. 'Look in the back.'

I turn the pages until I find the next set of photographs. This isn't a crime scene but an exhumation. The body was found in a shallow grave in the Lincolnshire Wolds.

'A runner tripped over what he thought was a root but turned out to be a human bone.'

'How did you know it was connected to this van?' I ask.

'The van was found two years ago near this spot. Although local law enforcement searched the area, they didn't find the grave or the remains at the time. It must have been covered up fairly well. However, the person who did this hadn't planned on nature's interference. The body was buried under an old oak tree; the roots grew through it and pushed it to the surface,' Martin explains.

'It wasn't buried deep enough then. Sloppy,' I say.

'Precisely. After being so scrupulous about burning the van, and possibly any clothing that might have contained evidence, the killer was a bit amateur about the body disposal.'

'First-time kill?'

'What do you think?' Ray says.

I read the autopsy report before replying, 'This wasn't a first kill. But it was a first-time clean-up.'

'Why?'

I return my attention to the folder, pointing to the description of the wound inflicted on the victim. 'Most amateurs stab downwards, or forwards. This one knew how to handle the knife and where to do the most damage. The stab was upwards, directly and precisely under the ribs. A killing blow.'

Ray nods. 'What I don't understand, though, is why they knew enough to destroy all DNA but not how to rid themselves of the body completely? Someone with that level of expertise should understand how to dissolve human flesh and bone with chemicals.'

I glance once more over the file before replying, taking in one forensic statement after another. Something nags at the back of my brain – a feeling I've had before when studying evidence. I see myself looking at the victim – a woman – through the perpetrator's eyes. Despite the execution, there is something sympathetic about the disposal of the body. Then my gaze falls on the photograph of the grave. Of course. The answer is there, so obvious, yet almost overlooked.

'This wasn't just a disposal of a corpse. The killer gave the victim a burial,' I conclude.

Ray leans forward and looks again at the pictures of the grave. I think he must have examined them many times before, but he can't see it. I almost didn't myself, but then I have been trained for this. To look and to really *perceive*.

'How do you know?'

'Aside from the fact that the death was clean. A straightforward kill, no dismemberment. No immolation – they could have let the body burn in the van. But look as this.' I point at the picture.

'Daffodils? So? They got crushed by the excavation team.'

'There,' I say. 'There's string wrapped around the stems. This isn't just a hole they dumped the body into; it's a grave. The killer laid their victim to rest, and then brought them flowers. These are fresh so I'd say the killer visits fairly regularly.'

Ray sits back and stares at me for a moment, holding his chin with his hand. He looks thoughtful and then his serious expression changes and his eyes focus on me as though he's seeing me for the first time.

'I'm going to need you to sign this,' he says. He produces a piece of paper and puts it down in front of me. 'Official Secrets Act.'

'I've already signed one. Should be on file,' I say.

'That was generic. This one is specific.'

I read the document, understanding completely. This is more detailed, and I acknowledge that by signing I'll be changing my life even more. It is the end of privacy as I've known it. I write my name across the bottom, then date the document. I push it back to Ray.

'So, what's this all really about?' I ask.

'As I've said, Archive is a very important department. To most in the know, we *are* about cold cases, but there's far more to us than that.'

I feel a growing exhilaration as I prepare for Ray to reveal all to me.

'Spies?' I ask.

'When we need to be,' says Ray. 'Mostly we take over suspicious cases from homicide.'

'Suspicious in what way?'

'Hits disguised as something else. Some cases involve persons of interest we've been watching. No two cases are the same and so it's difficult to fully describe what we do. Even so, I have no doubt you will fit in and form your own opinion of our significance within MI5.'

I digest this information; it's obvious that Ray can't give me a simple, straight answer as the taskforce doesn't have a specific definition. I'm intrigued though. My short time so far at MI5 has proved to be mundane and I've felt like little more than a pencil-pusher at times, with the occasional profile task to perform – despite the fact that I've done my job well enough to get Ray's attention. Now I'm wondering if that was the point. Were they waiting, watching me for a while before I was really brought into the fold? Did I have to prove myself first?

'Why do you take the hits on? Why does it matter?' I ask.

'Because these executions sometimes happen to former spies, or those we suspect of being hired assassins.'

'That makes sense in this case,' I say.

'Why?'

'This was one of their own. They killed them, but the burial aspect shows a great deal of empathy and deference. Anyone else would have been in a chemical vat for certain.'

'I think you're right,' says Ray. 'Maybe we'll learn that she's someone who's been on our wanted list.'

'You said that sometimes cases involve people you're interested in. Is there a connection with Archive? Is that why these people die?'

'No,' says Ray. 'Not that we've discovered. It's not generally our interest in them, but rather what they have accidentally or intentionally discovered that leads them down this path. But why our victims die is often the information we most want. Their murders could be important – we just don't know yet. In this case, if our victim was an assassin, judging by her age, she may have been killed because she was no use to them. *Retired*, if you like. She wasn't expecting it though. This woman may have known something that made it too dangerous for her to be allowed to simply *leave* her profession.'

I take in the inferences of Ray's revelations. If her employers had something to hide, this would make sense.

'Sometimes what we do is dangerous. That's why we are an armed division,' Ray continues. 'You should know that before you accept the transfer.'

'You already know I'm very adept with a firearm,' I say. 'I doubt I'd even be here if you thought I was the slightest bit coy about it.'

Ray laughs. 'We know *everything* about you.'

I process this. Ray means what he says. I'm ambitious enough not to mind. I find myself wanting in even more. I've examined killers across the spectrum, but so far not assassins. The appeal of this kind of work lies within the workings of the mind of sociopaths and how their narcissistic tendencies are hidden from the world in a semblance of normal behaviour. In effect, they are actors, playing the role of conforming. Assassins may have average lives, day jobs, partners – perhaps even children. To delve into these personalities and understand how they work is always the ultimate challenge. The idea thrills me in a way that other things in the world don't. It's a mystery I'm always keen to unravel.

Some would say it takes a sociopath to catch one.

'You'll have to be careful with future associations, girlfriends...' Ray says. 'But the pay and the pension are worth it. We look after our own.'

Did Ray just assume that I'm straight? No, he knows I am; they know 'everything' about me. I let that sit in the back of my mind. Does this change anything at all? No. I know what I'll be doing at Archive will be important. I want to be part of it despite the few drawbacks. What's a little privacy after all? Also, I'd like to see this file without the redactions. What will it tell me then about the killer? What other cases are they pursuing, and how will my mind be stretched to help solve them? I hide my anticipatory shudder as I move in my seat.

'You in?' asks Martin.

'You know I am.'

'Good,' says Ray.

I sign all the necessary paperwork and as Ray takes it from me, he says, 'Give my best to your uncle Andrew.'

'You know Andrew?' I say.

'We worked together. Back in my Ministry of Defence days.'

I don't ask him any more as I know from Andrew that he can't talk about his former government work.

'He's got his own company now,' I say.

'I know,' says Ray.

It leaves me feeling odd that they know each other, though I'm not sure why. Hadn't I suspected that Andrew was somehow involved in this? That he'd 'had a word' with someone at MI5 about a promotion for me? I decide I'll ask next time I see him.

Chapter Two

NEVA

Present day

S he is sitting at the bar when her mark comes in. He is tall and good-looking – just like his photograph. Not the sort they usually send her. This one is more like a male model than a clerk who opened the wrong folder on the wrong day and had been caught doing it. She hadn't asked them what was in the folder. Something dangerous, no doubt. Hazardous for this guy anyway. Risky for her too, should she learn the contents.

She knows better than to show any curiosity.

In the mirror that stretches across the back of the bar, she watches him, unnoticed. She has made certain that she is his type. The case file covered it all: how to dress (modest), what colour and style her hair should be (a black outgrown bob), and even the nerdy, black-rimmed glasses she doesn't need but which suit her anyway.

The inevitable happens soon after he sits: he meets her

eyes. She looks away, embarrassed. It is not difficult for her to avoid eye contact; looking directly into someone's eyes is far harder. There's a moment of hesitation. She knows he's studying her. She gives him a quick glance, a little more encouragement, and then he's moving seats.

He has so much confidence, as though he knows he'll have no trouble reeling her in.

'Look, I'm not interested…' she says. 'I came in here for a *quiet* drink…'

'Me too. Shit day?'

She doesn't answer.

'Let me buy you one drink … then I'll let you get on with your *lonely* evening,' he says.

'Like I haven't heard that before.'

He looks at her with an innocent puppy-dog expression that he's worked on for years. It's never failed him. It won't now. He doesn't know that this time is already more certain than previous ones.

She accepts the drink. There's no point in dragging it out: a James Bond special, but stirred, not shaken. Irony makes it so much more fun.

A few drinks later, and they are both giggling.

'Let me make you coffee,' he says. 'I make a mean cappuccino. Then I'll make sure you get home safe.'

She looks at him over the top of the Martini glasses. 'I shouldn't have drunk so much. You're not going to take advantage of me, are you?'

'Me? I'd never do such a thing.'

'Neva … that's unusual,' he says when they reach his flat. 'How do you spell it?'

'N.E.V.A.'

'I like that. It's different.'

'Yes.'

They are barely in the door when he comes on strong. Neva is ready for it. He pushes her up against the wall. Hands everywhere. She doesn't struggle. She lets him kiss and grope her, swaying as though the effects of the alcohol have somehow loosened her up. She drops the overlarge handbag she's carrying down to the floor, freeing her hands. It's then that she sees the vase of daffodils on a small table by the door. She shudders.

'I like girls like you. Always so prim on the outside but really…'

'That's enough.' She pushes at his chest, but the movement appears to be half-hearted.

He ignores her. Laughs a little in the back of his throat. He's not the sort of man who takes 'no' for an answer even if she really has changed her mind.

'I said stop—'

'You don't mean it—'

Neva punches him sharply in the throat.

He goes down fast, gasping for air.

'What is the converse of heaven?' she asks, running her fingers lightly over the petals of one of the daffodils. As if in slow motion, the petal breaks off and floats down onto the surface of the table. Neva's heart begins to pound in her chest. Her head hurts. Anger bubbles up to the surface.

Bright writhes on the floor, choking. He reaches out to

the wall beside him to try and lever himself to his feet. The look in his eyes tells her that he knows what this is about. He will never be able to admit that, though, not with a crushed larynx.

His eyes bulge; he's getting air, but not enough. She thinks about letting him suffer – perhaps for all those nerdy girls he's plied with drink and then forced himself on in the past – but Neva has bigger fish to fry and it will serve no purpose to delay. She reminds herself that she is not an avenging angel – that way madness lies; she is a woman with a paying job to do. The thought steadies her.

She picks up her handbag from the floor. It has everything she needs inside.

He tries to croak a plea for his life. *Pathetic really*. And pointless. That's when Neva lets her knife drop down from the holster around her wrist.

'I asked you a question. But it's clear you're not much of a thinker or you would know that your activities have been observed. But let me not frustrate you. The reverse of heaven is *hell*, or in my case—'

She stops as she becomes aware that she is talking more than usual. Babbling her thoughts like an amateur.

'Pl … ease…' he croaks.

He manages to get up onto his knees; the colour is returning to his cheeks.

'You have some fight left in you. Interesting. But this is what you get for being a nosey parker. Your employers were clear that they wanted you to know what you've done.'

The knife moves through the air, one clean swipe. She's adept at using it and it's still her first weapon of choice.

His hand grabs at his throat in a clumsy attempt to stop the flow but blood seeps through his fingers unchecked. Then, as shock takes effect, he pitches forward. Neva leaves him bleeding on the laminate floor. She observes that the cheap surface will soak up the blood and be damaged beyond repair. In the end, material things don't matter.

The hallway is warm, but not overly hot. There are four doors on the left. The first is the living room, the second a kitchen, the third is the bedroom and the fourth is the room she is looking for.

On entering the flat, she had slipped on a pair of leather gloves. Now she takes them off, putting them into a plastic bag that she withdraws from the pocket of her coat. She pulls on a fresh set of surgical gloves taken from the handbag, then opens the door to the bathroom. She glances inside, observing it is clean, and that no one else is there. Inside, she rinses her blade then stows it back in her wrist holster. From her purse she brings out a small bottle, containing bleach, which she splashes around the sink. She cleans it of all sign of the blood from the blade then returns the empty bottle to her bag.

In the kitchen she finds the mark's laptop. It is plugged in, charging. She opens it and finds his emails. Most people have their passwords stored on their personal machines, thinking them safe. The mark is no different and so it isn't long before Neva has full access. Without opening or reading anything, she deletes the contents of the inbox. Then she clears the deleted files, removing them permanently from the email handler. After that, she inserts a pen drive into the USB port, then initiates a complete reset of the device, wiping all files as part of the process using a specific programme. It won't be easy for anyone else to check what the mark has been doing.

Leaving the process running, she knocks over the tea and coffee canisters, spilling the contents over the work surface and onto the floor. Pushing over one of the breakfast bar stools, she finishes by pulling out and shattering his crockery. When this is done, the room looks as though it has been ransacked.

She does the same in the living room – tipping chairs, opening and rifling through the sideboard, knocking books from a shelf until everything is in turmoil. She destroys the bedroom in the same way.

After that she returns to the kitchen, takes back her pen drive, and goes back to the hallway.

The mark is lying on his side, dead. It hasn't taken long for him to bleed out.

She turns him over and searches his pockets, finding his mobile phone. Thankfully, there's no passcode on the device. She refreshes the mailbox and watches as everything clears out of the mobile app inbox and deleted files. Then she restores the phone to factory settings, erasing anything that might lead the authorities back to her employers. When the phone restarts, she returns it to his pocket. Next, Neva removes his wallet. She takes all cash and cards, placing them in another clear plastic bag that she withdraws from her jacket pocket. She folds the bag closed, then puts the package back in her pocket. After that, she drops the mark's wallet on the floor beside his corpse.

She hasn't touched anything without her gloves on, but she pulls a pack of wipes from her other pocket and wipes down the door handles in the hallway as an extra precaution. She bunches up the used wipes and puts them and the pack away in the inside pocket of her jacket.

She glances at the mark's face, looks at his glassy eyes, and presses her fingers to his pulse to confirm that he has gone. She notes again how good-looking he was.

Looks do not make the man…

Then she turns away and forgets all about this observation.

She takes a quick photograph of him on her mobile, then sends it to the only number stored on the phone. A few seconds later, the phone vibrates as a text arrives.

She glances at the message:

Payment sent

Then she takes the sim card out of the phone, snaps it in half, and places it in another clear bag and back into the pocket that holds the mark's money and cards.

Still wearing her gloves, she opens the flat door and looks down the corridor. They didn't pass anyone on the way up and Neva had been careful to keep her face turned away from the other doors, just in case one of them has a camera. She closes the door, then takes a short crowbar out of her bag. Casting a glance around, she uses the bar to break the lock, then she pushes the door half open. Her eyes fall once more on the vase of flowers, then she turns and walks away.

———————

Several streets away from the flat, a homeless man is sleeping in the doorway of a hardware shop. Neva takes the money and cards out of her pocket. Removing them from the plastic bag, she drops the wad down onto the man's sleeping bag. She hurries away.

Further along the street, she drops the sim card down into a drain at the side of the road. She drops the burner phone on the ground and smashes and grinds it with her heel, then dumps the pieces in a bin outside the off-licence.

Removing the wig and glasses, she stuffs them into another plastic bag. A few minutes later, she boards a bus heading out of town.

Chapter Three

MICHAEL

'Security Agent Michael Kensington,' I say, flashing the MI5 crest at Constable Ealing. Ealing recognises the badge and steps back to allow me entrance to the flat.

'What happened?' I ask.

'Neighbour found him. Looks like a robbery. His name is … *was* Aidan Bright.'

'I know.'

The constable goes quiet. He probably thinks I'm an arrogant tosser. I don't put him right because it doesn't really matter what the man thinks of me. I'm here to do my job and that is to study the crime scene first-hand to see if this gives me any insight into the killer. I examine the door, which has been forced and seems to back up the assumption that this was a robbery gone wrong.

I look down at the body in the hallway. He's slumped forward, as though he was on his knees begging for his life seconds before his life was taken. I bend down and see the clean wound at his throat. The cause of death is obvious. I don't disturb the body.

'Forensics are on the way. Did you touch anything?'

'Tried not to, sir.'

'Good.'

I walk away from the corpse and follow the route through the flat that I suspect the killer will have taken. In my mind's eye, I shadow the assassin's route to the bathroom, while pulling on a pair of surgical gloves. As I open the door, there is a strong smell of bleach – a sure sign that this room has been cleaned of all evidence. A jolt of anticipation rattles through my blood. I recognise the *modus operandi*: I've been tracking this assassin for years and they are always meticulous. All surfaces will be wiped down. Forensics won't find anything, but I search anyway. There is room for error; one day this killer will make a mistake and I will find it. But I know, as I look around, whose file this will go into and it's a profile I've been studying ever since I joined Archive.

I walk to the sink and look down, eyes scanning the porcelain for anything, even a strand of hair. Then I open the medicine cabinet. It appears that nothing has been touched.

Aidan Bright had been a person of interest for a while. He worked at Elgin Beeson, an armament manufacturer. Bright had been little more than a credit clerk with low-grade military clearance but MI5 saw him as a possible danger to security because the man had tendencies that made him open to future blackmail, or imprisonment. So, when the emergency call came through, the agency picked up on it. That's why I'm the first real authority to arrive on the scene.

I look around the flat, touching nothing, but taking photographs of the destruction for further study. Homicide are likely to come up with a scenario that shows Bright returning home, catching a burglar, and then the culprit turning on him. This isn't the case. This is a professional job, and Bright was dead before the ransack even took place.

'Robbery gone wrong?' the constable asks as I return to the hallway.

I don't answer, but I can tell the constable doubts what he sees too. The turning over of the flat is too precise. This, perhaps, is the flaw I've been looking for. Any opportunist burglary and would-be homicide would show signs of panic. There are none here, and I didn't expect to find any.

Even though I'm only a few years older than the constable, I think, *This young man will be one to watch for the future*. He's smart; I see it in his expression, despite his silence, or maybe because he knows when not to ask questions.

Sometimes I feel old, as though I've been in this line of work for longer than I have, because dealing with the things I see, on a daily basis, changes you. But would I ever change what I do? I doubt it. I analyse the joy I feel in discovering this is *the* assassin and I wonder what Ray would think if he knew that catching this one was something of an obsession.

'Thank you, constable,' I say. 'You may allow forensics to do what's needed and to take the body. They know who to report to.'

My eyes fall then on a vase of daffodils on the table by

the door. One of the petals has fallen onto the table. In my mind's eye, I see the assassin pausing to touch the flowers; days old, they were fragile and ready to break. Somehow it feels significant. It niggles at my mind but I don't know why.

———————————

'The flat was turned over,' I explain, 'but not for robbery. It was staged.'

Archive's office is based in central London, an unimposing building not far from Borough Market, and disguised as a publishing company. Archive is on the top floor. There the serious work takes place, not the real, and thriving, business we are disguised as. My office is just off a central room that my colleagues Bethany Cane and Leon Tchaikovsky work in. Down the hallway is Ray's office, which also doubles as our briefing room. We are in there now, and I flick through the photographs on a large screen as the four of us sit around the conference table, each behind a computer whose screen we can share. We have been working on this case for years but every new piece of the puzzle we find always leads us away from finding this assassin and, more importantly, the person hiring them. This time, however, I feel like I've learnt something about the killer that we didn't know before.

I am Ray's second, and Beth and Leon have equal status in our hierarchy. Beth is in her thirties. She's been with Archive a year less than me, and Leon, who is also in his mid-thirties, started a little before. We are a young team but for Ray, who is now approaching his fifties.

Although he tries not to show it, Leon has a little chip on his shoulder about the fact that I was promoted and he was overlooked. He's quieter than me at the briefings, but that's usually because I am sharing my insights with the team. I generally work better with Beth, as she is easy company and always contributes a great deal to any discussions, but also because I don't feel that underlying resentment for my position coming from her. She appears content with where she is.

'You think it's the same assassin?' Beth asks now.

'Yes. The use of the knife, the wiping and bleaching to remove evidence. It fits the MO of kills all in the last few years. But I also think it's the same person who buried and placed flowers on the grave of our mysterious Jane Doe some years back.' I explain the feeling I got when I saw the daffodils in Bright's flat.

'Could be a coincidence,' Ray chips in. 'But I'm all about gut instinct, as you know.'

I nod, as we've had this discussion many times. Instinct is everything in our job.

'Anyway,' I continue. 'That's why I think this is our girl...'

'*Girl*? How do you deduce that?' says Leon.

'Bright's death has given us a breakthrough. I believe he brought a woman back with him and she killed him.'

'We've known Bright's tendencies for a while,' Beth says, backing me up much to Leon's annoyance. 'So, it's likely they used a woman to lure him.'

In the past year, several women had come forward all claiming that Bright had raped them. Each time, somehow the slippery little bastard managed to get an alibi. There was never any DNA: he always used a condom, and then forced the girl to shower afterwards. Bright was a serial rapist who knew how to cover his tracks. The girls were often too shocked and afraid to come forward and those who did where made to look like liars. Even so, a case was being compiled against him. It was only a matter of time before he was arrested – an inconvenience for his employers, who, I'm sure, knew all about him.

'Which is why,' I conclude, 'I think someone at Elgin Beeson hired the killer.'

'But how can we prove that?' Leon asks, as he's all about fact and never lets us get away with conjecture.

'We can't,' I say. 'But we have to accept that the kind of power Beeson's has will give them access to someone who can "remove" a future problem. Bright was that problem, and he might not have had much security clearance, but he had enough to have access to something he could use if he were arrested. At least, that's my theory. But back to the girl. The assassin. What can we draw from this that will be a help?' I look around the room and find all eyes waiting for me to fill in these gaps. Even Leon appears to be interested. 'She'll be wearing a deliberate disguise. Bright's *type*. Beth, I have pictures here of all of the girls that were brave enough to come forward and report Bright. Take a look, will you? And let's see if there's any security footage in the area that might help to confirm my theory.'

'On it.' Beth turns back to the computer she's using.

Within a few seconds, she's accessed all the public cameras in the area and is fast forwarding through them looking for signs of anyone around the time of Aidan's death.

'We had a hit on Bright's credit card...' Leon says looking up from his computer. 'Off-licence a few streets from his flat, if that helps to narrow it down.'

Beth searches the cameras in that area.

'I've found something,' she says after a few minutes. 'Dark-haired woman with black-rimmed glasses passed by a hardware store near the Phoenix off-licence on the corner of Tate Street. That's Bright's fetish for sure. I think you were right, Mike. We are looking for a woman.'

'It still doesn't prove someone at Beeson's had him killed,' Leon points out, ever the devil's advocate.

'No, but he was a liability,' I say. 'Put the footage up on the large screen, please, Beth.'

Seeing her for the first time gives me something akin to an electric shock. My heart thumps in my chest as adrenaline rushes through my blood. The woman on the screen is exactly the type that Bright went for. But this one, although mousy on the surface, walks with magnificent confidence. There is a presence about her, a grace of movement, and I imagine that even the tap of her heels on the pavement is silent. A poet would compare her to something predatory, even though the walk itself does not say aggression. She's fascinating. This is the one we've been looking for. I just know it.

'She's about five-eight,' I say. 'Athletic, or with some dance training, judging by how she moves. She's fully aware of her surroundings, totally in command of them.

Look how she's turning her face away; she knows the camera is there. Beth, can we get anything from face recognition?'

'I'll try.'

'What was that?' I say. 'Rewind. She dropped something. On that vagrant. My guess is that he was the one using the card in the off-licence.'

Beth nods. 'Let's hope he wasn't as asleep as he appears. If we find him, we may have our very first living witness…'

My phone beeps then with a reminder. I have a meeting arranged.

'Lunch date?' Beth says.

'Yeah. Uncle Andrew,' I say. 'I'll pick this up with you all later.'

As I leave, I hear Beth say to Leon, 'Do you think that guy really *is* his uncle?'

I don't hear Leon's response.

———

I meet Andrew in an Italian restaurant nearby. He's never admitted that it was him who whispered in Ray Martin's ear to get me the job at Archive. Either way, it doesn't matter. It's all worked out for the best. Andrew never asks me about what I do, and I never volunteer information. Our meetings are, for the most part, quite simple. It's a relief, in many ways, from the darkness of my job.

Chapter Four

NEVA

'Hey! You can't get in that way!' says a male voice.

Neva looks at the man. She is wearing her long hair in two pigtails

'I'm locked out of my place,' she says.

'What? You live here? Haven't seen you before.'

'Just moved in. Dropped my keys down there,' she says, pointing into the darkest part of the alley.

'What were you doing out here anyway?' asks the man.

Neva looks sheepish.

'My folks are a bit strict about me going out sometimes. I snuck out.'

'Look. I'll let you in the back way, just this once. But you can't do this again.'

'You work here?'

The man nods. 'Maintenance.'

'Thanks.'

At the back door of the building, the man types in his security code. Neva waits while he opens the door.

'When you get inside, take the service lift to your floor. You don't need a pass to get in it from down here. Just from the floors themselves.'

'You've been really helpful. Can you show me where the lift is?'

'Sure, it's over—'

His cry is choked off as cheese wire cuts into his throat. Neva twists the cord, and blood leaks over and around it. A sickening gurgle bubbles from his lips before his knees give and the maintenance man slumps. Neva holds the line taut in her leather-gloved hands until she's certain he's dead.

She untangles the cable from his neck, placing it into one of her plastic wallets. Out of habit she checks his pulse. She looks into his wide, bulging eyes. She feels … *something*. A burst of unfamiliar emotion. He's a casualty she hadn't wanted. But as soon as he saw her his fate was decided.

'Who lives and who dies is dependent on what they know that can affect the Network,' her handler Tracey had said, and Neva reminds herself of this now. *There's no other logical choice; this is damage limitation.*

Once she has justified it to herself, Neva pushes the execution from her mind. She sees the man as nothing more than a problem she must now conceal. She closes the outer door and looks around for an appropriate storing place. She is in a loading-bay area. To her left is a large shutter door that can be opened to receive deliveries. To her right is the service lift and another door.

The corpse has a security pass clipped to his coat. Neva takes it. She goes to the door and swipes the card; it opens, revealing a small room where the maintenance man stores his tools. There's a strong smell of oil in the room and Neva notices the open can of grease that's been knocked over by the door. She wedges the door open and then returns to the body. Taking hold of the feet, she drags the carcass over to the room. She stows *it* inside. She looks down at the body for a moment. A small frown forms on her forehead.

'Sorry, old bean,' she says in a perfect royal English accent before closing the door.

She takes a breath before calling the service lift. In her gloved hand, she holds the security pass. She sees the man's name and tries not to remember it. The lift arrives. She straightens her right arm, ready to drop down her blade if the lift isn't empty. But when the door opens, she's relieved to find it free. She doesn't want any more work than she already has. This is supposed to be quick and easy. So far, things aren't going as well as they should.

She enters the lift and presses the button to take her up to the third floor. There, her target waits ... though *she* doesn't know it yet.

As planned, the lights are out all over this floor and the corridor is in darkness as she exits the lift. Neva's eyes adjust; she's never minded the dark. She moves down the corridor, keeping her head down until she reaches the flat in question. Then she removes a small pouch from the pocket of her jeans. She picks the lock with barely a sound.

With the power cut, the alarm is disconnected. This woman, Lily Devlin, lives alone and is security conscious. Neva doesn't know why she's been sent to erase her. Usually she doesn't care, but as she enters the flat, closing the door behind her, she comes face to face with a large canvas photograph on the wall. Lily Devlin, holding a small baby.

Neva staggers back as though someone has hit her. Her mind flies into a flash of memory. A woman, a baby, a man … all familiar faces but she cannot recall who they are.

'Mamma…' she hears a small voice say.

Neva looks around but there is no one in the hallway of the flat with her. This is a voice she's heard before. It is a unique moment of *déjà vu*. An echo from a past she doesn't remember.

She shakes away the evocation, then turns left towards her target's bedroom. She will do the job, quickly and efficiently. That's what she's paid for. Nothing needs to be dragged out or thought about.

Neva opens the bedroom door; the hinges creak. She pauses, waiting to see if her kill has been alerted, but no sound comes from within the room. She pushes the door further open. There is a shape outlined in the bed, but to launch in and kill, without being certain who it is, is not her way. She will look her victim in the eyes when she implements the contract. She'll make sure she's dead.

She comes into the room, aware of every sound, every movement. The woman isn't breathing loudly; silence comes from the bed. Behind her there is a movement in the air. Neva ducks down as something swings towards her head. She falls forward into a roll, launching herself back to her feet in one slick movement. She is facing someone now. A tall figure, taller than herself, and she is five-eight. The knife is released from the holster as she throws herself forward, knocking the person to the ground.

There is a groan as the person crashes to the floor. Light fills the room as the power comes back on; Neva sees the woman at her feet. It is the intended mark but she had not expected any resistance.

'Who are you?' the mark says.

'I'm here to kill you.'

'Why?'

'It's my job.'

Lily Devlin struggles to sit, pressing her back against the wall near the door. Neva makes no move to finish the job. She merely looks at her.

'Don't you ever ask why?'

'No.'

'You're *her*,' Devlin says.

Neva frowns. Someone else has said those words before, showing a recognition that they shouldn't have had.

'I never thought this day would come. Though I should have known. Especially after Ansell,' Devlin continues. 'But we all think ourselves immortal. We all believe we are indispensable.'

Neva never asks questions, but at the mention of the assassin, she is curious about Devlin.

'How did you know Ansell?' she asks.

Devlin pulls her knees up to her chest; it is an unconsciously defensive position. Neva knows that this woman doesn't want to die. But what Devlin wants will have no bearing on what will have to happen in the end.

'I used to be her handler.'

'Handler?' says Neva.

'Yes. You have one. Tracey.'

'You mean the person who pays me?'

'If you like…'

'You gave Ansell her assignments?' Neva says.

Devlin nods.

'And now you are mine—'

'Aren't you curious? Even a little?'

Neva thinks of Ansell. She remembers Ansell's grave. She hasn't returned since she saw the forensic van parked there. That day, they almost caught her taking flowers, which she'd done whenever she passed through the Lincolnshire Wolds. She didn't know why, but it was somehow important to her. Ansell's grave had become a symbol of what the future held. A surety that Neva had above all else. One day, she'd be disposed of, too.

She sits down on the bed and looks at Devlin but doesn't ask anything more. Instead, she waits for Devlin's desperate and hopeful chatter, knowing that the woman thinks her revelations will save her. It won't. It never does.

'They retire us all in the end. It's an ironic reward for our loyalty. You always believe you won't be next. Then, some psych evaluation you fail, or some small indiscretion, a display of inquisitiveness, a split second when you question the whole thing. They know. I don't know how, but they always know. I questioned. It was such a small thing. I asked whether we'd be able to retrieve Ansell's body from the mortuary. That's why you're here.'

'Ansell's body?'

'It was found. I know you buried her.'

'If you know, so must the Network,' Neva says. 'Yet it's me who's visiting you.'

'I covered for you. I excused your lack of knowledge in disposal and blamed it on the suddenness of them telling you to do it. It's not usual for the operative to clean up.'

'I know,' says Neva.

'Then someone is on standby to clean me away?'

'I haven't asked.'

'Didn't you even ask why they told you to clean up Ansell?' Devlin says.

'No. Why should I?'

'You're well trained,' she says. 'I bet no one has ever mentioned *his* name around you, have they? The one who gives all the orders.'

Neva continues to watch Devlin. Her face is passive, devoid of all emotion, but her eyes never move from Devlin's face.

'So, how will you do it? You favour the blade, don't you? May I choose?'

Neva nods.

'I'd prefer a bullet. Right in the back of the head. It would ultimately be the swiftest and most painless.'

Neva pushes the knife back into the holster. She pulls out the gun tucked into the back of her jeans. From her pocket she removes a silencer. It is a Glock 20, 10mm suppressed. A reliable weapon. It will do the job with minimal noise. It will also be clear to law enforcement that this was a hit, not a random robbery or accidental death. It's likely that a clean-up will be needed.

'You want an *obvious* death,' Neva says.

'Yes,' Devlin's answer is breathy. She sounds less scared, more excited. As though she feels her end will mean something more than her life has. 'I hope someone does the same for you when the time comes.'

Neva doesn't answer. She is happy to oblige and give Devlin the execution she deserves.

'Stand,' she says.

Devlin does as she's told. 'His name is Beech,' she says. 'Mr Beech. He'll be the one who makes the order for you one day, too.'

'Turn,' Neva says.

Devlin turns, and then she is running, making a break for the door in a last-ditch attempt to save herself. Neva expects her action. The gun goes off and Devlin collapses on the threshold of the bedroom door. Her head is turned. Neva stands over her. The bullet has penetrated the back of Devlin's skull. Neva cannot see the exit wound. She fires two more shots into Devlin's head. Then she takes a photograph and sends it to her employer with the words:

CLEAN-UP REQUIRED?

She receives confirmation of payment, and a short response:

NO

Neva finds herself wondering why. She's about to reply, but stops herself. Devlin's words ring inside her head.

I hope someone does the same for you when the time comes.

She finds herself wondering how it feels to be shot in the head.

Chapter Five

MICHAEL

'It doesn't make sense. Normally this sort of hit would become a disappearance,' I explain. 'But the body was left there.'

'What do we know about our victim?' asks Beth.

'She's the PA for Lib Dem backbencher Sylvester Engelman. She's worked for him for the past eleven years. Divorced. One child. A daughter, currently at university. She's clean. Not even a speeding ticket. No hint of scandal,' I explain.

'What about her university years? Caught smoking something?' asks Ray.

'That's the thing,' Leon says. 'There's not one hint of her being associated with anything scandalous. No drug abuse, no politically charged friends. By all accounts she was a homey, hard-working student. Political views are straight down the middle. Perfect for a politician's PA. *Too perfect.*'

I change the picture on the screen. It now shows an

image of Lily Devlin on graduation day. She looks like an average student. Normal. Forgettable, even.

'She's not what she seems,' I say. 'She can't be. Let's talk to her ex-husband.'

Anton Devlin's law firm in Surbiton is in a small building. There are several offices and three different solicitors working there. Though the practice is reasonably successful, Devlin is not a high-flyer. He is the senior partner, having branched out on his own after the divorce from Lily Devlin, ten years earlier. I already know that Devlin left a much more successful practice than his own current one will ever be because it is outside central London. He'd been earning a lot more money as one of the lesser partners in the previous firm than he was now. Devlin isn't in debt, but he isn't rolling in spare money either. The firm ticks over, he can pay his bills and have some extravaganzas, but he isn't living it up. Nor has he remarried. All of this has raised questions and Beth and I arrive at his office looking for answers.

I show my badge to the receptionist and ask to see Devlin. She raises her eyebrows, then tries to make her face expressionless.

'Please take a seat,' she says.

'Let's get this straight. You don't think the ex is involved?' Beth whispers as we sit in the waiting area.

'No. I really don't.'

'Then why are we in his office waiting to speak to him?'

'Because I think he may be able to shed some light on her life. He lived with her for ten years. He must know something about her.'

'Mr Devlin will see you now,' the receptionist says. 'Down the hall, second door on the left.'

We stand and walk down the corridor as instructed. The receptionist gives us a curious glance. I know it's the first time MI5 have ever visited their humble offices. Devlin is not on our radar. Neither had his former wife been.

Beth knocks on the door.

'Come in,' Devlin says.

We enter and I close the door behind us.

Devlin stands. He remains behind his huge table as we shake hands and make our introductions.

'I must admit, I don't understand why you would pay me a visit. Is it about a client? Only, I must remind you, client confidentiality is—'

'It's about your ex-wife,' I say.

'Lily?' The blush seeps ever so slightly from Devlin's cheeks. 'Look, we've been divorced for a long time. I don't see her and—'

'I'm afraid she's dead, Mr Devlin,' Beth says.

Devlin sinks down into his chair. '*Dead?* What happened?'

'She was shot,' I explain.

'My God! But how? *Why?*'

'That's what we want to ask you,' says Beth.

I sit down opposite Devlin; all colour has drained from the lawyer's face now. He is shocked and his hand trembles as he wipes it across his sweat-covered brow.

'You know what she was involved with, don't you?' I say.

Devlin appears to shrink in size, but he shakes his head in denial.

'I don't … have *any* idea who would do this. How would I?'

'When did you last see Lily?' Beth asks.

'I can't remember. It's been a while. Not since my daughter turned eighteen. We had no reason to talk or see each other much once Shellie was no longer a minor.'

'Think back to the past then. Where did you first meet Lily?' Beth asks.

'At university. She was studying economics.'

'Tell us about her. Hobbies? Any radical views?' Beth presses.

'*Lily?* God no. She was just an ordinary girl…'

'That's the official view, but what was she *really* like?' I say.

'I have to tell our daughter,' Devlin says. He's shaking. 'Oh my God. This is so awful.'

'I know this is a shock but we need you to focus. Your ex-wife wasn't just shot. It was a hit. An execution. Do you know what that means?' I say.

'No,' Devlin says. 'That's just—'

'It means she upset someone very dangerous. She might have been involved with something illegal. Someone made an example of her. We need to know everything you can tell us about your life with her,' I continue. 'Anything you can tell us may help.'

'There's nothing to tell. It was normal—'

'Normal doesn't usually get you shot in the skull three times,' I say.

'Please. I can't get my head round this.'

'Look … Anton, if you know anything then it's best you tell us now,' says Beth, her voice softer than my hard tones.

Devlin is too far gone to notice the good-cop/bad-cop routine.

'I don't know anything,' he repeats. 'I swear.'

'Why did you break up?' asks Beth.

'We … grew apart. Lily was… I thought she was having an affair. It was hard to understand as she had never been that … sexual.'

'What made you think there was someone else?' Beth asks.

'She was being very weird about her phone. It always had a lock on it, and then I found this other one in the house. A basic Nokia. She was texting someone on it, but she erased the messages each time so I couldn't see who it was, or what they said. When I questioned her about it, she said I'd better not ask as the answers she could give wouldn't satisfy me.'

'What about drugs?' I ask. 'Could she have been an addict? Maybe she couldn't pay her dealer.'

'Drugs? Lily? *Never*. She didn't even smoke and barely drank. The occasional glass of wine at Christmas and birthdays. She just wasn't into anything radical.'

'Did you ever find out who she was texting?' Beth says.

'No. And it drove a wedge between us. I told her if she didn't tell me the truth then I was done. She said that was probably for the best. It was uncharacteristically cruel. It was cold. And then it dawned on me that Lily was unemotional about most things. The only person she ever really showed any real affection for was our daughter.'

Michael considers this. 'Yet you married her?'

'I liked her. There was never any drama with her. We had a good life; she didn't mind if I worked late. After Shellie was born, we sort of did our own things. It was like I'd given her the thing she wanted – a child – and she didn't need *anything* else.'

'So, you're saying … you weren't having regular sex after that? Is that what added to your suspicions that she was having an affair?' Beth says.

'Like I said, she didn't seem that interested once she had the baby.'

'You broke up some … ten years ago. Why did you leave the law firm you worked for at the same time?' I ask. His eyes widen a little. He looks like the proverbial rabbit caught in very bright headlights.

'Look, that has nothing—'

'Please just answer the question.' I'm blunt. My patience is running thinner the longer this takes and there's something so weak about Devlin that I find him annoying.

'I wanted to set up alone.'

'It had nothing to do with the affair you had with a senior *male* partner?' Beth asks.

Devlin blinks. 'I don't have to discuss this with you. It has nothing to do with *this*. Look … what you've told me … it's not possible. Lily didn't know anyone odd. She was just so *ordinary*. She was the kind of person people just don't really take offence at. You know?'

I've pushed as hard as I can without bringing the man in for interrogation. I realise he can't tell us anything more.

'You've been very helpful,' I say.

As I open the door to leave, Beth turns. She walks back to Devlin and places her card on his desk. Devlin doesn't reach for it, but he stares down at the plain white card with bold black writing.

'If you think of anything that might help us find Lily's killer, please do get in touch.'

We don't speak again until we're in the car and driving back to the office.

'What do you make of that?' Beth asks.

'He was definitely stunned. And it was obvious he didn't know anything. He really believes that Lily had nothing interesting in her life. It was what we suspected though; she was his beard.'

'Yeah. But why in this day and age would anyone want to pretend otherwise when they're gay? I mean, who cares?' Beth says.

'Devlin cared enough to keep it secret. Even now he can't admit it.'

'That's a shame. Life's hard enough without not being yourself as well.'

We drive in silence for a while and then Beth says. 'Do you believe you can live with someone for ten years and they can keep secrets from you? Especially that?'

I glance at her. 'Isn't that what *we* do? Not the sexuality part.'

'I suppose. But it's different for us. My husband knows I

work for MI5 and he isn't to ask me anything. It's not a secret *where* I work, just *what* I do.'

'And you're in the habit of not talking about it,' I say. 'So, it doesn't count as secrets or lies, because you don't have to tell any?'

'Pretty much.'

'Hmm. Lily Devlin was keeping a secret from Anton, and we know he kept one from her. The phone he described sounds like a burner.'

'Yes. Why would an ordinary secretary need a burner?' Beth says.

'Whatever it was, it probably led to her execution.'

Chapter Six

NEVA

In her dream she sees a playground and a swing on which she sits. Someone pushes her and the swing goes higher and higher, until the unimaginable happens and she falls, face first, onto the tarmac. The swing hits her head as she tries to get up. There's shouting, sounds of a woman panicking, and then she's picked up off the ground. Sincere arms envelop her. She's dazed and shaken. Her face is wet with tears and blood.

'We'll get you home and wash this right away,' says the woman holding her.

Neva buries herself in loving arms. A feeling of warmth and safety lulls her and she dozes as she's carried from the playground.

Later, the woman kisses her head, and sings a lullaby. 'No more swings for you,' she says.

But she doesn't fear the swing. Instead, she experiences the lulling movement, as though she's still on it, moving back and forth, and it soothes her, along with the woman's sweet voice, until she slips into a dreamless sleep.

When she wakes, she keeps her eyes closed. She doesn't want to see the reflection in the skylight. She doesn't want to let go of that feeling of being held, of being loved. Eventually, the echo of the dream fades, despite how hard she tries to hold on. Then, and only then, does Neva pull herself up from the bed.

In the bathroom, she washes her hands over and over again. Then she splashes water over her face. The stinging cold makes her feel more awake. She recalls the splash of warmer water once, and the gentle pat of a soft towel that dried away the tears.

She pulls on a robe and goes downstairs to the kitchen. There she puts on the kettle; the habit of making morning tea she has got into means that she craves this as her first drink of the day. Afterwards she resorts to the purer liquid – water.

Water to cleanse in, water to drink, water to sweat from her pores as she does her usual morning workout. And then the cleansing and drinking start up again. It's nightfall before she realises she has fasted all day again. Another habit, two days a week, and all part of her conditioning. All necessary for her personal health. All to keep her at maximum fitness.

After a light supper, she looks at her new burner phone. There are no messages, no assignments. Without them, she almost has no purpose. It's rare that she considers her kills, but Ansell and Devlin are forefront in her mind. She sees them now, hand in hand on their journey to oblivion. No heaven for their sins. Neva's denied them that. Now only a cold, dark grave awaits.

She sits in the dark in the small snug. A television lurks in the corner but she doesn't seek that escapism tonight. Instead, she closes her eyes and tries to recapture the dream from the morning that gave her such profound comfort.

But the feeling doesn't return. After a while she gives up. The vision of innocence and childhood is gone, lost in the ether that has become her life.

She recites her mantra.

Follow orders. Curiosity kills. Fear nothing: you are death. No distractions. Fitness is key.

Her mind glitches. Follow orders. Curiosity kills. Fear nothing, fear nothing, fear...

Fear nothing: you are death.

She repeats this nine times.

There is no ego. No pride. She merely knows it is the truth. *For now.* She is death to anyone marked by her employers. *Follow orders.*

Neva feels the energy drain from her as though she is an automaton that needs winding.

Sleep, my little one.

Where had she heard those words? How she craves that soft whisper once more.

She goes to bed and lies in the dark, looking up at the skylight. The night is pure and she can see the stars, but her mind isn't clear. There is an impenetrable fog that comes over her whenever she isn't working, as though she's on standby, waiting to be activated, waiting for a directive. Inactivity weakens her.

She thinks again about her dream. The little girl who wanted to go higher and then fell is somehow connected to her. It is a memory of *before*. She feels this. She picks at the layers of recollection. Who was the woman whose loving arms held her? Where was the playground? Her mind tries to fill in the blanks of the hazy dream, but fails. There is a blackness surrounding the details. Part of her knows she was once this child. She must have been. But who that child was she has no idea.

Curiosity kills.

Neva closes her eyes; behind her lids she sees the stars framed in the lantern-roof skylight. She follows them on the flow to infinity. And still the mantra pushes at the edges of her mind, but its power over her is breaking down until only one fragment feels important.

You are death.

Sleep, my little one.

Death is sleep and sleep is death in her half-dreaming mind. And sleep becomes an eternal rest she almost craves. *But no.* The morbidity of it haunts her, down, down, into the darkest parts of her mind, where so often she's afraid to look. It shapes an unfathomable anxiety and a sure knowledge that something is crumbling the wall they built inside her head.

She cannot look, she cannot pass, yet the barrier continues to fail and Neva stumbles onwards towards an imagined precipice, where she stands, holding on to the fragile branch of her existence.

Days pass and Neva stops worrying about the lack of work. Her energy returns and she begins to imagine life without the texts, and deaths, and payments. Perhaps she no longer needs to be the bringer of some mysterious justice that her employers demand.

Sometimes she has experienced normality. Once they sent her on a long assignment. She lived as a regular person for six months before she had full access to her target. She worked in a bar which the mark frequented. She had to build trust, appear innocuous. And even after the deed was done, she remained there, continuing the lie, even when she didn't need to.

She'd enjoyed the routine. She'd built friendships, even though they were all based on the lie of her persona. As the barmaid, she could pretend to be something she wasn't. She immersed herself in it until she started to believe she could have this simple life. It was freeing.

Neva remembers this time and how Tracey had pulled her back, absorbing her into the Network as though she'd never been away, as though she'd never tasted independence. And Neva had railed inside against those invisible bars that Tracey represented.

Everything always comes back to Tracey; she will never let Neva go.

You're my protégée. I made you what you are! Oh, Tracey

loves to say this to her. But there is no soothing hand stroking her hair, or loving arms that hold her with pride. No, all of that is gone. A distant memory. A dream.

At night, when she's drifting to sleep, she thinks about Lily Devlin and Ansell. She wants to know why they had to die. Behind her eyes she sees the sincere face of Tracey; *she* has the answers Neva seeks.

To ask though…

The questions bubble up inside her and must be uttered. No matter what trouble it causes.

Chapter Seven

TRACEY

Tracey Herod looks up from her latte and meets the eyes of a beautiful young woman with long strawberry blonde hair and pale translucent skin that appears never to have seen daylight. For a moment she doesn't recognise Neva. Then, Tracey glances around the coffee bar checking if she and the girl are being observed.

'Come in the back,' she says.

Tracey stands, leaving the undrunk coffee on the table, and takes Neva through a door marked 'Staff Only'. Behind the door is a small staff area. Tracey locks the door and turns around facing into the room away from Neva. She presses her hand against the wall opposite the staff room door and a panel slides aside revealing the entrance to another room. This room is full of equipment that no coffee bar would ever have. Two computers stand on a broad wooden workstation next to two landline telephones. Neva knows these will be encrypted. Behind the desk is a cabinet big enough to store weapons in.

'You're not supposed to be here. How did you find me?' Tracey asks as she closes the inner door behind them.

'I've always known where to find you,' Neva says.

Tracey is rarely short of words and, even caught by surprise, she attempts to defuse the moment. Neva is behaving out of character. She usually works firmly in the realms of professionalism and never deviates from her tasks. It's why the Network uses her so often. It's why she is so very valuable to them. *This is a bad sign.* Something Tracey hasn't seen coming. Neva might be breaking down. She studies her, looking hard for signs of instability. Neva is natural today. No wig, no make-up. Herself. It's a look she rarely wears in public.

'New look?' she asks.

Neva smiles. 'Every day is a new look.'

'Why are you here?' Tracey asks.

'Aren't you even going to offer me a coffee?' Neva says.

'Do you want a coffee?' Tracey says.

'No, thank you. I need a new assignment,' Neva says. 'It's been a long time since the last one.'

'Nothing in, or I'd have contacted you. We're having a quiet time right now. Enjoy the rest while you can. You know sometimes they come one after another.'

'Okay.'

'So, I'll be in touch in the usual way—'

'It's very clean in here.' Neva runs a finger over the table top.

'What are you really doing here, Neva?' Tracey asks. Her voice is sharp. There's a tiny blush spreading over her cheeks that gives away the discomfort she's feeling. She doesn't like this intrusion. She glances at the weapons cabinet, wondering if she can make it in time.

'I wanted to see where you worked.'

'Curiosity is not usually your thing. Have you been practising your mantra?' The schoolmistress tone is there now. That voice of authority, designed to quell Neva.

Neva ignores the question. 'I wanted to ask you something.'

'What?'

'Why?'

'Why what?'

'Why Ansell? Why Devlin?'

'You know the answer to that already.'

'Because you *told* me to kill them?'

'Yes.'

'But what did they do?'

'Curiosity kills,' says Tracey, her voice still firm. 'Stand by for your next assignment. Don't come back here again.'

Tracey's face is stern now. Neva hasn't seen this expression before.

Tracey's cover is this place. Sometimes Neva watches her while she opens the coffee shop, unobserved. Again, it's an average life. One that Tracey is permitted to maintain. Neva doesn't think Tracey sees it just as a cover, but as her world. She probably has a family too, but Neva has avoided finding out. She knows such knowledge might change everything she plans to do.

Neva turns and opens the panel doorway that leads back into the regular staff area of the coffee shop.

'See you soon,' she says.

Tracey opens the top drawer on her desk. Next to a mobile phone is a loaded gun. She pushes it aside and picks up the phone. Something is wrong with Neva. She has to get clear of the coffee shop and then consider what action to take. The fact that she is asking questions is worrying enough but the girl's comment about seeing her 'soon' feels like a veiled threat. Tracey's hand is shaking as she selects a number.

'Tracey?'

'The coffee shop is compromised. Can you send in an extraction crew or should I just burn the place?'

'Leave it to me,' says the male voice on the other end. 'Protocol Two action. Then get out and make sure you aren't followed. What happened? Where is the breach?'

'I'll explain in person.'

'Come in immediately.'

'On my way.'

Tracey hangs up. The decision to hold back on her concerns for Neva has been made. She has to think about what she will say; she doesn't want to be blamed for Neva's behaviour as the girl's handler. They might say she has given her too much freedom of late and it would be true. She's never been concerned before about Neva because she is so predictable. When she wasn't on an assignment, she lived a solitary existence in her country cottage. Unlike some of the other operatives, she never looked to have a permanent relationship with anyone. Avoiding, for the most part, all human contact. Yes, there were the occasional sexual blowouts, accompanied by large amounts of vodka consumption. Tracey was aware of those times. They were necessary for the girl to let off steam. But she's never had any doubt that they were in control of Neva. *Until now.*

For the first time since she was recruited, Tracey feels an intense paranoia. She's always felt safe with the Network, as though her connection protected her somehow from other, less savoury, elements. Like other handlers, she believes in what they do. She considers her role to be important. She also earned a great deal of untraceable money from it. But now Neva, one of their own, has been watching her. How much does she know about Tracey's life? The intrusion upsets and worries her more than it would a person without her connections. Partly because it will concern her superiors, who may feel that Tracey has not been doing her job properly; she's become complacent.

Tracey unscrews the base unit of each of the computers and pulls out the hard drives. Behind the desk, she opens the weapons cabinet and takes out a pistol and some bullets. Ensuring the safety is on, she loads the pistol, then places it in her coat pocket. She pulls on the coat. Then she opens another panel at the back of the weapons cabinet. She slips through and comes out into the disabled toilet cubicle in the coffee shop. Another opening leads her into the kitchen. Ignoring the staff, she places the two hard drives in the microwave, switches it on, and then hurries from the coffee shop via the back door.

In the alley she hears the microwave fritz. Protocol Two achieved; the hard drives are now unreadable. Anything else left behind doesn't matter. When the extraction team arrives, they'll remove what they have to and destroy the rest.

Tracey looks up and down the alley. Both sides are clear, but at which end will Neva be waiting? She makes a decision and hurries left, heading towards the main road and Kings Cross Station. At the end of the alley, Tracey looks around. The road is busy; tourists pour up and down both sides of the street. She looks back down the alley and sees Neva at the other end, staring at her. Tracey pats the pocket of her coat as a warning. Then she rushes across the road and out in front of oncoming traffic. Horns blare; brakes screech. Tracey reaches the other side of the road unscathed. In a few seconds, she arrives at the front of Kings Cross Station and heads towards the steps that lead down to the tube. It doesn't matter which train she catches. She just has to lose Neva.

At the bottom of the steps she turns right towards the Piccadilly and Victoria lines; both will be busy. Either will do. She can lose her tail in any of the labyrinthine tunnels below. Glancing behind her, she presses her Oyster card against the turnstile. The barrier opens and she hurries through. Neva is nowhere to be seen.

Feeling more confident, Tracey takes the tunnels towards the Piccadilly line then, on the spur of the moment, cuts through a tunnel marked 'No Entry'. She is now on the opposite side. A train comes in, she glances around, then boards and takes the nearest available seat.

She looks out on the platform but there is no sign of Neva. Her last-minute deviation has worked.

Perhaps she's not following, Tracey thinks. Maybe I've overreacted!

The girl is dangerous. Tracey knows that. She's part of the team that trained her and they did the best job on Neva. She is at the top of her game. *So why this? Why now?*

Neva's best asset is her lack of emotion and empathy. She was cold from the start and she stood out from the others because of it. Tracey knew that this was not a natural condition but something she'd been conditioned to be. In those years of training, Neva had learnt to believe that everything was black and white. There was never any grey. She was a robot, designed to take orders and respond through logic, not emotion. And she's always remained that way. Until, perhaps, now. If Neva has begun to question, she is starting to think for herself more than is permissible in the world of the Network. If this is the case, the conditioning is deteriorating. It isn't usual at this stage in an operative's career that they would begin to crack. That sort of thing normally happened later and there would be signs. But there had been no warning of Neva's change in personality. It is sudden. Though Tracey knows that can't be the case. She must have been corroding for a while but she's hidden it well. Another failing on Tracey's part; she should have seen it.

Tracey wonders what has brought about this alteration and when it started. A fissure has appeared inside the carefully crafted mechanism that makes up the creature that is Neva. Tracey should have noticed something, had an indication that there was a problem before this occurred. But it wasn't all her fault! The last psych evaluation had shown nothing. But if Neva's gone rogue, what did she hope to achieve by breaking out now? She'll have every operative after her by morning when Tracey puts the word out. And Tracey *will* put the word out. She has to or her head will be on the chopping block.

Tracey tries to excuse Neva's behaviour as the train stops at the next station. But she can't. Especially after Neva had disobeyed her, waiting outside to watch Tracey flee. That action alone shows she can't be trusted any more. She can't let her get away with this!

Even so, the thought of turning Neva in concerns Tracey more than it should. She's always had a soft spot for the girl. Perhaps because once, she had been the underdog everyone thought would collapse under the pressure. Well, Neva had proved them wrong, and she was their best agent.

Perhaps they'll just bring her in for testing. It would be worthwhile knowing the extent of the damage. She might even be susceptible to reconditioning. They'd done that once before with another agent and it had worked well enough until the time came to retire him. They'd got five more years of use and the effort had been worth it for the good work he'd done during that time.

The tube train stops again. Tracey remains in her seat until the last possible moment and then she throws herself up and out of the carriage as the doors begin to close. She submerges herself in the commuters heading for the way out. At the exit, she notices she's at Hyde Park Corner. The place is familiar; she's passed through it before at some point, though precisely when she can't recall. Taking a breath, she turns around and heads back through the crowd to catch the next train going in the opposite direction. Neva won't expect that, if she has somehow followed, because it isn't the protocol.

On the platform, Tracey lets the strain leave her body. She is wired and tense, concerned, but no longer in flight mode. Her heartbeat finally steadies. She can hear the next train approaching. On instinct, she steps up to the yellow line and then Tracey is propelled onward. She plummets down onto the track. Someone cries out as she falls forward. Then the train exits the tunnel. Tracey hears the screech of brakes. A hand reaches out to help her back up and then she sees Neva stepping back, the offered hand withdrawn.

The look on the girl's face is unfathomable. Expressions Tracey has never seen before run over her normally serene features. Then the array of emotions slides away. Neva is back to the blank countenance she always wears at the point of a kill.

Though it is pointless, Tracey throws her arms across her face as the braking train slams into her.

Chapter Eight

NEVA

Neva walks away from the station. She is wearing a long black trench coat which covers the weapons that are secreted around her body. Her mind is in turmoil. A flash flood of memories and flashbacks drown her conscious thought.

She was five when she first met Tracey. She remembers the kind and smiling face that greeted her. There was a house. A large school-like property. Neva wasn't alone. There were six others her age: three boys and three girls.

There was a man with Tracey. She referred to him as Callan.

'As requested, this one is a back-up, in case any of the other girls don't make it,' Callan had said, nodding towards Neva.

Neva had thought his words were strange, his accent even more so. It was a kind of warped Northern twang that didn't fit into any particular place. She didn't know how she knew that but she hadn't liked Callan. There was something unpleasant and cold about the man. He strutted around the room, acting like he was in charge. Even at such a young age, Neva had thought him small and unimportant.

When he left, Tracey took her into the kitchen and gave her hot chocolate. That was the last kind act she did for Neva. After that, Neva was put in a small dormitory with the other three girls. Even so, she had always seen Tracey as stability and consistency. Tracey was a known element that she could rely on. Tracey told her what to do and where to go. Tracey gave her the assignments and sent her lots of money.

Now, Neva tries to recall the names of the other children. She can't. She picks at the layers of warped reminiscence, memories that someone has taken from her.

The times in the big house are blurred. As are the faces of the other children. She hasn't thought about the place for a long time. She remembers that, after a while, they all stopped talking to each other, and stopped playing. They behaved like strangers, even though they spent every waking and sleeping hour together.

Neva has a flash memory of a door, of a room that she went to, down a dully lit corridor. She recalls sitting on a wooden stool outside, waiting her turn to go inside, a feeling of ... apprehension swirling inside her, writhing like an eel infested pit.

'After today, you'll never be afraid again,' a voice says as the door opens 'Come inside. This is the start of the new you.'

The figure in the doorway is in shadow, but Neva knows

it's a man. 'The doctor', some of the others have called him. She thinks she must be sick and might need medicine.

The doctor steps back but Neva doesn't walk forward. She is afraid. The feeling consumes her until she turns away and tries to run.

Hands catch hold of her – not kind or loving but painful, cruel.

'Thought this one had potential?' says the doctor.

'She does,' says Tracey. 'You'll see. Start the process. She has an excellent pedigree.'

Neva stops walking. She's in the middle of the pavement but she doesn't notice. Tourists and commuters tut as they swarm around her. She recollects a sensation, like insects crawling all over her skin. Agony, white and intense. She hears again her own screams of fear and pain.

She presses her hand to her mouth and quells the cry that's been held inside her for twenty years. What happened in that room? The hurt and terror have blotted the memory. Or something else did.

'Miss? *Miss*? Is everything all right?'

Neva blinks. She looks at the man standing in front of her. His eyes are concerned. She has always valued kindness; it reminds her of the hot chocolate she once drank in a warm kitchen. The taste of delicious innocence and happiness.

Time slows. Such warmth in those brown eyes and he

doesn't even know her. She feels giddy with recognition, but what that is she doesn't understand.

'I'm ...' She finds she can't speak.

The man puts his arm around her waist. Too familiar? Only then does Neva realise that she is slumping, fainting. Incredibly, blackness is taking her. She snaps herself back with sheer will. She can't be weak; it's not an option, especially now.

'I need to get off the street,' she says.

'Come on,' the man answers.

Holding her with one arm, he raises his other hand and hails a cab. He helps her inside and then pauses.

'Where to?'

Neva shakes her head. 'I don't live around here.'

He nods, making a decision, and then he climbs into the cab with her and gives the driver an address. She hears it and remembers it. She looks at the man and tries to determine why he is helping. What kind of person does random acts of kindness for a stranger? He must have a motive. But for now, Neva doesn't care. If need be, she can take care of herself. She just needs to centre herself. Why is that so hard to do?

Chapter Nine

MICHAEL

'Drink this.'

I press a glass of brandy into her hand. She sniffs, smelling the strong liquid, before she sips. A few gulps later and that glazed expression falls from her face. She's pretty. Striking, even. The brandy appears to revive her.

'Where am I?'

'My place. Don't worry. You're safe.'

She looks at me. I take in her soft blue eyes and wonder what she's thinking as I keep my expression open. I don't want her to be scared or to feel I've scooped her off the street to take advantage of her. I don't know why I did it except that I had an overwhelming urge to protect her. But all the time three words course through my mind, *who is she?*

A range of emotions ripples over her features as she collects herself. I think I see concern, confusion, and then ... suspicion.

'You really are safe here,' I say. 'I didn't know where else to take you. You looked like you were in shock.'

'Thank you. I had a bit of a—'

'Did you see it?'

'See what?'

'The woman. The one that fell onto the track.'

'*Oh!*'

'I rang it in. I doubt there will be any proper witnesses. Most people spend time looking at their phones. They aren't paying attention. But you were so upset, I thought—'

'No. I didn't see *anything*. I just felt ill. Thank you for your help. I'd better leave.'

She stands but she has not recovered as well as she thought. She staggers, then sinks back into the chair as dizziness stops her leaving.

'I'm not used to feeling weak.'

'Rest. I'll get a doctor if you need—'

'No,' she replies.

The colour returns to her face along with her equilibrium. I almost feel like she's recovering from sheer willpower alone.

'I'm Michael,' I say. 'What's your name?'

'I … you said you called it in? The woman on the tracks? Are you a police officer?' she asks.

'I'm … *sort of*,' I answer, being vague. It isn't a conversation I can have with a total stranger.

'What happened?'

'She fell, I think. I was hoping someone saw it. Maybe she jumped,' I say.

'I'm feeling better now. I need to go. Thank you. Why

did you help me?'

'Why wouldn't I? I couldn't possibly leave you in such a vulnerable state.'

She glances around the room as though she's taking in the surroundings.

'Is that your wife?' she asks, seeing the photograph of Mia on the sideboard.

'I'm not married,' I say, feeling a strong urge to explain my status. 'It's my sister.'

'She's pretty,' she says.

I glance at Mia's photograph; I see the smiling young woman grown from a once tense and shy little girl and I understand in that instant my need to help and protect this total stranger. I'll always be Mia's protector, and something about this pretty young woman brings about the same intense emotion. I try to analyse it, but can't ground the sensation in any logical reality.

'I'd better go,' she says now, and her words bring a flutter of panic and a feeling of confusion. I don't want her to leave.

'Are you sure you're okay?' I ask, even though I can see she is recovered. It is somewhat miraculous.

'What do I owe you? For the taxi?'

'Nothing. Please. It was my pleasure to help.'

Her phone beeps in her pocket. She blinks, looking confused, and then she reaches for it. She looks at the phone as though she's forgotten how to use it.

'Is everything okay?' I ask.

'It's just work stuff. I have to go. Thank you again.'

She pushes the phone back into her pocket. When she

stands, she is more stable.

'Are you sure?' I ask.

She smiles at me then turns and makes her way to the door. 'I've taken up too much of your time.'

I look at her. Concern brings a small frown to my face but the woman doesn't see it. She doesn't meet my eyes. She appears to be embarrassed by what has happened. Understandable really. I feel the same.

'Before you go,' I say. 'Can I know your name?'

She takes a breath. A pause that shows she's uncertain whether to tell me or not.

'Anna,' she says. 'Thank you again.'

She looks at me then and it feels as though she can see right inside my head. She blinks. All signs of her earlier confusion have gone. I feel ... recognition – hers *and* mine.

'Have we met before?' I ask.

'I don't think so,' she says. She walks to the door and opens it, then glances back at me. There's a question hanging between us. I anticipate it as it lingers in the air, unspoken.

'Maybe I'd like to see you again,' she says.

'You know where to find me,' I say.

'That I do,' she says. And I see something then, something I wouldn't expect to see in this situation: an inner strength, confidence, and a sense of humour.

I smile at her.

When she's gone, I roll her name around my mouth, trying to reconcile its banality with the woman herself. Anna. Perhaps it's a simple nickname, short for something else?

Chapter Ten

NEVA

Neva hurries from the block of flats, shaken that she lost control and had some kind of 'episode'. She doesn't know what happened, only that thinking of – *remembering* – Tracey and her past caused some problem. It was as though the wall was not just crumbling but several of the bricks had crashed to the ground from it. In the back of her mind, another recollection floats. She pushes it back, away from her conscious mind. She can't think of it now. She needs to get away from the home of the 'sort of' cop. He may become suspicious, may try to follow her. She doesn't want to have to kill him, not after he has tried to help her. He is, after all, innocent. She never likes anyone on first sight, but she did like him. Could he be the first person she's met that has no agenda? She shakes the thought away.

She slips away into the nearest tube station, then pauses by the map, working out the route to her next destination. She has to get away from London, back to where they expect to find her. She has to regroup and then decide what the next move should be.

As she takes the next train, an odd sensation flutters in her stomach. She recognises it as some sort of unfamiliar emotion. Excitement maybe. It persists, growing in her chest until she finds herself smiling. This feeling is the start of something new that her rebellion, the removal of Tracey, has begun. Something inside her craves more. It is as though she has had a taste of revenge. It is sweet, like chocolate, and as tangy as wild berries. It gives her the same feeling of comfort that the dream of arms holding her did. The sensation is distracting and somehow ... important.

She almost misses her stop. She brings her mind back to the present. She's done something serious for which there will be severe consequences. Now is not the time to let any emotion in. Now is not the moment to be distracted.

Even so, she is preoccupied. Michael. Who is he? A cop. *Sort of.* A well-meaning citizen. A fool to have brought someone like her into his home. No matter. Despite her words, she won't see him again.

She takes her phone out of her pocket and looks at the message. The text is anonymous, as always. Someone in the Network telling her Tracey is dead. They've also sent a new contact number – for a new handler, no doubt. Was this standard protocol? After all, operatives like her could not be left without a handler, could they?

She shivers as she exits the train though there's no draught coming from within the tube tunnels at that time. She thinks again about the new handler, and her mind flashes to Michael almost straightaway, as though there is an indelible link between them. The feeling is disturbing.

Chapter Eleven

MICHAEL

'What happened to you?' Beth asks as I enter the main office.

'What do you mean?'

'The locals were expecting you to be there when they scraped the woman off the tracks.'

'Do we know who she was?' I ask, changing the subject.

'Not yet. What's left of her will give the coroner nightmares, I expect.'

'Any leads?'

'A couple. Leon is interviewing the last possible at the local station.'

'Really? I left it to the locals as I didn't think this was in our jurisdiction. Do you think it's something we should be involved with?' I say. 'I only called it in because I happened to be on the scene.'

'That's what we thought at first. Then we got these. Have a look. I printed them to leave on Ray's desk.'

She gives me a print-out of a few witness statements in a folder.

'See?'

Transcript of Witness Statement
Interviewer: Leon Tchaikovsky
Witness: Malcolm Radley

RADLEY
There was this woman in a black trench coat. She was holding out her hand to help. Then she must've got scared. She backed away and the train hit the woman who'd fallen on the tracks. It was horrible. I mean it, man. I'm traumatised.

TCHAIKOVSKY
Did you see the other woman fall?

RADLEY
No. Just heard a scream. Looked up. Then I saw the two of them.

TCHAIKOVSKY
Can you describe the woman in the trench coat?

RADLEY
Blonde, I think. Tallish. Didn't get a good look. I was looking at the woman on the track… She had brown hair. Her face … she knew she was finished, man…

'Radley might be able to give a better description of the victim,' Beth says. 'Might be helpful in identifying her if the coroner can't.'

I'm quiet for a moment as I absorb Radley's statement. *Anna was wearing a black trench coat.* I keep my face passive as I continue to read.

'Do we have any CCTV footage?' I ask.

'The camera on that track was smashed a few seconds before,' Beth says.

'*Vandalised?* Seems a bit of a coincidence,' I say.

'That's what I thought,' says Beth. 'Which is why Leon is doing the interviews. Something's amiss here. Maybe we should find this mystery woman in the trench coat. She might shed some light on it.'

I don't answer.

'Can I take this?'

'Sure. I'll print more for Ray.'

I leave Beth and take the folder into my office. Then I sit down and read it all.

I should have told Beth then and there about Anna. As well as the trench coat, she could be described as 'blonde' and 'tall'. After all, if Anna had seen the accident and she was genuinely traumatised by the death she'd witnessed, us interrogating her wouldn't have helped right then. Perhaps I should have taken her to hospital, instead of back to my place. And why had I done that?

It was down to that first moment I saw her. She stopped dead in the street as though she'd just been told the worst news possible. She looked bereft. Shocked. As though all her grief washed over her in one single moment. A realisation that life would never be the same. It was all there on her face. Then the colour blanched from her cheeks and she just looked sick. I was compelled to help her. Despite everything I knew I should have been doing. And when the police arrived, I'd put her in the cab and taken her out of there. Something I'd never dreamed of doing with a perfect stranger before. A man in my line of work needs to be more careful than that. *What was I thinking?*

I pick up my phone and ask Beth to put the CCTV footage from outside the station on the shared drive when she'd downloaded it all. Part of me is worried that I'd been caught on camera; part of me hopes I have. I am a man with very little mystery in my life, but Anna was something unfathomable. I almost believe I imagined her, so fleeting was the contact.

Beth messages me to say the footage is there. I reply,

I'll take a look and see if anything is amiss.

I look through the footage. Somehow, Anna has avoided being seen, even though I found her near the station.

Beth messages as though reading my mind.

There's no sign of her exiting the tube, maybe she got on another train?

I'm about to send a reply, but hold back. I can't reveal my accidental meeting with what could be the same woman without raising enquiries about my own somewhat reckless behaviour. It is out of character, I know that, and so I examine my reasons. Why had I taken care of her personally and not passed her on to the beat bobbies as they arrived? I could have. Should have. But she'd appeared to be so vulnerable. And I'd hoped I'd found a credible witness to the accident, hadn't I? In the back of my mind, I know I hadn't been thinking about her in those terms at all. It was a reaction. Something more primal than that. There was an affinity of sorts.

A flash of memory accompanies this emotion.

Mia and I are running and playing near a canal. That little boy … a friend of hers chasing behind us and then the splash of water. We both turn to see him going down, pulled by some fierce current. Mia screams. I pull her to me but she struggles in my arms.

'We have to save him!'

But I know we can't, and I won't let her risk her life for him.

'Jacob!' she calls. And then the adults are there and my father jumps into the water without a second thought.

There is an excruciating moment as we anticipate our father's superhero rescue. Jacob is tangled on something – reeds or garbage thrown haphazardly into the water buy uncaring, callous hands.

I cover Mia's face as they pull him free and our father, sodden to the bone, is helped out.

Jacob's body is worked on. There are torturous seconds of trying to make him breath. I watch it all but protect Mia from it as best as I can. Nothing they do, or even the paramedics that arrive soon after, can bring back the boy.

I shake these thoughts away. I had no responsibility for

Anna, unlike my sister. I should have been thinking like an agent. I should have turned her over to be questioned or taken care of by a medic. I should have known better.

I ask Beth on the message system:

No other sightings of the closest witness?

She answers,

Just a few others who said they looked up and the woman had already fallen

I go back into Beth's office.

'Do we know which of them screamed? That person must have seen it.'

Beth shakes her head. 'I don't know. No one has admitted to that so far. Maybe Leon will have more when he gets back.'

I go back into my office, closing the door. Without Beth's help, I access the CCTV cameras outside the hotel across the street from the station. I look through them until I see myself making the emergency call from my work mobile. I'd been on the underground, commuting into the office, when the incident occurred. I hadn't been on that particular line, just there when the uproar happened. After instructing the station staff to stop anyone leaving, I'd gone up and outside to make the call. I should have gone back inside and waited for the police to arrive to hand it over to them properly, but then I noticed Anna.

On the footage I see myself hang up the phone as I turn

to look at a disturbance off-camera. I walk away. I remember seeing Anna then, and how I'd hurried to help her. I'd been thinking I knew her. There had been something about her that was so familiar it was overwhelming. I didn't know what at the time. But now, looking at the footage, an idea occurs to me. I thought I knew her because I *have* seen her before. The way she moves. The way she holds her shoulders back. Her height, above average. The hair is different but…

I pause the recording, then open a folder on my computer containing information on the murder of Aidan Bright. In the folder, I find and open the saved camera footage near the off-licence. I watch it playing out, see the girl with the bobbed hair and glasses. Her height, build, and the walk. *Yes!* She had walked that way as she hurried down the corridor from my flat. Why hadn't I realised? Anna wasn't some random woman on the street; she was someone I'd been pursuing for three years.

I can't keep it to myself any more.

I open my office door.

'Beth? Can you come in here a minute?'

Beth leaves her computer terminal and walks over. 'What's up?'

'I did something stupid today. I think I helped a witness leave the crime scene.'

'A witness?' Beth says. 'Why do you think that?'

I shake my head, not wanting to voice what I really think. My gut tells me, even though I have no proof, that Anna isn't just a witness; she took an active role in this death.

'There was a woman. She was...' I explain helping Anna, but don't tell Beth how much I had helped.

Beth listens, making little comment. 'From what you've said, it sounds like you helped someone who wasn't feeling well. I don't see a problem with that.'

'That's what I thought at the time. But then the description in these statements. It was the same woman. She saw what happened.'

'You're not telling me everything,' Beth says.

'I can't. I don't know any more. It's just ... she reminded me of...' I glance back at my desk, and the computer that's still open, though paused, on the footage relating to Aidan Bright's death. 'She didn't look exactly like her, but she walks like her.'

'Like who?' Beth asks. She's frowning at me now, and I can't blame her because I'm being so vague.

'Like the suspect in Aidan Bright's killing.'

'Jesus. This could be a really lucky break,' says Beth. 'I mean, if she was there, then this probably wasn't an accident at all.'

'We don't know that,' I say. 'I can't accuse her as I don't have any evidence and there hasn't been anyone who saw the actual ... fall so far.'

'What do we know, Mike? Come on, there's no such thing as coincidences. Not like this. If she was the same woman and she was there, she more than likely did it.'

I remind Beth that we don't even know who the victim was yet, but she's on a roll now. Her eyes are shining. I've seen this kind of excitement before. She gets like this whenever she thinks we have a breakthrough. I still want to err on the side of caution though.

'The woman I spoke to did appear to be genuinely sick. Would an assassin get like that after a kill? Especially one confident enough to throw a credit card to a starving vagrant?' I point out. 'Let's not get ahead of ourselves.'

'I don't know,' Beth says now. 'There could be many factors at play here.'

'Such as?'

'This might not have been a hit. It may have been personal. And even to a sociopath, that will feel different.'

Beth's words strike a chord with me though I don't know why. Did Anna know the victim? Was she involved with her somehow? If so, what had the victim done to deserve such a violent death?

'You'd have to really hate someone to push them under a train and then watch as it ploughs into them, wouldn't you?' Beth says.

I try to imagine hatred that extreme and I can't.

Chapter Twelve

NEVA

The black cotton trench coat burns on the small pile of garden waste. All evidence of her association with Tracey is now gone. She has saved the new handler's number into a new burner phone, destroying the old one as per procedure and removing Tracey's number, eliminating a part of her past. Like a scab that's been picked, it bleeds and then closes over. The anger has gone. She feels numb as she now stands in the garden, burning the last pieces of Anna's identity. Though she had not been wearing a disguise, destroying the clothing gives her a sense of control.

She thinks about Michael. She knows his address. He's the only person of importance who has ever seen her true face. She should go back and kill him. But she doesn't want to.

Though she sent on her new phone number, the new handler has not been in touch. This is not an issue. Her employers are regrouping. It didn't take long for Neva to realise that they didn't know she killed Tracey. She doesn't understand why Tracey didn't tell them what she'd done before she ran, even though she knew Neva could no longer be trusted. Still, Neva hadn't planned this. Tracey's flight had spurred Neva on. She had wanted to know who was controlling her life. Spooking Tracey had been a means by which she might find out and the plan had been to follow.

The recent dreams and recollections had been crowding around her, screaming that her life was wrong. And then, something inside her ... snapped.

One deep, dark memory had informed her that this moment was important. It was her or Tracey. And she chose to live. It was the first step to destroying the link that tied her to *them*. The next stages, she hoped, would bring her closer to finding out who *they* were.

They'd taught her to have no fear, even of death. But Neva had decided she wouldn't make it easy for them to retire her. She was ready to fight. Readier than Ansell or Devlin had been.

She'd had an escape plan for a while. A strategy she put in place a few days after she killed Ansell. At the time, though, she had believed she had a long career ahead and the contingency had felt like a fantasy, something she'd never need but liked to toy with.

But things had changed. Her strength was being worn away, year by year, and the coldness that had once been inside her had thawed. She has no regrets for the kills she's made – that isn't in her make-up, though maybe once it had been, before they altered her – but Neva doesn't need to do this for much longer. She doesn't want to be someone else's puppet. If she kills, she has to know the reason for it.

Questions are not permitted within the Network and had she asked any, she would have found herself back at the house, back in that room at the end of the dark corridor, or worse, in a deep dark pit with her brains blown out.

With Tracey gone, she hopes for breathing space while she plans her future escape. She's been saving money. *They* pay well; it is a sweetener for the cost the job has on the recruits.

She snorts a laugh at the idea of being 'recruited'. As if she ever had a choice.

Neva never saw any need for extravagance and as a result she chose to live simply and she saved the money. It goes into a Swiss bank account that she's been careful to keep secret. There are three million pounds that she's put away over the last five years. Also, she has a flight bag, filled with £50,000 in cash and several different passports for various countries under different names. Some of which the Network provided so that she could do her job without detection, others … well, there's always a black market for everything if you have the money.

They trained her well: always be ready to go to ground. Have an exit plan. Neva does and she'll use their training against them the day they come after her.

The text she received after Tracey's death proves her situation needs a great deal more thought. It's why Neva is taking her time and not running immediately. To do so will mark her as guilty. She's clever – that's why they chose her – and only someone stupid would give themselves away like that.

The fire burns down to ashes. It's cold out, but the heat

from the flames keeps her warm. She waits until all the evidence is gone. She turns away.

In the field, wild daffodils grow in a patch. Her breath catches in her throat. She stops and looks at them. Then she picks one and places it on top of the pyre. There's enough heat remaining to cause the flower to shrivel and disintegrate.

Neva shudders. It's a fitting tribute for the end of Tracey's life.

When the flower is absorbed into the ashes, she walks back across the land towards the house.

The landline phone rings as she enters the kitchen. She goes to the sink, washes her hands, and the phone stops ringing. She doesn't check who's calling. No one important ever calls this landline.

The house is quiet. Neva has never disliked solitude, but now she craves noise. She wants company. Time to let off some steam...

As she pulls the drapes closed on the bedroom window, she notices a car parked down the lane. Periodically they watch her, and Tracey's death may well have raised suspicion. Neva goes about her daily business as though nothing has happened.

With the curtains now closed, she pulls on a short black dress, and covers her hair with a long black wig. She never goes anywhere without a weapon, and tonight is no exception. She stows her knife inside the leg holster of one of her knee-length boots.

She pauses, wondering who is monitoring her. She

glances at the window but doesn't look outside again. To do so will alert them that they have been noticed.

The house has a hive system installed. From her mobile phone, Neva closes the blinds in the kitchen and turns the lights on. In the small snug, she turns on the television and a side lamp.

Then she slips out of the house via the back door, walking across the land under cover of the growing darkness. They watch her main door but there's a hidden lane out the back, down through a copse of trees which emerges onto another road. Across that and through another field and there's an anonymous rented garage with another car stored in it. Just for her use. Just in case.

Neva wakes in a bed that is unfamiliar. For a moment, she doesn't recall where she is. She was careless. She drank too much, let herself go. Even if they had managed to follow her, this sort of blow-out behaviour was not uncommon. Sometimes she has to let her hair down. Sometimes she has to get laid to ease the tension and avoid the sense of loneliness that can destroy one of her kind. Tracey knew about these indiscretions; Neva is certain that the Network does too.

She runs her hand over her hair and notes that the pins have kept the black wig in place.

The man beside her is still sleeping. She slides from the bed, pulls on her dress and boots, and takes her purse. She doesn't glance back at him; she has no need to recall his face and doesn't care to know his name.

She slips away with the silence and stealth of someone who is used to disappearing.

It's only when she reaches the lobby that she realises she is in the same flat occupied by Michael. She pauses in the doorway, remembering his place and the taste of brandy. *His face.* Somehow, his image is ingrained in thoughts she saves for important things. Her heart is thudding as the lift behind her pings and she hears the doors open. She doesn't look around. She turns her face away. Brass panelling lines the lobby and Neva sees Michael reflected in it. He is walking towards the door. She bends her head, pretends to search in her purse, and doesn't look up as he passes her.

From the doorway she watches him hail a taxi. Then he is gone.

She stares out into the street for a while, and then turns and goes back to the lift, heading back upstairs to Michael's flat on the second floor.

She knocks on the door and waits, an excuse for her presence ready on her lips should anyone else be there. When there is no movement from within, Neva removes one of the pins from her hair. It doesn't take long to pop the lock, open the door, and go inside.

Michael's flat is tidy and minimalist. On a table by the door is a landline phone and one photograph. It is of the woman he said was his sister. Neva studies the face. She sees the similarity and knows he told the truth. They have the same sandy-coloured hair and the same colour eyes. Dark brown, warm, with the wry presence of humour.

She wanders around the flat, careful not to touch anything.

In Michael's bedroom, Neva looks around. Using the hem of her dress, she opens the chest of drawers. Then she looks inside his wardrobe. There is only male underwear and clothing inside, confirming what she already knows is true. He lives alone.

Neva considers this. A 'sort of' cop. No family – except perhaps the sister. His home does not appear to be 'lived in', as though it is nothing more than a base to him. This suggests he may work long hours and is rarely there. Dedicated to some kind of law enforcement job. Michael is the type of man she would normally steer clear of, yet Neva is fascinated by him. Something about him inspires an emotion she hasn't felt since she was a child. Warmth. Safety. Hot chocolate. This final thought makes no sense. He's a stranger to her. They had never met before. She explores her reaction to him, prodding and wiggling as though at a tooth that needs to come out.

She finds a photo album in one of the drawers. Flicking through, she sees pictures of Michael as a child with a girl the same age. Underneath each one is written 'Michael and Mia' along with their age. She understands then the closeness of the sister; they are twins – similar but not identical. And then the parents. The father in a police uniform, the mother wearing an apron as though she's just stepped out of a 1950s kitchen. A perfect family. Upstanding citizens all of them. She closes the album. A postcard of normality and a contrast to everything she's ever experienced.

She knows she should leave and never return but she has the overwhelming urge to talk to Michael again. She analyses her interest. Is it sexual? Or is she like a moth, attracted to the very light that shines brightly enough to burn? She's heard of others who take unnecessary risks, those to whom death and the kill have become sport. Neva has never been like this. She gets no delight from killing. It's a job. She's just good at it.

In a drawer in the kitchen she finds a cheque book. She sees his full name for the first time.

Michael Kensington.

She remembers another Michael. He was slightly older than Neva, six or seven to her five. In the early days he talked to her. Tracey never stopped them talking; it just happened after the third or fourth visit to the room when they all withdrew inside themselves.

None of them asked why Michael disappeared. Neva had not given him a second thought until now. What had happened to *that* Michael? What had happened to all the others she had spent time with?

She recalls leaving the house, thirteen years later. Fully combat trained, an expert in munitions. She'd even shown a talent for languages. They discouraged competitive behaviour, but Neva had prided herself on being the best of all of them. They weren't her friends; they were colleagues.

Then they'd set her up in the first house, a place in Bern, Switzerland, with a few others, slightly older and more experienced than she was. It was a 'halfway' house, Tracey had said. A base to work from until she was ready to go it alone. Neva knew they were just still keeping her under complete control.

There were three men and one other woman in the house. She had sex with one of the men to see if she liked it. It hadn't wowed her and she didn't bother with him again. Neva knew he was relieved. Her first proper assignment had her paired with him. He treated her like a novice until she beat him to the mark, a French ambassador, and took him out with a firm swipe of her blade across his throat. After that, the older operatives accepted her.

'She's top of the class,' Tracey had said to the handler who ran the house. 'She'll be out on her own before long.'

Two years later, Neva was in England and with Tracey's encouragement she bought the cottage with the savings she'd gathered during her term in Switzerland. Then, as Tracey predicted, she was out alone and working at full capacity.

Chapter Thirteen

MICHAEL

From the story I give Beth, my colleagues know I made an error in judgement. It's the first in years, and so I enter the conference room looking suitably embarrassed. Ray, Leon, and Beth are already there, and they stop talking when they see me. I imagine that Leon gloats a little, though Beth gives me an encouraging wink.

'Sit down, Michael,' Ray says. 'Beth's been filling us in on today's events.'

I sit down and find them all looking at me. It makes me feel oddly guilty, even though I've not done anything that would be considered that wrong. Taking Anna back to my place could be considered a mistake but I haven't told anyone that part. Not even Beth.

'I've pulled up all footage around the area but somehow, our girl always avoids being caught,' says Beth. 'Michael is the only one who saw her up close.'

'Describe her…' Ray says.

'Strawberry-blonde hair, fair skin. Blue eyes. About five-eight in flats, but she wore a small heel – two inch maybe. Slim, but athletic,' I say and then I explain my suspicion that she was the assassin who took out Aidan Bright. 'She's exactly the same build.'

'Our rail victim was a target, then?' Ray asks.

'I don't know,' I say.

'So, you saw her outside the station?' prompts Ray.

'Yes. As I told Beth, she was just standing in the middle of the pavement. I spoke to her and helped her get a cab.'

'You don't know where she went?' Ray asks.

'No,' I lie.

Ray grills me with fierce intensity. I don't change my story and I see him exchange a look with Beth.

'It's possible she was trying to help the woman who fell,' Beth suggests. 'Then realised she couldn't get involved.'

'I did question her about the accident. She said she hadn't seen anything,' I say.

'And you believed her?' Ray asks.

'Until the witness statements put her there, I had no reason not to,' I answer. 'Anyway, when I read Leon's transcripts, I knew she'd been right in the thick of it.'

The others speculate on who she might be and how they'll trace her. I listen in silence.

'She was English?' Beth asks.

I nod again.

'Accent?' Beth prompts.

'I'm not sure. RP. She spoke very carefully. Each word clipped, but I thought it was because she wasn't feeling well,' I explain.

'Could have been disguising her real voice perhaps? Any other observations?' Ray says.

I shake my head. Then I remember the brandy glass. It's in the dishwasher. I can't recall if I had started the machine that morning or not. If I haven't, we'll probably be able to pull a print from it. I shake my head again in a subconscious gesture. How on earth will I manage that one?

'Michael?' Ray says.

'I asked her name. She said she was called Anna. Other than that, nothing else. I just hope, somehow, our paths cross again,' I say, but I'm shamefaced as Ray studies me.

'Don't blame yourself. Any one of us could have been in the same situation,' says Beth.

'Well, if you do think of anything else, let us know,' says Ray.

Ray stands up and leaves the room.

'Welcome to the fuck-up podium, mate. It happens to us all from time to time,' says Leon. Then he stands and pats me on the arm to show some form of solidarity. I don't think it's sincere.

When he's gone, Beth says, 'It'll be all right. You didn't do anything wrong. Ray can be a bit of a dick about procedure sometimes, but we don't have one for this scenario. As agents, our priority is the public's safety. No one can say you didn't take the needs of someone you thought was a regular person into consideration. If you hadn't helped her, there might have been more hue and cry. Woman fainting in the street, MI5 security agent not helping – can you imagine the headlines?'

I thank her for the support and then we both go back to work on the incident.

Once in my office, I sink down into my chair, regretting my lack of honesty. I should have told the truth at the outset. Why had I lied? It wasn't as if I knew she was guilty of anything. I know the answer, even though I try not to admit it to myself. My whole life has been under scrutiny since I joined the taskforce. Anna was a secret I wanted to keep. A brief encounter that I'd enjoyed, but thought would go nowhere. That was, of course, before I began to suspect who she was.

I look through the glass windows into Beth's office. Beth has everything I've ever wanted. Unlike her, I find it difficult to live the lie that having a full-on relationship means. Beth and Leon don't have the same problem with lying to those they love. Beth is married and Leon is in a long-term live-in relationship. Both partners have been vetted and MI5 had no concerns about either of them. I never discuss their home lives with them, any more than they discuss their working day with their respective partners. But they seem to have the balance right. For me, though, I don't want to try that again. Those days ended with my former girlfriend, Kirstie.

We'd dated for a few years and I'd known that Kirstie wanted more from the relationship. I'd been willing to pursue it until Kirstie showed too much interest in my day job. Kirstie was a journalist, and despite passing the vetting process, I began to doubt her when she started asking too many questions. When I found her trying to open my work laptop, the relationship had ended. It had to when the trust was gone. That was two years ago now, and I hadn't been able to get involved with anyone since. I just couldn't face it.

So, what had changed?

Anna is the only woman I've been interested in since then and, of course, she turns out to be a potential person of interest. It's a major part of the frustration I'm feeling. But I had to tell them about her, otherwise I would be breaking my oath, and the job means everything to me.

In order to distract myself from further thought of Anna, I open the new transcripts Leon has provided about the incident.

Transcript of Witness Interview
Interviewer: Leon Tchaikovsky
Interviewee: Cara Harvey

HARVEY
I was rushing because I heard the train approach and that's when I saw this woman in front of me. She was clearing the path, so I ducked in behind her. I noticed her mostly because her hair was so lush. Long, straight hair. Blonde.

TCHIAKOVSKY
Did you notice what she was wearing?

HARVEY
Black coat, belted around the waist. Black jeans too, I think. I'm not sure. It was all a bit of a blur...

TCHAIKOVSKY
This woman, did you notice if she was in a hurry?

[Harvey thinks for a minute.]

HARVEY
I guess she was as keen as me to get on that train and people moved for her. Like I said, I followed. Then, she sort of ... rushed ... forward. I heard a scream and when I looked beyond her, I saw the other woman on the tracks. She'd fallen but was trying to climb back up...

TCHAIKOSKY
Who screamed?

HARVEY
I think it was the woman. The one I was following. It was like a cry of ... anguish. Like she was in real pain. Maybe she was shocked when this other woman fell? Anyway, she turned and pushed past me, running the other way, back off the platform. And then the train ... Jesus. It was ... [Harvey chokes back a sob]. I've never seen anything like it in my life...

I look over the top of my monitor and sigh. This account isn't exactly damning for Anna but I can see how it could be interpreted. I replay the witness's interpretation of what she'd seen, imagining how Anna threw herself forward, deliberately knocking the victim into the path of the oncoming train. And that cry she'd made? Was it one of torment as the witness suggested? Is Anna suffering?

The email software dings and a note from the coroner arrives. I open up the email and look at the report. The woman had been carrying identification that said her name was Tracey Herod.

A few moments later, Beth sends me an email confirming that Tracey Herod had been the owner of a coffee shop near King's Cross. What does this seemingly innocuous woman have to do with Anna?

'Michael?' Beth says from the doorway. 'The coffee shop Herod owned just went up in flames and the fire brigade have been called out.'

'Christ! Any casualties?'

'No. The place was evacuated when a gas leak was reported. Within minutes it was burning.'

'Let me have the fire officer's report when you we have it. This is getting very interesting,' I say.

'I know. It can't be a coincidence.'

Left alone again, I reread all the eye-witness transcripts. I'm not sure what I'm looking for that will tell me more than I already know but I want to try and understand Anna and her possible motivations.

Thinking about the small connection I've had with her, Anna doesn't closely fit the profile I had created for the assassin we are pursuing. Past history has shown such assassins to be high-functioning sociopaths, with narcissistic traits. They usually delight in death. After a while, a pattern emerges, showing how they play with their kill, elongating the moment of finality. This need to hold back the moment, as though gaining some kind of pleasure from the delay, often reveals a perversity found in serial killers. It is inevitable that an assassin will eventually become divorced from any form of inhibition. I have trouble reconciling this standard norm with the woman I met. If she is the killer, she is an anomaly. She didn't look like someone who had enjoyed committing a murder just seconds before. In fact, she was upset. Confused. Maybe even afraid.

I open the profile document I've been compiling for years on this particular assassin and look again at my notes. Though the kills are always quick and clean – often with a knife – there is no obvious deterioration into more psychotic behaviour. This *modus operandi* alone has made this killer stand out from others. Some perpetrators I've studied have fallen into common traits of over-cutting, leaving multiple secondary stab wounds, or excessive bullets shot into the victim's body – all of which display a level of disrespect for the person, dehumanising them completely in a frantic display of aggression. As though they hate the victim and the hits have become personal, not merely a job. For that reason, I think this killer might be the most professional of all. They seem strong, controlled. Like they've never lost it. They are perhaps incapable of resorting to torture, any more than they could break down with regret. Cold inside, feeling nothing, perhaps, other than the desire to follow orders.

I think about Anna. Did she behave like someone who had no emotions? Is she the person we've been looking for? My brief encounter with her suggests not. But my gut says otherwise.

Maybe I'm wrong about Anna. She might not be Bright's assassin at all. Or maybe she is and she knew who I was. Could the whole almost-fainting thing have been an act just for me?

I tell myself to stick to the facts. Anna couldn't have known who I was. And no, it wasn't faked. She did collapse in my arms. All the rest might be a fluke. Perhaps she was just a woman in the wrong place at the wrong time, probably shocked by what she'd witnessed.

But then where did that leave the victim? If this was a hit, then who was Tracey Herod and who wanted her dead?

I explore several scenarios. Some that show Anna as my killer, some that show her as a witness to a murder. I want to believe that they are two different people, but I keep coming back to the woman in the Aidan Bright case, and how similar her walk and frame are to Anna's.

I *know* it's her. And if this is true, and she did kill Tracey Herod, if she did give that shout of suffering, then this might mean that our assassin is finally losing control and the body count is only just beginning.

Chapter Fourteen

NEVA

When Neva returns home, the car that was stationed near her house is gone. Neva enters through the front door. It isn't important if she's seen returning, only that she wasn't followed when she left. It is a good sign that the tail has been pulled off. It means *they* don't think she is a problem.

She goes upstairs. Removing the black dress and wig, she showers and changes, putting on a simple silk blouse with a pair of black jeans. Then she braids her hair, tying it back into a French plait.

Once she is dressed, she opens the wardrobe. Pulling back the panels where her weapons are hidden, she removes her guns and knives, stowing them in two holdalls.

While the Network is running scared, it's time to leave. She hadn't decided to go until now; it is a difficult thing for her to actuate after years of imprisonment. She weighs up the pros and cons even as she packs her weapons.

What's the worst that can happen? If she stays, they'll be watching her over the next few months, albeit intermittently, and the opportunity may not arise again. They may even bring her in for conditioning. If she leaves, no more assignments and no more money. They'll know for certain she killed Tracey and will make every effort to locate her. *But this will always be the case, no matter when I go, now or later.* They'll try to track her. Is she prepared enough?

She pauses to think.

One of her new identities, a marketing manager, has been renting a flat in central London for the past six months. Another has had a flat in Madrid for over a year. She has two boltholes to retreat to, neither of which are on the radar of her employers. It's time to take on a new identity, an alter ego that Tracey hadn't known about. In fact, no one other than the man who created her papers has ever heard of Ingrid Rouille or Jessica Monroe and he isn't speaking to anyone from the dark sandy pit she put him in once he had finished his work.

'I'm ready,' she murmurs to herself in the mirror.

Looking out of her bedroom window, Neva notes that the road is still clear. No sign of the car. No sign of anyone at all. *It has to be now!*

She packs a small overnight bag with an auburn wig, make-up, and appropriate clothing for Ingrid's wardrobe; she is the twinset and pearls type, with designer bags and shoes. Neva has crafted an entire history for her, subtly creating an identity she can fall into. Neva adds a pair of Prada stilettos and a matching bag to the case, frivolous items she's bought just for this persona. She gets no pleasure from them at all.

Downstairs, she goes into the garage and unlocks the car. It's a ten-year-old Ford Mondeo, nothing flashy. She fills the boot of her car with the bags.

The burner phone makes a loud ding as she gets in behind the wheel. She's forgotten it's in her purse.

Meet me at the crossroads. Sharrick.

Sharrick, her new handler, is near. That's why there's no watch on her! They expect her to obey, or maybe they're ready to converge and this is just a trap to draw her from her place of safety.

Neva gets out of the car. She opens the boot and unzips one of the bags. She removes a Glock 61, checks the safety, loads it, and then gets back into the car. She puts the Glock in the central storage area amid the old receipts and pens and then picks up the burner and replies.

On my way

On her key fob is a remote control. She uses it now to open the garage door. She starts the engine and pulls out and away from the country house. She has called this place home for the past four years. She won't see it again.

She feels no regret.

The meeting point is a railway crossroads some five miles away. Neva pulls up alongside a silver Mercedes. She doesn't get out of the car. She waits for the man in the Mercedes to get out and walk towards her. He gets into her passenger seat, closing the door carefully.

Neva turns and looks at him. He is tall, over six feet, with silver hair cut short around the ears but flopping over his eyes at the front. She puts him at around forty but trying to look younger.

'I'm Sharrick,' he says. 'Your new handler.'

'What happened to Tracey?'

Sharrick looks at her. His eyes are cool blue, icy.

The hairs rise on the back of her neck. Neva's been trained to react or remain passive as a situation requires. There's a moment when she feels Sharrick's tension, as though he's steadying himself for a fight. Neva knows this pre-battle sensation. She forces herself to remain relaxed even though every reflex is screaming at her to reach for her gun. Any miscommunication at this point will dictate her future.

Sensing nothing from her, Sharrick's unease decreases. The slight stiffness in his shoulders lessens. The change is subtle but Neva is alert to every movement and she knows in that instant that the danger has passed.

'You had quite a history with her so you deserve to know. She said her location had been compromised. Next thing we know, the police are scraping her up off the tracks.'

'I see,' Neva says. 'You have an assignment for me?'

'No. I thought it best to meet first. See if this news upsets you. It doesn't.'

'Why should it?'

'Because she was with you … from the beginning.'

'Sentiment is a waste of energy,' Neva says.

'Good,' Sharrick says. 'Aren't you curious how she became compromised?'

'Curiosity kills.'

'If you have any suspicions, contact me.'

'I will.'

He gets out of the car without further comment. Neva backs up and turns the vehicle around as though she's heading back to the country house.

She glances through her rearview mirror and sees Sharrick driving away in the opposite direction.

The roads are wide open country lanes and no other cars are around. There's no one watching her. Can the Network be that stupid? Neva hopes so.

Chapter Fifteen

MICHAEL

I open the dishwasher and look inside. Cups, glasses, and plates fill it to the brim, still unwashed. I let out a slow breath. I'm not sure if I'm relieved or disappointed. Now I have the glass, I'm compelled to check for prints. If I come up with anything from that search, I'll also have to take this to Ray, which means I'll have a lot of explaining to do.

Taking a tea towel from one of the kitchen drawers, I pick up the glass and place it inside an evidence bag. I put it down on the kitchen counter above the dishwasher.

I take a beer from the fridge and open it, swigging from the bottle as though this will help me think. Who can I get to check this for prints who won't report back to Archive?

I can call in a favour.

I have a friend in Scotland Yard who can check out the prints on my behalf. That way no one at Archive need know and I'll be able to keep the information to myself if it proves to be a dead end. Of course, if the prints bring up something, then I'll have to come clean.

I think about what that will mean. With something to go on which might help us find Anna, it's likely that Ray won't give me anything worse than a bollocking for not speaking up sooner. Under other circumstances, withholding such information could mean serious repercussions, perhaps even suspension. The prospect of facing a disciplinary when I've so far had an exemplary career does not please me. But it's a real possibility. I'm faced with a decision that could change my life, possibly ruin my career.

I sip the beer again and try to put the issue from my mind. Tomorrow I'll meet DCI Drew Cartwright and ask him to check out the glass for prints and DNA. Drew owes me this; I won't even have to remind him that I once saved his career.

I finish the beer and get another one from the fridge, then I go into the living room. I sit down and reach for the remote control on the small table at the side of the sofa, but the gadget slips from my fingers and falls onto the floor.

'Shit!'

I place the beer bottle on the table and reach down for the remote. That's when I see the long strand of black hair.

I keep the place clean. Scrupulously clean.

Forgetting about the remote control, I pick up the hair. I glance around the room. I take the hair, walk back into the kitchen, and put it inside the evidence bag with the brandy glass.

I look around the room now with fresh eyes. Nothing appears to be disturbed but I know without doubt that someone has been here. Why didn't I realise sooner?

I walk through the flat, starting at the front door. Just as I would if I were at a crime scene, I study every inch of my floor and surfaces. The intruder came in through the front door. I put myself in their head. There has been no obvious ransack. Nothing was stolen or I'd have noticed immediately. So, what did they want?

I close my eyes and focus. If I were at a crime scene, what would I see? I need to search my flat and see if anything has gone.

I start with my bedroom. I haven't been in there since I got home. One of my drawers isn't quite closed. I can't be sure that I didn't leave it that way this morning as I rushed to get ready, but usually I'm tidy and always close the drawers. I open it up and see the photo album on top of a pile of old T-shirts. The album was always underneath, stowed, so that I could almost forget the family when I needed to, but knew where to go when I didn't. I'm in no doubt that I've had an intruder.

I go back into the kitchen to look again at the hair strand. Also, the thief may have gone in there. People leave money in jars in kitchens, after all. I scan the work tops, then I open the cupboards, one by one, trying to think like this person. Inside my cupboards I see … tins of food, dried pasta. Nothing appears to have been moved. What could you possibly want to find here anyway?

My eyes fall on the brandy glass. I pick it up and look at it through the evidence bag. The glass looks clean. Why hadn't I noticed that before? I open the bag and sniff. The odour of brandy has gone.

'Shit!'

I put the glass down. Trying to find prints or DNA might

now be a waste of time.

Then, a memory flashes through my mind. That morning I'd left early. There had been a woman standing near the door in the reception. She'd been wearing a short black dress; her long black hair was ruffled and it had crossed my mind that she was returning from an evening out – a 'walk of shame', they call it. She'd avoided looking at me. Kept her head averted. I hadn't thought too much of it.

I analyse the memory now, trying to pull out every detail. I was trained to be observant. She'd been tall, in four-inch heeled boots. But she was hunched, as though hiding her height. I'd thought this defensive because she might have been embarrassed to be seen. But … was it … *Anna*? Was she wearing yet another disguise?

Had Anna returned to my flat? I wander around, looking at everything, considering what she has touched and, more importantly, what her motive was for being here. Was the appearance of disarray intentional in order to make me dismiss her when I saw her? Or had she really spent the night with someone else in my block of flats? If that was the case, was it a coincidence or deliberate? I can't dismiss the possibility that she intended to come back, that she wanted to learn more about me.

I try to superimpose the long black hair onto Anna's face. I can imagine it, just. Then I remember that I've yet to work on the artist software to try and recreate her image to put into the database. This is now a priority, even ahead of taking the brandy glass to Drew Cartwright – not that he's likely to find anything on it now.

Feeling paranoid, I double-lock my flat door, ensuring the deadbolts are also run across the top and the bottom. It won't keep any trespasser out when I'm not home, but it will stop any attempt to come in while I sleep.

Then, a worrying thought occurs to me. Did she find my secure weapon box?

I hurry back into the bedroom, pull back the rug near the bed and look down at the floorboards. To the casual eye, the floor is immaculate, solid. Underneath the lamp on the bedside cabinet is a tiny button. I press it now and the floorboard slides aside, revealing the box. This little storage space was fitted by MI5 when I joined Archive. I lift out the secure metal box, key in the code, and use the finger print scanner as final security. The box opens and I look inside to see my gun, secure and safe. Untampered with.

I take out the gun. Standard MI5 issue, Glock 17. Making sure the safety is on, I load the weapon, then place it down under my bed, within easy reach.

When this is done, I lie down and try to sleep. But I'm wired, senses on hyper-drive, and so every little noise brings me back out of my shallow slumber. Twice I check the gun is still where I left it and then, just before dawn, too tired to fight sleep any longer, I finally give in and rest.

But my subconscious mind still worries at the problem. In my dreams I see Anna again near the station. This time she's wearing a black dress and her hair, loose over her shoulders, is flowing like a black cape around her. She smiles at me as I walk towards her. Then the air moves and my dream self falls back, hands held to my throat. Anna is standing over me, a sharp and bloody blade in her hand.

The blood pumps out of my body, over my fingers. I try to yell for help but no sound comes out of my destroyed throat.

I'm cold. So cold. This is what death feels like.

An irritating ringing pulls me out of this torturous nightmare. For a moment I'm paralysed, still in that place between dream and reality. I put my hands to my throat. Then I sit up, looking around my room. Light sifts around the curtains and still the ringing continues. It takes me a moment to realise it's my mobile phone on the bedside table. I reach for it.

'Hey? Where are you?' asks Ray.

'Oh shit!' I leap from the bed. 'Sorry. Alarm didn't go off. I didn't sleep too well last night.'

'Why?'

'Thinking about the case … you know how that is?'

'Nothing a stiff brandy doesn't cure. Come up with anything?' Ray asks

'Still working on it. I'll get there, a-sap.'

I hang up and place the phone back down beside me with a shaking hand. The dream presses again around my conscious mind. How can I tell Ray that my subconscious has connected and confirmed that Anna is our killer? That she's been here, in my flat, twice? Once because I brought her here, the second time of her own volition – motive still unknown.

I pick up the gun from under the bed and take it into the

bathroom. I lock the door, place the gun on the sink, then shower, shave, and brush my teeth.

Back in the bedroom I dress, adding my holster to my uniform, and I place my weapon inside it, before pulling my jacket on to cover the gun. I rarely ever take my gun into the office.

On the way out, I take a final glance around the flat and wonder what I'll do if Anna comes back. Part of me hopes she will. I want answers. Especially why she came back here. Was she curious about me too?

What am I thinking? This woman is dangerous. Her snooping isn't curiosity; it's something else. But what? Had I become a person of interest to her and her employers?

In the kitchen, I grab a bagel from the bread bin. Then I pick up my briefcase and leave the flat, double-locking the door, before heading off to the lift.

In the reception I take careful note of anyone around. There is a tourist asking for directions, a woman I recognise as one of my neighbours, and the cleaner mopping the tiled floor. Nothing unusual. Outside, I check up and down the street, noting any cars that appear to linger, or anyone that might be acting suspiciously.

At the kerb I hail a taxi and, even though it's quicker and easier to take the tube, I tell the driver the address and head off to the office. I glance back as the taxi pulls away. Every woman I see catches my eye. *Is she Anna?* I dismiss them automatically for height or shape or size. *This is ridiculous,* I tell myself. She could be anywhere. She could look like anybody.

Chapter Sixteen

NEVA

After following Michael from his flat to his place of work, Neva returns to her new home – an expensive flat in Hammersmith. Over the last few months she's spent the occasional night here, sneaking in wearing a headscarf and sunglasses, avoiding contact with any of the neighbours. Always careful, though, to wear Ingrid Rouille's clothing and wig.

She's thinking about what she's learnt about Michael as she enters the palatial reception and walks towards the lift. Head down, she tries to avoid contact with the few people she's aware of that are milling around.

'Hello? Miss Rouille, isn't it?'

She ignores the voice behind her and presses the call button on the lift.

'Excuse me, are you Miss Rouille?'

Neva turns to see a small, dark-haired woman, carrying a pointlessly small dog, possibly a shih-tzu. Neva smiles.

Then she answers the woman with a carefully crafted French accent.

'*Oui*. I am Ingrid Rouille.'

'I just wanted to introduce myself. I'm Carleen Calendar. I'm your neighbour. We're on the same floor. I also run the tenants' association and we're having a gathering this evening. I thought it might be the perfect time for you to meet us all.'

'That's kind. I'm afraid I'm busy this evening.'

The lift arrives and Neva enters, pressing the button for her floor. The pointless dog yaps as someone else comes into the reception. Neva glances at the newcomer. It's the postman. She puts her head down as he looks her way.

Opening the door of her flat, she enters with soundless stealth. The rooms are furnished with borrowed taste. Ingrid is a story she has written in her head. A play she is performing. Neva enjoys this idea; being someone else is the second-best thing she's good at.

In the kitchen she boils the kettle and begins to make some herbal tea but something is nagging at the back of her mind. The image of the postman flashes behind her eyes. The man is familiar. He looks like someone she's seen before. She shudders, shaking away the feeling of paranoia. No one knows she's here. She has to be imagining it. Besides, the man barely saw her as the lift doors closed, cutting the reception and Carleen Calendar from view.

Neva sits down on the expensive, but stiff, sofa and sips her tea.

Taking her mind off the postman, she thinks again about

Michael. The building he works in is listed as belonging to a publishing house but she's certain that really this is an MI5 or MI6 agency taskforce he's working for. Perhaps they're hidden there to make them a less obvious target.

Michael's behaviour interested her the most, however. He was acting as though he knew he was being followed. Neva was sure he hadn't seen her though, which meant one thing: he knew someone had been in his flat. She'd kept back and had remained unobserved. She'd even managed to snap some pictures of him and the building to use later. One of her contacts would know what this place really was; it would cost, but Neva could afford to pay. She had plans too for her future security, which involved taking contracts other than from the Network.

All of this needed to wait until such a time as she found herself safe. But that period wouldn't come until Neva discovered how far their influence reached and if it was just Europe, which she suspected, or worldwide. Either way, the Network couldn't do what they did without help. Throughout the years she'd worked for them, Neva had learnt more than Tracey suspected. She knew that there were government officials involved, operatives in the Ministry of Defence and even paid collaborators in British spy agencies. Names had been bandied about; her victims were often willing to tell her what they knew in the hope she'd show mercy. At first their blabbering meant nothing to her, but familiar names repeated time and again began to sink into her conditioned brain. She began to actively listen, even though she never asked questions.

There was mention of a Mr Beech on a few occasions, but Neva had trouble finding out more about this man. Those who uttered his name had been full of remorse, begging with more fervency than was normal.

Neva recalled one such man now. He was not the sort she was usually sent after. He had appeared to be just a rich upper-class wastrel. Someone the Network rarely took notice of. But this man, a lord of some kind – and even now she couldn't recall his actual name or title – had done something to bring down their wrath on his head.

Neva had picked him up at the theatre. She'd smiled at him in the bar, and the creep soon found his way over to where she was sitting. More, she discovered, to share the bottle of champagne she had on ice.

'Drinking that alone?' he'd asked.

'My date didn't show,' she said in her finest 'royal family' accent. 'A total cad.'

'Indeed.'

She'd asked him to join her. They didn't go in to the second act of the show. The play was awful and Neva's new friend was more interested in buying the next bottle, most of which he drank himself.

Neva persuaded him to come back to 'her place'. It was a penthouse flat in the docklands, all organised by her superiors. He was so drunk by then that he didn't notice the plastic sheets covering everything in the living room until she'd led him inside and closed the door.

'Oh God!' he said when he saw the knife in her hand. 'This is Beech's doing. That bastard. He wanted to steal my company and I let him. But he's never happy. Him and the Network ... they want it all ...'

Neva stopped advancing on him when she heard Beech's name. There was a flash of something behind her eyes, a painful memory that her conditioning quashed. She tried to recall it but the result was a blinding headache and an urge to cut her own throat.

Noticing her hesitation, the man had fallen to his knees.

'Don't kill me,' he said. 'I won't tell on him. I won't talk about the imports and exports. What he does ... I hardly know anything about it.'

But his jabbering implied otherwise.

Neva was on a strict time limit with this one. Clean-up would be here within the hour. She had to be long gone by then and the toff had to be dead. But she allowed him to talk, and she stored up the information, even though some of it didn't make any sense at the time. When the man had exhausted himself with pleading, she ended it quietly, and he didn't even fight. He knew, despite everything, that it was over.

The death had left her feeling empty, which was far worse than when she felt nothing at all. A lot of the kills had started to make her feel that way. Especially the ones that were pointless or somehow inconsequential. This man's end fell into the petty category. As though this Mr Beech had a personal score to settle and Neva had been used to do that.

Now, Neva analyses the thought of being 'used' by the Network. It isn't as if they had endowed her with a personal code. She'd watched a TV series like that once, where the killer did what he did because his victims were themselves killers or molesters who had evaded the police through luck or clever lawyers; they deserved to die. Neva had no such sentiments. She'd been taught not to care enough about the mark. It was a job, nothing more, and as such it shouldn't matter whether the target was justified or not. But it started to matter, and then gradually everything changed for her.

Like now. She should be leaving London, flying to a different country, and getting as far away from the Network as she possibly can. Instead she's here, biding her time and thinking about a man who might be a security agent. A man who means nothing to her.

Neva remembers the kindness Michael showed her. For some reason, that moment in the street was important. Michael Kensington, whoever he is, and whatever he does, is someone who can be relied on. Someone who might just be willing to help her find out more about Beech and more about the house in which she was made. For each of these things have grown into a significant part of her daily consciousness.

As if thinking about the house is some form of spell, Neva feels the coldness of the conditioning seeping back into her limbs. She stares at the wall of the flat. The mantra flows in and around her and then she presses back.

I *will* be curious. I *will* fight back. I am death.

'Who are you?' she says aloud. Mr Beech looms, real but as a shadow in her subconscious. 'Why can't I see your face?'

Behind the human-shaped shade she sees the house. A large monstrosity, sprawling as it does across impressive grounds. It was home for years, but she never knew where *there* was.

'I know you are part of this. I know you made me what I am. I'm coming for you, Beech,' she says. 'I'm coming for all of you.'

The teacup shatters in her hand.

Chapter Seventeen

SHARRICK

'Neva's gone,' says Sharrick to the person on the other end of the phone.

He's standing in the small hallway of the cottage while a team of four men systematically pull the rooms apart.

'Any idea where?' asks the voice on the other end.

'She's left her whole life behind, except, I suppose, for a few things. She's taken her laptop, a few clothes. And I assume passports. Although her regular ID was left behind in a top drawer in the bedroom. Weapons are cleaned out too.'

'I thought she "owned" that house. Why put down roots and then leave?'

'We found documents that say otherwise. It turns out she sold it some months ago. She's been renting it back ever since. I guess Herod hadn't thought to check on what she was doing. Neva has always been so ... *steady*.'

'And the money from the sale?'

'Switzerland is my guess. Can you get authority to find the account?' Sharrick asks.

'She won't have used a British ID. So asking for new account details from the Swiss won't be of any help. And she's more than likely used a bank whose discretion can be bought. Or a third party to buffer her. But I'll ask the question anyway. See what turns up. I'll put out some other feelers.'

Sharrick hangs up and walks into the living room. He curses himself for not noticing that Neva was compromised. She'd given no sign. But he should have pressed her harder; he'd known how good at this she was. She has to be caught, even though it's unlikely they can salvage her after this. It's a relief that Beech isn't blaming him ... yet.

'Anything?' he asks. The two men in the living room look up. They shake their heads in unison and then return to their task of slitting open the furniture.

'I found these,' says a voice from the hallway. Sharrick looks over to see Harman holding up a stack of passports in a clear plastic wallet.

He takes the wallet and opens it, rifling through the identities. 'All ones we gave her. She's taking no chances.'

'She planned this,' Harman says.

'For some time,' Sharrick agrees.

'Was that Mr Beech on the phone?' Harman asks.

'Yes.'

'I'm sorry,' says Harman. 'Is he...?'

'Calm at the moment. He thinks we can find her.'

'Then what?'

'We find out why she ran. If she's just … breaking down, well, there's ways of dealing with that.'

'What other reason can there be?' Harman says.

'Neva may have been warned by Herod. Perhaps she was compromised too and has been compelled to go into hiding.'

'But that would mean we have a major breach somewhere.'

Sharrick and Harman exchange a look. Sharrick is sure that if such a breach is suspected, Mr Beech would have been talking to him differently. He'd be in having a polygraph and so would everyone else.

'But the other possibility is … Neva is the problem,' Sharrick says.

'And she killed Herod… Do you think that's likely?' asks Harman.

Sharrick says nothing. No operative has ever killed their handler. Beech doesn't want to believe it's happened now, and neither does Sharrick. But the only way to know for sure is to bring Neva in.

'Anyway,' Sharrick says. 'It's why the protocol is changing. In future, if there's a compromise, we need to reveal to Mr Beech directly who and what, not do what Herod did. Because we can only speculate who was the cause now.'

Harman nods.

'Let's pack up Neva's stuff and get out of here,' Sharrick says. 'She won't be coming back here, no matter what.'

Chapter Eighteen

NEVA

In an internet café, Neva reaches out to a once trusted source. It is a forum, a place to which only those who know about it go. A place situated in the deepest, darkest parts of the Web. She negotiates through encryptions and navigates to a site she knows, leaving the Clearnet behind. She is now on the Tor dark Web, often referred to as Onionland. Neva has always thought the name amusing, and it makes this place sound unbelievable. But the dark Web is real, and she can find anything and anyone through its illegal resources with total anonymity.

She sends pictures of Michael and the location of his workplace in a private message to her source. Then she sits back and waits to hear the response, pretending to check a social media account she has just for this reason. It's a fake account, containing no pictures of herself, and no genuine information. But it makes her look innocent to anyone passing by her screen.

Her source comes back to her just before she's about to

give up and leave the café. There is only so much time she can stay in one place before her movements online become of interest.

Over the years, Neva has made some loyal contacts. This man, whom she knows as Ruben, is still, she hopes, one of them. She takes Ruben into a private chat to discuss what she's looking for.

Ruben tells her Michael Kensington is a security agent at MI5. He has full security clearance and is licenced to carry a firearm. Ruben tells her that Michael is working for a taskforce.

She types:

What does the taskforce do?

Ruben replies:

No one has clearance enough to know, but cold cases are among the things they are openly listed to investigate. It's called Archive. That's all I know.

He adds at the end of the message.

They're looking for you. Just be careful. Trust no one. Not even me.

Neva signs out from the computer. She's concerned that they're watching him. Ruben is too smart to be hacked, but the Network has ways of gathering information. Ruben knows that and so does she. It's why he encourages her to break contact as soon as she has the information she needs.

Neva returns to the Hammersmith flat. She's just about to cross the road when she sees the postman again. He's loitering near the reception door and he's on his phone. Neva goes into the café across the road from the building. She orders a coffee and watches. A few moments later, a black Mercedes pulls up. Neva recognises the standard black suit worn by bodyguards employed by the Network, but not the two operatives that get out of the car.

She expects them to go and talk to the postman, but instead they walk past him and go into the building next door to hers. A few seconds later, the two men come out and get back in the car. They drive away.

Is it a coincidence? The Network is everywhere, after all.

Neva sees a Royal Mail van arrive and the postman hangs up his phone. He gets in the van. Even though he never spoke to or acknowledged the men in the Mercedes, she's still suspicious of him.

She leaves the coffee shop and walks a few hundred metres down the road before she crosses over to the right side of the street. She doubles back, slipping behind the building. The janitor's office is accessible via the back door of the building. Neva has already established that he has a habit of leaving the fire exit open when he goes out back to smoke. This day is no exception. Neva is cautious as she traverses the back alley. No one is around, but she's now wary of the building next door and who might be there, watching, waiting for her to fall down.

She slips into the building and goes up to her floor by

the maintenance stairs. As she opens the door onto the landing, she checks to see if anyone is around. The corridor is quiet. She hurries along, retrieving her key from her jacket pocket. She reaches the flat and checks the bottom of her door. She had left a hair stuck across the jam and the door; if anyone opened the door, the hair would become dislodged. It is still in place.

She gets inside without incident. Then she closes all the blinds and curtains and begins to pack. She isn't sure if she's been noticed, but she prepares for the possibility of flight.

Then she lies low, lights off, as though she has not returned home at all that day. In the corridor outside her flat she hears people arriving at the flat opposite and realises that Carleen's tenants' party is in full swing.

Through her security camera – a discreet lens no larger than the size of a button hidden in the pattern of the brocade wallpaper in the hallway above her door – she watches on her laptop the movement of the residents as they go in and out of Carleen's flat. Then she notices the two men she saw earlier. They walk up to Carleen's door, but don't knock. One casts a glance over his shoulder at Neva's door. They exchange a look.

'Oh, gentlemen, come in!' says Carleen, opening the door to them. 'She's not returned...' she whispers, though Neva's camera microphone picks up every word. All three of them glance at Neva's door.

They go inside and Carleen closes the door with one last look at Neva's flat.

Neva is now sure that she's been compromised. Who is

Carleen Calendar? The name sounds too perfect to be genuine and this turn of events implies that she is connected to the Network. Is this how they found her? It would make sense that they had put the word out to all of their spies to watch for any new female moving in to their respective flats.

Neva turns away from the laptop screen. She shuts the machine down. She has to be ready to leave here, but passing Carleen's door will be dangerous and she has a lot to take with her.

She goes to the bedroom, picks up her flight bag and then returns to the kitchen. She unzips the bag, pushes in the laptop, and checks through her wallet to select a new ID.

She tosses Ingrid Rouille's passport down on the kitchen table.

She has four more under different names, but now she is uncertain if any of them are safe.

The kitchen is in darkness, with just the light from the street illuminating the room. She glances outside, down into the alley below. The reason she picked this flat was because of the fire escape stairs that frame the side. They're not common in London buildings but someone will be watching in case she returns and goes up the back steps. It's time to call in the cavalry.

Using the burner phone, she dials a number. The call is answered on the first ring.

'Janine?' she says.

'Yes?'

'It's time.'

Chapter Nineteen

SHARRICK

Sharrick waits outside, at the back of the building. Neva – or at least his source says it's her – has taken on the identity of a French woman, living in this block of flats. Harman is inside with another colleague and they wait in the flat opposite for Neva to return.

'There's been no sign of her since this morning,' Sharrick says into his phone.

'She may be on to you,' Mr Beech says.

'There's been no indication that she is. But possibly. Even so, she will need to return. My guess is that she has a flight bag inside with new ID. She'll want that no matter what.'

'Has anyone been inside the flat to investigate?'

'No opportunity,' Sharrick says.

At that moment, Harman speaks into his ear piece.

'Taxi arrived. She's getting out and coming inside.'

'I have to go,' says Sharrick down the phone. 'Our girl has returned.'

Sharrick leaves his post at the back and hurries around the building in time to see Neva paying the driver and going inside. He stays outside until she enters the lift and then he goes into the reception and up towards the stairs, which he takes two at a time.

He peers through the door on the second-floor landing and sees the lift arrive and Neva, wearing a red wig and a tweed twinset, exit and head towards the flat.

'Go. Go. Go,' he says and Carleen's door bursts open. Harman and the other operative are on Neva before she can escape.

'What are you doing?' she says in a thick French accent. 'Let me go!'

She screams as one of the men tugs at her hair.

'It's not a wig!' Harman gasps.

By now, Sharrick is beside them.

'Help!' screams the girl.

Sharrick looks at her face. She is the same height and build as Neva, but it isn't her.

'Ingrid Rouille?' Sharrick asks.

'*Oui*. What is the meaning of this?'

'I'm sorry. There's been some mistake.'

Ingrid looks over to a shocked Carleen, who stands by her front door watching the proceedings.

'All this because I said I had plans tonight?' Ingrid says.

The men release her and Ingrid staggers to her door.

'I'll be reporting this to the tenants' association!' she says.

They watch her unlock her door and go inside.

She switches on the light in the hallway before slamming the door on them all.

Behind the door, Neva smiles.

'Well done, Janine,' she mouths.

This small ruse has bought her the time she needs to escape.

They head silently to the kitchen. The operatives are probably listening at the door.

'Go into the kitchen,' Neva whispers to Janine. 'Make yourself a drink. Act like this is your home.'

Janine does as she asks and moves around the flat switching on lights. She goes into the bedroom, then the bathroom, and runs herself a bath. A few moments later someone knocks on the door. Neva checks the camera on an app on her phone, then takes position behind the door, a gun in her hand.

Janine comes out wearing Ingrid's robe and makes her way to the door.

'Who is it?'

'It's me, Carleen. I'm so sorry about the misunderstanding.'

'You should be,' Janine says.

Janine opens the door. 'What was that all about?'

'I'm sorry. It's a … well, I can't explain. Mistaken identity is the closest I can come.'

'Who were those thugs?'

'It's … an *official* matter,' Carleen said.

'Official? You think me some criminal or something? Just because I'm French?'

Through the crack in the door, Neva sees Carleen shake her head.

'I can only say how sorry I am.'

'I must go, my bath will run over.'

With that, she rudely closes the door on Carleen.

Janine and Neva exchange a look.

'Double-checking?' Janine says.

'Scared of losing her position on the tenants' board, I shouldn't wonder,' Neva answers.

Janine turns the light off in the kitchen and goes into the bathroom. While she's in there, Neva changes. She places on her head a short dirty-blonde urchin-cut wig that frames her face. She slips on black jeans and a black polo-neck top, over which she pulls on a black denim jacket. When Janine returns from her bath, Neva no longer looks like Ingrid Rouille.

'Stay until tomorrow,' Neva says. 'Then you know what to do. I've wired your money to the usual account.'

It's not the first time Janine has doubled for Neva. She wonders now, with the large sum paid, if it will be the last.

Janine settles down in front of the television and switches it on. Neva takes her bag and leaves the flat via the fire escape. She moves silently out and down until she reaches the alley. No one comes out of the shadows to stop her.

As she reaches the front of the building, she sees Sharrick and the other two operatives clustered at the front door talking. She turns away from them and walks casually down the street, losing herself in a bustle of evening revellers pouring out of a nearby pub. She remains among them as they flow across the road, and then she turns into a side street and begins to put some real distance between herself and Sharrick.

It was a close call that has confirmed how far-reaching the Network is. No one can be trusted and it proves that some kind of alert about her has been sent out. Carleen was an informant; how many more 'normal' people are on their payroll?

Down the next street she spots a car parked in a disabled spot outside a hotel. She toys with the idea of stealing it, then changes her mind and walks past. Then she sees a tube station up ahead.

She glances at her watch. It's 10pm. She needs to get out of the city and go somewhere there is less chance they will look for her. London is not as anonymous as it appears to be.

She pauses only to drop her burner phone, sim card and all, into a nearby bin after wiping it clean. If they find it, they can make of it what they will:

Chapter Twenty

BETH

Agent Beth Cane sifts through a pile of folders that Ray has placed on her desk. The series of murders that possibly link to Michael's mystery woman aren't the only things they're looking at. Beth has a backlog of cases that need to be examined. She puts aside the top file after a brief flick through; it appears to be a series of vigilante murders and since all the victims were rapists, she doesn't care to give this one more time. It crosses her mind that Ray would disapprove if he knew she thought this, saying that all investigations warranted their scrutiny. Beth can't help thinking that the men in question had all deserved what they got. They were scum, even if they were brutally murdered. For that reason, she gives her attention to something more deserving.

She opens up the next folder and sees the faces of seven small children. There are four girls and three boys, aged between four and seven years old.

Beth reads the notes and realises this is a twenty-year-old cold case. All the children vanished within days of each other. Goosebumps come up on her arms. The room isn't cold; it's how she always reacts to a hunch. She doesn't know why, but her gut tells her that this is worth pursuing.

She opens her computer and searches for similar examples in the database; she doesn't find anything that's been marked for their study and so she puts a wider search out onto the Web. It takes some time and she flicks through several unconnected links until she finds a newspaper report from thirty-five years ago; seven children disappeared in similar circumstances to the case she's been given but fifteen years previously. These occurrences don't appear to have been linked to each other, but Beth sees immediately that they are connected. It's too much of a coincidence for them not to be.

She reads all the information she can find and compiles a report which she emails to Ray. This case, cold though it is, is somehow significant. She wants Ray to approve her wish to reopen it and begin to investigate what happened and where those kids ended up.

Beth has worked for MI5 for over ten years. Like Michael, she was recruited at university and since then her whole working life has been dedicated to her job. Four years ago, Ray Martin pulled Beth into Archive, saying she was wasted in her previous position. It was a move she's yet to regret, even though her husband, Callum, often complains about her long hours.

As she waits for Ray's reply, she tries to look through the other folders, but her mind goes back to the children. All of them were incredibly gifted. Their disappearance disturbs her a great deal. At first, she thinks it's because she too is a mother, and the thought of one of her two boys going missing horrifies her, but Beth is a seasoned investigator and such things usually don't affect her.

Besides, I'm not made that way, she thinks.

She loves her children, but Beth, as Callum often says, is more interested in solving mysteries than being part of their family. From time to time a row erupts between them for which Callum, invariably, blames her job. It's been calm at home for months now, but Beth can feel another such argument brewing. *It's just a matter of time.*

Trying to take her mind from her personal problems, Beth forces her concentration back to the task at hand. This child abduction case niggles at her; she has an intense feeling that it's somehow connected to something else. This isn't a case of paedophilia or some other sicko stealing kids; she's sure of it.

'There's something more to this,' she murmurs. 'I just have to learn what it is.'

Chapter Twenty-One

MICHAEL

I stare at the screen; the face before me is taking shape but it still doesn't completely resemble Anna. The eyes are too close together, the nose is too wide. I tweak the settings, wishing I'd committed her face more to memory but for some reason I can't get her image, in this flat, two-dimensional re-creation, quite right. This is my second attempt in as many days. The first I abandoned as a complete disaster. I add hair, long, thick, with a slight wave on the ends. Then I search through the colour selections to try and match up the shade I remember. Once I find the strawberry-blonde shade, the picture begins to look more like her, though I know the features aren't quite right.

'How's it going?' Beth asks from the doorway.

'I'm not sure. It's harder to do this than it seems. How we expect normal people to identify someone like this, when they aren't trained to observe like we are, I don't know.'

'No easy task for sure,' Beth says. 'Let's see what you have so far.'

I turn the monitor so Beth can see the picture.

'She's pretty.'

'I suppose so,' I say.

Beth glances at me.

'The hair is striking and memorable. Email me this and I'll run it through our databases and see if we get any matches.'

I nod. Beth goes away and I finalise the image as best as I can and then send it on to her. After that I open my emails and begin to read the documents for a new case I've been sent but my mind drifts away from it and I continue to try and reconcile the photo-fit image I've devised with the real woman I've met. It frustrates me that it isn't close enough.

'Michael?' Beth is at my door once more and I'm surprised that I was unaware of her. 'Can you come and see this?'

I follow Beth into the outer office. There is an image on the large screen of a woman in her fifties.

'The photo-fit pulled up similarities with your woman.'

I draw a breath. 'The hair—'

'Yes. Very close in shade and thickness.'

'She's not the right age,' I say.

'Not to be our perp. But…'

'But what?'

'This is Simone Arquette. Her husband is Stefan Arquette, the French Ambassador. Their child vanished some twenty years ago.'

'Vanished?'

'Yes. Disappeared. A little girl with hair the colour of her mother's. She was only five at the time.'

'Where are you going with this, Beth?' I ask.

'The woman you met... If you're right, and she is the assassin who killed Aidan Bright, then she's a ghost. She has no real history or identity. But she came from somewhere,' she says.

'You think she could be Simone and Stefan's daughter? But how did she become ... a killer?'

'She wasn't the only missing child during that time. It's a case I've been looking at. It's a bit of a coincidence, but now I've made this link and I believe they're connected.'

'Usually, missing children are never found; they're more likely dead,' I say.

'I know. But there's something about this one. It's different.'

She explains her findings and the connection they appear to have to the other two cases she's found.

'All the children were mysteriously taken during the day from their schools. No witnesses. They just disappeared. But each of them was a savant in some way. Highly intelligent. Talented. Different and unique, and scoring way above their age.'

'All of them?' I ask.

'Without exception,' Beth says.

'Do you have a photograph of the Arquette girl?'

Beth nods. 'I'm running it through software to see what she'd look like now. It'll take a while. To be honest, I was surprised when we got this match so quickly. These things usually take days.'

I'm shocked by her possible lead too. Could Anna be the daughter of the Arquettes?

'Okay,' I say. 'Though it does seem a little unlikely that she'd turn up now… Where has she been the last twenty years?'

'Stranger things have happened.'

'Beth. We aren't this lucky. It's … too easy,' I say.

Beth shrugs. 'Sometimes we deserve a break. Otherwise it's just all a hard slog. And let's be honest, what we do is generally very difficult.'

I go back to my office and try to concentrate on profiling for another case, but my mind keeps going back to Beth's possible discovery and I can't get my head in the right place. A few minutes later I receive an email from Beth with the child's photograph attached. The Arquettes' daughter was called Amelie. I stare at the photograph on the screen, looking for Anna in the childish smile. The eyes hold an innocence that I find difficult to reconcile with the woman I've met, but that isn't surprising. I recall hearing somewhere that even as a child grows to adulthood, the eyes never really change in size and shape. I take a snip copy of Amelie's eyes and place them over Anna's photo-fit. The difference is astounding. Already this looks more like Anna.

'Let me see that aged picture as soon as you have it,' I call through to Beth. 'I think you've stumbled onto something.'

Chapter Twenty-Two

NEVA

For a time, she doesn't know where to go. She checks into a cheap hotel as a place to rest and regroup. Though the room is comfortable, she barely sleeps. She is sure that any moment Sharrick and his men will find her. The fear is not unreasonable, except that she has been trained to disappear. Even so, Sharrick and the Network have skills that help them find those in hiding. That's their job, just as hers is to kill. She's aware how easy it was for them to find her first hideaway, even though she and Janine have temporarily thwarted them. She knows it's only a matter of time before they locate her if she stays in England.

The next morning, she makes her way to Euston Station. She stares at the departure boards, wondering where to go. She needs to be near London; she hasn't finished her investigation into Michael Kensington. But the city feels like a prison and Neva's paranoia spikes. In the centre of this busy station, she feels even more vulnerable. The Network has eyes everywhere; yesterday proved that. She's tried to hide in plain sight under a new identity, but after this failure, she fears that nowhere is safe. She lets fate choose where she will end up, deciding that the next announcement will tell her where she's heading. Then she will decide what to do next.

'The next train to Manchester Piccadilly is now boarding at platform nine.'

Neva walks towards the platform, but her head turns left and right as her eyes scan her surroundings with practised ease; she's looking for anyone who might be taking too much interest in her. The station is full of commuters, all of whom appear to be focused on their own journeys. Despite her heightened adrenaline, she is reassured that she's not being observed.

She reaches the platform and gets on the train, going into the first-class cabin where she knows it'll be quiet and she'll be guaranteed a seat. She sits down and waits for the train to leave the station. Half an hour into the journey the ticket attendant accepts her cash payment for the seat. Neva is offered drinks and a light supper. She takes them and watches the world pass by through the window. She avoids eye contact with everyone she sees and does not engage with other passengers. She does not want to be remembered, even if she is noticed.

Two hours and forty-five minutes later, Neva leaves Piccadilly station in Manchester. She walks down the hill and finds herself on Market Street, the main high street of the city. The centre is bustling and it's easy for her to feel anonymous again. She doesn't take this for granted, reminding herself that this is a large city and the

Network's spies can be anywhere. This is a temporary reprieve.

She heads into a branch of CEX and emerges with a second-hand phone. A visit to a Tesco Express furnishes a sim card with data. She then checks on the phone for a hotel and finds one not far away. Using one of her fake IDs, she books a room for the night. Then she goes into a newsagent and purchases the *Manchester Evening News*. In the back she finds properties to let.

She checks in at the hotel and then changes her disguise as soon as she's in her room. The urchin-cut wig is packed away and Neva becomes a brunette with long flowing locks. She has very limited clothing with her so she goes out and walks back to Market Street. She's been to Manchester before, but the place is not that familiar. Even so, she remembers the Arndale Centre and makes her way there, knowing there is an abundance of clothing shops from which she can stock her new disguise.

She shops for an hour, making cash payments, and then returns to the hotel with her new wardrobe and an extra suitcase to carry everything in.

She orders room service while she looks through the newspaper, searching for a more permanent, less conspicuous place to stay. When the food arrives, she hides in the bathroom, instructing the waiter to leave it on the dressing table.

'There's a tip for you there,' she says. She doesn't wish to be seen up close by anyone who could be in the payroll of her enemies.

When the door closes, Neva comes out of the bathroom

and sets the secure lock on the door. She sits and eats her simple pasta dish as she looks again for somewhere to hide. In the paper she finds a small advert: a couple looking for a lodger. The location is out in the suburbs. It will be ideal. She calls the number and arranges a viewing for the next day.

Chapter Twenty-Three

MICHAEL

'It's probably her,' Beth says.

'It's not exact but it's close,' I agree. 'But then, this is computer software and nothing is perfect.'

'Yeah. She could have had surgery to change her appearance as well,' Ray says.

The picture has been manipulated to age Amelie to how she might look at twenty-five years old. It's taken two days for the computer to complete.

'I agree with Beth. It's her,' I say.

'If you're right, we've found her former identity. Not who she is or where she is right now,' Leon says. 'Even so, we can use our resources to search cameras for any possible sightings.'

'If this is our girl then she's already changed her appearance. We know that's her MO. But it's normally just disguises. To be honest, the hair is so easy to cut or colour, but she doesn't choose to do that,' I point out.

'I wonder what that says about her,' Ray says.

'Her personal, real identity is important to her, especially as she spends most of her time in disguise,' I say. 'Yet I wouldn't be surprised if she somehow denies this to herself.'

'In what way?' asks Beth.

'I've been thinking about our perp and, assuming she is the woman I met, she's a highly trained assassin, capable of remaining invisible. Looking back at the history of her suspected kills, I can't help but notice that she does not act at all like others in her trade. Yes, there's a coldness in the kill that's almost clinical. Then we get the furtive burial of the mystery woman we've still to identify. The marked respect for the grave. Summarising what else we know about the killer: there is no obvious enjoyment of killing, which is a trait that all too frequently drops in over time. We've placed this killer in several locations over the last five years. In all that time we've seen no major change in how she operates.' I pause.

'So?' Ray prompts.

'If she's the woman from outside the tube station, then she may be breaking down in a different way. Not falling into the pattern that others have by turning narcissistic and getting off on death. If anything, it's making her sick. Remorseful, maybe. Or…' I stop again. The team waits while I gather my thoughts. 'I'm not sure yet. But if she is – *was once* – Amelie Arquette, then maybe she's having flashbacks.'

'What made you think that?' asks Beth.

'Her behaviour that day. She was spaced out. Like she had just remembered something important. Or horrible.

And now I think about it, it's possible she had. Maybe she even recalled who she once was,' I say.

'We're assuming then that Amelie and the other missing children were somehow taken to be raised and trained to kill. Like some freaky experiment that the Nazis were reported to have done during World War Two?' Ray says.

'It seems a little far-fetched,' Leon says.

'I know. Very Cold War,' I say. 'But let's not forget what Henry Murray got up to at Harvard University, between 1959 and 1962. Just imagine it is the case. What if Amelie was taken and trained? Brainwashed, even. Like a sleeper agent. She's working fine, robotically obeying orders, and then something happens and cracks appear in the conditioning.'

'I've never known you to go off into these realms before,' Ray says. 'But I'm not going to shoot you down for it. We all have to think outside the box sometimes. Maybe you're onto something.'

'He could be,' Beth agrees. 'Some of the most formative years in a child's life are between the ages of four and seven. They are susceptible to their nurturing environment the most during this time.'

'Exactly,' I say. 'And it isn't impossible to imagine that someone out there has been developing techniques to create mindless soldiers to do their dirty work. Hell, I wouldn't put it past our own government to be working on this shit.'

The team laugh, but it isn't with humour; deep down they are open to this possibility.

'You think she's "mindless"?' Ray asks.

'That's the point really, Ray. I've been working on the

profile of this killer for some time. If it is Anna, and she was once Amelie Arquette, then she's probably been raised not to question anything. Even so, a high-functioning sociopath of this sort also has to operate within normal parameters when she's not on an assignment or when she's not activated if she's a sleeper. Throughout those times, and during a kill, she has to be capable of adapting to any circumstance. You can't completely turn a human into an automaton. Certainly not a highly skilled assassin. Or what you have is a creature that can only do as he or she is asked and cannot think for themselves. They'd be destined to fail in the end. Being a professional killer requires a great deal of planning and imagination,' I explain. 'We aren't looking at our usual serial murderer here. They aren't motivated to kill by emotion, insanity, or through some kind of obsession.'

Ray rubs his chin; there is three-day-old bristle growing there.

'If what you say is true then this thing is bigger than we thought. This girl is maybe one of many trained operatives and someone has to be in charge of a scheme this well organised. Think of the planning that has to go into it. Thirty-five years ago, seven children were taken and this thing began. Fifteen years later, presumably when the first seven were put to work, another seven are taken and groomed.'

'Which means that a further seven could have been taken five years ago and might still be undergoing their conditioning,' Leon says. 'And who's to say there aren't more children than these that Beth has linked.'

'I wonder what the significance of seven is,' Beth says.

I can't come up with an answer and, despite everything I've proposed, I still struggle to believe it myself. I'm amazed that my colleagues are even considering this is possible. But instinct tells me we are on the right track. We just need a lucky break now to find Anna and learn the truth.

Chapter Twenty-Four

NEVA

'So what do you do for a living?' Daz asks.

'I'm a regional manager for a hotel chain,' Neva says. 'I'm working here for the next six months, hence why I need something convenient for the city centre.'

'Oh, right. Well, my girlfriend is out at the moment so I can't really make a decision—'

'I'm willing to pay the entire rent up front,' Neva says. 'In cash.'

'Really? Well, just let me call her.'

Daz leaves Neva in the sitting room. It's a small semi-detached house in an area called Whitefield. He's shown her the tiny single bedroom with its minuscule wardrobe. There's a lock on the door and Neva has no doubt that Daz and his girlfriend will not snoop. He's desperate to please, but also nervous as he tells her they've never rented a room before. This is the perfect situation. One fleeting advert in a town newspaper, unlikely to come on the Network's radar.

'Nina?' Daz says returning to the room. 'Marie says yes. So when do you want to move in?'

'This afternoon?' she says. 'I don't have much at the hotel and I can go and get it and come back.'

'Oh. Right. *That* quick? Okay.'

She hands him the deposit, promising the remaining cash on her return.

A few hours later, she's settled into the small bedroom.

Downstairs in the kitchen, Daz shows her the shelf in the fridge where she can keep chilled food, and the cupboard where she can keep other items like tea and coffee.

'Thank you,' Neva says. 'Here's the rest of the rent.'

She hands him an envelope with four thousand pounds inside. Daz's eyes bulge as though he's never seen that much cash in one go before.

'I'll go and do a food shop now,' she says.

Daz nods.

She goes upstairs to fetch her purse and as she returns, she hears Daz on the phone to his girlfriend, Marie.

'The end of our money worries, babe,' he says. 'I told you it was a good idea to rent that spare room.'

Taking the set of keys he gave her, Neva slips out and walks down the street.

Earlier she passed a car dealership and she has to be mobile. She wanders around the lot and finds an inconspicuous car. A Toyota Yaris. Small, not that new, not that old. It's selling for five thousand. A man comes from the small office on the lot and smiles at her. He has a ridiculous comb-over and his hair smacks of a bad dye job.

'Need some help?' he asks.

'How much for cash? I can take this as seen today,' she says.

The dealer's grin widens.

'Pop the hood and let me look inside,' she says.

She checks over the engine after the dealer starts it for her.

'It's just had an MOT,' he says.

Neva sees nothing wrong. She's been taught a lot about engines. You never know when you might need to fix a getaway car. This one seems sound. They agree a cash price and then she produces a new ID and gives the address she's renting for the log book. Within an hour she's driving the car off the lot and back to her new home.

'Never put yourself in a position where others can observe you,' Tracey had once said.

Everything she's doing now is different from the training. It's why she's chosen this place, this house, and the two young people who are struggling to pay the mortgage. They'll observe her, but they won't *see* her. It's also not the kind of situation any operative would choose to be in. Living in someone else's home is too personal. She knows, therefore, that she's safe for now. They'll be looking in hotels, private flats, just like the one she rented as Ingrid. But she won't be in any of those places; she won't use an estate agent through which they can track her. She doesn't underestimate the power of their reach; it is infinite. True anonymity comes with sharing Daz and Marie's home.

When she returns with groceries, Marie is there. She

goes over ground rules with Neva, showing her the fridge and cupboard again.

'You're welcome to watch TV with us at night, but you might prefer your own in your room,' Marie says.

'I have a laptop. I tend to stream everything. Anyway, I'll probably be out a lot.'

Marie nods.

Neva stows her meagre clothing in the wardrobe. There's a small chest of drawers with a mirror on top so that it doubles as a dressing table. She pulls out the chest. Behind it, she tapes her Glock and bullets. Then she pushes it back against the wall. Neva places beauty products on top of it in a certain way. If either of her landlords get curious, she'll know that things have been moved. She hides another weapon under the bed, strapping it to the frame.

That night she gives Marie and Daz a bottle of red wine as a thank you for taking her in. She doesn't drink it with them, but chats to them as they down the bottle. Then she excuses herself and goes to her room.

Locking the door, she removes the brunette wig.

That night she sleeps soundly for the first time in days.

The next day she wakes early. She dresses in a smart skirt, blouse, and jacket. Then she pretends to leave for work. Soon afterwards, Marie and Daz leave the house. Marie works at the council offices in a small local town. Daz works in the city centre at a big retail store. He's working his way up into a managerial position but has yet to pass a few tests before he qualifies for the role. He hopes his pay will increase enough so he and Marie will be more secure.

Neva learnt all this in just one short conversation with him the evening before. It's surprising what people will tell you when you give them wine.

She returns to the house after they've gone and begins to plan the next few months in her new identity.

Chapter Twenty-Five

MICHAEL

I lift the white sheet back from the face of the corpse. It is a man in his early forties. Bearded. Flecks of red have coagulated in the facial hair where blood has seeped from his dying lips. I pull the sheet further back and examine the body. The man is naked, slightly overweight. There are several puncture wounds on his torso, and defensive wounds on the arms and hands of the body. He was attacked and it was sudden and brutal.

'His name is Alexander Olczak,' Beth explains. 'Russian national, visiting as a tourist. We're checking into him more but all indications are that he was no one of any importance.'

Olczak was found dead in his hotel by the maid service.

Olczak's death comes into the category of 'unusual' and that's why we've been called in. We've been on high alert now for the last three months since Tracey Herod's death, about which we have failed to learn more, and most disappointing of all is the lack of any further sighting of Anna.

'He arrived in the country on Wednesday. Checked into the hotel. Had dinner in the restaurant Thursday evening and no one saw him after that,' Beth explains.

'Any camera footage for the restaurant or reception?' I ask.

'Yes, security provided the recordings for the reception, bar, restaurant, and his floor. We'll wade through, see if he interacted with anyone. It looks like a deliberate, premeditated attack. This could be a lead,' Beth explains.

'We'll need your full profile on this one as soon as possible,' Ray says.

'No problem.' I take photos of the wounds and examine the body inch by inch.

Beth and Ray leave me to do my work and I'm already analysing the style of this perpetrator.

This one is possibly new to the job, one who might have panicked when the man fought back. It's not the experienced hit of the female assassin we've been looking for. This is a violent attack that shows a massive lack of control.

Once I've finished my examination, I return to Archive and look at the photographs Leon took of the room. There's also a report from our forensics experts; the blood splatter confirms the struggle that the injuries on Olczak suggest. As I read, I discover that they also have another blood group. I'd already guessed that this assassin was hurt during the fight. Olczak was a large man, fairly strong, even if he was overweight, and his death had not been easy.

Beth hangs up the phone as I come into her office.

'Glad you're here,' she says. 'I've been looking through the footage from the hotel.'

Beth opens up the video on her desk and shows me. We see Olczak arrive at the hotel. He checks in, then takes his luggage to the lift. No one gets in with him and he doesn't speak to anyone other than the receptionist.

Beth skips through recordings of the next few hours, pointing out Olczak when he comes down after stowing his luggage. He buys a vodka in the bar. He has one drink and then retires for the evening back to his room. The next day he leaves the hotel in the morning and doesn't return until the evening. As we were told, he ate in the hotel restaurant – a rare steak and a bottle of wine (confirmed by the autopsy) – and then he goes to his room. He doesn't act like a tourist; he appears to be waiting for something, or someone.

'Next I looked at the footage outside his room. The man died in his hotel room between the hours of midnight and 6am and so I reasoned someone must have been filmed going into his room,' she explains. 'But look.'

She fast-forwards to the evening of Thursday 25th February and we see Olczak exit the lift on his way to his room. Then the footage turns to snow.

'Mysteriously, the one bit of film that could help us in this case has been, I suspect, erased,' she says.

'Can we get a court order to seize the original hard drive? Nothing is erased permanently; it can probably be salvaged,' I say.

'That's Ray's call but I'll speak to him. Mike? You know this is weird, right?'

'It does seem like too much of a coincidence,' I agree.

'I mean, this goes deeper than a security guard being paid to destroy footage. The guard expected it to be okay. She copied it all for me while I was in her office. I didn't get any vibe that she was hiding anything.'

'Was this guard on that night?' I ask.

'I checked schedules and yes, she was working that night shift. She couldn't have been more helpful. I don't think she was hiding anything from me.'

'And yet the files are corrupted?' I say.

Beth lets out a slow breath. 'Not corrupted. Wiped.'

'Then maybe we need to interview who was on the shift after this guard,' I say.

Beth nods. 'I'll get on it.'

'Have you read the autopsy report yet?' I ask.

'No, I was waiting for your analysis of it and the wounds.'

'The assassin was hurt. They have his or her blood,' I say.

'That's a bit of a breakthrough. But only if we already have them on record somehow,' Beth says.

'I was thinking we should try and DNA match with the parents of the missing children.'

Beth blinks. 'Wow! Why didn't I think of that?'

'It could prove your theory that these are connected,' I say.

'If we prove one of these kids is still alive—'

'Then it might prove they *all* are,' I finish her sentence to confirm that we are both on the same page.

'Let's see what comes up on this original hard drive, then I'm on it,' Beth says.

A short time later, with the court order in hand, Beth and I arrive at the hotel and head straight to the reception; after a brief talk with the manager, we are escorted to the security office.

'Eric Smith is on today. He's the regular team leader,' the manager explains. 'He's been off for a few days so you'll have to brief him on what you need.'

We walk into the office and find Smith sitting in front of the camera monitors. There are six in all, covering the whole of the hotel and the car park as they flick from screen to screen. Smith is in his late fifties and has a short beard. His hair is long and pulled back in a ponytail. He turns to look at us briefly then returns his gaze to the screens.

'How can I help you?' he asks, not looking at us.

'We have a warrant for the security hard drives used to record a few nights ago,' I say.

'Yeah. Heard about the murder. Wouldn't have happened on my team's watch,' Smith says.

'Your team?' asks Beth.

'Yes, we were on our rest days.'

'Rest days?' says Beth.

'We work seven days on and four off. This can be a very tiring job. To get the best out of my people, we *rest* them. A new crew comes in each time to cover us. They're like temps – no fixed assignment,' Smith explains.

'So, you're saying this team that was on the other night weren't regular staff?' I say.

'Well, I guess we all work for the same company. But some teams are floaters; they move from place to place. Wherever they're needed.'

'I want access to the hard drive,' I say again, holding out the warrant.

'Let him have what he wants,' the manager says.

Eric Smith reads the document and then shakes his head.

'I can't really help you. I have a log here saying the drive was copied for you. But it's gone now so I can't give you the original.'

'What do you mean it's "gone"?' Beth asks.

'Well, the day after you came the system was replaced. New computers, monitors, and cameras all over the hotel. It's been planned for months. The old system was ripped out and taken away by the company that installed this one.'

'Taken where?' Michael says.

'It's all incinerated,' Eric says. 'It has to be to comply with data-protection laws.'

'Oh!' says the manager, 'Of course. I'd completely forgotten about that. Don't we keep any back-ups of what was on the drives?'

'We should have,' says Smith. 'But I'm sorry, I just booted up this new system and it's clean. There's no back-up footage at all. I think maybe one of the temp staff cocked up. I'm sorry.'

'We may be able to salvage the hard drive if we get in

touch with the company quickly,' says Beth, as we cross the street to where Beth's car is parked.

'It's already destroyed. Olczak's death was planned months ago,' I say.

'You can't know that,' says Beth.

'I don't know it, Beth, but I *feel* it. All these crazy coincidences and accidents. It's contrived. And that takes some major planning.'

'We still have some options. The security company must have records of who was working and who had access to the footage at the hotel. We bring them in and question them. Maybe we'll get lucky and they'll crack.'

I nod, but I'm expecting this to be a dead end as always.

'Why was Olczak killed?' Beth asks. 'Who was he?'

'Why were any of these people killed? Other than Aidan Bright, they'd all been off our radar. I'll speak to MI6 and see if they're in a sharing mood. More than likely Olczak was a spy,' I say. 'At least that might give us a clue as to who would want him dead.'

'It'll be a relief if we actually get an answer to one of our questions. We just keep on coming up with dead ends. I can't help thinking this case is linked to others we've been dealing with, but I have no idea why.'

'My gut tells me the same,' I say. 'Maybe the DNA of the killer will tell us what we need to know.'

'I hope so. But ... the *planning* that goes into these deaths. Who has those kinds of resources?' she says.

'I don't know, Beth, but I really want to find out,' I say.

They reach the car and I climb into the passenger seat as Beth gets behind the wheel.

'We've had no other leads on our mystery female, have we?' Beth asks.

'You know we haven't,' I say.

I feel Beth's eyes on me but don't look at her. I imagine the inquiring expression I've seen many times on her face. Despite all my efforts, I haven't found Anna. She's simply disappeared.

'You'd tell me if she made contact?' Beth says.

'*What*? Of course! Why wouldn't I?' I say.

Beth turns the engine on and pulls the car away from the kerb into the slow-moving London traffic. I use the switch of her attention to glance at her; she has a small frown on her face as she concentrates. I can't help feeling guilty, even though I haven't lied about any further contact with Anna. She hasn't been back to my flat, I'm sure of that. The day after I discovered she'd been there, I installed camera surveillance all over my home. I wish she *would* contact me, even though I don't know what I'd do if she does.

A few months earlier, my only lead, the brandy glass with her prints and DNA, drew a blank. As I suspected, the glass had been washed. It confirmed that Anna had returned, found the glass, and judiciously removed all trace of herself from it. Maybe that was why she'd broken into my flat in the first place.

The lack of evidence is disappointing but it removed the necessity for me to admit my indiscretion to the team. Even so, I regret what I've done. Finding Anna is all I can think about. So much so that I've pulled the files of her probable parents, the Arquettes, and I now have their DNA to compare with Anna if and when we ever find her. If she is

Amelie, I can only imagine what she's been through to turn her into what she is now. We should give someone in that situation a break, shouldn't we?

'How's the investigation going with the stolen kids, otherwise?' I ask.

'The only thing I've discovered so far is that the Arquettes met some of the other parents.'

'Really? When?'

'I have a meeting with Simone Arquette this afternoon if you want to tag along. Maybe she can tell us something we don't know,' Beth says. 'But let's not give anything we suspect away. I mean, your suggestion is the best lead I've had in months. I'd like to follow that before we make any real assumptions.'

'Sure. Makes sense.'

This is the first time I've heard about Beth's visit, and I wonder how long she has been planning to speak to Simone.

'You hadn't mentioned you were going to speak to the parents,' I say.

'I know this is a bit of a leap,' Beth says. 'But. Well. Without any leads, I'd been thinking about your mystery woman. This Anna. About her possibly remembering who she is. It occurred to me she might try to contact her parents.'

I don't say anything, thinking it unlikely. If Anna is the missing child then her life will be so far removed from her past that she'd never look back. But the idea of the parents meeting together does intrigue me. I don't know why. They probably just did it as a support-group thing – common grief shared – so I'm a little surprised that Beth has read into it. Even so, Beth's instincts are usually grounded. For that reason, I feel an urge to see Simone Arquette.

'Yes, I'll come with you. Give you my take on her,' I say.

'Good. I'd appreciate that!'

Chapter Twenty-Six

MICHAEL

The house is situated near Kingston about ten miles south of London. Commutable but out of the centre. It's a huge house, maybe six or seven bedrooms, with at least four large reception rooms and a downstairs office. We're led into the office by a formal butler. It seems that Simone and Anton Arquette are living the country-squire dream, enjoying all that their diplomatic position can afford.

Simone Arquette is tall and willowy. A former ballerina, she moves gracefully as she crosses her long legs. She sits on a sofa opposite us. Her grace does remind me of Anna but that could still be a coincidence. Behind her is the ambassador's desk, clear of any paperwork, though I notice a fountain pen is lying on the desk as though it has just been used.

I let Beth do the formal introductions while I find myself looking for Anna in Simone's features. Her eyes are slightly more upturned and they are green not blue. But then, I realise, Anna could have been wearing coloured lenses when I saw her.

'You're investigating Amelie's disappearance?' Simone says. 'You have a new lead?'

I give her the formal description for the taskforce but don't reveal more about our work than necessary. Simone's cat-like eyes study me.

'We look at old crimes with new eyes. We've had some success in solving them,' Beth adds. 'I'm hoping that some new things that have come to our attention may help in this case.'

'What new things?' Simone asks.

'A connection perhaps with some other missing children's cases,' Beth says. We've agreed to discuss only this with Simone, not any other possible links.

'You are a little late learning that. My private detective discovered the link in the case with other missing children. But still Amelie was not found,' Simone says.

'We know. And that's why we're here. We'd like to have access to everything your detective discovered and to know about your meeting with the other parents,' I say.

'I'll have my secretary send you everything, of course. But you should know I found out about the other missing children very quickly. I reported what I knew to the police, but they didn't take it seriously at the time.'

'I'm sorry to hear that,' Beth says. 'Can you tell us what you know?'

'It will be in your file, I'm sure,' Simone says.

'We'd just like you to tell us from your perspective what happened,' I say. 'I'm sorry if this is painful for you.'

Simone looks at me again as though assessing how serious I am about the case. Then she seems to make a decision; a slight nod of her head gives her thoughts away. She sees no harm in telling us what she knows.

'Amelie went missing from her school. She asked to go to the bathroom and never came back to class. There was no sign of her, or of a struggle, and no witnesses. When I learnt that more children had vanished, I tried to discover the connection. I learnt that all disappeared in similar circumstances. Yet each child was from a different part of the country.'

'So, you met the other parents?' Beth prompts.

'Yes. It didn't help much. The only thing we had in common was our clever children.'

Simone barely has an accent. Despite being born in Paris, her English is almost flawless. She is composed, overly so for a woman whose child had been stolen and never found. Maybe twenty years was enough for you to get over such a terrible tragedy. Not being a parent, I didn't know.

'Did you notice anything strange about any of the other parents?' I ask.

'*Strange?* No. All I saw were grieving families.'

'One last thing,' Beth says. 'Are you still in touch with any of the other couples?'

Simone blinks, and just for a second I see a rupture beneath her calm veneer. I stow it away in the back of my mind to analyse later.

'Occasionally one of them contacts me. They still have *hope…*'

'And what about you?' I ask. 'Do you have hope?'

'I don't think I will ever see Amelie again,' Simone says. 'I came to terms with that a long time ago.'

'That poor woman,' says Beth as we walk back towards the car.

'Poor isn't how I'd describe her. Cold is a better label,' I say. 'Don't you think she was … odd?'

'She lost her kid, Mike. Now she's just trying to hold her shit together.'

'She didn't react how any *normal* person would. We've reopened the case. You'd think she would ask more questions. I expected us to be managing her expectations but instead she managed ours.'

'I see what you mean. She was very definite that she wouldn't see her child again. With no corpse to confirm Amelie is dead, you'd think she would still hope for a miracle. I would. If it was one of my kids. At least she answered the question we really wanted to ask, without us having to open that can of worms,' Beth says. 'Amelie hasn't been in touch. So maybe she isn't this woman after all.'

'Or maybe she doesn't yet remember who she was,' I say.

But Simone's guarded expression concerns me. At one point I almost thought she was going to smile when she said she knew she wouldn't see her daughter again.

I have no understanding of what it's like to be a parent

and I don't ask Beth how it feels, not wanting to open our relationship up to our personal lives. It's something we try to avoid talking about amongst ourselves at Archive.

Beth's phone pings and she takes it out of her pocket. 'The PI file has already arrived. She's efficient – or her secretary is, at least.'

'Forward that to me, will you?'

I open the private investigator's folder as soon as I'm back at my desk but it's not very helpful. It appears that Simone had spent a lot of money for nothing more than we already knew.

I think about Anna again. I still believe she could be Amelie, which means that Simone might see her daughter again one day. But what good will it do to reveal that Amelie may have become a trained killer? Would any parent want to learn that?

I close the folder and stare at the blank screen as I recall the strange meeting with Simone. Was her coldness merely a defence mechanism? Did she cry as we walked back to the car parked in her driveway? Somehow, I can visualise her laughter more than her tears.

I try to picture Anna again. But my memory of her is warping with time. Instead I see Simone's cold green, cat-like eyes looking back at me as I hold out the brandy glass.

'Where are you, Anna?' I murmur, before I realise I've spoken aloud.

Chapter Twenty-Seven

NEVA

Neva watches Michael as he leaves the office that evening. She's been back in London for the past week. Tonight, unlike other nights, Michael does not go straight home. Instead, he heads into the tube. She watches him at a safe distance as he leaves Borough and makes his way to Covent Garden.

At a Japanese restaurant, he eats sushi alone and drinks Tsingtao beer direct from the bottle. By 8pm he's heading back to his lonely flat.

Neva doesn't know why she follows him, except that she has an urge to fill the void inside her. That emptiness is eased when she looks at Michael. When she studies his isolation. There is no partner – male or female – and no suggestion that he's looking. He doesn't appear unhappy as he wears his solitude like another layer of skin: familiar and comfortable. He is, in many ways, just like her.

Throughout her months in hiding she has been searching the dark Web for answers. But today she learns more about Michael and what he's investigating. It's not difficult to discover whose home he and his colleague visited. The French Ambassador is not a low-profile figure. And neither is his wife. At some point, Neva had a file on them as potential targets but at the last minute it was pulled.

To prevent discovery, she moves hotels every day. At this night's choice, Neva looks for answers and finds them on her laptop: Simone and Anton had a daughter.

A little girl who was abducted.

She looks at the pictures of Amelie and those of six others presumed to be taken by the same perpetrator.

With a thudding heart, she recognises the young faces.

'My name is Peter. What do they call you?'

She remembers Peter because he was so formal. The oldest of the group, he thought it was his place to take care of them all at first. Neva had looked up to him.

'You're not Peter,' Tracey Herod had told him. 'You're Kurt now.'

They were all given new names, but when they were alone, they recited their real ones to themselves in a form of meditation. They never wanted to forget who they were. It was somehow important. But after the treatments, their minor rebellion was quashed. Their former names no longer mattered, ceased to be repeated, and they became who and what the trainer and doctor wanted them to be.

Neva still does not know her real name, though she looks through the four familiar girls' faces. One of whom she thinks must be herself. They are all strangers and yet all too familiar. She sees a name now, listed as 'missing', and it feels like a world away. Like the moment when they told her she was Neva. She tries the other names on her lips but it feels as though they belong to someone else – another child in another dimension. Never hers. It's an abstract dream that sometimes she remembers while she's awake.

She closes her eyes and forces the memories to surface. It's painful and her head aches with the effort, even as she forces down a swirl of nausea. There they are: Katie, John, Melanie, Toby, Amelie, Peter (who became Kurt), Jennifer. Why didn't she pay more attention to the others? Why did she just let those minor friendships slip away? She thinks it's to do with the room. The mantras. The instructions forced on them day and night. Especially when they were so exhausted they could barely walk. After those times, Neva recalls rest periods. Days when they ate and slept and were sometimes allowed to watch television. But the films they watched were nightmares in themselves. Brutal, blood-filled visions of death were put before them until they were so desensitised that it neither scared nor disgusted them.

'I'd like to stab that knife into someone's ribs,' Kurt/Peter had said as they watched the footage of a vicious murder. He mimed the action, enjoying the killing as he watched it unfold.

Katie and John stared at the screen with dead, unemotional eyes. Melanie (what did they call her in the end?) watched Kurt, a slight smile on her lips. 'You'll do it soon enough,' she said. 'We all will.'

By then the training had been underway for the best part of ten years. Neva was the expert with a knife, something that rankled with Kurt. He was seventeen then, Neva almost fifteen. But she was taller than the other three girls, not much shorter than Kurt and just as strong because she never let emotions fuel her actions.

Now Neva remembers their final spar. She was placed with Kurt, knife in hand. Within minutes, Neva had broken Kurt's hold on his knife, expertly knocking it from his clenched fingers. She stepped back as she was supposed to, to allow Kurt to accept defeat, but anger got the better of him. He leapt towards her, grabbing Neva's knife.

'I'll kill you!' he said.

They fought. Neva held onto her blade, but only just. Tracey, Callan, and one of the other instructors pulled Kurt away. He was hauled out of the training area and taken down the corridor.

'He's history,' Katie had said.

'No, they'll just give him treatment. He's too emotional,' John told them.

Tracey came back into the training area then and the sparring resumed. Afterwards, Neva was taken into Tracey's office.

'You have your first assignment,' she said.

Neva felt a surge of excitement kindled by fear but she kept her face still.

'Good,' she said. 'What do you want me to do?'

'You're going to retire Kurt.'

Neva nodded but the thought of killing her sparring partner for real made her feel odd. Going too far, hurting each other seriously, had been against the rules; she knew that. But did Kurt deserve to die because of it? She had always been taught control and restraint and had won all of her spars because of her ability to do this. Kurt struggled to keep his emotions in check, even though the conditioning should make him capable of it. Neva vaguely wondered what it would feel like to end a life. Wasn't this ultimately what they were training her for?

'How do you wish to do it?' asked Tracey.

'Knife,' said Neva. 'I will cut his throat.'

Later she was taken to Kurt. He was strapped into the chair, having spent time with the doctor. He was quiet, drugged, and in the state they all were after intensive treatment.

Tracey gave her a knife. 'Kill him,' she said.

'No fight?' Neva asked.

'You don't have to win a fight to score a victory for the Network,' Tracey said. 'When you finish an enemy, or in this case a disappointment, you do it for the best reasons.'

Neva stepped forward. She had listened to Tracey's view on Kurt all afternoon. Reading between the lines, she knew she had to do it. It was Kurt or herself. Any failure now would make her a liability too. She *couldn't* be the one to die. They had almost retired her once before. Tracey, at that time, had saved her but Neva understood this was a one-time-only deal. She never lapsed again, and never would.

Neva looked at Kurt's drugged face. She thought he was unlikely to feel anything in this state. This was easy – a no-brainer. Even so, she hesitated. She was going to take a life, something they had trained her for all these years. Shouldn't she feel something about that?

Kurt's death meant she would be established.

She raised the knife and ran the razor-sharp edge across

his throat. The knife bit into his skin as though it was no more resistant than warm butter. She watched the blood bubble out of the wound and drip onto the wooden floor.

She felt *nothing*.

In a way, she had always known she would kill Kurt. It was a rite of passage, a thing she must do to graduate from this level to the next. Kurt himself should have moved on by now, but Tracey had held him back, saying he wasn't ready. Now he never would be. Maybe Tracey had only kept him around so that Neva could execute him.

Neva had glanced at Tracey but she kept her face passive. She was good at showing no curiosity. *Curiosity kills*, after all.

'Make sure he's dead before you leave him,' Tracey had said.

'I will.'

Neva waited until the blood stopped flowing, and then she pressed her fingers to Kurt's pulse as she had been trained to do. He was gone.

'Yes. It's done.'

'Good. Now, how do you feel?' Tracey asked.

'Feel?'

'Do you feel pleased he's dead?'

'No.'

'Do you feel sad?'

'No.'

'What do you feel?'

'Satisfaction. I did the job you asked. I'm proud of that.'

Tracey studied Neva's blank expression for a while and

then she sent her away, back to the dormitory and the bathroom to wash the blood from her hands.

Cleanliness was equally important. Removing evidence. Washing away any guilt.

As the water ran over Neva's hands, they had trembled slightly. It was the only response she allowed herself to mark the significance of Kurt's death.

Chapter Twenty-Eight

NEVA

I n the dreary hotel room, Neva's hand trembles again as she closes her laptop, removing the pictures of the other children from her sight. So many memories crowd into her mind and it hurts. Kurt is gone, and she hasn't thought about him for a long time. As though his death erased him from existence. She knows this is probably the conditioning. Maybe forgetting him helped her accept what she'd done. But seeing the others has damaged her equilibrium. She's recalling fragments of the house, those days spent learning her craft and all the torturous moments she endured as they took her personality and thoughts away. She's shaking as it all floods back. Her body is cold, as though she's going into shock. Just as she had been after Tracey...

Yes. She is broken. And there is no going back, only forward.

When she remembers all the deaths she has delivered – cold, decisive killings that meant nothing to her – she thinks about those people who created her. She also considers Kurt and Ansell. They were like her. They had been taken, groomed and changed, turned into killing machines. Ansell had been a success, graduating on to be an efficient operative, but Kurt hadn't survived the house. But in the end, they had both died by Neva's hand on the orders of the Network that had made them what they were. Loyalty went only one way, and that came from the threat her handlers had wielded.

Tracey's death has satisfied Neva for a while, but now she wants more blood. Not hits that her supervisors desire. Her *choice* of kills. She wants to discover who the people behind the Network are. The ones who made her kill. She wants to destroy them.

The urge to maim and kill intensifies with a passion that Neva has never experienced before. She prowls around the hotel room thinking, remembering. She has to know the details that they tried to hide from her. But it's like a jigsaw puzzle with too many missing pieces.

'One day you'll be a handler, Neva,' Tracey had told her once. 'I'm preparing you, because you're different. You are not like all the others.'

At the time she had been flattered. Tracey had encouraged this feeling at frequent intervals. 'Only you can do this; you're our special girl.'

Hadn't Tracey used those words often? Now she wonders who else Tracey said this to. It was likely that all handlers used such persuasive terms. It was a way to control them.

She glances at her laptop. John and the other girls –

women now – perhaps she could find them? They could fight against the Network … together.

She shakes away this thought, realising how ridiculous it is.

They weren't superheroes fighting for justice. They were killers, trained to take orders only from their masters. Of course, *they* might come looking for her. But it wouldn't be to compare notes on their warped childhoods; it would be to kill her for her betrayal.

For the first time since she was five years old, Neva feels alone. Tracey was a touchstone, even though her judgement was something to fear. Neva has no one to turn to, and until now, that has never been a problem.

Since she met Michael, she has been different. He was another link in the slow awareness that has been growing inside her since she killed Ansell. She remembers the concern in Michael's eyes, the day he helped her. Without realising it, he pulled her back from the dark void she almost fell into. Neva doesn't know where that blackness would have led her, but she knows she would not have easily escaped without Michael. He'd taken her away from Tracey's death. A pivotal moment of freedom, that had also left her bereft, confused, and terrified – all emotions she was unused to. He'd helped her regain a modicum of control, and it was enough to stabilise the growing anger. Michael's impromptu rescue had given her the breathing space she'd needed to start to *think*.

Since then, that's all she's done. When she's not thinking about revenge, she's focusing on Michael. She knows he can be part of her retaliation, but she's yet to figure out how.

The rage begins, cold and dark, a fury like she has never experienced. She hates the Network. She despises Tracey. She wishes she could kill her again!

'The only way to ease the pain is execute them all,' she murmurs.

But how? They kept her in the dark all along.

She knows nothing of where she's from. Nothing of the location of the house – the starting place. Nothing of how she got there.

Her fists clench and she grinds her teeth in frustration. She needs more than her own meagre resources to find them. She needs help. But who can she trust? Anyone could be part of the Network.

She sees Michael as he was that day. Kind. Caring. Gentle. The unfaltering way he took her out of that bad situation, never realising who she was.

But how can she go to him? He is MI5 and part of a taskforce whose nature is secret, all of which tells her that he can't be trusted. For all she knows, he too could be in the Network's employment. But no. She's followed him enough to know he isn't.

She forces her hands to unclench when the tension begins to make her fingers ache. She runs her palms over her knees as she sinks back down onto the edge of the uncomfortable hotel bed.

She turns off her unquiet mind with practised ease. *Anxiety causes weakness.*

Sleep, little one.

Neva removes her clothes and a soft, hypnotic mantra rolls over her as the pressure inside her grows quiet. Sleep cures all, wasn't that what her mother had once said? For a moment she tries to chase this memory, but it only results in pain.

She slips under the covers. The sheets are cool and the bed is more comfortable than she thought it would be. Her limbs relax as the warmth which accompanies sleep washes over her. Sleep will bring an answer; revenge can wait until the morning.

Chapter Twenty-Nine

MICHAEL

I take a beer from the fridge and switch on the television. I'm still unnerved by the meeting with Simone Arquette. I don't know why. But the more I think about it, the stranger it was. I replay the interview, reliving her responses, and facial expressions; the lack of emotion she displayed jars as much now as it did at the time. But my memory of it seems to accentuate the feeling.

I run over the moment when she admitted to still having contact with the other parents. That slight break in her façade is still unfathomable and was the only chink in her otherwise cold armour. I'll have to consider it when I have more information. Then it will make sense.

I swig the beer from the bottle – this is becoming a nightly habit – and then I swipe the back of my hand across my eyes, rubbing a knuckle in the corner to push away the sleep. I'm tired but wound up. Sometimes switching off is difficult for me and the job is one of constant frustrations, often leading to disappointment. The last few years have been unsatisfactory. *How many cases have we actually solved recently?* I'm beginning to wonder what the point is.

'Archive is not just about solving, but about cataloguing information that may help us in the future,' Ray had explained to me in the early days. 'We haven't failed as long as we are doing that.'

I wish I could have Ray's easy attitude to the job. Does Ray ever lie awake worrying that we aren't achieving anything? I doubt it.

I finish the beer and take myself off to bed, but not before I check my security.

A few hours later I jerk awake. I find myself slumped on the sofa, an all too familiar occurrence lately. The bottle of beer is half-full on the table and the room is cold as the heating has automatically turned off. I realise that I dreamed locking up and going to bed.

I go to the bathroom, pee, then go into the bedroom.

I set the alarm on my phone and then slip into the bed, aware that I'm repeating my dream. But I'm so tired that the thought is only fleeting. I'm asleep again within seconds.

Chapter Thirty

MICHAEL

'How's things?' my brother-in-law, Ben, asks as the bartender places two pints of beer in front of us. 'You look tired.'

Ben is always direct.

'I'm fine. Working too hard as usual. How are you?'

Ben smiles. 'Mia keeps me busy. She wants to move house.'

'Why? Thought you guys were happy in the country.'

'We are, but the owners of the farm next door are dicks. The woman has a meltdown if the leaves from our trees fall onto their side of the fence.'

'Jesus.'

'I know.'

'There's always a fly in the ointment somewhere.'

It's nice to see Ben on one of his rare visits to London. I find myself smiling.

'How's Mia otherwise?'

'Okay… We're trying for a baby,' Ben says.

'That's great news! But … I thought you two weren't the parenting kind.'

'Yeah. So did we. Then we both started to … *want* this, you know?'

I don't know. But I'm happy for Ben and Mia. My twin sister was always such a tomboy. Then she met Ben and everything changed. She became a woman overnight. They've been together since university and they're happy, as far as I can tell. Even our parents like Ben and that is no mean feat.

'So, is it serious? With the neighbours? I mean, what's a few leaves?' I ask.

'It's worse than that. We probably will move. Mia can't stand their dogs barking and the whiney kids that scream all the time like they're being murdered. I swear if they really were being killed, we'd ignore the screams because it's just another Tuesday.'

'Sounds awful,' I say. 'Can't you have a word with them about it?'

'We tried. The woman had a meltdown again and accused us of "spying" on them. Next, her husband comes round, all heavy-handed. I wasn't there and Mia had to deal with it. Upshot is, he says we're harassing them. But he admits his wife's neurotic. They aren't right in the head, either of them. Guess that's what happens when you start to believe that the piece of England you own is the only important stretch of land in the country. And it's a laughable few acres.'

Ben laughs but it lacks humour and seems punctuated

by genuine frustration. I pat him on the shoulder to show I understand.

'Have you spoken to Uncle Andrew lately?' Ben asks, as though to change the subject.

I nod. 'Yes, we have a talk about once a month. Sometimes we meet up, or he calls me. When did you last see him?'

'Last week. He's looking good. He's such a chick magnet. Silver fox. Am I right?'

I laugh. 'Yeah! I love that man!'

Chapter Thirty-One

NEVA

The surveillance equipment focuses Michael and Ben's voices through the crowded bar. Neva is in a booth with her back to them. There's a hairclip pulling back strands of golden-blonde hair from her face; it hides a directional microphone in her hair. She listens. For a moment she toys with the idea of finding the farm and killing the obnoxious neighbours, especially the neurotic whiney wife. It's a way to help, and she's killed for less important reasons. She stows this information away for future research and possible action.

As Michael drinks his beer, Neva observes him through a small mirror that she holds in her hand as she applies lipstick. The more she sees of Michael, the more she wants to approach him. But it has to be the right moment, when she's sure they won't be noticed.

After his third pint, Ben stands up and pushes his way through the crowd towards the bathroom. He sways a little when he walks, not quite in full control, but not too far gone either.

Reacting to this unexpected opportunity, Neva gets up. She walks to the bar and stands beside Michael. She leans close to his ear.

'I have a gun,' she whispers.

Chapter Thirty-Two

MICHAEL

I turn my head and look at the woman beside me. It takes a moment to recognise her. She's so good at disguise, how many more times has she been this close and I haven't noticed? When she says she has a gun, my body instinctively stiffens but I remain calm. This is a busy bar; there are too many witnesses. She's not here to kill me or she would have taken a shot in a better place.

'Are you going to use it?' I ask.

'I want to talk to you. Can I trust you?' she says.

'It depends what you tell me.'

She nods. 'I understand. You are part of a taskforce. Your search sometimes leads you to people and organisations that have great influence. More than they should have. Maybe more authority than the government has because they operate in more criminal conditions. Maybe you people even hope to bring such corporations down.'

I narrow my eyes a fraction before I can stop myself. She shouldn't know this, yet she does. She sees the slight tell and knows she's right. She glances around, then looks back at me.

'I worked for such an organisation. They are more powerful than you could possibly imagine,' she says.

'You mean you don't work for them now?'

She looks over her shoulder again, as though she expects that someone is watching us.

'I got away from them. They will eventually find me. It's inevitable,' she explains. 'And when they do, they won't just slap my wrists and say *don't do this again.*'

'Yet still you left?' I say.

She nods. 'I couldn't go on anymore.'

'What can I do to help you?' I ask.

Our eyes meet in the mirror above the bar.

'Are you willing to?'

It's my turn to nod.

A group of girls on a hen party converges on the bar. She tenses as the loud chatter takes up behind us. Her eyes dart from me and back to the bar. She frowns at the girls.

'Now's not the time. I'll be in touch,' she says.

As she disappears into the throng of bodies, I jump from the barstool. My heart thumps in my chest but it's not fear that causes the adrenaline, rather the excitement that Anna has made contact. This could be a breakthrough. I look round but cannot see her anywhere in the busy bar.

'You okay?' says Ben beside me.

'I have to go. A work thing came up.'

'Oh, right. Nothing to do with that blonde I saw you talking to then?'

I shake my head. 'No. Just work. Sorry. Give my love to Mia.'

'Sure,' Ben says. Then he sits back at the bar and orders another beer.

I weave through the groaning crowd and head towards the main exit, all the time searching the room. But there's no point. She's already gone. I reach into my jacket to take out my phone as I go outside, deciding that I'd better call this in. In my pocket, my hand falls on an unfamiliar shape. I pull it out. Anna has left me a phone of her own.

I look in the contacts list, but it's empty. I hear her words again: *I'll be in touch.* She wants to call all the shots. Well, that's fine with me.

I put the phone back in my pocket. I don't take out my work phone. I don't call it in.

I just don't want to.

Chapter Thirty-Three

MICHAEL

I'm unused to feeling paranoid but because Anna found me so easily, I start to take extra precautions. I toy with the idea of mentioning to Beth and Leon that she's made contact. The problem is, I can't help thinking that somehow Anna will know and she'll never get in touch again. This is how I justify my silence. It's so important to keep what's happening to myself, at least until I win her complete trust. Then, perhaps, she will believe that I can help her stay safe from her former employers.

Even though Anna said she had a gun on me, I hadn't felt threatened. I *know* she is dangerous. Her whole lifestyle revolves around death. Yet I knew she wasn't going to shoot me.

Anna's unexpected approach tells me a lot about her. Perhaps she's been waiting for her moment since we met a few months ago. This shows she's willing to play the long game to get what she wants. But what does she want?

Help. She asked for help and she took a risk in approaching me. She was sure I'd agree.

She could be setting me up, of course. The people she says she no longer works for might well be trying to compromise me. I was warned about these approaches as part of my training. This alone should make me cautious. I should at least tell Ray of her approach. But I have no intention of doing anything that will prevent Anna from contacting me again.

I'll share this with the team when the time is right.

I will. When I have something important to tell them. Before then, anything I say or do may jeopardise the next meeting. The thought of never seeing Anna again leaves a cold chill inside me that I can't explain.

'Use your gut and always follow your instincts,' Andrew would say if ever I discussed anything I was unsure about with him.

I feel the urge to arrange our regular lunch meeting, but I know I'll be unable to ask his advice, any more than I can my colleagues.

It's best, I think, that I leave my uncle out of this.

Chapter Thirty-Four

MICHAEL

It is a week before I hear from Anna again.

The call comes when I'm walking to the tube station after work. I've carried her phone all along, but during my working hours it is on silent. I don't want it to ring when I'm with my colleagues. I'd have to explain having a phone that isn't regulation, as well as the call received on it. But my worries are unfounded; Anna picks her moment with the usual attention to detail.

'Do you know Abney Park Cemetery?' she says.

'No.'

'Stoke Newington. Two hours.'

She hangs up as if she's expecting me to try to trace the call. Yet I'm sure she knows where I am and that it isn't possible.

I go into the tube station and start mapping the route to Stoke Newington. The burner phone vibrates in my pocket just before I pass the barrier. I take the phone out. There's a text from the same number that called me.

New location. The Langham Hotel, Marylebone. One hour.

I take the Jubilee Line to Bond Street. When I leave the station, I hail a cab to the Langham Hotel. I'll be there earlier than she wants me to be, but that's better than being late. And I'd prefer to choose a vantage point before she arrives.

But as the cab approaches the hotel, I receive yet another text.

Royal Opera House. Ticket booth. Give your name.

I redirect the taxi driver to the Opera House. As the car pulls up outside, I check the phone again. There are no further texts, but it's obvious that Anna is not taking chances. She's making sure I'm not being followed, and that I haven't betrayed her. She doesn't trust me, even though she's chosen to talk to me. I have no intention of deceiving her, even though this might be a trap and she may well be planning something for me. Perhaps I've somehow become a target. I subconsciously pat my jacket, feeling the gun in the holster beneath, then I get out of the taxi. I know this could be dangerous, and a serious mistake, but my curiosity is such that I'm willing to put myself at risk. I'm driven to explore this situation no matter where it leads.

There's a group of people standing outside the building wearing dinner suits; one of them is smoking, while other opera goers drift into the lobby. *La Bohème* is playing.

Feeling underdressed, I pay the taxi driver, then turn and walk towards the box-office door.

Inside, I approach the ticket booth.

'I believe there's a ticket for me? Michael Kensington.'

The girl behind the glass smiles at me, then reaches for an envelope that lies beside her keyboard.

'You're in a box. Best position directly over the stage. You'll love it there. Enjoy the show,' she says.

I take the envelope, open it, and find a ticket inside.

'That way,' says the girl.

A helpful usher directs me up the stairs and into the box. I enter with caution, expecting an ambush of some kind, but other than a few seats, as well as an ice bucket with a bottle of Bollinger chilling, the box is empty.

There are two glasses. *Is this some kind of bizarre date with Anna?* The thought makes me feel uncomfortable in a way that's difficult to express.

I choose a seat at the back – a position that grants me a clear view of the door to the booth, as well as the stage.

From this vantage point, I watch the theatre fill as people take their seats. I check the phone again, but there are no further messages. And so I put it on silent, but place it down on the table with the champagne bucket so I can see if the screen lights up.

The lights in the theatre dim. The orchestra starts playing and I look over the balcony, checking out all the other booths around the room. All of them are full, which suggests that Anna had to pull strings to get this one.

I pick up the phone and glance at it again but already I know there won't be any messages.

Then the curtains open on the stage.

Beside me, a figure slips into the booth and takes a seat. A female shape. Bobbed dark hair is all I can make out in the dim light. I hold my breath as she reaches for the champagne and expertly pops the cork. As the opening song begins, she sits down in front of me. I wait for her to turn around to talk to me but she says nothing as she pours the champagne into the two glasses. She doesn't offer me any, but takes one of the glasses herself and sips. I watch her as she appears to be concentrating on the show. I glance at the stage. Is opera so enthralling?

I can't understand the words, and the music, though vaguely familiar, does nothing for me.

After ten minutes, I lean forward and take the other glass of champagne. *If you can't beat them, join them.* I sip. The wine is perfect. Chilled. Delicious. Even so, I place it back down, concerned it might be drugged, or poisoned, as suspicion kicks in again. What is this all about?

Anna – *if* this is her, and I cannot be sure – tops up her own glass and continues to drink. I have no more. My eyes are on her back, not the stage, even as she remains riveted.

When the interval arrives and the lights in the house go up, I think I must have dozed off.

Then the woman turns: it is Anna. She looks … beautiful. The dark wig suits her, bringing out the blue of her eyes, and I'm taken by how chameleonic she is.

'My name is Neva,' she says. 'That's what they called me. Not Anna. Or any other name I've used in the process of working for them. This name has become who I am.'

'Who are *they*?' I ask.

'I know them only as "the Network". We were never told about our masters. I only ever saw a few faces, mostly handlers.'

'Tell me what you do know,' I say.

'I've been remembering things. I believe I was five when I was taken. From that day, I was conditioned. Trained. Made into who I am now.'

'Who was your handler?' I ask.

'I think you already know that.'

'No. I don't.'

'She went by the name Tracey Herod. She was one of the people who *trained* us,' Neva says.

I nod. It all makes sense.

Then Neva tells me what Beth and I already suspected. How she and six others were taken to a house and then their whole lives changed. Neva's story fills in some of the gaps for me, but she knows so little herself that the whole tale is still not revealed.

'This room they took you to, with the doctor. It was brainwashing?'

'They'd give us drugs, tell us the same thing over and over until we believed it. So, I guess brainwashing is what you would call it.'

'What things did they tell you?' I ask.

'That we'd always been theirs. We were born to serve the Network. After a while, we forgot our former homes and families. Our handlers became the only family we had.'

'And … you went against them. You killed your handler? You killed Tracey.'

'Yes.'

'Why?' Michael asks.

'I began to remember things. I knew what they'd done to me was wrong. I didn't want to be owned anymore,' she says.

'You're implicating yourself in several murders by telling me this.'

'I know,' she says.

'Then why tell me?'

Neva glances away and back at the stage.

'I speak seven languages,' she says. 'I discovered opera when I was on an assignment in Italy. *La Bohème* was playing then too. I heard it and loved it. I don't know why. I had no other emotions. Not for possessions, and none associated with life and death. But music. That is something else. I suppose I have an advantage because I can understand the words. But these people down here, most of them don't, yet they still engage with it. What that says is that music speaks to us on a primal level. It crosses language barriers. We don't need to know the words because the notes tell us the story.'

I'm not sure where she's going with this but I wait for her to explain. She looks back at me.

'The closest thing to this is the rhythm of death,' she says. 'There's a music to murder to.'

'And you *enjoy* that too?' I ask.

Neva smiles and shakes her head. 'Some do. Like opera, when you first hear it, you don't necessarily like it. But you can learn to appreciate it on a cultural level. Murder is an acquired taste, Michael. One I've learnt to be very good at. I feel no guilt or remorse when I take a life. If I ever did, some time in my life that emotion was removed from me. But equally I feel no enjoyment. There are plenty of us who do. But I'm not telling you anything you don't already know as a profiler.'

For a moment I don't know what to say. I absorb the information she's giving, acknowledging that she knows more about me than I do about her. But from what she's revealed, I know she must have been through so much, and it's made her who and what she is. This is the worst case of child abuse I've ever come across. I question again if she can be held responsible for everything these people made her do? Surely not? I use this to justify my contact with her now and the secret of it that I kept from my colleagues.

For all this, I don't see a victim before me. And I'm at odds with what she's told me and what I know of her crimes. Could someone like Neva be rehabilitated?

'You said you want my help,' I say. 'How? Do you want witness protection?'

'I do want your help and I want to offer you mine. You and Archive.'

I blink at the use of the taskforce's name. She obviously knows more than should be possible.

'In what way?' I ask.

'I have resources that can find your assassins. But more importantly, the people who control them.'

'How will you deliver this information to me? Will you let me take you in? Keep you safe?'

'I'd be in more danger in custody than I am out on my own,' she says. 'Right now, I'm invisible. They can't find me. By helping you I'll be opening a chink in my armour. I'm putting myself at risk. But let me worry about that, and also about getting you what you need. You just have to promise me you'll keep me a secret from your taskforce for as long as possible.'

I deep sigh. 'I don't know if I can.'

'At least you're honest.' Neva smiles again. 'Let me give you a helping hand with that. Here is your first lead.'

She leans towards me, retrieving a brown manila envelope from under my seat. She places it in my hands.

'Inside is information about someone. They call him Sharrick. He was assigned to me as my handler after … after I *killed* Tracey. They didn't know I did it at the time, but they probably do now. Sharrick is a lead that can get us closer to the hierarchy of the Network. But he's still a minor cog in the works. A mere handler and former assassin. All handlers are. But Tracey's death will have created a vacancy. I suspect Sharrick is next in line to fill it.'

'Next in line for what?'

'A seat at the table in the banquet hall of the Network. Think of it as a huge house, with many rooms. Promotions happen only from within. I only know about the ones immediately above me. And a little I learnt by spying on Tracey. She was more involved than the average handler, you see. She was also a trainer.'

I want to ask questions but instead I open the envelope and look at the photograph of Sharrick. He's a middle-aged man with white hair – possibly dyed. His face is clean-shaven. He's like a young Rutger Hauer. The picture captures him leaving a London club that I'm familiar with. He's carrying a briefcase and wearing a suit. For all intents and purposes, anyone would take him to be a businessman. But I notice other things about him: his well-built, strong frame. His lean, wiry, athletic appearance tells me more about him than the formal suit.

Even in the photograph I can tell this man will be light on his feet.

'This place...' I say. The location is a small gentlemen's club. I know it, but can't remember why.

'I'll leave you to figure that out,' Neva says. 'But he's there a lot. So that's a starting point to bringing him in.'

'How did you find him here?' I ask.

'One of my sources recommended I check the place out. I knew the lead was spot on when I saw Sharrick leaving the place.'

'But you didn't follow him, to see where he was staying?' I ask.

'No. He's a seasoned operative. I couldn't risk being seen,' she says.

The house lights go down as the orchestra strikes up again.

'You aren't staying for the second act?' I ask as she stands.

'I never stay anywhere too long...' she answers.

I don't try to stop her. I sit back in my chair as Neva slips out of the booth. I stay until the last song before I leave, taking the envelope with me.

Chapter Thirty-Five

SHARRICK

In a private office at the Methuselah Club, Sharrick opens his laptop and logs on. These offices are free and used by members on a first-come, first-served basis. It means that Sharrick, and others like him, can find refuge when away from their regular locations. In this building, all internet access is encrypted, so he can securely open his emails.

He flicks through the unimportant ones, quickly dismissing them, until he finds an encoded one from Mr Beech.

He opens the email and commits to memory a date, time, and location. This is not a meeting place for him, but one he needs to pass on to his charge, Samara. She's been newly assigned to him. He will take her through all subsequent stages of her career, starting today with a new and dangerous assignment.

Sharrick picks up his phone and dials Samara. He gives

her the instructions verbally, expecting her to memorise everything. Then he hangs up.

Business done, Sharrick closes his laptop and puts it away in the wide leather briefcase he carries. He doesn't concern himself with how Samara will perform her duties. She will, or she will die trying. All operatives are trained to perfection and he does not expect any problems with this one. Unlike the disaster that has happened with Neva.

Sharrick finds himself thinking of Neva now. Where is she? What would a girl who is so highly skilled do in order to avoid detection? The truth is, she should be doing everything they expect her to. They should be able to anticipate her every move. But Neva has broken away from her conditioning in every way possible. She's not falling foul of any of the safeguards they'd implanted in her brain. No, she's somehow managed to bypass all of that and is well and truly hidden from them.

Sharrick recalls his last conversation with Mr Beech, who is taking this defection better than expected. Though Sharrick has never seen it, Beech is known for his temper. Sometimes he's even killed agents in mid-flow of an explanation of why they had failed him. Sharrick heard of one such agent who dared to tell Beech that what he asked was 'impossible'. Beech stabbed the man in the eye with a fountain pen, before cutting his throat with a very sharp paper knife.

For these reasons, Sharrick is wary. He expects Beech's rage to be turned on him at any moment. Beech, however, appears to be taking it all in his stride. Sharrick wonders why.

'We've exhausted all of the possibilities she could have used,' Sharrick had explained. He waited for the angry outburst but Beech merely sighed down the phone as though the conversation bored him.

'Not surprising. Neva was trained by Tracey. She's more than an average operative because Tracey was our best trainer. Tracey delighted in her protégée's successes. Neva was something of a flagship for successful training. Now that has become the biggest joke of all.' Beech had laughed, displaying uncharacteristic humour. 'Find Tracey's last trainee and we may have an insight into Neva's disappearance. It has to be something they did during training.'

Mr Beech had hung up then, leaving Sharrick with the problem as usual.

'You could've at least told me who to speak to,' Sharrick had said to the dead phone.

Who Tracey trained was all a matter of 'need to know', after all. Sharrick was certain that this went beyond training: Neva was thinking for herself. Neva's programming should make it intolerable for her to function without *them*.

Sharrick had received a text from Mr Beech then, telling him to speak to someone called Vasquez. There was a number to call. At the same time, an email with a codeword arrived in his inbox. Sharrick had known that this was something he had to use with Vasquez – a keyword to allow the man to access the information he needed.

It had both pleased and concerned Sharrick that he had been given access to an important figure in the hierarchy of the Network. It meant he was moving up in the ranks. Possibly a good thing, but potentially a poisoned chalice.

Now, his meeting with Vasquez looming, he feels anxious.

He leaves the small communal office, switching on the 'vacant' sign as he does. Then he passes out into the main bar.

The Methuselah Club is a known haunt for stars of television and film. In the bar, Sharrick studies the other occupants, and he runs his eyes over the paintings of old stars that once attended the club. This place has always been more than just a gentlemen's club founded in the nineteenth century. It is home to the secret service too, and a neutral ground for other spies, many of whom attend with impunity.

Sharrick visits often. It is a good refuge when in London and feels like a truly safe location. The secret service won't become involved in anything taking place here. There is an agreement regarding anti-surveillance – more for the benefit of the British government than anyone else but the others take full advantage of it.

Sharrick sees Vasquez enter. He knows him because he is wearing a tie from a certain public school. Just as Sharrick himself is. Neither of them went to school there but it is a calling card for the Network.

Vasquez nods in the direction of the private offices and turns and walks away. A few seconds later, Sharrick follows.

Vasquez waits in the same office that Sharrick has just vacated.

Sharrick enters. There are two other men also in the room with Vasquez.

'Search him,' Vasquez orders and one of the thugs runs a weapon scanner over Sharrick, while the other pats him down. They both look like bouncers from a city-centre nightclub in their black suits.

'Mr Beech sent me,' Sharrick explains. He doesn't tell him that the thugs' search is pointless. No one gets into the Methuselah carrying a gun. Luggage, as well as physical bodies, are searched coming in.

'Leave,' Vasquez says to his goons. The two men leave the room and Vasquez takes a seat behind the desk. He places his own laptop down on the desk and opens it.

'Code?'

'Seventhchild. All one word. Uppercase S,' Sharrick says.

Vasquez types in the code and then stares at the screen. 'What do you want to know?'

'I need some names. Tracey Herod's trainees.'

Vasquez briefly glances back at Sharrick.

'Herod was an icon,' he says. 'Shame she got wasted.'

Sharrick nods, noting Vasquez's American accent. He doesn't speak while Vasquez does something with his computer.

'I've sent you a file. There are two of them residing in England. One just got promoted to the house.'

'Same batch as Neva?' Sharrick asks.

'The one above.'

'What about one from Neva's year group?'

Vasquez looks on his computer. 'Hmm. Not showing. That's odd.'

'Retired? *All of them?*'

'Only one is listed "retired". Kurt. He was Neva's graduation piece.'

'Then where are the others?'

Vasquez searches once more. 'Looks like they've been moved to a place above even my paygrade.'

'Thanks for the help,' Sharrick says.

'Forget we met,' Vasquez answers.

Vasquez leaves the room while Sharrick once more opens his laptop. Vasquez's emails are an introduction note to each of the operatives. Sharrick has two new codewords that will get him access to their information. It crosses his mind that he's wading into dangerous territory. How much will the Network permit him to learn before they feel he knows too much?

With little more to go on, Sharrick leaves the Methuselah Club and takes a cab back to his hotel. He now has two files, with two names. One is called Elba and the other Olive. Both from a class above Neva. It is possible, he thinks, that Tracey Herod had given these two some pearls of wisdom that Neva also took on board. They might be helpful. Surely, Tracey's radical methods had to be responsible for the way Neva had turned out.

Back in his hotel room he receives a text on his burner from Elba and arranges to meet him the next day.

Chapter Thirty-Six

SHARRICK

They meet in St James's Park. It's a bit of a cliché to Sharrick, but assassins like their games and in-jokes. Sharrick supposes that it makes them feel ordinary – as if their job is a normal nine-to-five.

Sharrick waits on a specified bench at a certain time until Elba joins him.

'Anarchy rules,' says Elba.

'Only in the suburbs...' Sharrick responds.

Sharrick is expecting a male, but he finds that Elba is female.

'I was never a very butch boy. It became evident when I was twelve that I had to become a girl.'

Sharrick wants to ask more but he remembers that *curiosity kills* and so he nods at Elba.

'I need to know about Tracey. The methods by which she trained you.'

A child screams in the distance. Elba looks coldly over to where a mother is chastising a small boy.

'Spare the rod, spoil the child,' Elba says. 'That was very much Tracey's motto. Therefore, she didn't spoil or spare. But she had favourites. She preferred the girls. For this reason, she also liked me. She recognised I was a girl *inside*.'

'She treated the girls differently? How?'

Elba smiles as though remembering a favourite aunt. 'Girls need more rules. Different protocols. She made us swear we'd never share this information with the boys.'

'What information?'

Elba frowns, struggling with her conditioning. 'I can't,' she says.

'Tracey is dead,' Sharrick reveals, although Tracey's demise is also on a need-to-know basis. He realises he has to free Elba from some of the conditioning restraints if he's to get what he wants from her.

Elba lets out a slow sigh. A slight shiver ripples through her. Sharrick wonders what it signifies. Relief? Fear? Shock? Maybe all those things. He can almost remember the feeling of his own conditioning, even though he's been permitted to go beyond it these past ten years since becoming a handler. But even that was under controlled post-conditioning circumstances.

'Girls have to have less emotion than the boys. We have to be devoid of fear. But I assume that is the same for boys? *It's harder for us girls*, Tracey used to say. We have more to prove, yet we're also so much stronger mentally than our male counterparts, if not physically.'

Sharrick's eyes follow the flow of muscles beneath the sleeve of his own shirt. There is little dispute that most of the males were physically stronger than the female operatives. The girls, however, always have the element of surprise on their side, as well as some dirty tricks to win a fight. They are 'unexpected' and cold too. Tracey was right in her assessment that they had to be. But the Network's training had always found ways to address the balance in the male/female physical concern. It would have been standard procedure to make the girls' mental strength impenetrable. In fact, they were taught to fight regardless of pain, injury, or fear of death. Like cornered rats, they'd come back at any assailant again and again and they'd either go down fighting or they'd win through sheer persistence.

'Did she tell you anything about protecting yourself? For the future?' Sharrick asks. He is feeling impatient now. He wants answers. He wants Neva. He wants to put her back in 'the room' and see if they can claw her back. He doesn't know why. Perhaps it's because she was the least likely to break and yet … she has. They need to learn how and why that happened. Neva ran. It was *planned*. She knew all along that one day she would have to go to ground and she was ready when the day arrived. That knowledge had to have come from somewhere, because it went against the standard conditioning. It went against everything the Network had worked for over the years.

'The mantra,' Elba says now, 'is there to protect us. Tracey was very strict about maintaining our equilibrium. It's something I'll pass on. When I go to the house to become a trainer.'

'You've just been promoted?' asked Sharrick.

'It's on the cards. I'll be able to choose from my favourite students.'

Sharrick remembers the house and the other six that grew and worked with him. He recalls how only five of them made the grade. He doesn't know if he would delight in taking others through this process; maybe Elba is well chosen for the role, because she will.

'If there is any piece of knowledge that Tracey gave you that you'll share with your future protégés what will it be?' Sharrick asks.

'Not to question your superiors,' Elba says. 'For they know better than you what you have to be.'

Chapter Thirty-Seven

MICHAEL

'Who's the guy?' asks Beth when I call her and Leon into the briefing room. I have the picture of Sharrick up on the large screen at the end of the room.

'Someone who might lead us to the people behind the series of murders we've been looking at,' I explain.

Beth and Leon sit down. We all study the screen.

'How did you get this?' asks Leon.

'I can't reveal my source,' I say.

'Okay. So, what do you know about him?' asks Beth.

'They call him Sharrick. He's an operative for "the Network". In fact, he's higher up than that: he's a handler,' I tell them.

'The Network? Unimaginative name, but it sounds familiar,' Beth says. She frowns at the screen as though trying to remember where she's heard the name of this organisation.

'This guy is a handler? Who does he look after?' asks Leon.

'Trained killers.'

'Like the one we've been searching for?' Leon says.

I nod. I've thought carefully about how much I will tell the team without giving Neva away. Half-truths are the best. 'My source told me Tracey Herod was his superior. She died because one of the assassins wants out.'

'The woman you met at the crime scene?' says Leon. 'Anna? It would explain why Herod had to die.'

I don't answer. I let them work it out for themselves.

'So, we find him, we find her?' Beth says.

'I'm hoping for more than that. We find him and we find those above him,' I say. 'My source wants to remain anonymous, as I said, but has given some inside information. These are dangerous people and any enquiries you guys make, please give away as little as possible. Sharrick is looking for the same woman we are. But he's not alone. From what I've been told, their spies are everywhere. It's why he's in town. He's staying in a hotel near Canary Wharf.'

'How d'you know?' Beth asks.

'I followed him from the Methuselah. He's had a few meetings there this week. He wasn't very cautious but I suppose he isn't expecting anyone to know who and what he is.'

After I parted from Neva, I remembered how I knew about the Methuselah: Ray Martin had told me about the club when I joined Archive. All the male members of the taskforce had free membership – a point that annoyed me as it excluded Beth.

'It's traditional,' Ray had explained. 'There is a female

version of this place, though I'm not at liberty to explain where.'

Despite Ray's explanation, I'd avoided the club, refusing to buy into something I believed was sexist and outmoded. But with this new development, I'd activated my membership for the first time. Then, all I'd had to do was wait and watch.

I'd texted Neva after I read her report. She rang me, willing to talk, but it was brief. I think she was still afraid to trust me. Given the information she had shared, I now understood why. After that call, I received one other text with a new contact number. Neva was taking no chances and had changed her phone.

After that I decided I'd follow Sharrick and see what I could learn. Sharrick had appeared on the second evening that I attended the club. He went into one of the private offices and remained there for an hour, before coming out and buying himself a brandy from the bar. Then he sipped the drink and sat in a corner, reading a book. He looked innocuous, but I knew that he was far from harmless. From the file that Neva had provided, I'd learnt about Sharrick's long relationship with the Network. However, this information was limited to speculation mostly and did not have any real evidence to back it up. Neva had devised the dossier based on what she knew, but the problem was, her access to the Network was limited to her own now deceased handler.

Even so, Neva had surmised that Sharrick was a former-operative-turned-handler. Because of his age, she concluded that Sharrick had succeeded in a long career. This made him trusted and eligible for promotion in the Network. Somehow – and Neva's report explained this – he had avoided being 'retired', just as Tracey had until Neva killed her. This meant one of two things. Either he was resourceful and had proved himself loyal time and again, or he always appeared to be under their control, never raising suspicion that he had doubts about his masters. Both could be true, of course. Neva's report also described how any doubt, no matter how small, often led to the termination of an operative. Therefore, Sharrick's longevity was significant.

Neva had ended the dossier with a comment confirming that she felt Sharrick was being groomed for future promotion. He would most likely skip a few levels and move up the ranks soon, especially if he found Neva and turned her in.

I was aware that most of this information was merely her conjecture, but I reasoned that it was enough to justify making Sharrick a person of interest to Archive.

'So, you're proposing we monitor this one?' Beth says. 'See where he leads?'

'He's a piece in a puzzle that I'd like to put together,' I say. 'He may well provide us with something we don't know about the Network. Beth, we've talked about the possibility that someone was taking kids and turning them into killers. I think Sharrick is linked to these people. He may be able to enlighten us about what happened to them. It's even possible that he was one such child himself. Perhaps we can study the faces of those recorded missing that might fit into Sharrick's age bracket.'

'That shouldn't be hard. This is a very clear shot you got,' Beth says.

I don't tell her that I hadn't taken the picture but I let her believe I had because it would only lead to more questions about my source.

'I must admit, I do want to know who brought you this,' Leon says.

I give them everything tangible we have on Sharrick, but no more about my informant.

'I'll put feelers out with my sources. The Network is ringing some bells with me. I'm sure I've come across them before,' Beth says.

'Okay. But reveal as little as possible. We don't want word getting back that Sharrick has appeared on our radar. Are there any surveillance cameras on the Methuselah Club?'

'The deal with that place is that there shouldn't be any. At any time,' Beth answers.

'But?'

'Well, if there are any, they aren't officially available to us,' she says.

'Unofficially?'

'I'll see what I can do,' Beth says. Then she winks.

I smile. If anyone can, Beth can.

'For now,' I say, 'I have a source in there keeping an eye out for him. We're taking careful note of anyone he interacts with as well.'

Chapter Thirty-Eight

SHARRICK

Sharrick leaves the park before Elba. He's frustrated that Elba has given him nothing. Except ... Sharrick now knows that Tracey was willing to go further than other trainers. Did Elba really suit being a girl? Or did Tracey change her because she needed a specific *type* for a precise role? He wishes he had access to Elba's full files. He would love to learn what her first job had been. Even so, this all shows him that Tracey did adapt the training. Maybe she even personalised it. In which case, what was it she gave Neva that was unlike the others?

Sharrick returns to his hotel room and opens the encrypted files that Vasquez sent him. He looks at the training sequence for both Elba and Olive. There was a combination of drugs, hypnosis, therapy, and physical training. Languages are a high point. Each of them is taught three different ones. Elba isn't particularly strong in this area. Olive is better. But other than the usual martial arts, weapons training, and body development exercises, there's nothing different to what Sharrick himself experienced. At least, nothing on record.

Much to Sharrick's surprise, Elba's gender change is mentioned. The male Elba was given hormones age 12 and then gender reassignment surgery at 13. There are no reports inside the document justifying this decision to change Elba at such a young age from male to female. It just occurs. Tracey signs off on it as casually as any of the treatments the trainees are given. Sharrick knows that no one would have questioned it. But he is beginning to wonder about Tracey even more now.

When he's read everything available, he sends an encrypted message to Olive. After a few hours Sharrick receives a reply. Olive agrees to meet. This is expected because an authority higher up will have given her clearance to speak with him.

I'm not sure I can be of any help

She says in the encrypted email.

But we must find Tracey's killer so I'll do my best to give you what you need.

This response, so open and informed, surprises Sharrick. Then he notes that Olive has asked him to attend her at 'the house'. She is going to be there, 'overseeing the training of the current batch'.

Sharrick agrees to go, a mixture of excitement and fear cramping his stomach. He hasn't suffered from such a feeling since he left the house thirty years ago. He wonders if it will be as he remembers. Then he realises he doesn't know the address. He's thinking how to word his response to ask the question of Olive when he receives another email. It reads:

> *I have been authorised to have you collected and taken to your destination.*
>
> *Meet at The Methuselah Club.*
>
> *Bring overnight bag.*

There is a time and date. With shock, Sharrick realises it is today, in less than an hour. He closes his laptop, packs a bag with a few things, and then heads off back to the club.

Chapter Thirty-Nine

SHARRICK

Alderley Edge in Cheshire is where highly paid footballers choose to live when they work for the Manchester clubs. It's a place of wealth and privilege and, above all, home to many who value their privacy. The house is located on the outskirts of the village in a rural setting, surrounded by several acres of land. It is obscure enough not to draw attention, and surrounded by further agricultural land which is also owned by the Network and rented out to farmers, making the location completely isolated and not overlooked by any other private landowners.

Sharrick is in the back of a limo, with the windows blacked out. He works on his laptop during the long drive from London, sipping from a glass of sparkling water.

The driver doesn't speak to him behind the film of black glass that separates them, and Sharrick makes no attempt to engage him.

When they reach their destination, Sharrick has no idea

in what part of the country he is, any more than he did when he was a child living in the house. Though he may be able to speculate because of the time it's taken, he makes a conscious effort not to think about it.

As the driver pulls up, the glass clears and Sharrick sees for the first time in years the place that had once been his home and his prison.

The chauffeur opens the door and Sharrick gets out.

A woman stands on the impressive steps at the front of the house. She is wearing a suit and looks ordinary, but Sharrick's practised eye notices the bulge in her jacket that signifies a gun and holster. Despite her plain looks, he knows this is Olive and that she is a dangerous operative.

Sharrick looks up beyond her, his gaze following the line of the house up to the third floor. The thought floats through his mind that the description of this place as 'the house' is modest. This is a palatial property. It's large enough to be a boarding school that can house students and teachers as well as have its own classrooms and training areas.

'Sharrick?' says Olive. She holds out her hand and Sharrick takes it. They shake hands.

'Thank you for agreeing to meet,' he says.

Olive nods and invites him inside. Sharrick enters the imposing front door and hallway, eyes wide with both curiosity and apprehension. The entrance is still as large as he remembers and it opens out onto a central staircase and two long corridors, one either side, that lead off into other areas of the house.

'It makes you feel strange, being here, doesn't it?' Olive

says as she leads him to the left of the staircase, into an office which is the first door. Sharrick doesn't answer; she accepts this as acknowledgement that she's right.

Sharrick doesn't recall the inside of this room; perhaps he was never permitted to enter it.

'Take a seat,' Olive says and she goes around to the other side of an exquisite antique desk made of polished oak.

Sharrick sits opposite her. Then he sees the plaque that sits on the desk.

OLIVE REDDING
Headteacher

'This is a school?' he says, surprised.

'It always was,' Olive says. 'Only now we find it is the best cover of all to admit what we are. It's a school for gifted children. The students think they are sent willingly by their parents. As you see, I warrant respect as the head. We must evolve, especially in how we condition each generation.'

The thought of this jars Sharrick. He feels nauseous. What was it they had told him during his time here? He can barely recall, possibly because after the conditioning it didn't matter. For certain, he and his peers stopped asking to go home and made no attempt to escape. He remembered being afraid when he arrived. The house was big, his guards intimidating. He had been so young, barely five years old.

'Can I get you something to drink?' Olive asks.

This courtesy also appears odd to Sharrick. 'No. Let's get

to business. Then I can let you get back to your important work. You know why I'm here?'

'Yes. You want to know about Tracey's methods?'

Sharrick nods.

'Brutal. Unforgiving. She really ran a very tight ship when she was in the house. Ruling us with pain and fear.'

'This was always the method,' Sharrick says. 'I'm looking for something diverse. Some training of hers that was different to that of others. As someone now familiar with how this is done, maybe you can enlighten me?'

'That's difficult,' Olive says. 'But I've put together a full dossier of all the regular methods of brainwashing that have been commonly used over the years. We are doing things slightly differently now, as I explained. Our students are no longer being *forced* to become operatives; they are conditioned to *want* to be one. There was always an element of competition before; now, the focus on this is heavier. Academic achievement is just as important as physical abilities. It is not an option to be a *good* assassin; they are taught to want to be the *greatest*.'

'What you say is the same philosophy we were taught from the beginning.'

Olive smiles. 'With all due respect, the torture you underwent made you believe that. Nowadays we encourage with positive reinforcement, and punish only when it is absolutely necessary. Obviously, on top of controlled conditioning. We are seeing great results. This round of students will be ready much younger to take up their duties. Their youth will be of great advantage. Theoretically, they will also be useful to us for longer.'

Sharrick quells the tremor of emotion that runs through him at Olive's revelations.

'Would you like to see what we do?' Olive asks. 'I've been authorised to show you around.'

Sharrick nods. 'That might be very beneficial to my inquiry.'

Olive stands. She walks back around the desk and Sharrick is aware of how young she is to have such responsibility, but also how powerful her bearing is. She is confident and at home in this environment. Unlike himself.

'Come,' Olive says. She studies his face as he stands and then she turns and leads him out of the office and into the house proper.

Sharrick pulls his emotions in check. He's always been in control, never falling down. As one of Doctor Mendez's first experiments, he was conditioned to fear failure as much as he feared his masters. He, like the others of his class group, had worked to please the trainers, looking for some recognition that they were worthy, but never receiving it.

He listens now as Olive explains the new methods. Drugs and hypnosis are used, but there is a conscious effort to praise and reward hard work too. It creates, she explains, the perfect slaves who adore their masters more than they fear them.

'But how do you factor in issues of breakdown? Of self-awareness that leads to disobedience?'

'These are children,' Olive says. 'They are taught to love and respect us. This generates far more loyalty than fear alone. Also, failure at times is seen as a learning curve.

Though, of course, the conditioning instils the innate horror of defiance. What we create these days are far more rounded individuals than before. They are taught that this is their vocation, not a forced enslavement. If you *think* you have free will, you have no reason to rebel. Also, because of this, we feel that all of them may well be able to retire in the traditional sense. As functioning human beings, they will not be a danger to the Network or themselves when set free.'

'How is this different then from the conditioning you received from Tracey?' Sharrick asks. 'And how is it that you seem so *rounded*?'

'There have been many breakdowns in recent years because of the old style of training. With the aid of psychologists, we've come to believe we need to deal with the underlying issues that cause such a breakdown. You and I were damaged badly by our experiences, but each of us was intelligent enough to rise above it and understand that we can choose to be part of the Network or we become retired. I have had therapy to help me become who I am. To make me into the best instructor for future generations. You have naturally evolved, haven't you? Though I suspect you suffer from many of the fears that were deliberately placed inside your psyche.'

Sharrick is shocked by Olive's blunt analysis of their mutual state. He doesn't acknowledge the truth of what she says, as her statements are not put as questions, to see if he agrees. This tactic frees him from responsibility. He can listen without acquiescence. Part of him realises that this is why Olive structures her words in this way. His loyalty is not in doubt. He is not required to question what his superiors did. Just as well, since he is incapable of doing so.

'I have been assured that lessons have been learnt and I'm permitted to analyse any possible mistakes in order to execute my role here effectively,' Olive explains. 'You are now being given the same permission. The Network has seen a great deal of strength in you, Sharrick. We are looking to move forward and develop you.'

Sharrick shudders at her words. Even though she's years younger than him, she is his superior, and therefore she has the right to say this. His head feels light as he thinks about the implication: he now has the right to ask questions. The feeling is difficult to comprehend and accept. It fights with his inner self. *Curiosity kills*.

'You'll get used to this freedom,' she says. 'Mr Beech believes it will help you in your search. It is also important for your future. Come.'

Sharrick follows Olive but a cold prickle puts the hairs on his scalp on edge. His teeth chatter with anxiety, but he forces his jaw to relax.

'You're remembering the fear,' Olive says. 'Watch this.'

They reach the door and Sharrick sees a girl sitting in a chair, unsupervised, outside the doctor's room. She is fourteen or fifteen years old. Petite but wiry. Her face is relaxed. She smiles at Olive and at Sharrick as though seeing them there is perfectly normal.

'Elsbeth is going for her treatment shortly. How do you like the treatments?' Olive asks the girl.

'Enjoyable. Relaxing,' says the girl smiling broadly.

Sharrick searches her face for signs of distress but finds

233

none. Then the door opens and a female nurse is standing in the doorway.

'Hello, Elsbeth,' the nurse says. She too smiles and appears benign. 'Ready?'

'Oh, yes please!' says Elsbeth. 'I've been looking forward to this all day!'

The child goes inside and the nurse closes the door.

'She wasn't scared,' Sharrick says.

'No. The treatments are considered to be rewards not punishment. What happens in there absolves the students of all future guilt about the path that has been chosen for them. They learn a morality.'

'Morality? That seems to be an oxymoron in light of their future job, and I say this with no judgement. It's how the world sees what we do, though we know our role is important.'

'They believe that what they do is for the good of humanity. The people they go after are *evil*. They don't consider anything else.'

Sharrick fights with his new freedom. He must ask more, but fears reprisals.

'Ask anything,' Olive says, as though she knows he is struggling.

'What I really need to understand is what changes Tracey Herod made to the conditioning of Neva that freed her. Can you answer that?'

'Possibly,' says Olive. 'Though we may need to find Neva and study her to be sure. Our failures can inform our future successes.'

'But the trouble is,' Sharrick says, 'this very thing is how she has learnt to escape us. I need to know how to unpick her mind. I need insight into how she might warp her training.'

Olive nods. 'I thought you might need help with this. We have the doctor who worked on her here. He's not working anymore. His mind is a little confused these days, but we take care of him. He deserves that loyalty. And if we have him in our control then he can never be a threat.'

'*Mendez*? Can I see him?' Sharrick asks, even though the thought strikes terror in his heart.

'He's ready for you,' Olive says.

Sharrick follows her away from the treatment room and to the entrance hall. Then Olive leads him upstairs to the second floor.

'This is our medical zone,' she says. 'Was it the same in your time?'

'I don't recall. Maybe there was a treatment room, and a doctor occasionally examined us other than Doctor Mendez.'

'Mendez was such a pioneer. We owe so much of our success to his experiments.'

Sharrick says nothing.

'His room is in the west wing,' Olive says as they turn left at the top of the stairs. 'His appearance may shock you. He is quite frail. And thirty years older than the last time you saw him.'

They pass two doors before Olive stops and knocks on the third one on the right.

'Come in,' says a small voice.

Olive opens the door and walks confidently inside as though Mendez holds no terror for her at all.

Sharrick pauses at the door. He feels the same sick, scared sensation that once accompanied all visits to Mendez, but even more so the treatment room.

'Good day, doctor,' says Olive. 'Here is the visitor I told you about. You remember Sharrick, don't you?'

Mendez is indeed frail in appearance but his eyes are steely cold mirrors that inform Sharrick more about the character of the man than his infirm body. Sharrick remembers Mendez as strong, tall, and young, but now he appears shrivelled. He realises that if the man is eighty or older then he must have been at least fifty when he worked on Sharrick's group. How many other assassins had he created before then?

'I remember you,' says Mendez. 'The acrobat…'

This reference to Sharrick's particular physical skills jars him somewhat. He hadn't expected Mendez to remember him at all because the doctor had always made them feel so unimportant. He treated them like lab rats, as something less than human. Sharrick hadn't felt like that since he left this house and gained a modicum of freedom as an operative. Now he is plummeted back into that awful position.

Mendez studies him as if he knows exactly how Sharrick is feeling. A small smile curves the wrinkled lips upwards, and yet the humour doesn't reach the doctor's eyes. It is cruelty that Sharrick sees there, and disgust.

'Do you want a drink?' Mendez says and suddenly his face becomes more congenial, less frightening and brutal. 'I don't get visitors much and it will be nice to hear about your successes. You may not know this, but I am proud of you, Sharrick. You reached heights that others only dreamed of.'

Sharrick sinks down into a chair that's been placed beside Mendez's by the window, but facing inwards. There is a teapot on a small table beside the doctor and he begins to pour tea into two cups.

'Milk and sugar?' he asks politely.

The scene is surreal and Sharrick almost believes he's still in the limo and has fallen into a vivid and fantastical dream.

'Sugar, no milk,' Sharrick says.

The doctor adds a spoon of sugar to Sharrick's cup, and milk to his own. Then he stirs them with separate spoons.

'I don't have a sweet tooth,' he says. 'But I could never have tea black.'

He holds out the cup with black tea and sugar and Sharrick automatically takes it. He sips, wincing because it is still not sweet enough for his taste but he doesn't ask for more sugar.

'I need to know about the work you did. With Tracey.'

'I'll be in my office,' Olive says. 'This is for your ears only.'

Then she turns and leaves Sharrick alone with the man who tortured him for more than twelve years.

Chapter Forty

NEVA

'Rent's due again tomorrow,' Daz says.

As though anticipating her arrival, Daz is waiting by the stairs as Neva comes in the front door.

'Yes. I know,' she says. She smiles. 'I have it for you. I'll just go upstairs and put my coat away. I'll bring it to the living room in a minute.'

Daz smiles back. Neva knows that he thinks she is a good tenant. They barely see her and she pays on time. If only they knew what she really was? Would Daz feel so comfortable knowing she had an arsenal of weapons hidden in her room?

Daz goes into the living room and Neva hears him switch on the television. A short time later, she comes downstairs and goes in the room holding a wad of cash in a white envelope.

'Six months again?' he says.

Neva nods.

Daz takes the envelope. His eyes show avarice. Neva

238

thinks he had been planning to increase the rent but has weighed this up against her reliability and decided to leave things as they are. She was prepared for the greed though, and had planned to deal with it diplomatically. It is a relief that this obstacle has not come up. Dealing with normal people is harder than dealing with killers. At least you know where you are with someone when they are trying to murder you.

'Have a great evening,' she says. Then she goes back to her room.

Inside, she locks the door and pulls her guns from their hiding places. Even though they haven't been used, she begins her weekly ritual of cleaning the weapons. She's soothed by the routine, as though this task is a touchstone to her true nature. She meditates while she polishes the barrel of the Uzi. But she doesn't repeat the mantra of old. These days, she has her own chant. She tells herself how she can be free. She promises herself revenge.

There is a knock on the door and Neva hides her weapons under the duvet of the single bed. She opens the door and finds Marie there.

'Hi. Just wondered if you wanted takeaway as we're ordering?'

This is the first time they've asked her this question, and Neva knows they have takeout once a week.

'What are you getting?'

'Chinese.'

'Lovely,' says Neva. 'A quarter crispy duck would be great!'

'I'll call you down when it arrives.'

Neva closes the door, wondering about Marie's sudden friendliness.

Forty minutes later, Marie calls upstairs. Neva has finished cleaning her guns and has hidden them again. She now leaves her room and goes downstairs. Marie has put some candles on the kitchen table and laid four places.

'Expecting company?' Neva says.

'Yeah. My brother Anthony is visiting. He'll be staying in the spare room. Red or white?'

'Huh?'

'Wine,' says Marie.

'I prefer red.'

Marie places a bottle of merlot on the table alongside an average bottle of pinot grigio. Neva smiles a little at this. Pinot is always the choice of someone who knows nothing about wine. Both bottles are screw tops, although the choice of red isn't a bad one – Chilean, and a respectable brand that has a consistent quality.

Daz comes into the kitchen followed by Anthony. He introduces her and they all sit while Marie dishes out the food. The wine flows and Neva enjoys this normal company despite herself. Anthony is cute; under normal circumstances she would have made him a one-night stand. But you don't crap where you eat, and so she doesn't encourage his flirting and pretends not to notice.

After dinner, Neva says goodnight to them all and goes back to her room.

Once there, she opens her laptop and looks at the three of them on her surveillance cameras. They're still in the kitchen, opening another bottle. She puts earphones in and listens to their idle conversation.

'So,' Daz says, 'is she a dyke?'

'I don't think so,' Anthony says. 'I think she's just socially awkward. Probably a bit on the spectrum.'

'Well, you'd know,' says Marie, 'being a shrink and all.'

'I'm a psychologist.'

'Same thing. You mess with people's minds.'

Anthony shakes his head and laughs. 'You're incorrigible.'

Neva listens to them for another hour. She doesn't need television; people are entertaining when they don't know they're being overheard and Neva has been studying Marie and Daz now for six months. She may use Marie's personality one day if she needs it. Her appearance would be easy to replicate, and her identity easy to clone. She wonders about Anthony. She thinks back to many conversations Marie and Daz have had. Anthony has been mentioned here and there; Neva knew there was a brother, even though this is the first time he's visited. If he is a medical person, is he somehow a threat?

She squashes down her mistrust. She is not complacent, hence the cameras all over the house, but she knows for now that she is safe. No one would ever think she was here, among these ordinary people. She is more off the radar now than she's ever been.

Out of habit she switches on her burner phone to check for messages. She sees a message from Michael's phone asking her to meet him. She mulls this over. Then she types a reply.

Why?

He answers,

We lost Sharrick. Need to pick your brains about where he could have disappeared to.

Neva wonders if this is a trap. But no. She realises that she has been sitting too much on the sidelines since she moved in with Marie and Daz. Hiding, yes, she had to, but also avoiding what has to be done. She thinks about Michael again. Can she trust him? Really? After all, he's in MI5 and she is a killer. It's his job to put her behind bars for her crimes, no matter how much information she shares with him.

Can I really trust you?

The reply is immediate.

Yes.

So is hers.

I'll be in touch.

Neva turns off the burner and stows it in her handbag. Perhaps now is the time to adopt Marie's identity? Tomorrow she will return to London.

Chapter Forty-One

SHARRICK

Sharrick has been allocated a single room in the personnel quarters. He drops his laptop bag down on the bed and looks round. There's no outside window and it's cramped but it has a small en suite bathroom which affords a modicum of privacy.

He leaves his holdall at the foot of the bed and then goes out of the room, closing the door behind him. He pauses. He's on the third-floor landing, another area he has not seen before. Olive told him he has full access. He can look around the facility to help him understand their processes. The thought terrifies him but he is also curious about the place.

He mulls over his conversation with Doctor Mendez. The old man was formidable, despite his frailty, and Sharrick is disturbed by the contact they've had. Even so, he feels he's learnt something that may help him find Neva. Mendez had confirmed a deviation in her conditioning that could allow her more mental freedom. It had been requested by Tracey, and Mendez had done it, not because she was his superior, but because he enjoyed experimenting. Neither he nor Tracey could have predicted the way Neva would go. Mendez, in a very lucid moment, had revealed his knowledge of Neva's defection as well as what he knew of her.

'We were experimenting with different methods then. Trying a few new things. She was an odd child. Different from the rest in that she was already quiet, as though she had been waiting during the first part of her life for us to find her. It was always her calling,' Mendez told him.

'Was she afraid of you?' Sharrick had asked.

'It was hard to tell. She didn't cry after the first time, unlike some of the others. Just … accepted the hypnosis and didn't fight when we injected her with the drugs. She came to the room. Lay down. Responded to whatever we did. I didn't like her initially, but Tracey was adamant that she had potential. She didn't show it at first, just this passivity, then when she came out of her shell, we all knew she was something very special indeed.'

'What was special about her?' Sharrick had asked.

'She didn't do anything how you expected. Like the knife. She loved wielding that thing, though it's normal for the boys to be more into the up-close killing and girls frequently favour a gun. Tracey encouraged her. She wanted her to be brutal. I think she even encouraged enjoyment in death, but Neva never gave her the satisfaction of that. She always remained indifferent, barely even lost her breath during a fight. She never at any point showed any serious emotions. Because of that alone, we would never have thought her capable of running. She was the most controlled of them all.'

The conversation with Mendez has left Sharrick drained. He is weakened by it, but he hides this from the doctor and from Olive when she returns for him. Even that is convenient, arriving as she does when Mendez has said all he wants to, as if Olive knows exactly when that is. Sharrick suspects the room is bugged, if not wired with cameras. He thinks the whole house is rigged with surveillance. He would make sure it was if he ran this facility.

Now, he leaves the room and forces himself to walk down the stairs. He appears in control, as he draws in all of the resources he has at his disposal – the major benefit of his training. He can operate in any circumstance, and even though he gives assignments and no longer takes them, he will never forget how he must behave. Inconspicuous. This, after all, is just another role to play.

On the second floor he glances into one of the small dormitories. This is the girls' area, judging by the clothing that is hung up on the rail and the shoes that stand neatly under each bed. He has a flashback of his own time here. The terror of the first night... Whispered conversations with the other equally scared boys.

'I want to go home, Benji...' said a boy called Paul. He was taller than the others, but was still so young. Like himself.

Was he the one they referred to as Benji?

Sharrick finds he is standing still on the stairs. That feeling of terror he'd once experienced here now threatens to consume him.

It's just the conditioning, he tells himself. It's only natural.

He shakes off the feeling as if it's nothing more than a minor phobia. Then he propels himself downwards.

Reaching the ground floor, he decides to explore this level. He knows that the classrooms are here. He wants to see the students; he wants to see if they are all smiling like Elsbeth. For some reason, he hopes they are. He hopes that the old torturous methods are long gone. He doesn't know where this empathy for the current batch comes from. He has no children, has never wanted them, and yet he doesn't want to see any harmed. This, too, is at odds with his conditioning: anyone is a target if they are an enemy of the Network.

In the hallway, he opens the door opposite the study and finds himself in another corridor. He walks down it, observing the closed doors on his left and right. Then a spark of memory makes him pause once more. Here. This door.

He opens it without knocking and finds himself looking into the gym. A judo mat lies in the centre. Around the edges is a variety of exercise equipment: a trampoline; ropes hanging from the ceiling for students to climb up; a vault; a gymnastic beam.

Sharrick remembers climbing up to the top of the rope in triumph and a first failed attempt at walking across the beam. Then he looks up and sees the trapeze high above. It isn't enough for them to be strong, and tough, and to be able to fight. They have to be everything. Gymnasts of the highest standard. Mendez was right; Sharrick had excelled in this area.

'One day, what you know about using a trapeze will save your life,' his trainer had said. Then a terrified child, he was forced to climb to the top and throw himself off onto the net below. Later, there were no nets.

'There are no nets in real life,' his trainer had said, lowering it down before the students' frightened eyes.

That was the day Paul fell. He broke his spine. They took him away, crying in agony. He was nine years old; Sharrick was ten. They never saw Paul again, and by then, none of them would dare ask what had happened to him. But Sharrick had worked hard after that. He didn't want to fall down onto the hard floor and end his career like Paul. So he became the best and, even now, he knew he could use that trapeze and fly across this high-ceilinged gym, catching the swing gracefully on the other side.

He finds himself climbing up the stepladder. It was so much higher when he was a boy. Not so frightening now. Sharrick had taken on greater heights than this and survived them. At the top he sets the swing going, catches it on its return, then sends it back out across the room, harder and stronger this time. He catches it again. Then he leaps out with it. Strong hands hold the bar as he swings across the ceiling. His mind slips back into memory as he swings back and forth. Turning himself easily on the swing until he's facing the platform again.

'Swing to me, Benji! I'll catch you!' calls Paul.

Sharrick, turns himself again and sees Paul waiting on the other platform, his hand holding the second swing.

Paul pushes the swing towards him. They are in tandem; Sharrick knows how to flip from this one onto the other. His swing pulls back and Paul catches the other. He is laughing and smiling.

'Coward!' he says. 'It's so easy once you know how. Just let go and reach out, Benji!'

Sharrick swings back; the other swing comes to meet him. Perfect. Harmonious.

Sharrick lets go with one hand like a tentative child. He reaches out for the other swing but already it's gone.

His hand paws back at his own swing, gripping it.

'Come on, you big baby,' says Paul. 'You have to let go with both hands and fly across to it. You know how it's done.'

Sharrick swings back into the middle and back again. Paul catches the other swing.

'On three!' he calls.

Then Paul throws out the swing to meet him once more. Sharrick lets go.

'Sharrick, no!' There is a scream from below and then his hands are grasping, reaching for Paul's swing, but the only thing that meets him is empty air. He falls. Falls down so fast, hitting the ground hard. His leg crunches under him. His collarbone shatters. Sharrick feels it all through a veil of confusion.

'Oh my God!' Olive says. 'Get help!'

Sharrick sees the boy, so like Paul, running towards the door, shouting 'Medic! Accident!'

Olive is over him now. 'What were you doing?' she asks.

'Paul. I saw Paul.'

Olive's face is pale as she looks at him.

'Who's Paul?'

'My friend. He was so good at trapeze.'

'We don't have friends,' says Olive. 'You shouldn't have gone up there. The drug was just to make you pliable. Someone should have been watching over you!'

'I climbed the ladder … Paul … he was waiting for me.'

Olive looks up at the still moving swing, then back down at Sharrick. She sighs.

'Mr Beech was wrong about you,' she says. 'You're broken.'

She reaches inside her jacket.

Sharrick sees the gun a spilt second before Olive fires two shots into his head. Then he feels no more pain.

Chapter Forty-Two

MICHAEL

'I like pizza,' Neva says.

'We've gone from opera to as basic as it gets,' I say with a laugh.

Neva smiles. There's more humour in her eyes than usual. She is less cold, less distant. I wonder why. Maybe she's finally trusting me. On this second meeting, I too am feeling more relaxed with her, though I'm aware that I should never really let my guard down.

'It's very public. I was able to observe if you were being followed,' she says.

'How?' I ask.

She shows me the screen of the phone she's holding. She's connected to the internal camera system of the pizza restaurant, as well as the cameras outside.

'I would ask how again but I doubt you'll tell me.'

She gives me a lopsided grin. It's very endearing. It also makes her appear far younger than she is.

Her look today is very different from my idea of her real,

sophisticated self. Mousy, shoulder-length hair, a cheap T-shirt under a grubby-looking denim jacket and a pair of jeans ripped through at the knees. She looks ordinary, slightly grungy. Not someone you'd notice in a crowd. The clothes are also slightly too big – as though she's borrowed them, or recently lost weight, which I don't think is the case.

'Let's get to the point,' she says. 'Sharrick wasn't my handler long, and although I studied Tracey, knew most of her movements, I didn't have time to do this with him. Tracey was easy for me anyway. She'd been with me since I was a child. She trusted me. The last thing she expected was that I'd stalk her. So, in answer to your query, before you ask it, I don't know where Sharrick's base is. If I did, I might well have gone there and interrogated him myself.'

'It doesn't matter now anyway,' I say. I look around the busy restaurant to make sure no one is observing us and that our conversation is not overheard. 'Sharrick's dead.'

'*What?*'

'He was found in a flat over in Devon. We discovered that he's lived there for the last five years under the name Damon Sharrick,' I say.

'What happened to him?' Neva asks.

'Well, it looks like a hit. Two shots in the head. That's what finished him. But here's the thing. He had a broken leg and his collarbone and arm were fractured. The coroner said he could only have sustained such injuries if he'd fallen from a great height. At least thirty feet. Not enough to kill him, but enough to damage him significantly. Then someone put the bullets in him and finished the job.'

Neva shook her head. 'Why? He was *in* with them.

Rumour has it he was about to be promoted. It was why I chose him for you. He was about to enter the inner circle of the Network.'

'And now he's dead,' I say.

'It doesn't make sense,' Neva says. 'Who did you share my dossier about Sharrick with?'

'No one. I shared my *lead* on Sharrick with two of my colleagues. But they can be trusted.'

'Are you sure?'

'With my life,' I say.

'I have to go,' Neva says.

'Don't go. Come in with me. I can guarantee your safety.'

'No, you can't, Michael. Listen. This is really wrong. Sharrick … he was strong. He'd survived all this time. He wouldn't have been retired without cause. Someone leaked the information that he was being watched,' she says.

'No. It's not possible,' I say.

'Can you do one more thing?' she says.

'What?'

'Toxicology. On Sharrick's body. Pull up the report. See if there were any *substances* in his system. If they were in doubt about him, they'd drug and question him.'

'Okay. But I'm not expecting anything. I suspect he was thrown off something in an attempt to kill him. When that failed, he was shot. They retired him. It's that simple. You said yourself they never let anyone go into old age. Sharrick was past his prime and no more use to them,' I say.

'So you think this was just bad luck? Our timing was off?' Neva says.

'Yes.'

She frowns and shakes her head a little, as though she thinks I'm the naivest person she's ever met.

'We can't meet again,' Neva says.

'You're being paranoid. No one knows you're my source,' I say. 'And I have no plan to reveal it.'

Neva stands. 'Goodbye, Michael.'

'Wait,' I say. '*Please*. I'm sure I wasn't followed and you made doubly sure. Let's talk this through.'

'Okay,' she says relenting. 'But … I need the bathroom. I'll be right back.'

She leaves and I watch her walk towards the ladies. Just then the waitress comes up and asks if we're ready to order. I take my eyes away from Neva and look at the waitress.

'A beer for me,' I say. 'The lady will decide when she returns.'

I wait. It doesn't take me long to realise that Neva is not coming back. I hoped she'd trust me, but given the information I'd shared, I couldn't blame her for being suspicious.

Despite her fears, I don't believe there is a leak in Archive. I've worked with Beth, Ray, and Leon for a long time. There has never been any doubt of their intention to resolve the cases they work on. Even so, Neva's words sow a seed of doubt in my mind. What if one of them was a mole for the Network? A double agent, even? I shake my head in subconscious denial. The waitress returns with the beer. I take a sip, then pay her, and stand up from the small cafeteria-style table. There's no point staying here alone.

Plus, I feel self-conscious that I'll be remembered, especially since my date has ducked out on me.

Outside, I look around. There is a man standing in a doorway opposite me, for example. He's not looking at the pizza restaurant, but he looks suspicious, as though he's averting his gaze too much. He is turned away, his body almost blocking the restaurant from view. Is it possible I *have* been followed?

I cross the road and walk towards the guy.

'Hey,' I say. 'Do you have the time?'

The man looks at me and panic crosses his face.

'Look, I'm just waiting for my wife!' he says.

'I only asked you for the time,' I say.

'Yeah. But … I know what that means … round here…' stammers the man.

'It means I left my watch at home.'

'I'm not gay! *Okay*?' says the man.

I blink, shake my head in surprise, and then move on. *When you begin to feel paranoid you can imagine things*, I think.

As I walk away, I chuckle. The man has issues and I can't help being amused at my own insecurity. I think I've been around Neva too much.

Chapter Forty-Three

NEVA

Neva walks away from Michael and heads towards the ladies' room, but before she gets there she slips sideways and into the restaurant kitchen.

None of the chefs look at her. She's paid them already for their discretion in anticipation of having to use this as a contingency.

In the kitchen she takes the phone she's been using to contact Michael out of her pocket. She removes the sim and drops the phone into the nearest bin. At the back door she pauses, looking out down the dark alley. Then she slips outside, skulking along the wall where she feels she is best sheltered. Before she exits the back street, she removes the mousy wig, takes off the jacket and drops them and the sim card in the nearest dumpster. Behind the dumpster is another bag containing a long black coat. She pulls it on, fastens it up and slips the hood up to hide her hair. Then she leaves the shelter of the alley and walks away as fast as she can.

Just in case Michael has led them to her, Neva decides not to take a train back to Manchester that night. Over the next few days, they will be watching all exit points.

She walks the streets, carefully checking behind and around her until she finds a car that will be easy to steal. It's an ancient Morris Minor, in racing green. She's always disliked green, but old cars are so easy to take. She could walk around for hours and not find such a gift.

A few minutes later she's inside and hot-wiring the car.

Neva drives the stolen car to Birmingham and leaves it at the train station. There she buys another cheap phone and sim and catches a train to Manchester.

Back at Marie and Daz's house she packs a small travel bag. She takes one of her fake passports and places it in the overnight bag. After that she stows her weapons in another holdall along with all her other IDs.

'It's time to get out of Dodge,' she murmurs, as though to convince herself she has to leave.

She leaves a note for Daz and Marie, telling them she will be absent for a few months. She doubts they will care about her absence until the next rent period comes around and she probably won't return anyway.

Before she leaves, she glances around the room that has been her home for more than six months. This exit has more impact than the one from her former country home. She examines the emotion. It is like the beginnings of toothache, a dull, annoying pain that you somehow know will get worse if left unattended. Neva doesn't know how to address it, or how to understand what it is that's making her unhappy. Is it the small comfort of this house, or the thought of leaving England altogether?

Taking the two bags, Neva closes the bedroom door and locks it. She's left some belongings, though there is nothing she is attached to. She knows she will have no need to return here. Then she walks downstairs and out of the house.

Out of habit she looks up and down the street, then under her car, just in case something has been placed there. She is a dangerous enemy and any potential assassin will know this. It wouldn't be wise to get into close combat with her. Once she's satisfied, she climbs into the car and drives away.

After dropping her weapons bag into her retained storage unit, she abandons the car and makes her way to Manchester Airport in a taxi.

By the time she arrives, she has bought a one-way ticket to Geneva and a first night's stay in a hotel there.

Chapter Forty-Four

MICHAEL

Following up on Neva's request, I arrive at the mortuary after hours. I could have waited until tomorrow, but Serge will be on duty and he is always the most helpful diener of all of the mortuary assistants.

I show my identification at reception and then walk down the corridor to the lift. Exiting at the basement, I walk down a corridor which smells of bleach towards the mortuary. The door is locked, with a keypad on the side next to a bell. I press the button and a few seconds later Serge comes out of a side room and hurries towards the door. He sees me and presses the door release button on the other side.

The body is being kept in a private facility run by MI5 and MI6. I have been here many times and I've built relationships with the coroner and his orderlies. Particularly Serge Kostow.

'What brings you over this late?' Serge asks.

'I need to see the toxicology on Damon Sharrick,' I explain.

'Ah! The corpse with the bullets in his head.'

I smirk at Serge's blunt answer. 'Yeah, him.'

'Doctor Wendler didn't do any tests on him,' Serge says.

'Really? I thought that was a matter of course?'

'Normally. But he got word from your office not to bother.'

I'm surprised by this but keep my expression deliberately blank.

'Can I change that? *Discreetly?*'

'Sure. What are you looking for?' Serge says.

'Anything unusual. Doping, hallucinogens, poison, that sort of thing.'

I follow Serge into his office and watch as he fills out the paperwork on a red form.

'This form is used to ensure only the person requesting the information gets the results. That'll be me, and then I'll pass it to you,' Serge explains. 'You want this sent to your office email?'

'No. I'll come and see you when you have the report,' I say.

Serge nods. Serge is used to these requests from agents. Some want to keep information for their own personal reveal at briefings; others have different reasons for secrecy. It's all in a day's work. In my case, I'm not really sure why I want to keep this secret at the moment, but instinct tells me I should.

'I'd like to see the body,' I say.

Serge leads me into the storage room.

'He's in number three,' Serge says. Then he opens the fridge and pulls out the drawer.

There is a sheet over the body. I've never understood why they do this. What's the point? The guy isn't feeling the cold now. But it's a tradition, relating to respect for the corpse, I suppose.

Serge pulls back the sheet. I can see the state of the injuries Sharrick sustained prior to his death. The collarbone is jutting out at a weird angle. There are two neat bullet wounds in his forehead.

'Were the bullets still in?' I ask.

'No.' Serge turns the head of the corpse to show me the exit wounds, wider and messier than the way in. 'The corpse was washed, wearing a fresh, dry-cleaned suit. No blood where he was found, so he died elsewhere.'

I feel the frown on my forehead before I can straighten my face. Why would the killer go to such trouble, and then return Sharrick to his home? It was almost as though they wanted him found. Maybe Neva was right and this is some sort of message to show they are on to her.

Serge pulls back the sheet further. I look at the man's hands. They are chafed, as though he had been gripping something hard to prevent himself from falling. There are signs of old callouses across the palm in the same place.

'What did you make of these?' I ask.

Serge looks at the wound. 'I've seen these types of callouses before. Usually builders have them.'

'He doesn't look like a builder to me,' I say.

Serge nods. 'Doctor Wendler noted them in the report.'

'Thanks, I'll take a copy of the full report and if you can

get a rush job on the tests there'll be a bottle of whisky in it for you.'

'You know me too well,' Serge says.

Once outside I tense up. Hairs prickle at the back of my neck and I feel like someone is watching me. I look around but see no one in the car park and all the parked vehicles appear to be empty.

I order a taxi and wait by the reception door until the driver turns into the car park. Then I get inside and we drive away. Out of instinct I turn to look at the parking area again behind me. At that moment a car starts up and begins to follow. From the back of my cab, I watch the other vehicle. It stays behind us through most of the journey and then, a few streets from my flat, the car turns off and drives away in a different direction. I'm uncertain whether I was being followed or if this was just a coincidence.

I'm just being paranoid.

But the hairs are still standing up on the back of my neck. I feel odd. It's as if I'm in a goldfish bowl being watched by a superior being.

The taxi pulls up outside my flat and I get out. I force myself not to look around as I push open the reception door and enter the building.

I can't shake the feeling that I'm being observed even as I reach my front door.

Once inside my flat I check the surveillance equipment I've installed, looking at the recordings of each room on my laptop. Nothing has happened; all is as expected. But even so, I'm uneasy. Then I realise why.

If it was possible for Neva to access the restaurant and

street cameras, then what could someone with the resources of Archive, or the Network, do? The thought occurs to me that I may well have given my life up to surveillance without realising it.

I disconnect the equipment from my WIFI and switch it all off. If there is any possibility that I'm being monitored, by Neva or anyone else, I won't make it easy for them.

Chapter Forty-Five

MICHAEL

A week later I meet Serge in a sushi bar in Soho. We sit side by side, selecting food from the conveyor that goes around the room. As Serge tucks into his first plate, I open my briefcase and put it down on the floor beside us. Without a word, Serge drops a manila envelope inside. Next, I place a bottle of Jack Daniels down on the counter. It's in a brown paper bag. Serge takes it and puts it into his rucksack. We eat in silence, pay separate bills, and then I leave, taking the briefcase with me.

Back at my flat I open the envelope and look at the toxicology report. All seems normal with one exception; there are traces of LSD in Sharrick's blood. I don't know what to make of it. Or why the report was not done immediately. All it shows me is that Sharrick had taken something prior to his death. Was that willingly, or was he doped? Seeing how well Sharrick had looked after himself, I find it difficult to imagine that he would resort to drug taking, especially something as difficult to control as LSD. I come to the conclusion that he was drugged.

I read the rest of the report. Wendler noted the hand chafing but has made no speculation as to what caused it. That, it seems, is down to me to discover. Maybe Neva can shed some light on this.

I use the burner phone to dial Neva's number, only to discover that the phone has been switched off. I haven't heard from her since the pizza restaurant. I stare at the phone, disappointed. I send a quick text, just in case. But other than this, I now have no way of contacting her and cannot share this news or, more importantly, discuss with her what it all means.

It seems I'm back to square one, out on a limb, and totally alone with anything I learn.

Chapter Forty-Six

MICHAEL

I wake with a nagging feeling in the pit of my stomach. The thought that the toxicology information was being deliberately ignored in relation to Sharrick's death just keeps looping around in my head. I can't recall any other time when a drugs report on a body hasn't been made as a standard part of an investigation.

When I get into work, I look back at the records and see Ray Martin's name signing off on the autopsy. This throws me: why would Ray tell the coroner not to do a complete report?

Beth, Leon, and I have been investigating Sharrick but hadn't run this by Ray because there was no need to. I now look at the records and notice that Ray has accessed the files on Sharrick that I'd put on the system. This means that Ray has been looking at what we were working on. I wonder why. Perhaps Ray always checks on us, as part of his own managerial role? But no. The system doesn't show his name against any of the other files. Ray has only read records in the past where we have asked for his opinion and expertise. He has enough work without looking for more. So why has Ray shown an interest in Sharrick's case, when it hasn't even been discussed with him?

Neva's suspicions come floating back to me. She was certain that there was a leak in Archive. If the Network had known of MI5's interest in him, Sharrick would be seen as a threat or a weakness. It would give them a motive to terminate an operative who had, until then, been very useful. Well, Sharrick was no use to them now, or to Archive. And Neva has cut ties with me, which means no more leads.

It frustrates me that this case, like so many others, will probably fall down around our ears with nothing to show for all the research I've done so far.

'Hey,' says Beth from the door. 'You look glum.'

'Bit gutted about Sharrick,' I say.

'What did your source say?'

'My source is frightened and has stopped contact.'

'That's crap,' Beth says. 'I was hoping we'd pull Sharrick in for an interrogation. This is very disappointing.'

'Tell me about it,' I say.

'I thought he might know about the kids. The missing kids. Call me soft but I'd like to get the bastards behind that,' Beth says.

'Me too,' I say.

'Did your source ever give you anything on that?'

I shake my head. 'No,' I lie, because I can't reveal what Neva's told me about the house and her kidnap without admitting it's her.

Beth frowns a little, then she shrugs. 'I can't help searching for anyone to blame for it. How awful it is for the parents. And I'd like to learn one way or another what happened to those kids.'

'Well, if there was any link to Sharrick, we'll probably never know.' I say. 'Sorry to be so negative.'

Beth turns to go.

'Beth? Did *you* see a tox report for Sharrick? There isn't one on the system.'

'No. Ray said not to bother,' she says.

'Oh?'

'Yeah. He said it wouldn't tell us anything and he'd rather the doctors put their effort elsewhere,' Beth explains.

'Oh. Right.'

I'm full of doubts as Beth walks away. Ray has made a point on this case of changing normal protocol. But the outcome of the toxicology report gave me no leads anyway, so ultimately he was right. It was potentially a waste of time. Unless Neva can shed some light on it and that isn't going to happen anytime soon.

This is ridiculous! Ray isn't corrupt! I shake away any doubts I have about my boss. How can I question Ray on this? Ray brought me into Archive; he promoted me, gave me a purpose. Neva was wrong; Sharrick's death was a coincidence and her disappearance was an overreaction.

No matter what, I just can't believe there is a leak in Archive. But even as I try to convince myself of this, I find myself analysing my colleagues and the way they work. Is there anything off about any of them?

Chapter Forty-Seven

NEVA

The chalet is in the mountains in Saint-Cergue, a resort some six miles from the small village of La Cure. For most of Neva's time here it has been out of season, and therefore secluded. However, the surrounding flats have recently started to fill. For anyone else this would be a lonely experience, but Neva is used to her own company.

As the season starts, she avoids the arriving tourists. Even so, she doesn't truly relax, remembering to train her body daily, as though she expects the onslaught of the Network's silent army of assassins at any time.

Once every few weeks, she drives out to buy food. Sometimes she shops in the Swiss side of La Cure, at other times she passes deeper into France. She doesn't make eye contact with the sales assistants at the stores and doesn't engage in conversation with them above asking for what she needs. She wears various disguises so that her appearance is never the same. She tries to limit the frequency with which she attends any particular shop.

When she has exhausted the area, and begins to feel that the shopkeepers are paying her too much attention, she drives further away for her groceries.

This takes her longer each time.

Two months into this routine, she returns from a whole day driving to and from a shopping mall. Before she enters the chalet, she notes that the hair positioned as usual across the bottom of the door is missing. The hairs stand up on the nape of her neck. She glances around the open-plan living space, trying to assess what is different. The room is large with a sofa and an armchair facing a big television. There's a low coffee table in front of the sofa, and a sideboard below a wide hatch that looks into the kitchen. To the left is a family bathroom that also leads into a fairly big double bedroom. On the right is a door leading to another twin room that Neva doesn't use.

Then she sees the anomaly. The television remote control has been moved from its usual spot. Normally it is on the arm of the chair facing the TV, but now it rests on the sideboard near the kitchen. Neva is meticulous about the placement of her gadgets, though she does briefly consider that she may have moved the device herself and has forgotten. But no. She wouldn't have placed it there. It is almost as though someone has been using the TV while waiting for her arrival.

She walks into the room as though all is normal and places the bag of groceries down on the sideboard. Then she bends down and pulls her knife from a sheath hidden in her boot. Simultaneously, she removes her Glock from the holster strapped under the sideboard.

At that moment, a maid comes out of the family bathroom.

'Sorry…' she says in broken English. 'Late today, miss!'

Nevá hides her weapons inside the grocery bag before the woman sees them. Then she turns away as the maid finishes her final sweep of the room.

She watches the woman move towards the door and follows, intending to run the lock behind her as she leaves. Normally she puts the 'Do not disturb' sign up on the door when she's out. She doesn't like the maids to be in the chalet without her presence and she only allows them in once a week.

I'm lapsing, she thinks. *Getting too comfortable here.* Perhaps it is time to move again.

The maid is holding a bucket full of cleaning products. She opens the door and then with a sharp movement she swings the bucket, almost catching Neva in the face. But Neva falls back, rolling with the potential blow and is up on her feet before the woman is on her.

The maid is holding a syringe – a clear liquid inside it – in one hand and a gun in the other.

Neva steps back around the coffee table in the centre of the room and keeps it between them. Without looking away, the maid closes the chalet door and locks it. Then she moves forward into the room and begins to circle the table.

'I can take you in alive or leave you here dead,' the woman says. Her English is perfect.

Neva studies her. She's in her late thirties, an older class than herself, but still strong and her reflexes are good. She must be confident of her abilities in order to get this close.

Neva curses herself for her stupidity as she moves around the table opposite the woman. They will do this until one of them makes a move. *I did put the 'Do not disturb' sign up on the door,* she thinks. This woman has removed it and tried to catch her off guard. It almost worked too. But at the last moment, Neva saw the slight movement that indicated she was going to use the bucket as an initial weapon. There has never been anything wrong with Neva's reflexes.

Now she takes in the woman's stance and the self-assured way she holds the gun and the syringe.

There is no way she will let herself be taken alive.

Neva leaps over the table, taking the woman by surprise. Hitting the assassin's wrist hard, she knocks the syringe from her grasp. It tumbles to the tiled floor, and skitters across the room, coming to rest by the armchair near the TV.

Neva's full weight throws the woman to the ground even as she brings the gun forward. The assassin fires; the bullet passes Neva's right cheek. She feels the heat from it, but is unharmed.

The world goes into slow motion. Neva pushes at the woman's wrist, but she is strong. They roll on the ground. With her now free left hand, the assassin delivers a blow to Neva's face. Pain shoots through her cheek bone but she responds by elbowing the woman hard in the chest. The assassin is winded but still she comes. Blows are exchanged again. The assassin's nose breaks. Blood splatters over Neva's face.

Then the gun goes off again.

Outside, Neva can hear shouting.

Neva frees the gun from the assassin's fingers and throws it across the room. She grabs the woman's head, smashing it down on the tiled floor, brutally, over and over. She wants her dead. She hears the crack of the skull as time speeds up again.

Someone is hammering on the chalet door.

'*Was ist da drin los*?'

Neva hears the German and automatically translates it to 'What's happening in there?'

She lets go of the assassin when the woman's eyes glaze over. She's dead or brain-damaged. It's all the same to Neva. She stands now, walking calmly to the bathroom where she washes the blood from her hands and face. Then she returns to the living area, takes her weapons from the grocery bag and walks into the kitchen. She opens the back door and exits the chalet just as she hears the front door cave in. It could be security or even some more of the Network's people. She doesn't wait to discover. She hurries between the chalets and flats and heads out via a route she has already planned for such a contingency.

Out in the woods she has buried an escape bag with passports, money, and more weapons. Covering her tracks, Neva makes her way to her hiding place.

Chapter Forty-Eight

VASQUEZ

After receiving the news that his assassin is dead, Vasquez hangs up the phone and looks around the small office in the Methuselah Club.

Neva's escape has left drama and chaos that need to be dealt with. It is a situation that neither he nor the Network will find easy to cover up. Even so, any decisions are not his to make. He needs to pass this up the chain, to a much higher authority.

He pulls up the number for Mr Beech in his phone. Inside this room, conversations are protected. Even so, he hesitates to make the call. Beech will not be happy and, like Sharrick before him, Vasquez fears his wrath.

Vasquez takes a moment to regroup. He experiences a flash of panic – something he's very unused to. Everything has been spiralling out of control since he was told of Sharrick's retirement, and how the man had 'broken' – a term no operative would ever want applied to themselves. Sharrick had been strong for so long; the whole situation appeared to be impossible, unlikely, and somehow wrong. Now, Vasquez is beginning to wonder if there are some issues inside the Network that he should be aware of. It won't be the first time that a lesser agent has made a play for leadership. Is it a coincidence that these minor problems and retirements have occurred since Tracey's death and Neva's defection? Somehow, he doesn't think so.

One thing Vasquez understands: there was very little 'accident' in coincidences. Someone is always behind them. The question is, who?

He looks again at Mr Beech's number. He has to report this. Beech is his direct superior and the chairman of the board at the Network. A seat there is Vasquez's ambition.

If Vasquez fails to tell Beech what's happened, the consequences could be terminal. But Vasquez isn't ready to face up to such a catastrophic failure to capture or kill Neva, because Beech has expressed that he only expects success on this mission. They had, after all, sent one of their most successful operatives after her.

Vasquez takes a deep breath and places his phone down on the desk. He has to compose himself and think how to word his explanation.

Just then, his phone begins to ring. Vasquez jumps and glances down at the flashing screen. Mr Beech's number is lit up.

He can no longer avoid it; the decision has been taken out of his hands. He answers and launches straight into a matter-of-fact explanation. It's all he can think to do.

'Inga is dead. Neva gave our agents the slip.'

Vasquez expects rage but Mr Beech is quiet. It is more

terrifying than when he loses his temper. Vasquez continues to talk to fill the silence.

'We don't know where she's gone, but the trail will still be warm. I have our best people working on it.'

'Then Inga was not as good as she appeared,' Beech says.

'Inga tried to bring Neva in alive, as you wanted. Unfortunately, she was overpowered.'

Vasquez explains what his agents have told him.

'What do you want us to do?' Vasquez asks now.

'I had hoped that the distance put between her and us would have made Neva less cautious,' Mr Beech says. 'Now she will be on full alert. If she's seen, tell your agents not to hesitate. Kill on sight. The time for recovery has passed.'

Beech terminates the call and Vasquez places his phone in his pocket. The conversation has gone better than he expected. He had expected to be blamed, but Beech sounded calm and philosophical about Neva's loss.

Vasquez opens his laptop and sends out a blanket email to all handlers.

NOTIFY ALL AGENTS: NEVA TO BE EXECUTED ON SIGHT.

He then attaches Neva's photograph and all known aliases. He gives as much information as he can without compromising himself or the Network, then he clicks send.

Sending the email is a relief. Neva is now everyone's responsibility. And, because of who and what she is, this is one job they will be vying for. Vasquez lets out a slow breath and sits back. He can almost see the handlers jumping over themselves to notify their operatives that a hunt is on. Now that the gloves are well and truly off, Neva *will* be found.

It is all just a matter of time.

Chapter Forty-Nine

MICHAEL

'Don't turn the light on,' says a voice in the darkness of my living room. 'Close the curtains first.'

After all these months with no contact, I'm shocked to find Neva in my flat. Even so, I follow her directions, closing the curtains before switching on a lamp near the window.

Neva is sitting in the chair by the door near my bedroom.

'I'd given up hope of ever seeing you again,' I say.

'I had to go to ground. I've also been doing my own investigations. I couldn't contact you until I was certain you weren't being monitored.'

The past few months I've been wary. Despite reinforcing my belief that all of my colleagues in Archive are clean, Neva's words reinforce the nagging doubt.

'Am I?' I ask.

'Have you noticed anything odd?'

'If I'm being followed, the tail is good. I haven't seen anything. What can you tell me?'

'The word from my sources is that they are certain you're being watched. They don't know by whom, or why. But that was months ago and now I'm no longer in a position to use those sources anymore.'

'Why?' I ask.

'The Network no longer wants to capture me; they've put a kill order out instead. When I learnt that, I had to sever ties with all my informants, just in case they were playing a double game.'

'Then you've taken a massive risk,' I say. 'Why did you come? Surely if I'm being watched, it's not safe for you.'

Neva sighs. Then she meets my eyes.

'I realised that it's time I took a few risks. I'm trying to find out who kidnapped me as a child and made me what I am. I still need your help and resources. I think you're in a position to find out more than I can right now. I've been watching and I didn't see anyone on you. So perhaps my source way back was wrong. I also searched your flat when I got here. I didn't find anything, other than your own security system which you have wisely disconnected.'

I sit down on the sofa opposite her. 'Maybe it's time to tell me what you remember.'

She sighs again, as though all thoughts of the past create great pain.

'There's a recurring memory. I was in a park,' she says. 'I don't know where.'

Neva's mind slips back to the park.

'I could feel the rush of air as the swing went higher and

higher and then, somehow, my grip loosened and I fell, face first, onto the tarmac. I didn't feel any pain at first. I was stunned by the fall. The *au pair* came running, yelling and frantic. Until then, she had been talking to a man. Giggling. Flirting … I think.

'When the *au pair* lifted me from the floor, the man was there too. "Her face … is she going to be scarred?" he'd asked. "No, it's just a scrape," said the girl. My face began to sting then and I could feel blood trickling down my cheek.

'He told her to take me home and wash it. The *au pair* nodded as though *he* was her boss and not my parents. I remember him telling her to look after me. That I was somehow precious.'

'Did you know the man?' I ask.

Neva nods. 'I think so. He might have worked for my parents too. I thought at the time he was scared they'd both get into trouble because they were paying too much attention to each other and not watching me. So I told my mother that I had let go of the girl's hand and fallen as I ran towards the swings. I didn't want her to lose her job, you see. She was always sweet to me and I liked her.'

'Describe your mother,' I say.

'I can't. All I see is this blank place where her face should be. Her image was taken from me.'

I think for a moment and then prompt her again for information that might help us both.

'What do you remember about the day you were taken?' I ask.

Neva thinks. 'They spent a lot of time and energy trying

to make us forget our past. I can only recall a few details. I was at school. I needed the bathroom and the teacher let me leave the classroom. On the way back ... someone I knew was there. But the face is blank as well. I can't see who it was.'

'Could it have been the *au pair*?'

Neva frowns as she tries to bring the person's face up. Then she shakes her head. 'I just can't remember. I didn't feel unsafe, or afraid. It was someone *familiar*.'

I frown. 'Perhaps it was one of the teachers at the school. That's something I can do. I can look into that, see if there is any connection between the staff present at the time and other missing kids.'

'It *could* have been a teacher, I suppose,' Neva says. 'Whoever it was, they took me outside and there was a black car waiting. I was put in the back and fastened in. Then I was given a carton of juice. I remember it tasted odd, and that was the last thing I recalled.'

Neva explains how she woke to find herself being carried into a huge house.

'Tell me more about the house.'

Neva describes a large, old building. She tells me about the kitchen and the hot chocolate Tracey made for her.

'It was the sort of place you could get lost in. A big rambling estate house. After Tracey gave me the hot chocolate, I was taken into a dormitory. There were three other girls of a similar age to me. The eldest told me we were in a boarding school. I asked why we were there and she told me that she'd been told it was because we were all "special". We'd been chosen. None of it made sense, and I just wanted to go home. I soon learnt that was never going to happen.'

I listen to Neva's description of her first days at the house. It is a shocking tale of fear, and abuse, and treatments that are tantamount to torture.

'Do you remember any other people, other than Tracey?' I ask.

'The doctor. Mendez. We were all so scared of him. When they told me the first time that I was going down the corridor to see a doctor, I wasn't afraid. The few doctors I'd seen before had always been kind, there to help you if you were sick. But Mendez was cold. He spoke with an accent, very subtle, not originally English. He ordered me to sit in a chair and then yanked the sleeve of my cardigan up. He stabbed a needle into my arm without even pretending he wasn't going to hurt me; he just didn't care. We were cattle to him, you see. He had no feelings for us beyond his medical curiosity as he warped our minds. I think now that he actually got off on it.'

I remain quiet as she speaks. I don't offer comfort, or show any signs of sympathy, but inside I'm sickened that a child could be treated so viciously.

'I wasn't allowed to object to his rough treatment; no one was,' Neva continues. 'And tears ... I cried that first time. I was scared and shocked, and Mendez slapped me hard across the face. He said my tears were wasted on him. He was going to make me into someone important, worthy, strong. Someone my parents would be proud of. If I was weak, though, they'd call me a failure and then I would never see my parents again. I never cried again and I learnt to show no emotion. That way it was all over with quicker.'

Her eyes are shining when she finishes speaking. I wonder if this is the first time since then that she has allowed herself to be close to tears. As if she knows what I'm thinking, Neva swipes her hand over her face and pushes away any sign of the water that almost leaks out.

'On my way here, I saw a baby bird in a park. It was on the pathway, chirping for its mother. I looked up at the tree above its head and realised the creature had fallen from its nest. I picked it up and put it back. I don't know why, but I had to.'

'You were feeling empathy for the bird,' I say. 'You've never felt that before?'

'Since I last saw you, I've been picking at the memories. They haven't all come back. There are so many gaps, but something else has come: *emotion*,' Neva explains.

'Understandable. They tried to take all feeling from you. It's obvious, though, that you were stronger than they knew, Neva. You're finding your way back.'

'I've been thinking about you. A lot,' she says.

Neva stands and walks over to me. She kneels. There is a slight tremor in her hand as she touches my face.

'What are you doing?' I say.

'I want to feel. I want to experience something with you, Michael.'

'I can't,' I tell her. 'You're vulnerable right now. I'm not going to take advantage of that.'

'Then I'll have to take advantage of you,' Neva says.

She leans towards me. I try to turn my face away but Neva doesn't let me.

'No,' I say.

She kisses me. I'm a man. She's beautiful and sexy and so mysterious. I stop speaking and respond. There has always been sexual tension between us, but only Neva is willing to acknowledge it.

'We can't,' I say again, pulling away.

'We can.'

I get to my feet in an attempt to change the dynamic and get away from her. Neva sees the tell-tale bulge that shows my protests are a struggle.

I help her stand. We stare at each other for a moment, then I pull her to me. I hold her. She lets me embrace her, wrapping her own arms around me. The hug is awkward, but I'm trying to show her that she's safe. That this is the only touching she should have from me right now.

I step back and look at her again.

'You know I'm attracted to you. Far more than I should be. But this … it will blur the lines between us.'

Neva nods and then as I begin to let go of her, she forces her way back into my arms and kisses me again. I feel a surge of lust as she presses against me. My tentative self-control is slipping. I kiss her back, pushing my tongue into her mouth and then she's pulling me down again to the sofa.

She tugs at my shirt. White buttons fall on the carpet.

'Stop!' I repeat, but my protest is weak.

She kisses me again and my hand cradles her head, pulling her harder to my lips. I'm lost and she knows it.

'Not here,' I say when we break again.

'The bedroom?' She laughs. 'How very traditional!'

She stands, holding out her hand to me, and, unable to resist her any longer, I take it and lead her to my bedroom.

We shed clothing at the foot of the bed. I look over her naked body as she lies down beside me. My hand traces a scar along her thigh, but I don't ask her about it. The truth is, she hasn't been far from my mind since that day in front of the tube station.

As though Neva fears I will pull away again, she climbs on top of me. Her strawberry blonde hair streams down over her breasts and as she leans over me her silky hair falls on my chest.

Her expression changes as I become buried inside her. She works me and I enjoy the play of emotions that crosses her features. I pull her down, taking her lips again and then I flip us both on the bed until she's under me.

Neva closes her eyes as I run my hands over her. I know what she's thinking, as if our minds, as well as our bodies, are joined.

This is pleasure. This is pain. This is what I wanted from the moment we met. I forget everything else. Does it really matter anyway?

Chapter Fifty

NEVA

S he watches him as he sleeps. Something about his face makes her feel ... happy? Sad? She toys with the emotions which are at opposite ends of the spectrum, and yet she wants to experience it all. If she was still working for the Network, this would be the moment she'd pick to kill Michael. She would have to do it, because of what he knows. But the conditioning has broken down, and those urges are gone. Especially the compulsion to protect herself from becoming attached to anyone. Michael has *seen* her now. Neva wonders what her passion face told him about her.

Michael stirs and turns over, facing away.

Neva fights the urge to run. She lies back down. It is comfortable here, but not quiet. Central London never is. Oblivious to the police siren that screeches past, Michael sleeps on.

Neva knows she should slip away now, before daylight,

but she doesn't want to leave. She'd told herself that she would contact him to help her find her enemies and gain her revenge. But, really, *this* was always on the cards. She'd wanted him from the beginning; she just hadn't recognised it for what it was. Because Michael is not a one-night stand. He's not some anonymous male who can help her relieve some frustration.

But she should leave and let him get on with his life without the risk she brings to it, even though she has nowhere else to go.

She ponders sharing this information with Michael, knowing he will most likely suggest bringing her in under MI5 protection. But her sources told her that Archive is not free of corruption. It's unfortunate they weren't more specific. She wishes now she could have been more persuasive, but the informant who told her this had been running scared and no amount of money would secure more than he was willing to reveal.

The leak at Archive, however, will not be easy to find unless she can convince Michael to act as her informant and such behaviour will put him at further risk. Neva isn't sure she wants that.

She closes her eyes and tries to go back to sleep. She's unafraid here, as though Michael's flat is a safe haven. Yet Michael can't be off the radar. There are people in the Network whose job it is to watch MI5 and MI6 agents. Especially a taskforce like Archive, whose job is to find them. As such, it stands to reason that they know all about Michael and his colleagues. Her source told her he was being watched by someone close. Any one of his co-workers could be a double agent. It had to be one of them, for Neva knows Michael has no one else in his life.

Her mind begins to drift. *Just a small nap* and then she will leave before she causes him a problem.

Chapter Fifty-One

MICHAEL

I hear running water. It pulls me up from the comfort of my sleep. I am dreaming about passion, the lover I've always craved crushed in my arms. I open my eyes and look at the slit of light peeking above and around my curtains. On the side of the bed is a travel bag. It's not mine, and for a brief second I wonder why it is there. Then I remember the previous night. *Neva.*

I'm swamped with remorse. How had I let myself be led so easily? I sit up as the shower in the en suite bathroom switches off. There is the gentle rustle as Neva dries herself. My mind sees the towel touch her beautiful and toned bare skin. She is perfection; even the scars tell her story.

She comes out of the bathroom. Her skin is glowing with the blush of heat from the water and the rub of the towel that is now wrapped around her. Her hair is wet. It looks darker, redder, and longer as the water clings to it. She is beautiful. My heart hurts. It's not a feeling I'm used to.

'Sorry if I woke you,' she says.

'You didn't. But I have to go to work anyway,' I say.

'On a Saturday?'

'Oh!' I close my eyes.

I think I must be hungover, but I didn't drink the previous night. There was no time. We'd had sex and I couldn't even blame alcohol for my lack of control. I remember now that yesterday was Friday, and as a rule I don't work weekends unless a case comes up. As if the thought of a work emergency instigates it, my mobile rings. I find it at the side of the bed. At least last night – *after* – I'd had the presence of mind to put it on charge.

Beth's number flashes up on the screen.

'I have to take this,' I say to Neva.

I get up, take the phone, and grab my robe from the back of the bedroom door. Then I go into the kitchen. I answer the phone as I put the kettle on.

Neva stays in the bedroom.

'Hey, Mike,' says Beth. 'I'm flying to Switzerland. Just wanted you to be in the loop.'

'Why are you going there?'

'Ray was contacted by Interpol. Suspicious death in a resort not far from the Swiss border. The victim has been identified as a British resident.'

'That's not usually our problem,' I say, keeping my voice low. I stick my head out of the kitchen and glance across the living room to the bedroom door: it remains shut.

'True. But we think this is linked to the Network.'

I reach for the tea canister.

'Ray thinks they cornered the assassin we were looking for,' Beth continues.

I stop making tea and start paying more attention.

'Really? You think the assassin killed this person too?'

'No … the assassin *is* the victim. Killed by someone else. It's all very confused which is why I'm heading over there.'

'Okay. So how long do they think you'll be there?' I ask.

'A few days at least. I'm sure you'll hear about it all from Ray on Monday. I'll send you a photo of the dead woman. Then you can let us know if it's the one you saw.'

'Sure,' I say.

Beth hangs up and I continue to make tea. *Does Neva even drink it?* I make two anyway. Placing the two cups, some sugar, a spoon and a carton of milk on a tray, I take it through the living room to the bedroom. When I enter, Neva is dressed in black jeans, a black sweater and a short black wig.

'Going somewhere?' I say.

'I can't stay here. It's not safe for either of us if I do.'

'Right now, it's probably the safest place to be. You were in a resort near Switzerland all this time, I take it?' I say, getting right to the point.

'How do you know?'

'Dead body. Want to tell me about it?'

Neva looks at me. She sits down on the bed. I notice that she's made it.

She sighs. 'I think that's unnecessary, don't you?'

'They came after you and you killed.' I put the tray down on the chest of drawers by the window. 'Tea?'

Neva smiles. 'Okay.'

The moment is surreal.

'The thing is, I was careful, yet they still found me,' she explains.

'It can't be easy to live in a constant state of red alert,' I say. 'Maybe you did let your guard down. Or maybe you were spotted by someone who was on the lookout for you by pure coincidence. Either way it doesn't matter.'

'I have to stay below the radar but it'll be harder now.'

'Sugar?'

Neva shakes her head. 'A little milk though.'

I pour some milk in the tea, stir it, and hand her the mug. Neva sips. The tea is boiling hot and the heat seems to warm and soothe her. Despite her words, she makes no move to leave.

'Let me help you,' I say, aware that I'm always offering my help, though she rarely takes it.

'I don't know how you can. I need to get to the top and take them all down. Expose them. Kill them. It doesn't matter. The Network has to crumble before I can live a normal life. How I'm going to do that without learning who's behind it all, I just don't know.'

'Is that what you really want?'

'What do you mean?'

'Well, I'm not sure how you can ever live a "normal life",' I say. 'You killed the assassin who came after you, right?'

Neva nods. 'Of course. They wanted to bring me in. The alternative to agreeing was death. I had no choice.'

'I agree, but the thing is, you're always going to be a killer. How do you switch that off?'

'If I'm not forced to defend myself, I don't need to kill. I don't take a life for pleasure...'

'I already know that,' I say.

'You can't help me,' she says. 'I don't know why I'm here. I know that someone close is watching you. You're more of a risk to me than anything else.'

'Someone close? But you don't know who?' I ask.

She takes a big gulp of the tea, then she lies back on the bed. Relaxed. 'I'm so tired.'

I nod. 'I understand. You've been hiding. It's all too hard for you. No one should live like this.'

I pour a little milk in my drink and stir.

'No ... I mean, I'm really ... the tea ... *don't...*'

The mug falls from her hand and spills on the carpet beside the bed. I look at my own mug and then place it back on the tray.

'*Neva?*' I say, concerned.

I lean over her. Check her pulse. Lift one closed eyelid. Then I glance down at the fallen mug. The drink was drugged! *What the hell is going on?*

I hurry to the front door of the flat and ensure the security bolts are all in place. Then I check the windows and look out across the cityscape. I examine the building opposite for signs that I'm being observed. I see nothing irregular.

When was the last time I drank this tea? Last weekend. During the week I buy coffee on my way to work.

In the kitchen, I sniff at the canister. The tea smells ordinary, musty. Then I return to the milk and smell it. I'm not sure but I think the milk has an atypical odour. I know it isn't the sugar, so it *has* to be the milk. The person who did this must have known that Neva doesn't take sugar, but always takes milk. Then a terrible thought occurs to me: *no one knows Neva is here.*

The drug was meant for me!

I take a tea towel from the top drawer in the kitchen and collect a canister of carpet cleaning solution from under the sink. Then I return to Neva. I check her over again. She is sleeping soundly. Drugged but apparently not harmed.

I clean up the spilt tea. Afterwards, I leave Neva on the bed, close the bedroom door and then sit down on my sofa in the living room.

Someone has been in my flat. Neva said that someone close was watching me. But who? And why did they attempt to drug me?

I begin to search the flat. Neva said she had combed it, but I have to make sure she's right. I know what to look for, though I'm sure I'd have noticed if my home was bugged. I look for an hour, taking out light bulbs, taking apart the phone by the front door, but I come up with nothing. Whoever has drugged my milk is being careful to make sure to leave nothing an experienced MI5 agent would notice. Maybe the plan is to come in as I sleep? I pause, wondering how they would know if I've drunk the tea or milk.

I check the front door again. All the locks are in place. I can't imagine how they'd get inside, short of using something to smash the door in, and then one of my neighbours would hear and raise the alarm.

When I finish sweeping my home, I find Neva standing

by the bedroom door. She looks awake, but I soon realise she is walking in her sleep.

I lead her back to the bed.

'Rest,' I say. 'You're safe here. I'll get to the bottom of this.'

'Yes, Doctor Mendez,' she says.

I encourage her to lie down. She doesn't object; she is pliable. Once again, I wonder what was in this milk.

'Sleep,' I say.

She closes her eyes again.

I search the bedroom for bugs or cameras. There's nothing to find. After searching the en suite bathroom, I remember that I haven't had a chance to shower or dress yet. While Neva sleeps, I go into the bathroom, brush my teeth, and shower.

When I'm dressed, I return to the bedroom, pull up a chair, and sit by the bed, watching over her. I don't know if we are safe. I only know I couldn't find any bugs or cameras, so for now I assume that no one knows she's here. And as for whoever drugged my milk, I have no idea what they intended.

Chapter Fifty-Two

MICHAEL

She wakes a few hours later, going from unconscious to wide awake with no interim grogginess.

'Hello,' she says, smiling at me as if nothing has happened.

It's late afternoon. I have only left her side to fetch a glass of water.

'Are you hungry?' I ask, then regret it, wondering what other items of food or drink in the kitchen may have been tampered with.

'Yes,' she answers. 'I feel like I haven't eaten for days!'

I order Thai food on an app on my phone, reasoning that whoever did this wouldn't have access to a random restaurant I might find on an app. I put the flat opposite mine as the delivery address as a precaution. I know this neighbour, a little old lady who goes to Australia for three months every year to see her daughter. She's away at the moment and I have a key to go in and water her plants. 'It'll be delivered in an hour.'

I go into the kitchen and open a bottle of wine. The bottle is a screw top and is sealed, though I'm still nervous that it might have been tampered with. I pour a little into a glass and sniff it. Then I sip a little and wait for that lethargy I'd seen affect Neva. I don't feel anything and consider the wine to be safe. I take it into the living room. Neva is sitting on the sofa. I hold out a glass to her.

'Why do I feel like I've lost time?' she frowns.

'I gave you tea this morning,' I prompt.

She takes the wine glass and sips it.

'Oh yes, I remember ... then. Oh my God! You *drugged* me!'

Before I can move, Neva has put the wine down, and has a blade at my throat. I remain stock still.

'I didn't drug you; it was intended for me,' I say. 'In the milk.'

Neva studies me for a few seconds and then pulls the knife away.

'You drank the tea first, but I think I was the target,' I say again, then nod towards the wine glass. 'That's fine.'

'I don't understand. Why would someone want to drug you? What would they gain?'

'I don't know. But I'm beginning to think it's not the first time it's happened. It's like someone knows my habits. I don't drink tea most days, and I always have milk with it. Unlike coffee, which I take black.'

I see panic in Neva's eyes for the first time. I guess she is debating leaving and staying clear of me in future, but something tells me last night meant more to her than casual sex. Maybe that's wishful thinking on my part, as I am far more invested in getting to know her than I should be.

'Do you remember when I told you about Sharrick and you asked me to check his toxicology report?'

Neva nods.

'There was LSD in his bloodstream. When he died, he was most likely taking the trip of his life.'

'Can I see the report? And the autopsy?' she asks.

I open my briefcase and pass it to her.

'You've been keeping it in there all this time?' she says.

'I hoped we'd meet again. So I could show you.'

She opens the folder and reads the report and looks at the pictures of Sharrick's dead body.

'Execution for certain, but why dope him first?' I ask.

'He was being tested. They sometimes used hallucinogens to make us drop our guard. They gave him the LSD so they could question him while he was tripping. He'd be incapable of lying to them in that state. Whatever he said convinced them that he was broken. Hence the bullets in the head.'

'Broken?'

'Yes. Like me. I'm broken. Or at least, I've ripped through the barriers of their conditioning. If they'd taken me back in, they might have been able to brainwash me again, but I doubt it. I'm too far away from it all now.'

'Neva, when you were drugged this morning, you walked in your sleep. You called me Doctor Mendez.'

'If I did that, then the stuff that was put in your tea—'

'Milk,' I say.

'Milk then. It was something similar to what they gave

us. As children. To condition us. Which can only mean one thing.'

I frown as I wait for her to continue.

'The Network is watching you, and they are planning to … turn you maybe? Make you one of theirs.'

'That's ridiculous!' I say.

'I've never heard of this before, to be fair. They usually work on children as they are more susceptible. It's odd that they are targeting you this way. Perhaps they know we've been in contact and they want to learn what you know.'

'But how could they? No one knows about our contact.' I say.

'Someone does, Michael. Who did you share this with?'

'No one. I swear. Even my colleagues at Archive don't know you were my source. They just knew we met once. At the train station.'

'Maybe that was enough for your rogue agent to make an assumption that you were dealing with me,' she says.

'I've never deviated from protocol so that's a bit of a leap,' I say. I know I'm being defensive.

There are only three other colleagues with the same access as me, all of whom I have trusted with my life before today. But because my milk was tampered with and the nature of the drug that was put in it, I am now in a great deal of doubt. Is Neva right? Could one of them really be working with the Network? If so, who? And what do they hope to gain by drugging me?

As if she knows what I'm thinking Neva touches my arm. 'It might be that they wanted you to reveal who your source was.'

'That's the most likely,' I say. 'But how would they know if and when I drank the milk?'

Neva shakes her head. 'I don't know. That's the biggest mystery here. But your place has been compromised. We need to get out of here.'

'I've been thinking about that. I had all day while you slept. If they're watching me, leaving will alert them that I'm onto them. Even so, I'm concerned that they may realise you're here with me. I checked the flat and I couldn't find any surveillance, but that doesn't mean there isn't any,' I say.

'What do you propose?'

I don't speak. But I open the front door and point to the flat across the hall and show her the key, which was in the cutlery drawer in my kitchen.

Then, I say loudly, as a precaution, 'We sit tight and see what happens.'

Chapter Fifty-Three

MICHAEL

Mrs Kendal's flat is the reverse of mine, and other than the furniture, it feels like I'm in the mirror image of my own. A knock at the door signifies the arrival of the Thai food. I nod towards Mrs Kendal's bedroom door, and Neva takes my cue to go in there. I open the door to a spotty kid who works the delivery slot to earn his way through university. I'm pleasant to him as I take the food. He shows no curiosity, and doesn't even attempt to glance into the flat as I place a tip in his hand. After he's gone, I close and bar the door again. Neva comes out of the bedroom and she fetches plates and cutlery from the kitchen.

After the strange enforced fast created by the events of the day, we are both hungry. We eat in silence. The food is delicious and I try to clear my mind as I chew, sipping the wine in between bites. But the awful thing is, I can't really switch off. I'm still processing what's happened, both with Neva and with the drugged milk.

After dinner, I go back into my own flat. Neva helps me carry Mrs Kendal's crockery, which we load into my dishwasher. Then we begin to empty my cupboard and fridge of any foods that could have been tampered with. I'm left with a few cans of soup, a can of plum tomatoes, a can of baked beans and some eggs, as I reason that any piercing of the eggs would become evident as the eggs would leak in their box. But at the last minute, I throw away the eggs as well. I'm just not sure enough that they haven't been touched.

With a full bin bag, I go out of the flat and throw it down the garbage chute.

When I return, Neva is replacing the black bag in the kitchen bin. She looks at me with complete understanding.

I feel invaded. My home no longer feels like the safe haven it once was, but I'm not sure what to do about that. I take a few personal items and we go back to Mrs Kendal's flat, but not before I pretend to go through my regular evening routine, ending with turning the light off in my bedroom as though I'm going to sleep.

In Mrs Kendal's standard double bed, we are a little cramped. Despite the previous evening, we don't touch. It doesn't seem appropriate in the old woman's room.

The next day, I go out and get some proper provisions, replacing the eggs and other perishables while Neva stays back at Mrs Kendal's flat. When I return, briefly, to my own place to collect her crockery from the dishwasher, I see the carton of contaminated milk still in there.

'I could get this analysed,' I say to Neva, bringing it back with me.

'But how do you know you can trust anyone in MI5's lab?' Neva asks.

I don't answer but I know she's right. If I take the milk in, then whoever is responsible may learn that I found it. I can't risk showing my hand. Not yet. I must remain beyond suspicion until I find out what I need to know.

Neva helps me unpack the groceries. We put them away in companionable silence, and then I make us a sandwich.

She's making no attempt to leave, which I'm pleased about. Her presence makes this easier somehow, but I'm concerned about what's happened and her safety. We need to find out who's behind the drugged milk.

'We need to explore ways in which you can observe your colleagues,' Neva says, as though she's reading my thoughts, 'without them realising.'

We discuss this, though I don't talk about who those colleagues are, and she doesn't ask.

'Are any of them acting out of character?' she asks.

I think about it and can't come up with a definite answer. The autopsy report on Sharrick, the lack of toxicology, is the only thing I can pinpoint as strange. And that was all down to Ray. It doesn't make sense that he would be behind this.

After supper we go to bed. We still don't touch each other; we merely sleep. It's been a very strange weekend.

Chapter Fifty-Four

MICHAEL

When Monday arrives, my paranoia is heightened. I dress and behave just as I do every work day, but all the time I'm struggling with the change in my feelings about Archive. Part of me wants to just go into the office and tell Ray what happened, get him on side, but I still have a nagging doubt about him. Despite the fact that I had previously excused his behaviour to myself, I now re-examine it, because it was out of character. It's difficult to acknowledge that he, or any of the team, could be playing double sides. But after what's happened, I can't take any chances.

'You'll be here when I get back?' I ask Neva. She's lounging in bed, watching me dress. She looks incredibly sexy and I'm almost tempted to get back in with her.

'As long as no one sees me, I should be safe here. Your neighbour isn't likely to come back early, is she?'

'No. She's away for at least another month,' I say.

'I'll keep my eye on your place. If someone comes in and tries to spike your milk again, I'll have to deal with them.'

'I know.' I don't tell her that it's a relief to think she will be there making sure that doesn't happen. 'Try not to kill them; they may be able to tell us something.'

On impulse, I lean over and kiss her. She kisses me back and when I pull away, she is reluctant to let me go.

'I'll be back about six,' I say.

At Archive, I work alone in my office. Beth is in Switzerland and Ray and Leon are huddled together working on another case. I'm relieved that they're all busy; it gives me the opportunity to study their activity unobserved. I think back over the years and try to identify any time when Ray, Leon, or Beth haven't been a hundred percent straight with me. I can't remember any such occasion.

With Beth's office unmanned, I go in and do a quick search of her desk. The drawers are unexpectedly messy, with stationary stuffed in randomly. I'm surprised by this as I've always found Beth to be well organised. Without finding anything of interest, I close the drawers and return to my office. I don't know what I expected to learn anyway.

A few moments later, Ray emails me and asks me to come to his office. I head down the corridor to see him. Having snooped in Beth's office – but also because I'm keeping Neva a secret from everyone – I'm feeling a little guilty. I take a breath before I open Ray's door.

'Hey, Mike,' he says as I enter.

He's sitting at his desk with a brown folder in front of him. I find myself examining his friendly, open expression, and analysing his tone. Is it ever so slightly forced? Does he know I'm hiding something major from him?

'Take a seat,' he says. 'I'd like to give you a new case. The missing kids.'

'Beth was working on that,' I say.

Ray nods. 'She's going to be away for a few more days. I'd like you to look at this.'

Ray pushes the folder at me. I open it and immediately feel confused. I see photographs of all the missing children, and a cohesive dossier on each of them.

'But this is Beth's case,' I repeat. 'I'm sure she'll pick it up again when she gets back. She's been very invested in it.'

'I know. And that's the problem, Mike. Beth is too close to this one. I've taken it back. I want you to deal with it from now on. Plus, I'd like to see some actual progress on this too. We're getting pressure from above since you and Beth saw Simone Arquette. And Beth doesn't seem to be going anywhere with it.'

I take the folder back to my office and flick through it. I then remember the line of enquiry I'd passed on to Beth – my suspicion of a teacher or other employee involvement at the schools. There is nothing in the file to suggest she followed it up. In fact, the dossier has no additional notes from Beth at all.

I look on the shared drive and try to find Beth's transcripts. *Surely, she has a document showing her progress so far?* But I can't find anything despite checking several directories. The only explanation for this is that she didn't save her work to the shared drive. Sometimes I don't either, so this is not uncommon. I plan to ask her for it all when she returns, but in the back of my mind I'm beginning to wonder if she deliberately sat on this and did nothing. There would be only one reason she would do that, and that would be if she was involved somehow in the Network.

My mind runs away with the idea of her working for the enemy. I can't imagine it. She was so passionate about finding out what had become of the missing children. Even so, this lack of activity is strange. I only hope I'm wrong, and that she's been doing something that I just can't access right now.

Well, no matter what, I decide to follow the line of enquiry I'd previously suggested to Beth. Putting aside what I'd been working on, I pick up the phone and ring one of the schools in question. I decide to look up the Janice Brayford Preparatory School. This one is nearby and it's the one that Amelie Arquette went missing from – the same child I believe that Neva once was, but I haven't built up to broaching that question with her yet. Though maybe I will soon. In the meantime, I'll try and give Ray something we can feed back to Amelie's family. That at least would take the pressure off Archive and will allow me, with Neva's help, to look into this in more detail.

Chapter Fifty-Five

MICHAEL

The headteacher was very helpful on the phone and agreed to let me come to the school that afternoon. Now I wait in the small office occupied by her secretary, but I'm not there long before the imposing woman opens the door to her office and invites me in.

'Sorry to have kept you,' she says.

I show her my ID and give her one of my formal business cards. 'I appreciate you seeing me at such short notice.'

She offers me a seat and coffee; I decline the drink, and sit down in a small area of the office where two sofas face each other with a coffee table in between.

I study Mrs Denton. She is in her late forties, with brunette hair that's going grey. She has a faded look about her. Doesn't wear make-up, though plenty of women her age still do; it's almost as though she doesn't want to be noticed as a woman, but recognised as a powerful figure ruling her school with a rod of iron.

'So, how can I help you?' she says after a few moments of awkward silence. 'You said this was important.'

'It is. I want access to your employment records,' I say.

'If I might ask why?' she says.

'I'm looking at who worked here at the same time that Amelie Arquette attended, and if they remember the day she disappeared.'

Denton's face pales. I keep my expression blank but I watch her for any sign, any *tell*, that will show me she knows more about this than she should.

'My entire career has been at this school,' she says. 'I was Amelie's teacher at the time. But you probably already know that. I've struggled with this so much since. I shouldn't have let her go to the toilet unattended but my classroom assistant had taken another child to the sick bay. I was alone with the class and couldn't leave them.'

'Children go to the bathroom alone all the time,' I point out. 'You couldn't have known.'

'Yes. That was true. *Then*. The school has a policy now of escorting to and from during class times. I initiated it myself when I took over as head five years ago.'

'Well, you obviously have an alibi, Mrs Denton,' I say. 'But what of other members of staff?'

She tells me about the rigorous investigation made by the local police, how all the teaching staff were interviewed.

'Because Amelie was a diplomat's daughter, the investigation was taken very seriously,' she says. 'I take it they never found her?'

'No,' I say. 'But we've reopened the case recently.'

She doesn't ask me why, which I am expecting. Instead

she looks thoughtful. 'But surely you have the police records of who worked here at the time?' she says. 'And their interview transcripts.'

'I do.'

'So then what more can I give you?'

'I believe Amelie went willingly with her kidnapper; she knew them,' I reveal to see her reaction.

She looks startled. 'You don't really think one of the teaching staff was behind this?'

Instead of answering her question, I ask her about security at the time. The doors were locked when I arrived today, and my identification was studied before I was allowed in. But could a stranger just enter the school in any other way?

'Security wasn't as it is now,' she admits. 'Reception doors were unlocked. Parents often walked in and went to their child's classroom to collect them. Now they aren't allowed to do that. The world has changed. *This* changed our school!'

I leave her office with a promise that her secretary will send over a list of former employees. I want to see if any of them *aren't* mentioned in the police report. I have a feeling about this case, and although I'm not suspicious of Denton, I think she may still know more than she realises.

As I walk through the reception, I see a pile of prospectuses left on a table for potential students. I take one, for future reference.

When I return to my office, I pull the prospectus out of my briefcase and flick through it. There is a section inside about the history of the school: a four-page spread telling the story of how Janice Brayford founded it in the 1950s. Brayford was still alive, and almost ninety when Amelie Arquette went missing, but by then someone else had taken over the running of the school.

I look back at the folder Ray gave me earlier and see that Jacqueline Brayford-Bell was the headmistress from 1995. It isn't much of a surprise to learn that Jacqueline is Janice's only daughter.

Denton had said she took over five years ago, so I assume that this was when Jacqueline retired. I try to work out what age Jacqueline was by then, but can't because I don't know what age Janice had been when she had her daughter. It is certainly research for later if I think it will help, but for now I'm merely curious.

I put the prospectus down, then, looking once more through the file, I make a list of who I need to contact.

I spend the rest of the afternoon ringing a few of the other schools. It's difficult to get to speak to the heads for most of them, and so I arrange a few telephone appointments for the next day. Then, at 5pm, I put the prospectus, and the folder, in my briefcase and shut down my computer.

Tonight, I have every intention of speaking to Neva about her past.

Chapter Fifty-Six

MICHAEL

When I return home, I go into my flat as usual. I turn on lamps and close curtains as though I'm home. Then I go across to Mrs Kendal's.

Neva is in the kitchen. There are two pans boiling on the hob. She holds out a glass of red wine to me, then she returns to stirring something she's cooking in one of the pans.

'I hope you like spaghetti bolognese,' she says.

I'm a little shocked by this display of domesticity; it isn't something I've ever considered that she does.

'I like cooking,' she says. She looks at me and her eyes dip shyly. 'Remember, I was taught to fit in. Cooking is a useful skill.'

It's very odd for me to have anyone cook for me. There's been no one in my life since Kirstie, and that hadn't turned out so well in the end. I feel more than a little uncomfortable with it, but I force myself to stand and watch her while I sip my wine.

'Can I help?' I say after a few seconds.

'This is weird, isn't it?' she says.

'Yes. Very.'

She stops stirring the wooden spoon around the pan and reaches for her own glass of wine.

'Yeah. For me too. I usually do this alone,' she says.

We are very similar. And very different. Both of us live in a less-than-normal world. Mine at least pretends to be normal, but since she's alone all the time other than when she is on an assignment, I wonder how Neva's universe can come anywhere close. And yet she does this so well. She looks so natural. Is this a performance or am I seeing the real her?

'Sieve?' she says.

'Huh?'

'To strain the spaghetti.'

I search through Mrs Kendal's cupboards until I find what she's looking for. Then I hold out the sieve. She takes it, places it in the sink, and then she takes the second pan off the hob and tips the contents into it. She shakes it, straining away the water. Then she returns the pasta to the pan. From the fridge she cuts a piece of butter from a bar and swirls it around the spaghetti, returning the pan briefly to the hob until it all melts.

'Plates?' she says.

I get the plates and she serves up her creation.

We sit at the breakfast bar. We eat. We sip wine. The bolognese sauce is delicious. I try not to stare at her, or make a big deal of the fact that she's cooked for us. It doesn't mean anything, other than a practical need being filled. But she looks so at home here it makes me feel relaxed as well. I wonder about this, how she can just be so calm, and then I realise it is all a facade. Something she does to hide her real emotions.

She's natural today. No wig, just that luscious hair and a little make-up. It makes her appear very young and sweet. The perfect girl next door.

'I take it you had no issues today?' I say.

'No one came to your place. So no one got killed,' she says.

I laugh. It is an amusing thought that someone might sneak into my home and Neva would dispatch them. I play out the scenario in my mind as though I'm watching a movie. I see Neva karate chop the intruder. I chuckle a little at the thought.

Neva gives me a look and frowns a little, even as she takes a bite of food. I don't explain how far the small joke went inside my head.

After dinner, when the dishwasher is full, we go back into the living room with our newly replenished glasses.

On Mrs Kendal's coffee table is the autopsy report for Sharrick.

'Did you look at this again?' I ask.

'Yes, and I think I know where he disappeared to.'

I look at her and wait.

'They took him to the house. I'd say that's where he died,' she says.

'How do you know?'

'The chafing on his hands. Sharrick went up on the

trapeze. He'd probably not used it for years, but the old scarring confirms he once did,' Neva says.

'Trapeze? I don't understand.'

Then Neva explains about the rigorous training that all operatives go through.

'If an escape calls for it, I could launch myself from one rooftop to another with a lot of confidence that I'll reach the other side,' she tells me.

'It explains what he fell from,' I say.

Neva nods. She's quiet, as though she's imagining Sharrick on the trapeze, seeing him fall.

'I wish I could find this place. We'd have a whole load of answers in one go,' I say.

Neva curls up on the sofa and I open my briefcase and return the report to its former place. Then I pull out the prospectus for Janice Brayford's prep school.

'What's that?' she asks.

I hold it out to her, watching her expression as she takes it.

'Do you recognise this place?' I ask.

She shakes her head.

'Look inside; maybe something will spark a memory.'

Neva opens the booklet. She studies the opening pages, examines the pictures of small children in uniform, and then she opens the page to the history section. She's relaxed as she reads and then she turns the page again and is faced with the photograph of a young Janice Brayford. It's an old black and white taken in front of an imposing building.

Neva sits upright.

'Look!'

I join her on the sofa and she points to the photograph and the building behind Janice. All we can see are steps, going up to a grand double doorway.

'I recognise this place,' she says.

On the opposite page is a more modern photograph of the woman. I identify it as the head teacher's office at the school, even though the décor has changed since this photograph.

'Oh my God,' says Neva. 'The house.'

'What?' I look at the picture. Janice was probably in her eighties at this point. 'What am I looking at?'

'Behind her.'

Above Janice's head is an old black and white picture taken at a distance of a sprawling mansion. At the front is a row of steps leading up to the big double front doors. The same steps that Janice looks very comfortable in front of in her youth.

'This is *the* house. The one where they took me.'

'Are you sure?' I ask.

'I spent twelve years of my life there,' she says. 'I'm positive.'

I take the prospectus and read the story of Janice Brayford's life once more, this time looking for information on the house. The only credit given to the black and white picture of her is 'Janice as a trainee teacher in her early twenties'.

I think we've just had a breakthrough, but I don't say anything.

The rest of the evening, Neva is quiet. She wades

through the prospectus but whatever she gleans from it she doesn't share.

I tell her about my visit to the school that day. She listens, but says nothing. Eventually I ask her outright if she recognises the place.

'No,' she says. 'It doesn't fit in with the memory I have of my school,' she says. 'It seemed much smaller somehow.'

I don't press her on it. She's probably shocked that she has found some link to the house. Or perhaps seeing the building again is causing her some massive stress. It's hard to tell because she shuts herself down as a defence mechanism.

'Now we have a photograph, it should be easier to find this house,' I tell her.

She gazes into my eyes, her own quizzical and glinting in the candlelight.

Then she stands, takes my hand, and leads me to the bedroom without a word.

I let her. The time for coyness is gone.

Chapter Fifty-Seven

MICHAEL

The next day, I return to the Janice Brayford Prep School unannounced. I ask to see Denton, but I'm told she's called in sick.

'I need to see her office,' I say.

The secretary is reluctant to take me in there without the head's permission, but I threaten to get a warrant and the girl is so intimidated that she unlocks the door.

Inside the room, I look at the pictures on the walls. Janice Brayford's photo isn't there, and neither is the picture Neva and I had seen behind the woman in the colour photograph. Now, in its place, is a simple landscape print.

'Where did that picture go?' I ask the secretary. When she looks at me blankly, I describe it to her. 'It's there in your prospectus.'

I go and fetch one from the pile in the reception and show the girl the photograph.

'I don't know,' she says. 'It wasn't there when I started here. It's always been the landscape.'

I ask for Denton's mobile number but the secretary refuses to give it. 'I can't!' she says. 'I'll lose my job. That's data protection!'

'Then ring her and put me on the phone to her.'

I follow the girl back to her office where she pulls out Denton's mobile number and, hiding it from me, dials the number on the landline telephone on her desk.

After a few rings it goes to voicemail. She leaves a message for her to call me, reading out my mobile number from the card I hold out to her.

After that I leave the school and return to the office, but on the way, I buy two new phone handsets and sim cards for cash. One that I'll give to Neva later and one that I'll keep for myself just to communicate with her.

When I get into the office, I find Ray and Leon are absent. Like me, they will be out doing their own investigations for whatever cases they are working on.

In my inbox I find an email from Beth. She asks about the child disappearance case. I don't know what to answer. Ray has given it to me now, but he didn't ban me from discussing it with her. I reply with a noncommittal response about catching up with her when she's back.

Using this time alone, I go into Leon's office. I'm not expecting to find anything in there, but I search his desk drawers and look inside his office diary. Nothing jumps out at me as being out of the ordinary.

Getting into Ray's office will be a different matter however. He always locks the door when none of us are in the office. Even so, I go down the corridor and try the handle. As predicted, it doesn't budge, so I walk on past towards the coffee machine to give me an excuse for being down here.

I bring back a drink to my office, open my briefcase, and take out the prospectus again. The picture stands out to me so much as an odd one for the old woman to have in her office. I look up Janice Brayford and discover she was ninety-one when she died. I search the name Jacqueline Brayford-Bell and other than finding a few photographs of her on her retirement, there is little to go on. I'll have to get permission to search DVLA to see if the woman still holds a driving licence. New data protection laws mean that all of these searches need justifying, even for MI5.

Later, I scan the image of the house in the prospectus and set up an online image search to see if the house can be recognised by our systems. There are always a lot of avenues to go down.

Chapter Fifty-Eight

NEVA

After Michael leaves for work, Neva showers and dresses, and puts on a shoulder-length black wig.

She smiles when she sees the two empty wine glasses in the living room as she briefly remembers the sex from the night before

She can't stay here all day today, despite her promise to guard Michael's place from further invasion; she has a source to meet and her own investigations to continue. The picture of the house has haunted her thoughts. Memories merge with horrible scenes that form part of bizarre, disjointed fragments of her dreams. Now she's awake, she tries to make sense of it all. A signpost saying 'Manchester 17 miles' is one thing she recalls, but she doesn't remember ever going there until her recent stay – not even for an assignment.

She realises now that this memory was always there. It's why she subliminally chose Manchester as the place for her bolthole with Daz and Marie.

Out of habit, she takes all of her belongings in the rucksack she brought with her and tucks a small pistol into a holster at the small of her back. She pulls a loose jacket over the ensemble. She looks like a rock-chick or goth, especially when she pulls on a sleeve that makes her arm look as though it has a large Celtic cross tattooed on it. In truth she has no tattoos, and no piercings – not even in her ears.

She takes the rucksack and exits the flat, taking with her Michael's spare keys.

Outside, she heads to the tube station, avoiding any cameras along the way.

Her source works at the Royal Botanic Gardens in Kew, managing the Orchid display.

It's still early and the gardens are otherwise quiet. Neva walks over, holding a map, and the woman gives her a slightly impatient sideways glance that suggests she's already sick of being asked directions.

Her name is Sophia Birling. She's worked at the gardens for years, but she's also a hacker with a sideline in selling information she's gleaned about huge corporations. She's not smart enough to know what she's actually stealing though, and this is why Neva has decided not only to converse with her online but also to meet Sophia in person. Neva's interest in the woman was piqued when she casually mentioned she'd come across financial records for a company that has so far been off the radar. What alerted

Neva to this was the mention of the company's CEO: Mr M. A. Beech.

Lily Devlin had said the order for her death had come from Mr Beech. Neva hadn't really digested the name – not until the information came up for sale in Onionland – and then she'd remembered the conversation. *Mr Beech. He'll give the order for you too.*

Neva doesn't think too deeply about why she hadn't thought of the name since Devlin's death. Key words and phrases often become obscure to her. It is, she thinks, a side-effect of the conditioning. Though she remembers more now than she ever did, Beech's name had been taboo. She had forgotten it the instant she heard it. But not now. Now it's beginning to make sense to her. And Beech himself is a figure somewhere in her past, though she's yet to find that memory.

'Act as though you're giving me directions,' Neva says.

Sophia's face registers a moment of shock and then she starts to gesture after the woman with the buggy, and then to another part of the gardens.

'Good,' says Neva. 'Where's the document?'

Sophia looks around. Neva casts a glance too but she's more circumspect than Sophia, whose lack of sophistication is obvious. How did this ridiculous woman come across this information?

Sophia takes a folder in a plastic wallet out from under her blouse. She passes it to Neva.

'What about my money?' Sophia says.

Neva looks at Sophia for a long moment. She's taken a big risk meeting her, but she wouldn't let her have the information remotely. Really, she should kill her for even getting this close. She weighs it up. If this was a Network job, she would have to silence the girl. But no, those days are over. Sophia isn't working for, or against, the Network. Neva reasons that she is not important enough to come up on their radar. And even if she does, she couldn't tell them anything about Neva other than what she looked like and the Network already knows that.

'It'll be transferred this afternoon if this doesn't prove to be a red herring,' Neva says, making her decision. Then she turns and walks away.

She's careful to make sure she hasn't been seen as she leaves the gardens. She hails a taxi and then heads into Richmond. There she goes to an internet café and logs on and reviews the email servers and chatrooms she uses in the dark Web via a VPN she already has set up. Another source has sent her a file on Mr M. A. Beech and his company, along with a photograph of the man. Neva frowns at the picture, wondering if she's seen him before. She can't remember. He has white-blond hair, is in his late fifties, and dresses with a great deal of finesse. Some would call him a silver fox, though he's really too young for that epithet. She googles him. The man is generally private and so she doesn't find much about him online with the exception of his attendance at various charity functions with a different supermodel on his arm each time.

She sends the information in an encrypted email to herself to access later. Then she logs off and leaves the café before any suspicions are aroused.

In another taxi back to Michael's flat, she removes the

tattoo sleeve and puts on a jacket she takes from her rucksack. Then she looks inside the folder that Sophia gave her. Inside is the complete financial history of Beech's company, along with an address.

She decides she's going to stake out the place a little before returning to Michael's. She gives the driver instructions to take her to the nearest tube station instead.

Then she stuffs the folder back into the plastic wallet and puts it into her rucksack.

Chapter Fifty-Nine

MICHAEL

'I'm glad you're here!' says Ray as I enter my office.

'What's up?' I ask.

'There've been some more abductions,' Leon says.

'From schools?'

'No, this time our perp took them from a variety of play areas. Simultaneously,' Ray explains.

I shouldn't have had the second glass of wine at lunch, because I'm feeling a little woozy.

A few hours earlier, Uncle Andrew called and said he was in town. I had slipped out for a long lunch. It's not something I usually do, but it's not often Andrew is in the area.

I sit down at my desk, wondering how I allowed Andrew to tempt me with that second chardonnay during the working day. But I don't suppose it matters.

I shake the fugue off after a coffee and I wade through all the paperwork generated by the recent abductions. While I wait for more information and Ray's instructions, it occurs to me that we don't normally get pulled in to such cases so quickly. Usually there's something else that makes a regular abduction come to our attention. But this isn't ordinary, I can see that, and it's linked, I'm sure, to everything else we're working on, and especially to Neva.

There are seven children missing. Four boys, three girls, and it's obvious that this is connected to the previous abductions that Beth and I have been working on. What is the significance of seven, I wonder? Odd numbers are always conspicuous. I make a note to ask Neva about this and see if my words prompt some memory that may help us find the answers we seek.

'Mike?'

I look up and find Ray standing by the door.

'You okay?' he says.

'Sorry, yes. I was thinking about this case.'

'The local police are still collating evidence but we may need you and Leon to travel to the locations and find out what you can,' Ray says. 'Interview some of these parents, or whoever was with the kids at the time.'

'Of course. It's connected. It has to be.'

Ray nods. 'I'm sure of that too.'

He walks away and I return my attention to the information I've received so far.

Like the others, the children are aged between five and seven. All from wealthy or middle-class families. One of the parents is a CEO of a conglomerate. There's a footnote on this file; they are expecting a ransom note, but I doubt they will ever get one.

The day finishes and I find myself still looking at my

computer as silence descends on the building. It's not that the place is particularly noisy during the day but there is a sudden absence of sound. A vacuum that becomes stillness. As though the air stops moving.

I blink. I hear the security guard sweeping the rooms to make sure everything is locked up. My computer is still on, but it's in privacy mode – an extra security that screens what I'm looking at even from colleagues. I shut it all down and stand. I'm stiff, and annoyed with myself for having fallen asleep. Neva must be wondering where I am and why I've not come home. Perhaps she's even worried.

I make sure my office and any private documents are locked up, then I take my briefcase and leave.

It's only when I'm halfway home that I realise I didn't check up on the image search I'd started for the house using the picture scanned from the Brayford Prep School prospectus. It's not like me to be so forgetful. I really shouldn't drink at all during the day. I'm a total lightweight these days.

I get back to the flat after 9pm and walk in to find Neva sitting by the door.

She has a gun pointed straight at my head.

Chapter Sixty

NEVA

Earlier that day

Beech Corp is in central London, not far from Piccadilly. Neva takes the tube to Piccadilly Circus. It is risky being here, especially if Beech is involved with the Network. They may have operatives looking out for her, even though she shouldn't know about him or his involvement.

Across the road she pretends to window shop. From there she locates all the street cameras and takes note of the front door that leads into the building. Beech's business is in an impressive white structure, and it takes up two floors above a popular store. It isn't what she expected to find, because this company makes several billion a year. In many ways, it's lost among the shops around Piccadilly Circus. The sign above the door doesn't stand out, but what Neva does notice is the security guard just inside, and the camera covering the door.

Neva stays clear of all the cameras. She goes inside a store and pretends to browse the clothing, while glancing occasionally out through the window and across the road to Beech Corp. From her vantage point she could be there within minutes, but what would be gained by exposing her presence?

She leaves the store when an assistant starts to take too much notice of her. Then she walks away, browsing in another shop window, using the highly polished glass to observe the building across the road.

By lunchtime, Neva begins to wonder what she can learn from this observation. No one has gone in or out of the building all the time she's been there. She is about to give up when a black limousine pulls up nearby. Because this area is busy, and stopping is awkward, the driver doesn't get out, but the passengers do.

She sees Beech emerge and right behind him is ... Michael.

Chapter Sixty-One

MICHAEL

'Hey!' I say. 'It's me. You can put that thing away.'

Neva does not lower the gun.

Without taking my eyes from her, I push the front door closed. It wouldn't do for a neighbour to casually walk by and see this situation.

'What's happened?' I ask.

Neva's face is blank. I realise I am looking at her professional facade.

'Before you kill me,' I say, 'I'd at least like to know why.'

'Sit down. Over there,' she says, pointing to the sofa. 'Take it slow.'

I pass her and the gun follows me; all the time I'm wondering how the fuck I'm getting out of this one. My eyes search her face for any sign of empathy. Have I been played these last few days? Have I let myself be lulled into a false sense of security? Have I made a complete and utter dick of myself?

I sit down and look at her. Then I place my hands on my knees.

'I'm going to ask you some questions,' she says, 'and if I don't like the answers or I feel you're lying, I'm going to kill you.'

I study her and know she means every word. The gun has a silencer; no one will even hear it happen. My heart is thudding in my chest. I wonder if she can hear it.

'Okay,' I say.

Where is this going? She's cold and deadly, ready to end our blossoming relationship with one twitch of the trigger. I'm disappointed, but shouldn't be so surprised. This is, after all, who she is.

'Where were you today?' she asks.

'This is all because I'm late, right?' I try to laugh but see she's deadly serious. 'All right. Let's talk about my day. First thing, I went back to the prep school and tried to see the head again. I wanted to ask about the house,' I say. 'She wasn't there and neither was the photograph.'

'Where did you go after that?'

'I bought us some phones. Used cash. I wanted to be able to keep in touch with you.'

She nods. I'm still staring down the barrel of the gun; she hasn't finished asking me everything, but I'm not dead yet so maybe that's a good sign that we can sort out whatever is upsetting her.

'Then?'

'Into the office. But you know I can't discuss what happened there, no matter how much you threaten me,' I say.

'You're working for a spy taskforce, Michael, I wouldn't expect anything else. What about this afternoon?'

'I met my uncle for lunch. At Borough Market. We ate lobster and drank chardonnay. I drank two glasses.'

Neva's eyes narrow as though she doesn't believe me.

'Did you hear yourself then?' she says. 'That last bit sounded rehearsed. Like it's something you've been told to say.'

'What are you talking about? I met my uncle for lunch. At Borough Market. We ate lobster and drank chardonnay. I drank two glasses...' I say. She's right; it feels practised, even on my tongue. Like something I've learnt to say that day.

She points with the gun to her mobile phone on the coffee table.

'Look in the photographs on that thing. Try to ring anyone and I'll put a bullet in your brain.'

I pick up the phone and open it to recent photos. Then I see an image of a white building, a limo, and myself.

'What is this?' I say.

'Who's the man with you?' she asks.

'My uncle, Andrew. But...' I tail off. 'I wasn't anywhere near his offices today.'

'Your uncle? He's ... *Mr Beech*...' she says.

'Yes. Michael Andrew Beech, but everyone calls him Andrew. My parents named me Michael after him.'

Neva lowers the gun but she doesn't put it down.

'Look, what is this?' I say. I'm feeling more confident now that there's been a misunderstanding. But I'm totally confused by the photos.

'Tell me what you did today,' she says again. 'Every detail. This is important.'

'When I got into the office, I received a call from Andrew inviting me to lunch. He's not in London that often; he lives...' My mind has gone blank on where Andrew lives. 'Anyway, it doesn't matter where. He just comes in for business occasionally.'

'You say you went to lunch? But then?'

'Back to work.'

'What time did you return to work?' she asks.

I close my eyes, trying to think.

'I took a long break, maybe two hours. So I think I got back at about 2pm.'

'Michael, you arrived at that building at 12.30pm and you didn't leave until three. You were there two and a half hours. I was outside the whole time.'

'No,' I deny. 'I remember every bite of that food, and I felt tipsy when I got back. I shouldn't have—'

'Have you ever lost time before?' Neva interrupts.

Her words shock me. I want to deny it. But then I recall that a few days ago my milk was drugged.

'Think, Michael! This is important.'

'I ... don't know.'

'Who is Andrew?' she persists.

'My uncle, I told you.'

'Your dad's brother? Your mother's?'

'He's not a blood relation. He was a close friend of my dad. He's my godfather,' I say. 'Mine and Mia's.'

Neva nods. 'Yes, your sister, Mia. Does she meet him for lunch occasionally too?'

I shake my head, confused. There is a memory of Mia and Andrew sitting talking. Something back when we were kids. And Ben had mentioned he had gone to visit them, so yes, they must meet up sometimes. I'm confused and struggling to believe what Neva has captured in her pictures. I look through them again. Yes, there is Andrew. There is me. And they show today's date. I don't know how she could have faked them but my brain won't accept it.

'It's not me,' I say. 'I wasn't there. We were in a restaurant at Borough. Perhaps I have a doppelgänger.'

'And your uncle does too then presumably?'

Neva stands. She clicks the safety back on the gun and puts it down on the seat she's just vacated.

'I have a theory for you,' she says.

'I'm listening.' Anything to explain this madness. This loss of time.

Then she begins to tell me about the house again.

———

I'm exhausted when she finishes outlining her thoughts. I don't believe it, but I can't deny the day was bizarre. I'd even blacked out at my desk while working, only to wake confused. And that thing of using privacy mode, I had known what it was, but not how I knew it, or how I'd achieved it. I still didn't.

'I think they've been drugging you for a while,' she says again. 'They want to use you for something, perhaps to tell them secrets.'

'But I've known Andrew my entire life. I just can't believe he'd be involved in this.'

Neva goes into the kitchen. I hear the tap running and she returns with a glass of water.

'Hydrate,' she says.

I'm nervous as she holds out the glass. What if she's behind the drugging and all of this is some elaborate ruse?

As if she can sense my doubt, she lifts the glass to her lips and glugs down a large amount. Then she holds it out to me again.

'Drink. You need this.'

The water is like nectar to my tongue. I hadn't realised how thirsty I was. Neva watches me gulp the last dregs and then she goes back to the kitchen and refills it. I don't doubt her this time and I take the glass and drain it quickly.

'It's the drugs,' she says. 'I remember the feeling well.'

'You think it's the same stuff they gave you as a child? But why me? How is this even possible? It would mean we are both connected to the Network. And I swear I have no memory of anything like this happening before.'

'Let's get some sleep,' she says.

'But your theory. What you just said ...'

'It's just a theory, Michael. We don't know. But I have an idea where we can find out. Where're those burners you bought?'

I open my briefcase and pull out the phones. We unpack them and activate them both, exchanging numbers. I take them into the kitchen and plug them in to charge overnight.

Then I follow Neva, gun now back in her hand, to our borrowed bedroom.

'You take the bed,' she says. Then she sits in the chair by the window.

'We could do shifts?' I suggest.

'No. I'll sleep, but in the chair, so I'm ready if anything happens.'

The thought that something might happen is not conducive to relaxation and sleep, but I do as she says and get into the bed.

'Just for the record, I doubt anyone will come here. They had you earlier – whatever their motive. And if you'd betrayed me, they'd have been here today before you got back.'

'Betrayed you? No, I'd never—'

'You wouldn't have a choice, Michael! They'd ask you and you'd answer under their influence. But I can only assume that they don't suspect we've even met and so they never ask you about me.'

I process this, feeling frightened and sick and out of control. Can this really be happening? I voice my disbelief again.

'The camera doesn't lie. I saw you there. It may be hard to comprehend but you were there. On some level you were operating normally, but they make you forget what you did. No one knows that better than me,' she says.

'But how did they make me forget?' I ask. I have to understand.

'It's been a long day. Get some rest,' she says. 'Tomorrow we travel and get some answers. Hopefully the ones you really need to get through this.'

I lie down, turn the lamp off beside the bed, and close my eyes.

Behind my eyes I see her again, waiting for my return, gun pointing at the door, and then at me. My heart speeds up. A surge of adrenaline is residual from that moment. Yet I feel safe that she's there in the room, watching over me like an avenging angel.

'Michael!'

I open my eyes and find a little girl with fair hair staring at me. It's dark in the room, but a shaft of light seeps in from the open door.

I'm in the dormitory of my school. I've only been here a few weeks and already I wish I was home with my parents. What they teach us is strange.

'What is it?' I whisper back at the girl.

She looks over her shoulder at the door. She moves from one foot to the other as though ready to flee at a second's notice. Then she drops down beside my bed, and climbs underneath it. I lean over the edge and look at her hiding there.

'What are you doing?' I ask.

'They're coming for you...' she says.

Chapter Sixty-Two

MICHAEL

I jerk awake and see Neva's shape slumped in the chair. I can hear her gentle breathing as she naps. I consider turning over and going back to sleep but the dream is still floating in the back of my mind. I tremble as I pull myself up into a sitting position. The vivid dream has disturbed me. It felt real, though I know it is just angst that has created this scenario in my subconscious. Probably the distressing news that more kids have been taken is preying on my mind. I'm sure this means that more young people are going to be moulded into something like Neva. I feel like I should be doing something about that, but have no idea what or how. What was it like for Neva, living in that house? No child should live with such fear.

Neva is an enigma. She hadn't been blessed with a normal childhood, reared as she was to be a killer. Yet she is capable of so much. I feel a little pathetic when compared to her. She is strong and I feel weak and vulnerable, struggling as I am to make sense of my changing world.

Neva stretches in the chair and yawns. I glance at the clock beside the bed. It's early but it would be pointless now to go back to sleep.

I pick up my phone and unplug it from the charger on my bedside table.

'What time is it?' Neva asks.

'Just after five,' I say.

I start composing a text to send to Ray, excusing my absence from work. Claiming man-flu. I've never had any time off sick so Ray may be suspicious. Even so, I press send. I'm half expecting a reply telling me to 'man up', but no immediate response comes.

'Should we get out of here?' I say.

'Bagsy the bathroom first,' Neva answers.

I let her take care of her ablutions as I get up and go into the kitchen. Out of caution, I sniff the milk in the fridge. Neva wasn't home all day yesterday and I'm nervous that somehow Mrs Kendal's home has been compromised too.

I decide that it might be a good idea to reactivate my security cameras again while we're gone. I go into my flat and I plug in the wires and reactivate the system on my laptop. Then I bring it and all of my overnight things back to my neighbour's home.

Neva comes into the kitchen as I pour boiling water onto the teabags.

'I'll take it black,' she says.

'Probably wise,' I say.

I finish our drinks, then I take mine into the bedroom. Leaving it on the chest of drawers to cool, I go into the bathroom and shower. Neglecting my usual shaving routine, I go back into the bedroom, a towel around my hips, then I dry and dress, before I repack my overnight bag.

Before closing the zip on the holdall, I hesitate. Am I really going to see my parents to ask about Andrew?

At the last minute, I stuff my gun in the bag, then I zip it closed. I take the holdall with me out of the room, dumping it down on the coffee table.

'You'll need to bring your stuff,' I tell Neva.

She's sitting in the chair by the door again, but this time the mug of tea is clutched in her hand, not a gun.

'Already packed while you were in the shower,' she says.

I then notice the bag by her feet.

'How do you feel?' she asks.

'Odd. I haven't seen Mum and Dad for a while,' I say.

'Not close then?'

'I'm closer to Mia,' I say. 'But there's been no falling-out. They're just … more into each other than us. If you understand?'

Neva nods.

My parents live in Cambridge. They moved out of London when my father retired last year.

'I'll hire a car,' I say. 'Drive us.'

'I can steal one,' Neva suggests.

I'm shocked that I actually consider her offer for a second. But the car hire, although it requires ID, seems like the best bet. The last thing we need is to be spotted and chased down by police looking for a stolen vehicle.

'We'll hire,' I say.

'Okay. But I'll use one of my fake IDs,' she says.

'What about paying? They won't take cash; they'll want a card.'

'I have those too,' she says.

Though I shouldn't be surprised, I am. I don't ask her how she has managed to obtain all of these things. Perhaps the less I know the better. Even so, Neva knows what she's doing. She's hidden herself well for the last few months.

My regular phone pings as I pull on my jacket. I look at it and see a text from Ray.

You looked under the weather yesterday. Get some rest! Take a couple of days if you need it.

I thank him and switch off the phone.

'Leave that here. It's traceable,' Neva says. Then she goes into the kitchen and brings out both of the burner phones and their chargers. I take one, put it in my pocket, and I stow the charger in my bag. Neva does the same.

'Just in case you're being watched, I go first,' Neva says.

She pulls on a knitted hat, pushing her shiny fair hair up into it. Then she slings her rucksack over her back and goes out.

As discussed, I wait ten minutes and then follow. But first I drop my work phone and charger back into my flat. I make sure the place is locked up, as well as Mrs Kendal's flat. By the time I get downstairs, Neva is already walking towards our meeting point.

I exit the front of the building and walk towards the tube station, which is about ten minutes away, taking the precaution of observing those around me. Then I join the queue at the taxi rank. Neva comes up and stands behind me. When I reach the front of the queue, we both get into the same cab.

As the taxi pulls away, Neva looks through the rear window, studying cars and people that might be paying attention to us.

'I think we're okay,' she says.

I direct the taxi four streets away and get the driver to drop us off at a local hotel. Then we walk around the corner to the car hire company.

A short time later, we are driving away in an inconspicuous dark-blue Corsa.

The sat nav says Cambridge is only sixty-two miles away and it should take one hour and thirty-two minutes. On normal roads, this would only be a little over an hour's journey, but getting out of central London and onto the M11 is always slow. In the end, it takes us almost half an hour longer than the sat nav predicted.

'I know it's risky, but I'm coming in with you,' Neva says. 'I have to see if either of your parents are lying.'

'Oh, believe me, my bullshit detector will be hiked up to full scan too,' I say.

I'm shocked I'm saying this. At the moment, there is no reason to suspect my parents of anything. But the hairs are prickling on the back of my neck as I turn the car into their street and directly onto the driveway next to my father's car.

The house is fairly ordinary, though much bigger than they could afford in London. Last year, they sold their small townhouse there and, with the freed-up capital, were able to find a four-bedroom detached home in Cambridge, with a reasonably sized garden, for a fraction of the cost of the townhouse. Dad had never been one for gardening, but he fancied trying his hand now he was retired. I'd been to the house just once before – the day they moved in – and now that memory imposed itself again in my mind. Mia and Ben had been there to help too. At the end of the day, we'd ordered pizza and sat around Mum's kitchen table drinking beer. It had been pleasant, so why didn't I see them more?

'Ready?' says Neva at my side.

I nod but I feel nervous. It's almost as if I'm at a stranger's house.

I get out of the car and so does Neva. Then I approach the door, knock, and wait.

Chapter Sixty-Three

MICHAEL

Mum answers and takes a step back.

'Michael? What are you doing here?'

Mum looks homey. She's wearing an apron and there's a smear of flour on her cheek as though she's in the middle of baking. She always looks like this. And for a moment it feels staged just for me, but I know she wasn't expecting me and that this is a ridiculous notion.

'Hey, Mum,' I say. I open my arms. She blinks and then moves towards me for a hug.

'So, who's this?' she asks, looking at Neva, when she pulls away.

'I'm Anna,' Neva says.

Neva holds out her hand and she and Mum shake.

'Where're my manners! Come in! Your dad is in the garden.'

Mum chatters as she leads me into the house. The living room is in much better order than the last time I was here.

That day, unopened boxes were stacked against one wall. Since then, Mum has made this place a home.

'I've been baking so your timing is perfect!' Mum says. 'Sit down. I'll put the kettle on and fetch your father.'

I sit on the familiar plush sofa. She's had this one for years, though you'd never know as it's still perfect. Neva doesn't sit; she stands by the window watching the road outside.

'Well, this is a nice surprise!' Dad says, coming in from the kitchen. 'Anna, is it?'

Anna studies him and then takes the hand he holds out to her.

'Must be serious,' Dad says. 'I don't remember Michael ever bringing a girl home before.'

Neva smiles at him. Dad sits down in his favourite chair and Neva sinks down on the sofa beside me. There's an ornate mahogany coffee table between us and Dad. I don't think I've seen this table before and suspect it's new.

'How long have you two...?' says Dad.

'Dad, that's not why I'm here.'

'Hold that thought. I'll just see if your mother needs help.'

Dad gets up; he moves slower than the last time I saw him. He looks older too. He goes back into the kitchen. A short time later he returns with a tray. On it is Mum's best china teapot with matching teacups and saucers. He places it on the coffee table. There's also a matching jug with milk in it and a small dish containing sugar cubes. Mum's brought out the big guns today. I can only imagine what she is thinking about me turning up here with a woman.

'Can I take your jacket and hat?' Dad says now to Neva.

'I'm fine, thank you,' she says but she pulls the hat off out of politeness.

Dad stares at her beautiful strawberry-blonde hair as it falls down over her shoulders. He looks at me and winks. Then he bends over the tray and starts to pour the tea. He holds a cup out to Neva; she takes it but doesn't drink.

'Help yourself to milk and sugar,' he says.

After taking a cup from him, I place it down on a coaster on the table. I want to cut to the chase now, and ask my questions about Andrew. But I have to wait a little longer until Mum comes in.

She enters soon with a plate of perfect cupcakes which she puts down on the table before us, along with a stack of small plates.

'Mum's a great cook,' I say to Neva but neither of us reaches for one of the cakes. 'Mum, sit down, will you? I'd like to talk to you guys.'

Mum sits on the small two-seater sofa she often occupies. She's smiling at me.

'Well, I wondered when this day would come,' she says.

'I saw Andrew a couple of days ago,' I say, moving the subject away from their assumption that I'm here to introduce Neva as my girlfriend.

'Really? How was he?' Dad asks. 'Haven't seen him for some time.'

'You guys are close though? I mean, you chose him as my godfather,' I say.

'More tea?' Mum asks.

I shake my head.

'How did you meet Andrew, Dad?' I ask. Then I pick up my teacup. Both my parents stare at the cup but say nothing. I put it down again and wait for them to answer.

'We went into the force together. I told you that,' Dad says. 'Andrew lasted a couple of years, then his dad died and left him the business. He quit the force and became a big fancy CEO instead.'

I remember hearing this before, almost word for word. I glance at Neva. She's quiet but observant under an appearance of shyness.

'What is Andrew's business?' Neva asks.

'Didn't Michael tell you?' Mum says.

'No. I've only just been made aware of him...'

'It's some import/export thing, I believe,' Dad says. 'I don't pry. But he must be up for retirement himself one day soon.'

'But he left the city a while ago, didn't he?' I say. 'Where's his house again?'

Mum picks up a cupcake and places it on a plate. 'These used to be your favourite,' she says holding it out to me.

'I'm okay right now, Mum,' I say.

She looks disappointed as she places the plate down on the table. Neva takes it and smiles at Mum.

She lifts the cake and peels away the case, then she nibbles the sponge at the bottom.

'It's delicious,' she says.

'You've known Andrew a long time then,' I say. 'Dad, you're a cop; have you ever suspected Andrew of ... not being what he says he is?'

'What are you talking about?' Dad says. 'Andrew is

Andrew. He's always the same. Now, let's talk about you two. When's the big day?'

Neva laughs at this. She uses the laughter as an excuse to put down the cake.

'We're just…' I stop. How to explain Neva to my parents. Is it best to let them think this rather than to have them wondering too deeply who and what she is? 'Okay. You've figured it out. Anna and I are planning to get engaged!'

Neva laughs a little harder. I doubt she's ever been in such an embarrassing position before.

'Anyway, I'm trying to tell her about my family. You guys, Mia, Uncle Andrew. Just so she knows what she's letting herself in for,' I continue.

'He's not been very fluent on this subject,' Neva says, falling into the lie.

'Oh, Michael! I'm so happy for you!' Mum says.

My parents begin to relax then and I realise the odd, alert, way they had been looking at us both was because they weren't sure about the situation. I know it's unusual for me to turn up unannounced so I cut them both some slack. Even so, I need to find out more about Andrew.

I sip my tea finally but I take it black and Neva tries the icing on the cupcake. She praises Mum for her cooking but she avoids the tea. Then she asks if she can go to the bathroom. Mum gives her directions and Neva leaves the room.

'She seems nice,' Mum says. 'A little shy perhaps, but she'll get to know us.'

I nod.

Mum pours more tea and stirs in milk, then she passes my cup back to me.

'How did you meet?' she asks.

I sip the tea. It tastes too milky after the black cup I've just consumed.

'Travelling on the tube,' I say. 'Then we just kept bumping into each other.'

'Is he under yet?' Dad says.

'What?' I slur.

'Nearly,' says Mum. 'I'll take care of this.'

'*Mum*?'

'Now, Michael, why didn't you *kill* her?'

I'm torn between reality and my dream state. Part of me is denying that this is happening. That my mother just drugged me. I haven't had much of the milky tea, but it was enough to make me lose control. The cup slips from my fingers and falls down onto the floor with a clatter.

'You have to execute her, Michael. She's a risk to us all!'

'Kill *her*?' I say.

'Yes,' says Mum. 'Here. Go and find her and finish this.'

Mum presses a gun into my fingers. I look down at it and realise it's my Glock, now with a silencer. I don't know where it came from. I stand, gripping the weapon with grim determination. I feel strong and cold and full of purpose. I check the barrel, take off the safety, and then I go in search of Neva.

Mum had sent her upstairs to the main bathroom. It had occurred to me that this was peculiar, when there was a toilet in the hallway, but for some reason I didn't correct her. Now I understand why: they recognised her immediately which means they are high up in the Network. I remember. Yes. They have a seat each at the table. They are both on Mr Beech's committee.

I know now too that Neva is a traitor to the Network. She has to die.

I remember a lot of things: how they took me as a child. I was only gone a few weeks, and then I was placed back with my 'parents'. They knew all about it. They were part of my training. But this allowed me the appearance of a normal life. I'd worked hard at school, while training at 'the house' at weekends. Unlike Neva, I knew exactly where that place was. But only when I was truly awake. *Like now.*

I walk through the hall, gun held in both hands and pointed down. Neva won't suspect, or see me coming, until it's too late. The other part of me, the Michael that does not know the truth, stirs inside me and I try to quiet him. I have to do this. I am loyal to the Network. Besides, if you aren't working *for* them, then you're *against* them. There's no surer way to retire than to start to breakdown.

I take the stairs with the stealth of a dancer. The training was rigorous – no room for failure or lack of stamina until you had mastered all of the principles. I can call on reflexive movement, strength and endurance under pressure and go for days without sleep and not lose any of these faculties. I'd done it before. Many times.

At the top of the stairs I expect Neva to burst from the bathroom, gun in hand, but the door remains closed. I walk towards it, light on my feet; there's barely a creak on the landing as I reach the door.

White light bursts behind my eyes as something knocks

me down from behind. My head feels like it's been cracked open. I try to turn but my knees buckle; I've been hit in precisely the right place. Only one of *us* would know how to do that.

I slip down into unconsciousness long before I hit the floor.

Chapter Sixty-Four

MICHAEL

I'm tied to one of the wooden kitchen chairs when I wake. I struggle against the bonds but they've been secured so well that my struggles only make them tighter, not looser. Neva is taking no chances and I wouldn't either in her shoes.

Mum and Dad are secured next to me. Dad's bleeding at the temple; Mum has a bruise smudge on her cheek in place of the habitual flour. They are both unconscious. We are all in the back room, which Mum was using as the dining room. The dining table is not centred anymore; it's pushed aside, and we three occupy its former space.

Neva is sitting on one of the plush velvet dining chairs Mum spent a small fortune buying some years ago.

'After I saw you with Beech, I knew who you were,' Neva says. 'The drug is still in your system and so I'm going to tell you this now while it will have the most impact. *Remember everything* when you come around. And then you'll have to make an informed decision about which Michael you want to be.'

'I'll be any Michael you want, Neva,' I say. 'Why not untie me and let's thrash this out.'

She half laughs, knowing I'm not the Michael she wants to speak to right now.

'You can fight this, Michael. Your natural self is a good man. This ... sleeper-you is not real. It's a child that was badly abused and used by his own parents.'

I glance at Mum and Dad. They are both gagged. Wise move on her part; she probably recalls that there are trigger words they can use to control me. I don't remember what those words are, but I know that if they are used, I will fight and kill; I've done so before. Even Neva's bonds won't hold me then.

'I'm going to feed you some water,' she says. 'It'll help get this shit out of your system.'

I try to refuse the water, but eventually give in. What does it matter? If I play along, she may untie me and I'll take this treacherous bitch down at the first opportunity.

After drinking the water, I begin to feel tired again.

Darkness gathers around my eyes and for a moment I *see* the other Michael. So hard-working at Archive. I have his knowledge when I need it, but I don't share his emotions. He feels like a dream I once had and then he comes into sharp focus. He pushes at me, punching and kicking. I jerk, try to fight back, but I can't. He's strong, this Michael; he's inhabited this body more than I have.

Chapter Sixty-Five

NEVA

Neva watches over Michael as his body repels the drug. She holds the back of the chair to prevent this odd seizure from throwing him to the ground. She doesn't want him to be accidentally hurt. Once he's still, she knows he's going to remain asleep while his mind reorders. The awakening will be hard for him. He'll remember things he'd rather forget. This was how she was the day she killed her handler. The day she forced her own personality to the surface to join with the one that the Network had given her.

Once he's still, she fetches a pitcher of water and throws it over Michael's mother. The woman jerks awake, sodden, bruised, and tenderised for interrogation. She wants to do this before Michael wakes; he doesn't need to see it.

'Okay. You're now going to tell me all about Andrew and where the house is,' Neva says. 'And then, I just might let you all live.'

Michael's mum looks shocked and horrified. 'I'm not one of them,' she says. 'I don't know anything.'

'Really? Only I just watched you drug your son,' Neva says. 'I heard everything you said to him. Don't lie to me. I take no joy in being able to stomach what you people taught me to do. But stomach it I will. I'll torture you if I have to.'

It takes a little physical persuasion to get the woman to talk. But smashed toes and a broken collarbone are the least she deserves. When Neva learns where the house is, she stops the torture. Others would have continued, but Neva does not revel in what she has been forced to become. In fact, she makes a conscious decision to do only what is necessary.

Neva gags Michael's mother again, then drags her, and the chair, out of the dining room and into the lounge. She returns immediately and drags the still unconscious father away too.

Michael *shouldn't* see them when he wakes.

Chapter Sixty-Six

MICHAEL

I hear four dull thuds. Like the noise of a muffled hammer smacking against unset cement. My head hurts. I'm woozy, nauseous, and confused. I try to move but find that I'm restricted. It's hard to open my eyes. My lids feel gritty and swollen. They don't respond to my unspoken command. I tug at my bonds and then water is being pressed to my lips again. I take it, grateful for the liquid washing into my sand-dry mouth.

'How do you feel?' asks a voice at my side.

'Like something smacked me over the head,' I slur. My tongue feels thick in my mouth.

More water is offered. It helps and I find I'm able to open my eyes. The light in the room stings them, like a blaring light that's turned directly to my face.

'Who are you?' says the voice.

'Michael Kensington. Where … am I?'

'Don't you remember?' It's a female voice. I know that much, but I can't recall who she is. My mind is fried. Then there is a rush of memories, like dreams I've had but forgotten, and they swamp me until I feel like I'm drowning, or going insane.

There's a little girl beside my bed. She's a bit younger than me, and she's scared. 'They're coming for you,' she says.

I turn my head as a bulb goes on outside the room. Then the dormitory lights up. There are three other boys in here, but the girl has vanished. Then I remember that she's hidden under my bed to avoid detection.

The other boys wake when the light goes on, but the new arrivals – a woman and a man – ignore them and come to my bed.

'You'll bring him up as though he's your own,' says a male voice.

'Of course,' replies the woman. 'Come on, Michael, let's go home.'

The man beside her reaches for me. 'I'm your dad,' he says.

I feel confused. I try to remember them from before I came to the school. A flash of memory skirts around the edges of my mind. Another mother calling out to me as I ran around in the garden, a Labrador puppy bouncing at my feet, barking in excitement.

'John...' I say.

'No. You're Michael,' says the other man. He's standing by the door. Blond hair, tall. Smartly dressed. I've seen him here before, though he just watches our transformations and never comments. 'Take him now. But bring him in at the weekend for top-up treatment.'

Ah! This must be a hospital. I've been ill; that's why I'm confused.

The woman helps me dress, then they take me from the … ward? Perhaps that's the name?

'Have I been sick?' I say as they lead me down a huge flight of stairs.

'Yes, and now you're better,' says the woman.

I see her and the man exchange an expression as they take me down the front steps of the house and put me in the car. It's dark outside. The woman, Mum, makes sure my seatbelt is secured. I thank her. She gives me a bottle of water and sandwiches wrapped in foil.

'For the journey,' she says.

We drive for a few hours; I drink some of the water and eat one half of a sandwich. It's chicken and mayonnaise, a personal favourite. Then I drift off to sleep, even though the day is beginning to dawn.

I wake later in a bedroom. It's nicer than where I've been. There are toys, and posters, and it's painted pale blue. I can smell the fresh chemical scent of the paint.

Mum comes in as if she knows I'm awake. She gives me water again and a spoon of medicine that will help me 'settle'. Then she shows me around the house. I don't remember it, or my room, but Mum explains this is normal.

'You had a very serious illness,' she says. 'Meningitis. It made you forget lots of things.'

There's a girl in the kitchen, sitting at a small table. She's eating a bowl of cereal.

'This is Mia,' says Mum. 'Your twin sister.'

Looking at Mia makes me happy. I sit next to her and

Mum gives me the same bowl and cereal. Mia holds my hand.

'We've both been ill,' Mia says. 'But now we're together we're going to get better.'

'You had the mengies as well?' I ask.

Mum laughs, 'Meningitis. And yes, you both had it.'

I let go of Mia's hand and eat my food.

'Do you have a pink room?' I ask. 'Mine's blue.'

'Mia's room is lilac,' Mum says. 'It's her favourite colour.'

Mia doesn't look certain but she nods. Then she takes a swig of the milk that Mum places down before her.

'Time to visit Uncle Andrew,' she says.

Mia falls asleep on the chair and Mum picks her up and carries her outside. I follow them both to the front door and look out on the street as Mum places Mia in the car. Dad is in the driving seat.

'See you both tonight,' he calls, then he drives away.

'Don't worry, Mia will be back later,' Mum says. 'Now, you and I are going shopping. So, go and get dressed. I put your clothes on the chair by your bed.'

We go out, taking a bus ride into what Mum refers to as 'town'. There we go to a shop that says 'School Uniforms' in the window. I try things on. We leave with new clothes and shoes for school.

'You start your new school on Monday,' Mum explains.

'What day is it now?' I ask.

'Tuesday,' she answers.

That evening, Dad returns with Mia. She's still sleepy when we all sit at the table to eat. She struggles to eat the roast chicken dinner, even though Mum insists it is her favourite. After dinner, Mum takes Mia upstairs to bed; half an hour later, I follow.

When I wake the next day, the room feels more like mine. I hear Mia laughing with Mum in the bathroom as she encourages her to brush her teeth. The sounds are familiar. This is home. How could I have forgotten any of it?

Chapter Sixty-Seven

MICHAEL

The dream of my childhood slips away as I come around to the sound of knocking. I jerk my head up and find I'm in a bedroom, an unfamiliar one, and the blinds are drawn.

'Housekeeping!'

I struggle from the bed, find I'm only wearing my boxers, and I go to the door. I open it and peep round it, explaining I'm not ready yet. The woman frowns at me, then nods. 'Check-out is at eleven,' she says.

'Okay.'

I close the door and blink, looking at the hotel room. There's a gap in my memory: I have no idea how I got here or even what time it is. My watch is not on my wrist. I walk back to the bed and look for my personal belongings. My hand is shaking as I find my watch on the chest of drawers beneath the wall-hung TV. My wallet, my phone, and my clothes are all piled on a chair by the window.

I pick up the phone. It's fully charged and there's a text message on it.

We have to talk. N x

The memory of the last few days comes flooding back. Neva and I went to my parents' house to ask them about Andrew. My mother drugged me.

I sink down onto the bed. My head hurts. I run my hand over the back of my neck and find the lump there. Neva knocked me out. She tied up my parents. Where the hell are they now?

'Oh God!'

My mind is a jumble of mixed-up recollections, some that don't feel like mine. But I know what this is. The memories *are* mine; I've been living a double life. Neva instructed me to remember it all when the meds were still in my system. My brain couldn't cope with the rush of knowledge and so I'd blacked out again and again until finally I became coherent.

She'd half untied me then, knowing I'd be able to get free. Then she'd left.

I'd struggled out of my bonds and gone into the lounge. That's when I found the bodies. Mum and Dad were dead. Executed. Still tied and gagged. Neva had done it and I knew why.

I had run to the downstairs toilet and thrown up. My stomach was empty bar the water Neva had fed me. God, what was I going to do? I cursed myself for being an idiot. Why had I brought her here? What did I expect would happen? Did I think this would be some kind of family reunion and Mum and Dad would reassure me that there was no problem with Andrew? Deep down I'd hoped it had been all some horrible mistake that Mum and her baking would put right. Just like when I was a child.

But I hadn't known how involved they were, had I? I'd thought maybe the Network had tainted my family only through Andrew. I couldn't have predicted Neva would kill them – even if it was necessary.

But I could. On some level I'd always known they were *wrong*. All those trips to visit our uncle, how sick and woozy and miserable Mia and I would feel on the return. Then Mum's baking would soothe us and we'd drift off to sleep and forget the whole horrible experience – until next time.

In my parents' house I'd found my wallet and the keys for the Corsa by the door but Neva was long gone. I got into the car and drove away.

Even as I'd fled the house, my mind was a mess. I worried what I would do. I had to ring work and tell them *everything*. But the other memories pushed against me, telling me this would be a stupid move. I should call the police, hand myself over to them. But no. I'd be dead in twenty-four hours if I did that. The Network's reach was limitless; wasn't that what I'd been told?

A telephone number had popped into my head then.

I pulled over when I saw a phone booth and dialled the number. It was answered on the second ring.

'I need clean-up,' I said. My throat was dry. 'Codename Neva killed my parents.'

'We'll deal with it. Come in. You know the procedure,'

said the voice on the other end. It was a familiar voice, but the name of the person evaded me.

'On my way,' I'd said.

I got back in the car and drove to Cambridge train station instead of the meeting point I knew I should be going to. Because I'm not *that* Michael. I'm *me*. And despite the flood of information about what I'd done under the Network's influence, they didn't own me. Neva had been right to trust that I'd feel this way.

At the station I'd abandoned the car and caught a train to Manchester. I didn't know why there, but some inner logic said it was the place to go. There were still so many gaps in my memory, so much I had to process before I could use what I knew and decide what I had to do.

On the train I was consumed with more information about my parents – my parents who weren't my parents at all – and Mia. She wasn't my twin! But what did all of this mean for her too? She'd been an innocent child once; we both had.

I'd found a hotel and paid top rate to get a room instantly. Then I'd undressed and fallen asleep again. It had been the only way to cope with everything.

Now I stare at the phone, wondering if I should call Neva. Part of me is fighting the urge to murder her. There'd be a great deal of pain inflicted before I gave her final retirement. I feel anger and hatred boil up inside me. But these aren't the assassin Michael's emotions, they are mine. I've been lied to. Used. But … none of this is Neva's fault. She's just forced me to face it. The other side of me wants to silence her – but not because he cares; he's just been taught to be loyal always to the Network. He's an automaton, responding to instructions and barely thinking about what he does or why.

I think about my parents and their lie. I'd never met them before that day when they took me from the house. They had deserved to die for their part in this. They all did. And the house, one phone call to Archive and I can bring the place down and everyone in it.

I toy with the idea again of calling Ray Martin and telling him everything that's happened. Can I trust him? I just don't know.

The ache behind my eyes starts to lessen and I pick up the burner phone again. I pull Neva's phone number up and press call.

'Michael,' she says.

'I don't know what to do,' I say.

'I'm in the lobby. Come down and talk to me.'

'How do you know where I am?' I ask

'I told you to meet me here.'

I take this information in as I pull on my clothes, then pick up my holdall and look inside. My service revolver is still in the bag. I scan the room, make sure I've left nothing behind, and then I go downstairs to the reception.

Neva is wearing the long black wig again but I recognise her anyway. She's sitting in the lobby, pretending to read the local newspaper. I sit down in the empty chair beside her.

'How are you feeling?' she asks without looking at me.

'As though I've been beaten around the head several times. Oh wait, you did hit me over the head.'

'You were pretty dangerous; I had to do something.'

She puts down the paper and looks at me.

'I'm sorry. I didn't want to have to kill you. We are the same, you and I,' she says. 'A terrible thing was done to us, but we have the capability of being free of it.'

I hear her words but can't believe I'll ever be free of this pain I'm feeling.

'I was lied to. Misled. Brainwashed. Nothing in my life was actually real.' I'm filled with rage. 'I ... I know now that my flat wasn't bugged. I put the drug in my own tea. They conditioned me to ... check in. So, on Saturdays ... not every week ... I'd sometimes drink the tea. The other me would emerge and I'd go and meet Beech. I just don't remember everything I'd tell him. It's like ... the information is *unavailable*.'

She nods. She is the only person who can really understand what I'm saying, and yet my anger wants to focus on her too, as part of this. She was part of them, even if she wasn't really complicit.

'You murdered my parents,' I say. It hurts. Deep. Like someone is sticking a knife in my heart and twisting it.

'You know why,' she says.

'I do but—'

'You're still dealing with the attachment you had to them. But remember what you said to me as we drove there. You weren't close. This is why. They weren't your *real* parents and they knew it, even if you didn't. And every time they were with you, those interactions were a performance to them. They manipulated you, and your sister too.'

'Oh God! *Mia*. What am I going to do about her?' I say.

'Right now, nothing. They may activate her to find and kill you. Then—'

'No! I can't.'

'I'm with you, Michael,' she says. 'I'll take care of what needs to be done.'

'You don't understand. She's pregnant.'

'Interesting.'

I shake my head in confusion. 'What's interesting?'

'They *let* her get pregnant. Maybe she's not one of us but one of *them*.'

'I don't understand,' I say.

'You will. But let's get out of here now. I have another safe house set up.'

———————

Neva's safe house is a forty-minute drive out of Manchester centre, the other side of Altrincham. It's a small country cottage in a rural location. I take my holdall containing my meagre belongings inside and find it cosily furnished.

'Nice place,' I say.

'Airbnb,' she says. 'Surprisingly anonymous.'

In the bedroom I find she's bought me some basics – more underwear and clothing – as I only brought enough things for one night. I'm surprised by her practicality.

I take a shower and change into the new clothing: a pair of jeans and a T-shirt. In the bathroom is shaving gel and a new razor. I scrape away the two-day-old stubble and feel more human again.

Downstairs, Neva fixes us some lunch. She offers me tap water to drink.

'Screw tea,' she says.

I laugh.

Over a tuna sandwich, I ask her what the plan is.

'We could just get the hell out of here,' she says. 'But they won't stop looking for us.'

'I can't do that. I have a life. A job.'

'You don't understand, Michael. None of that is real.'

I have a hard time processing this and I tell her so.

'Don't get me wrong,' she says. 'The person you have been ... the MI5 agent, that's mostly you. But you're more than that. You're a sleeper and the Network isn't going to let you fall into the hands of your colleagues now that the cat is well and truly out of the bag. You know too much and you're aware of it all, no longer compartmentalising the bits they didn't want the real you to know. If they know you're compromised, they can't let you live.'

'So we run? Hide?'

'We could. Or we could fight back,' she says.

'How?'

'Your mother told me where the house is. But she lied. They knew I wouldn't torture her further if I believed what she said. She was good. I'll give her that. She put up with just enough to make me believe she'd cracked.'

I feel sickened by her words.

'I'm sorry,' she says. 'But I had to do it.'

'I know,' I say. I understand completely who and what she is, more now than ever. I'd have done the same in her shoes. Yet I still can't believe I think like this.

'She told you it was in Bristol. That's a default location. When you started on her, other conditioning kicked in. She would have believed she was telling the truth. She lied. But I *know* where the real house is. I remembered. When I was … the other Michael.'

Neva put her hand on my arm, 'I was hoping that would be the case. We just have to think of a way to get in there and shut them down.'

'I can do that,' I say.

'Michael, you've been compromised. They'd never trust you.'

'There's a lot you don't know, Neva. Andrew will trust me. He's always trusted me. I'm his heir.'

Chapter Sixty-Eight

MICHAEL

The house is in several acres of land in rural Cheshire. I know the security rituals and how to get in there. What I'm not sure about is how to get Neva in.

I draw a plan of the place, showing her all the weaknesses in their defences. They may have upped their game as a precaution though, and I explain this to Neva.

'I want to bring Archive into this,' I tell her. 'We can do with their help.'

'Michael, you can't trust them.'

'But wouldn't I remember now if one of the others was in the Network?'

Neva shakes her head. 'They may have kept you in the dark about each other. Hell, for all I know, Archive is a front to help, not stop, them.'

I'm not surprised that she thinks this. The Network has many fingers in many pies, particularly the government, which is full of people facilitating them for the backhanders, or other privileges. I write down a list for Neva of all those I know of.

'The thing is, most of these people don't know what the Network really does. They take bribes to push bills through that suit the company, or help Beech Corp – whose money mostly finances the whole operation. My parents talked a lot when they thought we were drugged,' I explain. 'All this stuff has been hiding in my brain.'

I tell her some more things I overheard.

'There's something else you should know. That last day when I was in work, seven children were reported abducted. I was waiting on instructions to go and interview the parents. It's likely that all of these kids were taken to the house. They haven't finished with the last batch; they're overlapping the new with the old. For some reason they need more operatives. But here's the thing. There's something nagging me. About the parents ... I just can't remember what it is.'

'Give it time. There's a lot of information in your head that needs to be processed and made sense of,' she explains.

A short time later we go out for a drive in Neva's car. I don't know where she got this one – perhaps it's another rental – but I drive far enough away from the cottage until I find another phone box. The woman I'd spoken to was at the house. I'm late checking in. Now I have to convince them I'm still under their influence.

I dial the number again and she answers with an abrupt 'Yes?'

'I'm not far away. Made several detours to make sure I wasn't tailed,' I say.

'And have you been followed?' she asks.

'No. I'm free and clear.'

'Mr Beech will be here to debrief you. What's your ETA?' she asks.

This voice is familiar. It's the same one that took my call last time and there's a trace of an accent, though I can't place it. I know who she is – or at least my other self does – but I still can't access this information. It's as though it's hidden behind even greater barriers than the other things I can remember.

I glance at my watch. 'An hour.'

When I get back in the car, Neva is waiting in the passenger seat.

'Any problems?' she asks.

'None. My explanation was accepted. Andrew is there too,' I say.

Neva nods. We now both recall that Andrew is always at the house when the new children are brought in. He plays an important role as the figure of authority.

The plan is simple: when we get nearer, she'll hide in the boot of the car. I'm not expecting them to search it, but if they're suspicious, she'll be armed and ready if the trunk is opened by anyone other than me. Then all hell will be let loose and we'll be in for a fight. But I'm ready for that. I almost welcome it. The other Michael inside me will know what to do when the time is right, and I'll use his knowledge to bring down the house, and the Network.

With more time we might well have come up with a better plan. I'd wanted to go in alone, but Neva wouldn't hear of it. She wants her revenge, and now I know how I've been manipulated, so do I.

Twenty minutes away from the border of the house, I pull over and help Neva settle in the boot. Then I drive straight for the impressive walled and gated driveway.

There's a security guard waiting in a small booth. I pull up and wait for him to approach. I open the window and say the expected codeword; he glances briefly into the back seat, then turns and points a remote control at the gates. They begin to open with barely a creak. I close my window and make my way sedately into the grounds and drive up the long approach to the house. I behave exactly how I would if the other Michael was in charge.

The house looks just like the photograph I saw in the school. It's been years since I was last here myself but I marvel that they could have so easily suppressed my memories of the place. I hadn't even recognised it from the pictures, but Neva had. So powerful is their control that I know I'm going to have to be on my guard. I don't want any opportunity for Beech or anyone else to make me slip back under their influence. As I draw nearer, a wave of anxiety rises in my chest, followed by slight nausea. I remember feeling this way; approaching the house always brings a rush of unwelcome memories.

I recall sitting in Mendez's surgery, my eyes wedged open as I am forced to watch horrible images on a large screen. All the time, the drugs were pumping into my system through a drip. These are not pleasant recollections. I was a child being tortured.

Now my recalled memories reveal that back in the

Second World War, Hitler's doctors had used drugs and torture as a way of brainwashing agents they later sent out into the world. Mendez wasn't old enough to be a Nazi, but sometime after the war, as a young medic, he'd gained access to notes that should have long been destroyed. These early experiments became the basis of Mendez's conditioning. A conditioning that he evolved over time once he realised that young minds were the best to work on.

It was sick. Abusive. The evillest thing I can ever imagine one human being doing to another, especially a child. At least I was given the semblance of a normal life around the training and they'd allowed me, albeit for their own reasons, not to remember the torment most of the time. But I do now, and all that pain eats at me even as the house looms ahead. I push back, trying not to let my awful past swallow me whole. I remember reading files on Mendez's methods. The old guy has Alzheimer's now. Andrew shared that with me during one of the times he pulled me in to see him.

Andrew had shared a lot of information with me. He'd trusted me; hopefully he still did. I understand now what my role had been. I was their mole in Archive. For this reason, I was sure that no one else in there was. This thought brings me to an important conclusion.

As I pull up to the front of the house, I remember that parking is around the back. I drive around the house and see the large carport, which is full of various other vehicles. I back into a slot beside Andrew's Porsche so the front of my car faces the cameras at the back of the house and the boot of my car is obscured. Then I pull out my burner phone and, making the decision to tell Ray Martin where I am, I send him a text. The message is in code, but it tells Ray my location and makes reference to the children. I wonder what Ray will make of this, considering I've taken sick leave. He'll realise that this was a lie. How he'll respond, I don't know. I hope he'll bring in some help. I've a strong suspicion Neva and I will need it.

I erase the message from the phone, then get out of the car. Taking my jacket from the backseat, I go around the back of the car and open the boot. I make a show of pulling on my jacket and then lift out my holdall. Meanwhile, Neva slips out of the boot and hides behind the car. I slam the boot shut, lift my holdall onto my shoulder and walk towards the back entrance of the building. I'm sure that any observing security will think this is all normal.

The backdoor is locked, as per protocol. I press the intercom and stand in front of the camera. There is a piercing buzz and the door unlocks, allowing me to enter.

I go in, leaving Neva outside, trusting she'll find her way into the house without too much difficulty. One thing I know about her is that she's very good at getting in and out of places and not being seen. The Network taught her well.

I pass down a long corridor and out into the main entrance. I'm surprised that no security guard comes to greet me. I had at least expected to be patted down, but no.

Olive Redding is waiting for me at the door to her office. We've met before and I know that she is the current caretaker of the house.

'Come in, Michael,' she says.

I enter and see the slender frame of another woman sitting by Olive's desk.

'Hello, Michael,' says the woman, turning to me. Of course! I had recognised her voice and now the memories rush back into my mind. I am almost plummeted back to the moment I first arrived at the house, when Simone Arquette brought me here along with her own daughter.

'It was so amusing when you came to talk to me with your colleague,' Simone says. 'About Amelie. When you two were in the house together.'

'*Simone*,' chides Olive.

'Oh, Michael is fine!' Simone says. 'He knows I mean no harm. This is our life here, after all. I'm a breeder. He's a sleeper. And Amelie became an assassin. We are all the property of the Network. We all understand our roles.'

Olive asks me to sit. I do as she says, falling easily into the conditioning, respecting her position here. She is a powerful woman. I know she is a former-operative-turned-trainer. Does she still get tremors when she walks down the corridor to Mendez's consulting rooms? Or does she still play the mantra over and over inside her head, reaffirming her loyalty to the people who took her from her home and brought her here as a child?

'Mr Beech will want to see you,' Olive says. 'But first, how did Neva find your parents?'

I tell her the story that Neva and I planned on the way here. Mostly the truth, with just one tiny twist, that Neva had knocked me out, killed my parents, and left me in the house to take the rap. I don't tell them that I now remember everything. They assume I'm still in agent mode – a default if my other self becomes compromised.

'When I came to, I remembered who I was and what to do. My mother had followed protocol and activated me. Neva had fled, and so I called you, as I was supposed to, for clean-up.'

'We picked up the bodies,' Simone says. 'There's a team waiting in Bristol for Neva to appear at the other house. When she does, we'll have her, Michael, and you can wreak your own revenge on her, if you like?'

'Good,' I say. 'I wasn't sure if Mum had given her the Bristol location, though I hoped. Which is why I didn't come here until I was certain I wasn't being watched.'

As the casual interrogation ends, Andrew comes into the room. I stand and bow my head to him. I don't address him as Andrew – though my real self always did; instead, I call him Mr Beech, like everyone else does. This appears to be the right behaviour as Andrew is relaxed around me, sure that I am genuinely on their side.

'Come to my study,' Andrew says.

I follow him out of Olive's office and down to the next room on the left of the expansive hallway.

'The death of your parents changes things. Their disappearance will raise questions. Therefore, you are compromised,' Andrew says. 'That being said, there's no cause for alarm.'

'What do you mean?' I say.

'I will one day need a successor, as you know. I think it's time you took a more active role. Maybe take on my duties here at the house. Then you'll be shadowing me properly, learning the ropes. It's time.'

I bow my head, showing how humbled I am at this suggestion. The thought horrifies me, but also excites the other side of me, who has always known this was coming. I find myself wondering why I'm so privileged. Questions that have never been asked before pop into my head. Who were my real parents? Why has Andrew taken such a personal interest in me all these years? I don't ask the questions, hoping instead that the answers will be forthcoming.

Andrew pours us both a liberal shot of brandy from a decanter on his study desk.

'To the Network, dear boy.' He takes a generous swig.

I pick up my glass and sip the warming liquid, trying not to show how distrustful I feel about drinking or eating anything here.

'But now, you must tell me everything. How did Neva know who you were?'

The only way to deal with this is to tell mostly the truth. Andrew will know if I'm lying anyway. And so, I start at the beginning.

'I met her outside the tube station the day Tracey Herod was killed…'

Chapter Sixty-Nine

NEVA

S he passes by, as invisible as a ghost and as silent as the dead. The kitchen is empty but Neva can hear movement in a small pantry on the left-hand side of the room. Inside the room, Neva sees the cook, stuffing a handful of chocolate chip cookies into her mouth. The woman chomps noisily, oblivious of the assassin behind her. For what is about to go down, Neva intends to leave no adult witnesses. All are facilitators, abusers, abductors. She enters the pantry, reaches out and grabs the woman's neck. One precise twist, and the woman slips to the ground at her feet. The half-chewed cookies crumble from her dead mouth, even as the eyes glaze over. It's grotesque, but nothing worse than Neva has seen before.

Neva remembers this woman as she looks down at her face. She's older now, but no less mean. There are flashes of memory, how she tormented the children with food, half-starving them mostly, then sitting eating cookies even as one of them fainted with hunger.

Maybe I am an avenging angel after all.

Neva leaves the pantry, closing the door as she goes.

At the kitchen door she encounters a small child. She is a little girl of five or six. The girl is small and frail-looking. Neva realises that nothing has changed at the house, despite the story that Michael told her of their 'new' methods.

'I want my mummy,' says the girl. Her eyes, over-large in her too-thin face, are red from crying.

'Where are the others?' Neva whispers.

'In the gym room. We have to climb the ropes.' The little girl holds out hands showing red and sore blisters.

'How many teachers are in the gym?' Neva asks.

'Just Mistress Mercy.'

'You're going to be okay. Go to the bathroom. Stay in there until I come back for you.'

'You're not one of *them*, are you?' says the girl, barely able to trust this new adult stranger.

'No. I'm not. I'm here to help.'

The little girl goes into the small toilet by the cloakroom. Neva presses her fingers to her lips to warn the child to remain silent. As the girl closes and locks the door, Neva hears soft tuneless whistling. She ducks into the broom cupboard under the stairs. Peering through the cracks, she sees an armed guard walking towards the kitchen. It's only a matter of time before the guard finds the cook, then the alarm will go up and her chances of taking revenge will be gone.

Neva leaves the closet and follows the guard into the kitchen. He is totally relaxed and unaware of her. Behind him, Neva picks up one of the breakfast barstools. She hits the man with all her strength. The guard goes down, but he's not unconscious. Neva delivers a precise kick to his throat. He falls back, gasping for breath. Another blow to the head and the guard falls back lifeless. There was some noise, but the house is big and Neva hopes no one was near enough to hear it. She pauses, catching her breath and listening. No alarm; all is quiet.

Neva pulls the guard into the pantry. She checks his pulse; he's alive. She takes her knife from her boot, and slits his carotid artery.

There is a popping, gurgling sound as the guard's last breath hisses from his mouth. Neva removes her knife and wipes it clean on the cook's apron. Blood pools briefly from the guard's throat, spilling onto the pantry floor, and then peters out as the heart stops pumping.

Knife in hand, she slips out of the kitchen, leaving the two bodies hidden in the pantry.

Down the corridor, Neva hears voices.

She presses her ear to the door and recognises Michael's voice.

'I don't know what more I can tell you,' he says.

'Neva's defection could be catastrophic. If we don't find and retire her soon, we may find the Network itself is exposed,' says Beech.

It's been a long time since she heard Mr Beech's voice but Neva would know it anywhere.

She sees him now, younger, wielding a cane, like an intimidating school master. She doesn't recall if Beech ever used the cane on anyone. He carried it almost as an affectation. She had not remembered this when she saw him with Michael in London or before that when she googled him. It was as if the conditioning disallowed any memory of Mr Beech and only now, back in the house, can Neva permit it. Other information is returning to her as well. Things she had forgotten. Things she never wanted to remember.

There is a rush of terrifying recollections. Further abuse. A beating for one of the boys who they thought wasn't toeing the line. He was black and blue for weeks, but was used as an example for the others who were made to inflict the thrashing on him in the first place.

You aren't with us, you're against us, they'd all been forced to chant as the blows fell.

Toby, she thinks. Or at least that was the name they gave him eventually. Where is he now? Does he work here? Or is he out in the field like she had been?

She wonders if Michael is experiencing returned, uncontrollable memories. She hopes this does not have a negative impact on him. She takes a tremulous breath; there's no choice now either way. They are here and the plan must go ahead.

Neva moves away from Beech's deep tones. His voice, though muffled through the door, has an ill effect on her. The hand holding the knife trembles. She is weakened here. Doubts seep into her mind that weren't there before. *The Network is everywhere. We are nothing without them. We are weak.* What can she and Michael do alone?

Neva takes a controlled breath. She stills these uncertainties, strengthening her belief that they have to end this, no matter how hard it becomes. There is so much she doesn't know, or can't remember. But these qualms were placed in her mind to stop her betrayal, weren't they? She calms herself. I'm strong; *I'm death*. Once again, she sees Ansell's grave, daffodils marking the final certainty. The doubts are hard to suppress but this memory reinforces her resolve. She is sure of one thing: she will face expiry before she gives in.

She walks along the corridor, breathing deeply as she fights for control. Beech's voice, now in the distance, feels less intrusive. The anxiety attack stills and she reins in her wayward emotions.

Neva reaches the staircase. The huge house remains silent. She recalls how very few people actually live or work here. A few teachers, trainers, who perhaps only come in a few hours a day. Back in her time, the recruits were kept in conditioning for most of the day. Quiet and controlled. But sometimes, like now, they are working on their physical strength and so are alert.

Neva weighs up what to do. The house is probably only a small part of the Network. There are new children here as well as some that are almost fully operative. Those will be dangerous. Their conditioned minds will fight hard for the Network. If nothing else, fear of their trainers will stop them from easy capitulation. She and Michael can get them out, but then where would they take them, and what was to prevent the Network taking others? It is odd that they only ever take seven in at a time. Neva doesn't know why that is or if it matters. But Beech is behind it all. He has to die, and so do all of the trainers they find here. Maybe then the Network will be thrown into enough chaos that their defences are down. Without leadership, the whole thing will fall apart.

But even as she thinks this, Neva feels the tug of fear that always accompanies any rebellion.

I can do this, she thinks. *I killed Tracey and no one had more control over me. Not even Beech.*

But first, as agreed with Michael, security needs to be cut off from raising any alarms in or outside the house.

Neva presses against her stifled memories. Where did they keep the monitors? Ah yes. Next to the conditioning room. She passes the staircase and walks down the opposite corridor. The walk does not feel as long or as terrifying as it once had. This at least has little impact on her. Her eyes dart left and right as she studies the hallway, looking for signs of cameras even though Michael told her there are none.

They watch the children but not the trainers, Michael had explained as the plan was formed. That way there is no evidence of what has been done to them, should this place ever be discovered.

And so the dormitories are to be avoided, as well as the exterior. But not the bulk of the interior of the school, nor the conditioning room. No, the Network is too clever for that.

Neva reaches the security office. She doesn't knock.

The guard is sitting with his feet on the desk. He has a mug in one hand and a sandwich in the other. As the door opens, he quickly removes his feet. Then, seeing Neva and not one of the teachers or other guards, he drops both the sandwich and coffee and leaps to his feet. The coffee cup smashes on the floor splashing coffee over the guard's boots.

Neva's knife is knocked from her hand as the guard throws himself on her. She crashes back into the door, slamming it shut and blocking herself and the guard from the hallway. She swings at him, lands a punch, but he has her by the throat with both hands and starts to squeeze. Neva brings her knee up, aiming between his legs, but the guard jerks his lower body out of reach; her blow brushes against his stomach, but not with enough impact to wind or injure.

They struggle. The guard smacks Neva's head back against the door. She's dazed for a second but then her training kicks in. She cuffs the guard hard on both sides of his head simultaneously, boxing his ears. The impact hurts enough to make him yelp and loosen his grip on her throat. Neva gasps in air before throwing her body weight into the guard, propelling him backwards and smashing him against the desk. She delivers a hard kick to his calf and the guard's knee gives out under him, but he saves himself from falling and still fights back, punching her in the face. Despite receiving a hard blow, Neva doesn't stop until her knee connects with the man's groin. He crumples.

Neva kicks him in the stomach and then the head, over and over again until the guard no longer moves.

Then she turns to look at the security monitors and flicks through the various screens until she's located all of the guards that might be an issue. There are five more outside walking the perimeter, all armed to the teeth. Getting in was easier than getting out will be.

The guard on the floor isn't wearing a gun belt, but Neva finds his weapon in the top drawer of the desk along with a box of bullets. She checks the clip, then fills the pocket of her jacket with the bullets. She puts the gun in the waistband of her jeans at the small of her back. She'll use it when necessary but until then, stealth is important. She picks up her knife and holds it down by her side.

Neva turns off the security cameras and monitors. She rips out the wires, making them useless. She takes a breath and opens the security room door.

Chapter Seventy

OLIVE

Olive is unsettled. Michael's presence and reception at the house unnerve her. After Mr Beech takes him from her office, she sinks down into her executive chair and leans on her desk, her head in her hands. She doesn't feel well. She feels sick, as though she's eaten something bad.

'Why does he warrant such special privileges?' Simone asks, and Olive has to agree she doesn't understand Beech's leniency towards Michael. He should have been searched on arrival. Instead they were told to greet him like normal. Yet here they are, knowing he should have come in sooner. None of it adds up. Olive doesn't trust him at all.

They've all made sacrifices to be where they are. Olive perhaps more than most. She is brave to a point. She's taken lives many times for the Network. A fight holds no fear for her, just the same as all of the operatives trained in the house. Failure to fight is never an option. Losing a battle even less so. Olive manages to cope with being here, day in and day out, passing those kids into the clutches of the new doctor. She cares for Mendez, despite what he did to her. And yet there isn't a day that passes that she doesn't want to press a pillow down on his face and feel him struggle under it. At those moments, Olive tells herself that Mendez suffers more being alive, old, decrepit, and now losing his mental faculties, than he would if she just put the old bastard out of his misery.

Now she tells herself all is well and meditates, saying her mantra over and over in her head to keep herself grounded. Sane. The house, after all, is her personal hell. At least, it would be if she let it get to her.

She's never spoken out of turn, and she doesn't now, even though Simone bitches about Beech. Olive won't tell on her though; Simone isn't her superior but she won't risk saying anything that could bring about an early retirement for either of them. Silence, as she sees it, is not betrayal. Silence is the biggest lesson they have taught her. Even now, as the cracks begin to appear, the thought of *breaking* terrifies her. It would mean the end of everything. She'd be finished off by someone just as she'd ended Sharrick.

'I don't know how you do it,' Simone says.

'Do what?' Olive asks. For a moment she's glad of the distraction. She's scared to think right now. Thinking is always dangerous. Sometimes, lost inside her own head, she fans the flames of her own destruction.

'You know,' says Simone. 'What they do here. They took Amelie; I had to let them. That's what happens when you sell your soul to the devil.'

'You got what you wanted out of it,' Olive says. 'The money, your husband's career.'

'Every day he asked me, why not try for another one? But they wouldn't let me, and I'm too old now. They have that much control.'

'Would you really have wanted another child? After all, they might try to claim that one too.'

Simone weighs her up. 'You know where Amelie is, don't you?'

'You know I don't.'

For the first time, Olive sees real emotion in Simone's face. It shakes her stoicism more than Simone's questions. She sits back in the chair, turning her expression blank as Simone talks. She doesn't want to hear more, but she also won't stop her.

'The day she was born, I looked at her and I knew I couldn't keep her. She was so small! Born a month early, too. I tried not to love her. Every day, I did what I was supposed to as a mother. Then I got the nanny. I had to put distance between me and this fragile thing. Part of me hoped she'd have a defect, being so little. But she thrived and grew and was so intelligent. There was no way they wouldn't take her. And then, one day she was gone. They made me bring her in myself. It was only then that I realised how much of my heart Amelie had. I rang Beech. I *begged* him. *Please, not her. I can find you someone else.* He said, "Simone, if you break our deal, you know what will happen. You and your husband will be finished, in every way." I cried and he hung up on me. Cold bastard.'

Olive says nothing. She feels … nothing. Though this is just her telling herself not to feel. She repeats her mantra to deflect Simone's tears.

'Is she good at the job?' Simone asks. 'Tell me that at least.'

'I can't. I don't know anything about her. You know this, Simone. They don't ever tell anyone all of it. I only know about the ones I'm working with now. Nothing more.'

Simone stands. 'My week here is over. I need to get back to London.'

'You should,' Olive says. 'At least you don't have to do it again for a while.'

Simone sighs, rubbing at her eyes. 'I'll go and pack. Then I'll come back for you to sign my pass to leave.'

Olive can't help feeling some sympathy as she nods her agreement. This place ... this *entity* ... has that impact on all of them. Except Beech, who is always happier here than anywhere else. *This*, the heart of everything his father started and he continued, brings him joy. Olive can't imagine such glee in anything, especially not the house.

Simone leaves.

Olive sits again with her head in her hands, waiting for her to return, hoping she'll be a long time. She's feeling fragmented. She lied; she knows all about Amelie and where she is. Her predecessor did not redact as many documents as she should have. The filing cabinets are full of information about all the previous children. The truth is, Olive needed the access in order to do the right things with these new kids. The only file she hasn't looked at is her own. She can't bear it, knowing that her own parents, like Simone, probably sold her to the Network for some monetary gain. One day she may look them up. Perhaps they deserve a taste of what they created. She has the documents, hidden on a cloud space – should she ever find it impossible to resist.

But Olive knows she will never do this. She has to stay strong. Who else will make sure that these children don't go through everything she did? Everything they *all* did.

She goes to her filing cabinet now and pulls out Amelie's and Michael's files to remind herself of the details. She opens Amelie's first. The picture of the small, fragile child arriving at the house haunts Olive. She finds herself often looking at Amelie because she uses her as an example of how not to start the training. It's why they changed things, almost twenty years ago. This is the reason they ended up with Neva and the knock-on of her defection.

Olive torments herself with the gory details for a time, then she closes the file and looks around her office. She doesn't open Michael's file. She's saving that for later, when she feels stronger.

The house should feel like her own personal empire. How she'd delighted in the promotion! Then Sharrick came, bringing change in his wake. It was the moment that had started her own fall. But she'll struggle against it. Remembering the past is not all it's cracked up to be. For her it brings pain. She is fighting it, though. She doesn't want to break; she wants to bend like a reed in the wind. Let it all flow over her. Look how well she's held up! She has a lot to be proud of; at every turn, Olive has done what the Network asked.

Ten years here. That's all they want from her and then she'll be free.

She's saved a lot of the money they rewarded her with

for the assignments. Now, she is on a retainer of £120,000 a year. It is a cushy job too. She just has to make sure everyone else plays their part and instils the mantra in the trainees to prevent betrayal. No risk. It is simple. Easy.

But then there are the 'Simones' she has to deal with. Those who have graduated to a different status, lesser than Olive's but with more freedom. Simone can come here and cry, and regret, but she only has to attend one week, and not every year. Just when the Network feels it is time. She doesn't even have to be conditioned. No, Simone was a *willing* recruit, unlike most who come for the week's 'top-up', and she will go home now, and forget for a while that she sold her child into torture and a lifetime of servitude.

Olive's irritation with Simone grows to anger followed by disgust. What was her deal anyway? *The ungrateful bitch! She has it all!*

Olive has never wanted children. Or a lasting relationship. She finds any form of commitment inconvenient. Early on, she underwent surgery. A minor procedure in the scheme of things, a sterilisation. She doesn't regret it. She knows that any child she might have had would have been taken from her. She saw it with another recruit, a girl in her own year. They called her Creda. She was sixteen at the time, and, first assignment under her belt, she'd been ready to move on to the halfway house. But Creda was stupid. After her first kill, she had sex with two of the security guards. She'd been active with one of them for a while, but the house leader had turned a blind eye until she became pregnant. They'd kept her back at the house until the kid was born. Then the baby, a girl, was taken away. Fostered probably, until the day she'd be brought in and become absorbed into the Network.

A year later, Creda, now seventeen, had joined Olive at the halfway house but she was subdued. She had confided that the security guards in question had been 'retired'. Their punishment was not for sleeping with her, but for not taking precautions with a valuable asset. Olive hadn't been sad for the guards. They had tried to interfere with all the girls, Olive included. They were forceful about their interest, and Creda and Florence had given in, thinking it would gain them some privileges in the future. But Olive avoided being 'caught' alone with any of the men. She saw them looking at her, heard crude comments about how they had 'broken in' the other two, and she didn't want to be used that way. She went through enough at the house as it was. The policy regarding interaction with the trainees and the guards had changed dramatically since then. They were warned they were not to have anything to do with the students at any time. Any deviation was quickly dealt with. Olive took a personal interest in this and made sure the guards were never permitted alone with either the boys or the girls. She'd also implemented a vetting system.

Even so, Olive has never forgotten the lesson Creda learnt: don't do anything that the Network doesn't allow. But as soon as she was given freedom to live alone, Olive had made sure she couldn't conceive. She kept it secret from her handler, and the issue had never been raised of her viability, because her role was as a killer, not a breeder.

Now she has children to care for anyway. 'Care' being a loose phrase that she bandies about in the meetings she has with the trainers. She will see this batch of trainees through to their first assignments, and then they'll move on to the next house. After that, the guards and the head teacher will change and the new influx will be someone else's problem. It's always the way in the house and the Network. In her own mind, she makes things better for the trainees now. It's all she can do to make sure she sleeps at night. Olive hopes to leave this new legacy in place. But she has to hold it together in the meantime. She has to make it through the next ten years.

Adrenaline floods through her veins at the thought of real freedom. Olive walks around her office, trying to relieve the tension that Simone started and which her memories now compound, but it doesn't work. There's only one way to feel better and that's to go to the shooting range.

From her weapons chest she takes her automatic crossbow and arrows. This has always been her weapon of choice; all of the operatives have them, but most like the finality and ease of a gun. Olive loves to watch the movement in the air when she releases an arrow, and that fierce and intrusive thump as it hits home. That sound, like the last beat of a heart, eases the pain inside her. Pain that she refuses to acknowledge in any other way.

Locking her office door, she walks around the staircase and heads towards the back of the house where the range is located in a long extension. As she passes the security room, something smacks hard against the door.

Olive freezes. She considers raising the alarm, but instead her training kicks in. She becomes calm and she loads her crossbow. She's been ready for this, ever since she heard Michael was coming in. She doesn't know Neva, and her file is closed to all but those who need to see it, but this has to be her. From what she was told, Neva is the best they've ever had. Olive is determined to be the one to bring her down. Surely that will count for something with Beech? Maybe she'll even make committee level after this?

She waits by the door, bow raised.

Chapter Seventy-One

NEVA

As the door opens, Neva hears a familiar hum as the air shifts. She heaves herself aside a split second before an arrow flies into the room. Even as more arrows follow, she weaves forward, deftly avoiding being hit. The security guard behind her isn't so lucky and an arrow thuds into his leg.

The arrows stop and Neva draws the gun from the small of her back as Olive frantically pulls at the trigger of the jammed crossbow. As Neva's and Olive's eyes meet, Olive's expression changes. She stops trying to shoot. She takes a step back.

'No! You're hers. You can't be!'

Olive lowers the crossbow, shaking her head.

Neva looks at the woman, her gun held steady, pointing at her chest. Even as she expects the alarm to be raised by the commotion they've caused, she waits to hear what Olive will say next.

'I suppose I'm on your target list,' Neva prompts.

'You're *her* daughter. I *never* knew.'

'You know who my mother is?'

Olive nods.

'Who are you?' Neva says.

'Olive. I'm the headteacher here.'

Neva's face hardens. 'Then I'm going to kill you.'

Olive raises the crossbow between them. 'Wait! I can *help* you.'

'Why would you?'

Olive shakes her head. She looks confused, frightened. 'I don't know. But I feel I *have* to. She staggers back against the wood panelling surrounding the staircase. Tears flow down her cheeks. 'I'm ... *broken*. It hurts!'

Neva watches. She can almost hear the snap as the Network's control over Olive ends.

Olive lets the crossbow drop to the hardwood floor. The loud clatter echoes through the hallway. Her hands fly to her head as though she has a headache and then a soft moan escapes her lips and builds into a cry of pure anguish.

Neva understands this moment – this feeling of breaking apart as you fight against everything that they made you become. She feels a further crack in the cold place of her own heart. Olive is shaking and no longer a danger. But how can she be trusted? This could all be an act to get Neva to lower her guard.

Neva steps out of the security room and casts a glance either side. There is no one around. Olive's fall hasn't been heard. Neva stands over her as the woman becomes a blubbering wreck.

She considers shooting her and ending her misery but

such a kill would be rash and pointless. Olive has information that Neva needs. Her mind is in turmoil, torn by this difficult decision. To destroy Olive will finish the house. But why is she here if not to save *someone*? The children, yes, but what about this woman, faced as she is with some inner torment that has broken the conditioning?

Neva grabs Olive's arm. 'Come on. Let's get the children and get out of here. This ends now!'

Olive nods but she's shaking and in shock.

'Hold it together,' Neva says. 'You can do this, Olive. You're broken but you're alive!'

Glancing around, Neva pulls the security room door closed.

'Is Michael still with Beech?'

'Yes,' Olive says, her voice breaking.

Neva picks up the crossbow. She unblocks it and then presses it back into Olive's hands. 'The only way to be free is to take down your handler. You've been questioning your life a long time, haven't you? It's time to end this.'

Olive shakes her head in denial. 'I can't.'

'I can,' says Neva. 'And you will too if you want to be free.'

Holding Olive's arm, Neva leads her back around to where she heard Beech's voice. This time she knows he will have no effect on her.

'He's in there, I know,' Neva says.

Olive is shivering, in shock, and incapable of speech. But she still manages a nod.

Neva reaches for the study door as Michael opens it.

'Michael?' she says.

'Don't, he'll be—' Olive gasps at her side.

Michael lifts a gun and fires.

Neva pushes Olive aside and dives at Michael. They grapple. His knee jerks up into her side, winding her. Neva staggers back. Olive backs away; the crossbow is up in front of her.

'Amelie!' screams a voice.

Simone Arquette throws herself in front of Neva. Michael fires again. The bullet hits Simone. Her hands fly to her stomach. She looks at Michael and then crumples down on the floor between him and Neva. Blood pours from the wound, but Neva doesn't bend to see if Simone is alive because it's crucial that she doesn't take her eyes from Michael.

'Michael,' Neva says, 'This isn't you. Please. *Listen*. They've sparked your conditioning but you can fight it. Remember all of yourself, not just this part.'

Michael levels the gun at Neva.

'Wait!' says Beech. He comes out of the room and looks around at the carnage. 'I'm afraid Michael can't break free, my dear. He's been activated with a deeply embedded word that only I know, which means he'll fight until I stop him. You've caused me a great deal of trouble these last few months, Neva. Operatives are dead because of you. My organisation's work has been disrupted and we've lost the support of politicians that were once very firmly in my pocket. I can get that back, but I have to make a clear example of you. And as for you, Olive, what a disappointment after all my confidence in you! Of course, I can't say I'm surprised. You were always substandard material. Even to Creda.'

'*Michael*?' Neva ignores Beech's speech and focuses on Michael. He is indifferent, cold. She's seen this killer side of him briefly before and now she doesn't have the element of surprise to take him down.

'Kill her, Michael,' Beech says.

The weapon moves up, levelling with her chest as Michael aims his killing shot. Then Neva notices a bead of sweat dripping down Michael's face. *He's trying.*

'Only you can do this,' she says. 'Break away, Michael.'

'I said, kill her!' Beech orders. His voice is sharper, higher pitched than usual, and shows an element of hysteria. His personal weakness leaks through.

Neva knows then that Beech is afraid. It strengthens her resolve to pull Michael from his clutches, to save the children, and even Olive too. All is not lost and for the first time in her life a new emotion works its way into her chest and stomach. A feeling of warmth, of ... hope. For the future is still not set and she can still walk away from this. She even risks a glance at Simone Arquette.

When Michael doesn't comply, Beech reaches for the gun. He tries to pry it from Michael's hand and then there is a hard, sharp thrum as something zings through the air towards them. Beech staggers back, releasing the gun. Michael turns it towards him. Both he and Neva see the crossbow arrow that's buried in Beech's side.

Using his other hand, Michael forces the hand holding the gun down.

'It's over … Beech,' Michael says, his voice forced and struggling against the conditioning. 'You corrupt bastard!'

Beech slides down the wall, feet splayed, hands on the arrow. He tugs at it.

'What's that sound?' Olive says.

Michael glances at her, then back at Beech.

'I wouldn't do that if I were you,' Michael says. 'You'll do more damage and you'll bleed out faster.'

'I didn't think you cared, dear boy,' Beech says.

There is a loud whirring sound, like a tornedo is taking up outside the building.

'I don't. But that sound you hear is Archive arriving here in helicopters with a SWAT team. I called this in when I arrived. I'd like to see you brought to justice.'

A gurgling, blood-filled chuckle slips from Beech's lips. He tries once more to tug out the arrow but the strength is no longer in his hands. His breath rasps in his chest.

Neva bends down and examines Simone. 'She's dead.'

'I'm sorry. His control was too strong,' Michael says.

'I think she was my mother,' Neva says.

'I suspected as much,' Michael says. 'Olive? Where is she?'

Neva looks around. 'She's slipped away. Good for her.'

'Good for her? She was running this place.'

'Do you think she had any more choice than you did when you fired at Simone?' Neva says.

'Oh God! What a mess,' Michael says.

Gunfire starts outside. They hear shouts and cries as the last remaining security guards are taken down.

'I need to get out of here too,' Neva says.

'I can help you. Get you immunity from prosecution.'

'How will you manage that? No one but us will understand how hard it is to resist the Network.'

'Exactly. I can tell them, from my own experience.'

'Michael, the last thing you should do is admit you've been a double agent. Even though you couldn't help it,' says Neva.

The front doors burst open and Michael turns, holding his hands up in the air as the SWAT team pours in.

'I'm Security Agent Michael Kensington!' he calls. 'I'm holding a gun but I'm going to put it down.' Michael bends and lowers the gun to the floor and then he stands again, hands held up.

'Michael, look out!' calls Ray Martin.

Beech snatches up the gun. Michael sees the man aim and he throws himself aside and then there is a barrage of automatic gunfire. Michael is deafened by the shots, and he watches Beech jerk and twitch as each bullet penetrates his body. The gun falls from Beech's lifeless fingers and skitters across the floor.

'Neva!' Michael calls, looking around to see if she was caught in the crossfire.

But she's nowhere to be seen.

Chapter Seventy-Two

MICHAEL

'So, you're saying that Neva was Simone Arquette's daughter Amelie? That Arquette was willingly involved with the disappearance and grooming of her own child, and so are the parents of all the other missing children?' Ray says.

We are back at Archive. After the SWAT team arrived, I was bundled into one of the helicopters and brought back. They told me they found all the children and some arrests were made.

I'm now in an interview room with Ray and Beth and they've been grilling me for what seems like hours. I'm tired but all I want to do is tell them the truth.

I nod. 'This thing has been going on for years. People exchanging power and wealth for their children. Though in some cases it might only be one parent involved and not the other. Ambassador Arquette isn't involved. I know that much.'

'That's like a fairy tale or something, Mike,' Beth says. 'One I read to my kids, like *Rapunzel*.'

'It may seem far-fetched but people have done worse for money,' I say. How can they possibly understand how real this is to me? And how awful. 'My own godfather was running this thing. My parents were both involved. In fact, they weren't my real parents at all. But I didn't know. My whole life ... it's been a lie. I don't even know who my real parents were.'

'Okay,' says Ray. 'We've been through that, and I sympathise, Mike. We're going to sort this out. But what you're telling us is wrong. Neva *isn't* Amelie.'

'What do you mean?' I ask.

'She isn't Arquette's daughter, though she does *look* like her.'

'But...' I say, 'Simone saved Neva's life. She believed—'

'We found this on Olive Redding's desk,' Ray interrupts.

Ray places a brown folder in front of me. I open it and begin to read the contents.

'Amelie *died* during the first week of her conditioning,' Ray explains, even though I can see this for myself. 'It seems she had a heart condition. She was a premature baby. There were complications that the parents hadn't known about. The poor kid couldn't take the drugs and hypnosis. They killed her.'

I put the folder aside. I feel sick. I know I saw Neva back in the house when I was there for a few short weeks of initial conditioning. They were calling her Amelie. I remembered it all once I entered the place. It had given me physical pain. I *knew* her then; she'd tried to warn me. Somehow, despite the circumstances, we'd been friends. But regardless of wishing we had resolved her parentage, she wasn't the girl in the photograph I'm now looking at. Similar – *very* similar – but not the same.

'If she isn't Amelie, who is she?' I ask.

'The file just admits they brought in a replacement. It seems that they were afraid to let Beech know the girl had died. I'm combing missing persons to find out who she was but I've had no luck so far,' Beth says.

'Mike, you're going to have to be detained until we can straighten this out. You see, we found some very irregular activity on your computer. You understand how this goes, don't you? You need to tell us the *whole* truth,' Ray says.

I sigh and rub my hand across his forehead. It's been a long day and still I can't get them to understand how I didn't know about my involvement. *Will this ever end?*

But I know now what they found. *I* was *changing* records, making Ray and Beth appear guilty, directing the heat away from myself. It was *me* that sent that initial email cancelling Sharrick's toxicology, though I made it seem as though it was from Ray. Then at some point, too, I'd also put things in Beth's reports that would make Ray worry about her ability to work on the case, all designed so he would give the case to me. And the *other* me would have made sure it was never solved. Beth was getting too close to the truth; she'd found a link between Arquette and one of the other parents, an old photograph of them together at school. So, while I thought she wasn't doing anything, she was just keeping this knowledge close to her chest until she had all the evidence she needed.

'I'm willing to do what I can to help you bring the Network down. Start at Beech's company offices... Here's what I remember of my visits there...'

Chapter Seventy-Three

MICHAEL

I've been in custody for a couple of months. They don't tell me much about the ongoing investigation, but Ray has said they found the documentation I told them about at Beech's offices. He's implied, but not said, that they have SWAT teams taking out several locations in the UK, and Interpol are involved for those locations in Europe.

'We know more about your real parentage,' Ray told me soon after they'd brought me to this facility. They'd found a file on Olive's desk that told them everything about my conditioning. 'They used a surrogate mother. Unnamed. And you were left with her for the first few years of your life. Then you were handed to the house. Beech was your biological father.'

I'd taken this information in and tried to recall *before* but nothing came to me. Perhaps they had successfully erased all recollection of the woman who'd raised me in the beginning. Was she nurturing? Loving? Did she cry as

Simone Arquette collected me and took me, with Amelie, to the house of killers?

'Beech was preparing me to take over from him one day. Like his father did with him.'

I'm in an unknown location, where political criminals are kept. I'm being considered highly dangerous. But because I have no hope of escape, they've given me the file and I've read it over and over. Seeing what they did to turn me into their perfect sleeper operative is difficult to take, but the more I read it, the more in control of myself I feel.

Mia is a problem for them. She's also Beech's child, by a different surrogate, and we were born within hours of each other. *Almost twins.* They brought her in and interviewed her. She doesn't remember anything of those visits to the house. I didn't tell Archive what I know about her involvement; she will be guiltless unless activated. She has a beautiful baby daughter now, who is only a few weeks old. They showed me photographs, and seeing that tiny innocent creature brought me to tears. I hope that everything I've done will help to protect her and the child in the future. The Network will not be getting my niece. Come hell or high water, I'll make sure of that.

When he visits, I ask Ray about the children we rescued.

'I can't tell you much,' he says. 'But we found the recent kids and they are relatively unharmed. There were seven teenagers though. Four boys and three girls. They are undergoing intense psychiatric help. I have no idea if they will ever be let out into the real world at this point, but we're doing what we can.'

Then he tells me that the parents are still under

observation. Some they were able to prove were involved. But the majority do appear to be innocent. Perhaps Beech had trouble buying the children from these people after all? Maybe Simone Arquette was a rarity. Either way, they are safe and sound and happy to be home, even if social services will be in their lives until adulthood. Better that than they are taken away again, this time never to be found.

'The file on Amelie gave us the location of her grave,' Ray tells me. 'She's been returned now to her father and given a proper burial.'

The thought makes me cry again. I'm so emotional these days; the pain of it all can no longer be held in check.

I think about Neva a lot – who she is, where she's going, and what her future holds now. It's worrying that there are operatives out there still. Some, like myself, may be sleepers. Others are trained killers with no direction now that their leadership is gone. I hope they feel they can be free, as Neva did, as Olive learnt.

I find the two of them in dreams sometimes. They lie on a beach like two friends without a care in the world, the sprawling sand pale as bone, kissed by silver waves. It's a hope-filled fantasy that I want to believe in.

'Good for you!' I say when I wake.

Ray says I shouldn't concern myself with them. I need to think about me, and they have me in therapy to help with the trauma of everything. The counselling helps, but the truth is, I'll always be a child of the house. What they did, who they made me, will never leave me. With time, however, I'll learn to live with it.

Ray says the work I've done, the efforts I'm still making,

have gone a long way to securing my future. But the job at Archive, high classification, probably won't be open to me after this. I don't blame him for his caution. I'd say the same if it was him, or Beth, or Leon.

I don't think they will ever trust me again, but I hope that one day, one distant impossible day, I'll be lying on a beach of white sand and Neva will find me.

THE END

Michael and Neva will return in *Kill or Die*...

Acknowledgments

What an exciting, and terrifying, day it was when I sent *The House of Killers to* my lovely agent Camilla Shestopal for her thoughts. I knew that *The House of Killers* was a very different novel and for that reason I was somewhat apprehensive. So, I was thrilled when Camilla came back to tell me that she 'loved' it and that One More Chapter wanted to not only publish this one, but were invested enough in the series to commit to the next two also. Hence *The House of Killers* series was born.

Huge thanks go to Camilla as always for being such a wonderful support and for the amazing guidance she gives me on my writing and career. And for absolutely being a friend too, whom I love to just chat with and see whenever we get the opportunity.

A massive thank you needs to go to my editor Bethan Morgan, whose amazing and insightful observations of character, plot and setting have helped me immensely to focus this novel into the work it is today. I've never been more excited to read feedback on one of my works because it had such energy and enthusiasm as well as helping me clarify everything I wanted to achieve within these pages. I was delighted by how completely Bethan 'got it'. And I've absolutely loved the editing process, which is always a joy at HarperCollins. I feel like I learnt so much from the process that I could then carry forward into the next two books.

Thank you to Charlotte Ledger, who with Bethan, thought I was worth taking a chance on and who also got the vision for this series. And also to the fantastic marketing team, Claire Fenby and Melanie Price, who never let a good opportunity pass by when it can help the authors at One More Chapter promote their books. Seriously, what a team!

And of course I will not forget Holly Macdonald and Lucy Bennett for such fantastic cover design, all of which helps to show *The House of Killers* in its best possible light.

Final thanks must go to my friends Tracey Herod (what an appropriate name) and Andrew Beech, who happily let me use their names to become such great villains in the series. You guys rock!

ONE MORE CHAPTER

One More Chapter is an
award-winning global
division of HarperCollins.

Sign up to our newsletter to get our
latest eBook deals and stay up to date
with our weekly Book Club!
<u>Subscribe here.</u>

Meet the team at
<u>www.onemorechapter.com</u>

Follow us!

 @OneMoreChapter_

 @OneMoreChapter

 @onemorechapterhc

Do you write unputdownable fiction?
We love to hear from new voices.
Find out how to submit your novel at
<u>www.onemorechapter.com/submissions</u>